To my guardian angel,
my abuelita

CHAPTER 1

"Hey, it's me, Lenny. Where the hell are you?"

I KNEW IT WAS A SHITTY IDEA TO CLICK ON THE LINK ON MY HOME screen.

But I did it anyway.

Because as I'd learned over the course of my life, I liked pissing myself off.

Hadn't I *just* told myself to clear the damn cookies and the history on my computer? Yeah, I had. I *knew* I had. It had just been a few weeks ago when the last article had popped up on my home page, and it had ended up forcing me to jump on a stationary bike so that I wouldn't do something stupid.

Except that time, all I had done was give my screen the middle finger and then clicked on a different article to read... cussing under my breath the whole time.

Unfortunately for me, I was grumpy, petty, and a little bored, and that's why I followed the link for the first time in a while, watching my computer screen blink for a second before it led me to a website that in the past I had been on more times than I would ever be willing to admit.

…Months ago. A year ago. Not lately. Not in a long time.

There was that at least.

It's not a bad idea to have an idea of what this asshole is up to, I told myself as the same subject line that had reeled me in reappeared on the screen in big bold letters. I read the title of the article, and then read it again.

The words on the screen weren't going to affect me in any way, even if my stomach soured and my fingers jerked around the mouse under my palm because I suddenly wanted to throw it at someone who was across an ocean from me. I wasn't going to do that, because I didn't care.

The last few months had made it easier to read the name featured on the headline without wanting to go break something. If anything, all I felt was the slightest hint of aggravation. Just the *smallest* little baby hint of aggravation.

JONAH COLLINS TO DITCH RACING CLUB DE PARIS

Honestly, I was really proud of my eyelid for not twitching. At least not like the first time I had seen that name after a one-year blackout. Luckily I had been home with just Mo, and she would never rat me out for how I'd said "motherfucking asshole" at the sight of it.

Or tell anyone about how I'd put a pillow up to my face and screamed "FUCK YOU" into it.

And if I swallowed just a little hard as I read a few more words on the New Zealand news site, it was only because I hadn't drunk enough water yet and my throat was dry.

Jonah Hema Collins has confirmed that he is leaving Racing Club de Paris but has not confirmed any future plans.

Former All Black Collins has just completed a rocky two-year deal with the famed Paris club—

And, for the sake of the rest of my day and the life of my mouse, I hit the red icon at the top left of the window and exited out of the page, coming face to screen again with a list of news articles that *did* matter.

So he wasn't staying in France. Who cared? It didn't mean anything.

Fucking asshole.

I pushed that thought away instantly, feeling my back teeth grinding down, and focused on the list of news that I should have been focusing on. News that actually affected my life and the lives of my loved ones and friends. This news was *work*.

MACHIDO SET TO RETURN TO UFL 238

But it only took a second for me to decide that I didn't give a single shit about Machido coming back to the United Fighting League—or any of the other news on the, arguably, most popular MMA—mixed martial arts—website I was on daily. I *should* care. MMA was my business, my family's business, but right then, I didn't give a single fuck. My mind just strayed right back to that damn article about The Asshole not signing a new deal in Paris.

And that did it.

My eye started fucking twitching.

I didn't have to look at my desk to open the top drawer, grab the stress ball that my best friend had given me a year ago, and squeeze the hell out of it with all my strength.

All of it.

I could feel the tension at my elbow from how hard I was choking the innocent ball that had never done anything to me but had probably saved more than a couple of the people at the gym from murder when they screwed up or were just flat-out dumbasses. The soft yellow ball was honestly one of the most thoughtful gifts anyone had ever given me. It was a decent replacement for the nut sacks I wished I could squeeze the hell out of when someone pissed me off.

I had promised myself eight long months ago that I was done. That I was over this shit. That I had moved on with my life.

Six months ago, when I had seen that first, middle, and last name on my tablet screen and my blood pressure went up, I had confirmed to myself *again* that I was over giving a shit—after I'd screamed into the pillow and punched my mattress a few times.

I had done everything I possibly could.

I was done wasting time and energy being pissed.

And it was totally fine that I hoped someone tripped and landed face-first into a pile of warm, fresh dog shit at some point in their near future, wasn't it? If it happened, awesome. If it didn't happen, there was always tomorrow. All I did was cross my fucking fingers that eventually the day would come, and I'd find out that it happened, and if there was visual proof of it, *fabulous*.

Everything was *great*. I didn't need to look around the office I was working in to know that. The office that had been the equivalent of my grandpa's throne. The same grandpa who owned the building it was located in and the building next door to it. The same building that had our last name plastered on a giant sign outside.

MAIO HOUSE

FITNESS AND MMA

Our family legacy.

That sign alone made me smile every day I saw it. It was home, and it was love. It might not be the same building I had grown up in before Grandpa had moved the business, but it was still a place that was directly linked to my heart and more than half the best memories in my life. I now ran this MMA gym, and I always would.

I took a breath in through my nose, one that I didn't hold for longer than a second, and then let it right back out.

Fuck it.

What that dipshit did with his life was none of my business and hadn't been... ever. He could go wherever he wanted and do whatever and whoever he wanted. In short: he could go fuck himself.

Dumbass.

That thought had barely entered my brain when the office

phone beeped with an incoming call from another phone in the building. I didn't even get a chance to say a word before a familiar voice said, "Lenny, I need your help."

I instantly forgot the article, that fucker's name, Paris, and everything associated with my computer screen. I sighed, knowing there were a few reasons why Bianca, the full-time front desk employee, would need me, and I wasn't in the mood to deal with any of them. Every reason stemmed from one truth: someone had to be acting like an idiot.

As a kid, I had spent what felt like half my life at the original Maio House building. It had been small, dark, and a little rough around the edges. And I had loved the shit out of it—from the way it smelled after a long day of sweaty, musky bodies to the way it smelled after Grandpa had put me to work, not giving a shit about child labor laws, mopping down the floors and wiping equipment. Back then, I hadn't been able to envision a job better than the one Grandpa Gus had, owning a gym, managing it, getting involved with fighters' training. It had seemed so cool and laidback, especially after he'd gotten a computer that had been loaded with solitaire that I got to play for hours while waiting around to go home if there was nothing else to do. When I'd gotten older and discovered chat rooms, it had gotten just that much better. Hanging around the floor with people I loved or messing around the computer had been the best.

I had looked forward to managing Maio House when I'd been younger.

For some reason, my brain had chosen to block out most of the other shit that went along with the job—specifically, the moments when I would get yelled at to go break up an argument or a fight between two grown-ass men. Or act like I gave a shit when members complained or threatened to cancel over really basic-ass reasons like when the butt blaster machine was out of order.

"What's up?" I asked, feeling almost exhausted even after sleeping a whole six hours.

"John just came by and told me he was in the locker room in your building and he saw two of the MMA guys getting ugly with each other," Bianca said, not bothering to explain what that implied because we both knew damn well what it meant.

Someone had to go stop it, and none of the employees got paid enough to want to get involved with two grown-ass men arguing.

That was my job.

I just didn't get why John, the custodian, didn't just stop by my office and tell me. I hadn't been an asshole to him or anything that morning... I didn't think. I'd have to make time to go talk to him and make sure we were good later, when I didn't have two idiots to go deal with.

"All right, Bianca, thanks. I've got it," I told her with another sigh as I got to my feet.

"Sorry! Good luck!" she replied in her happy, likable voice that had won me over when I'd interviewed her four months ago.

Who the hell was dumb enough to be arguing right now and over *what?* I left the office and headed out to the main floor. I looked around for a clue, taking in the empty sea of blue mats. There were four guys hanging around the cage, but they were in their own little worlds. Just about everyone from the morning session was gone.

I made it to the doorway that opened into the hallway that led into the showers and lockers and didn't slow down my pace as I yelled, "Hide your ding-dongs. I'm coming in!"

I wasn't in the mood to see any dicks flapping around or anybody's buttholes winking at me. I could go the rest of my life without walking in on someone bent over naked. If I was going to see any balding, brown-eyed demons, I wanted to choose whose.

No one called out in response. All right then.

Maybe it was my lucky day and they had left, but I still had to check to make sure nobody was knocked out unconscious on the floor. That had fortunately never happened, but it was only because the rules at Maio House were so strict about fighting. The smart ones knew better than to do something that stupid, and even the cocky idiots could usually be reasoned with before they did something they'd regret.

Usually.

I barely had to clear the short hallway into the locker rooms when I immediately spotted the two guys standing in front of each other, silently, face-to-face. Forehead to forehead more like it. *Really?*

There were a lot of things I had always loved about having Maio House be a part of my life. About it being in my heart. In my blood. About knowing it was mine as much as it was Grandpa Gus's. Like princes and princesses who knew the kingdoms they would inherit, I had always known what would one day become mine too. So I had known, even back when I had been about Grandpa's hips' height, what happened when you got into a fight when it wasn't for training purposes.

Time and time again, he had made me sit at the tiny foldout couch he'd had in the corner of his office back in the old building where Maio House had been born while he suspended one person after another for violating the rules. The rules that were posted right in front of the main doors everyone walked through to get into the building. The very same rules that had been around since before I was born.

1. NO BRAWLING
2. NO DRUGS
3. NO CHEAP SHOTS (LEAVE GENITALS AND NECKS/SPINES ALONE)

***Violating the rules is cause for suspension or termination.
It had always seemed easy enough for me and for most of

the people who had come and gone throughout the years to follow them. They were common sense. Don't fight without a reason—which, *hello,* you had to be an idiot to cross that line. Don't take drugs on the premises that weren't prescription or over-the-counter painkillers. Leave each other's ding-a-lings, egg sacks, and spinal cords alone. We wanted people to be able to walk out of the gym *and* reproduce if they wanted to. Basic shit.

It was rare that anyone broke the rules, but it happened. Just two weeks ago, I'd had to suspend one of the guys for purposely hitting the guy he'd been sparring with in the balls. Needless to say, he'd been fucking pissed and had tried to play dumb.

I really didn't want to have to suspend someone else again, not so soon.

I recognized the smaller of the two as a nineteen-ish kid with cornrows named Carlos. He was bucking his chest out. The other man was Vince, who topped the younger guy by about fifty pounds and four inches and was five or six years older. He hadn't been a member of Maio House for long. And they were both lovingly gazing into each other's eyes.

Not.

"Are you two for real right now?" I asked, honest to God disappointed in both of them. What the hell could they possibly get so mad over that they were in the locker room millimeters away from being able to kiss each other? "Would at least one of you fucking stop?"

It was Vince who blinked first, maybe being the first one to have some fucking sense in him.

"Now, please."

Vince blinked again, but he still didn't take a step back, and Carlos, if anything, puffed out his chest even more.

I rolled my eyes. These two idiots might make their livings fighting people, or at least make part of their living doing that, but I had been in more fights than either of them… even if mine were always with a referee and for points, not because someone made me mad, and I wanted to prove something. *Thank you, judo.*

"Look," I told them, reaching up to tug on the corner of my eye from how annoying these two were being, "I don't give a shit if you get into a fight with each other, I really don't, but I'm not going to feel bad suspending either of you if you do. And it'll be for a month, and, Carlos, you have a fight coming up, and Vince, you've got one in two months. So… what do you want to do?"

It was Vince who reacted first. Him being a light heavy-weight, I was relieved he snapped out of it, taking a step back and opening his mouth, loosening his jaw. Meanwhile, Carlos stood exactly where he was, tipping his chin up higher than it had been and basically fucking asking to get popped. His choice in friends suddenly made a hell of a lot of sense.

God needed to grant me some strength. Soon.

"Do I need to ask what happened or are you both good?" I asked, not giving a shit which of them replied.

"We're good as long as he shuts the fuck up and minds his own business," Carlos answered, and I didn't miss the way Vince shook his head just a little bit in what seemed like disbelief. "I don't need your advice, *Vince.*"

That's what this was over? I tugged on the corner of my eye again. "Vince?"

The bigger guy smiled smugly, and after a moment, he shook his head and glanced back at me, his face intense. His eyes slid toward Carlos once more before yet again coming back to me. "I'm fine," he responded after a second. "I'll keep my advice to myself next time, *Carlos.*"

God help me.

"You're sure you're both done then?" I asked again.

Carlos didn't look at me, but the hand holding his phone twitched as he mumbled, "Yeah."

Vince nodded.

Good enough for me. With that, I turned around and headed back toward my office, hearing them trade muffled words with each other and not giving a single fuck. Maybe I should have eavesdropped, but… it didn't really matter, did it?

I was going to need to tell Peter about that little scene so he'd keep an eye on them.

By the time I made it back to my office and sat down in my chair, I convinced myself to try and focus again. Shoving the rest of my thoughts and feelings about everything other than work aside, I refreshed the page of the MMA news site I was on and instantly regretted it.

POLANSKI REQUESTS REMATCH, IS READY TO REGAIN TITLE

Noah.

Ugh.

I had already forgotten he'd lost his fight three days ago. I'd fallen asleep watching it, and the only reason I knew he'd lost was because my grandfather had mentioned it—with a gleeful little look in his evil eyes.

I fucking loved that man.

I snickered at the memory and clicked on another link, not in the mood to even read Noah's name, and made myself read the next post down the list on the MMA site's homepage. Then I made myself read it again because I couldn't remember a word of it once I had finished. Something about an upcoming event between two well-known fighters that I didn't have history or beef with.

It was at the end of the second read through that a soft knock on my door had me looking up and smiling at the man already coming in, hands shoved into the pockets of his black track pants. I could tell instantly by the expression on Peter's face that he had already heard about the two idiots in the locker room. No surprise there. He had a radar for stuff like that.

I wrinkled my nose at the man who was basically my second

dad. "At least nothing happened," I told him, knowing exactly what he was thinking.

His face, his coffee-and-cream skin still youthful looking even in his sixties, twisted up into a look of distaste. "What was it over?" asked the man who emphasized the importance of discipline and control on a regular basis. He stopped behind one of the chairs in front of the desk that Grandpa and I shared.

I shrugged, feeling a familiar pinch at my shoulder again. Damn it. "Vince said something to Carlos. Carlos got butthurt." I rolled my eyes.

That got me an eye roll out of the deceptively serious man. There were a handful of lines at each of his eyes and down the sides of his mouth, but he was still almost as fit as he had been almost thirty years ago when he'd come into our lives, unaware that he was going to become the third leg in our family. "I don't know what to do with these children sometimes." ·

"Let's call their moms and tattle."

Peter snorted in that laidback way that was everything about him. You never would have figured that this almost slender, just slightly above average height man could take down just about any man's ass if he wanted to. I had always thought of him as kind of being like Clark Kent. Quiet, kind, and laidback, he seemed like the last person who would have a seventh-degree coral belt—black and red actually—in Brazilian jiu-jitsu by day and help me with my math homework at night.

"Did you see Gus this morning?" Peter asked.

"Just for a second. He was on the phone with someone talking about joining a basketball tournament for the elderly."

My second dad grinned and shook his head before the expression dropped away and he asked, "Are you okay?"

I shrugged both my shoulders.

The way Peter narrowed his eyes told me he knew I wasn't exactly lying or telling the truth, but he didn't pry. He never pried too hard. It was one of my favorite things about him. If I wanted to tell him something, I would, and he knew that. And there were very, very few things I didn't tell him.

Just the big shit.

I had just grabbed my stress ball from where it was sitting beside my keyboard so I could put it back into its drawer when Peter snapped his fingers suddenly. "I got this message from the front desk a minute ago, saying you referred him to me," he said as he stood there. "But I've never heard of the guy."

"What's the name?" I hitched my shoulder up again and rolled it back, feeling that pinch again. Since when did I get all these random aches and pains from just sleeping wrong? Was this what happened when you hit your thirties? I needed to start going to my physical therapist. Maybe the chiropractor too.

Peter didn't hesitate to stick a hand in his pocket and pull out a bright pink Post-it note. He drew the scrap of paper away from him before squinting at it. "A... Jonah Collins?"

I dropped my shoulder back into place and stared at him.

Fucking *shit.*

CHAPTER 2

"Hey, it's Lenny again. Where the hell are you? I went by your apartment and banged on your door for half an hour. Let me know you're alive, okay? I'm worried about you."

I HADN'T KNOWN WHEN I'D WOKEN UP THAT MORNING THAT MY life had been about to change with that name coming out of Peter's mouth.

But it happened.

And he had to have known when I stared at him silently, feeling almost faint for probably the second time in my life.

I had no idea what to *say*. What to think. How to even react.

Growing a magical penis out of nowhere would have been less surprising than Peter saying the Fucker's name.

But what hit me the strongest—the hardest—was the knowledge that time had finally run out.

It was a testament to how well Peter knew me that he reacted the way he did. Carefully, being watchful as he did it, he pulled out the chair in front of the desk and took a seat, neatly, an example of the effortless control he had over his body. I doubted it was my imagination that he seemed to almost brace himself.

"You don't like him?"

Like it was that easy. Whether I liked him or not.

I didn't even realize I had raised my hands up to my face before they were scrubbing over my cheeks and forehead, sliding back through the ponytail that I had thrown my hair into that morning because I hadn't been in the mood to do much else. I hadn't appreciated all the years that I'd made it a priority to sleep eight to ten hours a night; that was for fucking sure.

The "Elena" that came out of Peter's mouth was the gauntlet he threw down between us.

Not Lenny. Not Len.

Peter had gone with *Elena,* pulling out the dad card he rarely used.

I was fucked.

The option to lie to him didn't even pop into my head. We didn't do that. None of us did. There was just stuff we... didn't say to one another. We didn't ask each other certain questions because there was that underlying factor that we knew we didn't lie. If you didn't ask, you didn't know. And if we wanted you to know, we would tell you. It was the way that Grandpa Gus, Peter, and I had always been. We didn't ever have to say it, but the trust between us was reinforced with miles of rebar and concrete.

Because in thirty years, there were only a handful of things I hadn't told them about. And I was sure that there had to be a handful of things they hadn't told me too.

Slowly, I dropped my hands away from my face and straightened in my rolling chair, shoving my shoulders back and meeting Peter's dark brown gaze. I took in the face that had cheered for me at nearly every judo competition I had been in—the exception being the time he'd had pneumonia and the other time when his sister had died and he hadn't wanted me to miss out on the tournament. Peter's face was the one that had tucked me into bed for countless years, right along with Grandpa Gus's. The face that had reassured me more times than I could ever count that I was loved, that I could do anything, and that I was always capable of doing better.

So I told him the two words that would need to be enough. Two words I didn't want to let out but had to. Because time was up.

It was one thing to try your hardest and pretend someone didn't exist, and a totally different thing to lie in order to keep that charade going.

"It's him."

His eyebrows furrowed.

He wasn't getting it. Not yet at least. But he was going to need to because I didn't exactly want to go into details. Not with the door open. Not *here*. So I raised my eyebrows and stared at him, trying to project the words back into his head.

It's him. It's him, it's him, it's him.

I saw the moment it clicked. The moment he realized what the hell I was trying to get across. *It's him.* Him.

Peter shifted in his seat, crossing one leg over the other and leaning back as he asked with a funny look on his face, like he didn't want to believe it, "*Him?*"

"Yeah." Him.

Peter's dark brown eyes shifted over the bluish-green wall behind my head as he processed even more what I was saying, *really* thinking about it and what the hell it all meant.

Because I already knew what it meant for me, at least to a certain extent.

It meant I needed to start saving up bail money for Grandpa Gus for when he got arrested for either aggravated assault, harassment, conspiracy to commit murder, or whatever the charge for acting a fool in public was.

That idea shouldn't have amused me, but it did. It really

fucking did. At least it did until the other half of what that would entail really hit me.

I'd have to see that prick in court when he pressed charges against my grandpa.

I would have to look at the fucking man who had disappeared for a year, only to suddenly reappear again in the same country I had last seen him. The asshole who had left me hanging. Who hadn't even had the balls to call, text, or email me back. Not *once* after the three hundred times I had tried to contact him.

Sure, right after he'd bounced, he'd sent four total postcards that had his signature on them—but only that. There hadn't been a return address. There hadn't been *shit* on them. Not even a message. Not even some kind of code I could have cracked. Just his scribbled signature, a postmark and stamp from New Zealand, my name and previous address in France.

I grabbed my stress ball again, immediately squeezing the fuck out of it.

And if I was imagining it was somebody's balls… whatever.

"What…?" He didn't even know what to say. I wondered if he'd written off finding out about *him.* "Ah… I… he… does MMA?" he finally got out.

I shook my head.

Peter thought about that for a moment but had to come up with the same question I had: why was Jonah calling him? Peter didn't understand as well as I did how random of a call it was. He didn't know who Jonah was or what he did for a living. But what Peter did know was that *we* were family. And he proved that to me instantly.

"What do you want me to do?" he asked. "Has he… called you?"

I sat there still hung up on the fact that name had come out of Peter's mouth. What were the chances? Seriously, *why was he calling him?* Why now?

I squeezed my ball some more. "No. I blocked his number."

Those questions bounced around in my skull. *Why? Why? Why? Why? Why?*

I couldn't help but scratch at my throat and eyeball the framed picture sitting right beside the monitor of my computer.

It didn't matter why. All that mattered was that he had called.

"I don't know why he's contacting you instead of me," I told him, still eyeing the picture in the frame. "But I talked about you enough when we... knew each other. He knows who you are. He knows my last name. He knows Grandpa owns this place. It's not a coincidence."

When we knew each other. God, I could almost laugh at that. And I could only laugh at the idea of *him* contacting Peter as an accident. There was no way that was possible.

Rubbing my fingers over my face again, I held back a sigh.

Peter leaned forward in his seat, his face even more serious than usual—at least while we were within these walls. When we were out of Maio House, that was a different story. That was the Peter that I knew, the one I had grown up loving from the moment he had knocked on Grandpa Gus's office door, asking for a job. We had all fallen in love with him. According to Grandpa Gus, I had let the strange man sit by himself for all of two minutes before I'd climbed up onto his lap at the age of three and passed out against him, holding his hand.

None of us had known back then that it would be the first of many, many times I'd do the same thing over the years.

I loved this man as much as I loved my grandpa, and God knows—everyone knew—that I thought that old creature of ancient evil was the greatest thing ever, even when he was driving me nuts, and that was always.

"Why now?"

My fingers made circles against my brow bones. "I don't know. He hasn't called or emailed since the last time I saw him." Fucker. "I stopped trying to contact him eight months ago." I had to clear my throat because all of a sudden it felt too damn tight and dry. "The last email I sent, I told him that was the last time, and I meant it. I didn't reach out again." I would rather cut both my hands off. Sew my vagina shut. Give up caffeine for the rest of my life. But I didn't tell him that. Not when even his silence was thoughtful as he processed this shit I was laying on him.

"Do you want me to call him back? We can find out what he wants," he said after a beat.

Fuck.

"Unless you would rather wait and see what he does." Peter lowered his voice, knowing damn well that I didn't want anyone else to hear or put the pieces together. "Or if you would rather call him."

I didn't want to do shit.

All I wanted to do was tell Jonah Collins to fuck off into another galaxy. But I wouldn't. Even if it killed me. Even if it went against every instinct in my body. I was done with wanting to scream at him. Beat the shit out of him. Tell him he was a piece of shit. Rip off his balls and soak in his blood. Curse the day we had met on that tour.

But I wouldn't.

I eyed the picture frame again.

I wasn't going to do shit.

We don't always get what we want, Grandpa had told me once when I'd been acting like a brat after losing a match. And he was totally right.

Knowing all of that though didn't ease even a little of the frustration and annoyance that set up camp in my chest. "I reached out to him, Peter. Not once or twice, but over and over again. It was his choice; not mine," I explained.

Peter looked at me for so long, I had no idea what the hell he could possibly be thinking.

"Then we don't do anything," he finally said. "See if he calls back. See what he wants."

See what he wants.

I knew what he didn't want. Peter and I both did. Just about everyone in my life knew, for that matter.

"If he calls again… if he comes here, we'll handle it. Are you fine with that?"

I squeezed the hell out of my stress ball again but nodded. We were going to have to handle this, one way or the other. I didn't exactly have a choice.

That had me getting a small smile from Peter, who still seemed different than usual. I couldn't blame him. But luckily, this was Peter and not my grandfather.

God, I wasn't looking forward to that conversation.

"Can we wait before we tell Grandpa?" I asked him, shaking my leg underneath the desk. *Why now? Why period?* I knew I was a selfish asshole for thinking that, but I couldn't help it. Why today?

God, and since when was I so *whiny?* I disgusted myself, damn it. Why, why, why? Boo-hoo. Ugh.

I could see the argument in Peter's eyes at my request, but fortunately, that quick mind came to the same conclusion mine did too.

We were going to need bail money if Jonah Hema Collins came here—not that I expected him to. All he'd done was call. For some reason I couldn't even begin to fucking understand.

And if the thought of him coming here raised my blood pressure—and my middle finger—I was going to need to be an adult and suck it up. This wasn't about me. So I focused on the topic of my grandfather.

"I don't want him to know unless he has to," I told Peter. "He doesn't need to be getting riled up for no reason. He's finally just now getting over it," I explained, knowing this was one of those things that fell into the gray area of not lying to each other.

Peter's nod was tighter than it should have been, but I understood that too. Of course, I understood. I hated putting any of them into this position in the first place. *I* hated being in this position to start with, but here we were. It was no one else's fault but mine. "Okay," he agreed, clearly slightly torn. But we both knew what the greater of the two evils was.

Neither one of us said anything for so long it almost got awkward.

After what might have been three minutes or ten, Peter stood again and shot me an intense look that immediately had me pressing my lips together and forming something close to a smile.

"Everything is fine," he stated, calmly, projecting the thought into me.

"I know."

His eyes flicked up toward the wall behind me, where I figured he was probably looking at a framed picture of the three of us on my eighteenth birthday, crowded around a birthday cake with candles that could have been fireworks. His slim chest expanded and then went back down as he came to terms with whatever it was he was worried about. Everything, probably.

Those eyes took their time moving from the wall to me, but when they did, he managed to give me a smile that was definitely a little strained. "Come work out with the team for an hour. You need to get that look off your face."

"What look?"

He raised his eyebrows. "That one."

I pressed my lips together, temporarily shoving the *why, why, why* aside. "I'll think about it. My shoulder is extra achy today."

Peter shot me a knowing half smile as he left the room, not needing to insist. We both knew he was right. I was too wound up, shoulder pain or no shoulder pain. No shit.

Jonah had called Peter. Why would he do that? And did it really have to make me feel almost fucking sick?

With a deep breath in through my nose and out of my

mouth, I tipped my head toward the ceiling and tried to ease the tension out of my body.

I hated not knowing what was going to happen.

I hated surprises.

There was a reason that jackass had called him. I'd grown up around men with insane amounts of testosterone. When they wanted something, they usually got it.

And when they didn't want something... well, they didn't, and sometimes they left without a trace.

I was a lot of things, but I wasn't dumb or a chicken.

If that fuckface called, he called. Whatever happened, I could handle it.

Chances were, he'd change his mind and keep up his disappearing act, and I could continue to live my life the exact same way I had been.

I was going to work out, maybe hop on a bike so I didn't aggravate my shoulder more. I was going to fucking calm down. Regardless of whatever else happened, if I was going to have to kill anyone, I had people to help. There was no way for me to stop anything from happening, but I could and would deal with it.

Jonah Collins had no idea what he was going to be walking into, *if* he did. If, if, if.

If he even walked into anything in the first place.

CHAPTER 3

> *"It's me. Again. Lenny. I went by your apartment. Akira told me they haven't heard from you either. Look, a ruptured Achilles isn't the end of the world, even though it feels that way, okay? And I'm sure your face will be fine once the swelling goes down. Don't be all vain and shit. At least text me back."*

I KNEW THAT I WASN'T EVEN TRYING TO HIDE MY BAD MOOD WHEN the second person in less than an hour walked into the office, looked at me, and then turned around and walked right back out, not saying a word.

It was that shitty.

Never, ever had I been the kind of person who bottled shit up and let it fester in the first place. For as long as I could remember, Grandpa Gus had made me talk things out to get whatever out of my system. If that didn't work, then there were other things I could do to calm down again. To reel back. To *center*. Pressure makes everything pop, he said.

But despite being fully aware that meditation helped me relax and focus—some days it helped me not think, and other days it helped me think about things that were bothering me but without raging—I didn't do it. I hadn't woken up and hopped on the stationary bike either to get out of my head. I knew better.

I had tossed and turned the entire night, staring up at the ceiling and then listening to a true crime podcast because I hadn't wanted to turn on the television or go downstairs because I didn't want to risk running into Grandpa Gus, having him *see* that something—someone—was up my ass and wondering about it. Because he always knew when something was up. Always.

And I wasn't ready to tell him the things he needed to know.

Not yet. Not while I wasn't completely convinced I could be rational. So I was going to blame keeping things from him as the reason for my crappy mood the next day. That and a night of sleeping like shit, mixed with the anticipation, anger, and hurt, made this uncomfortable stone that didn't want to pass through my system.

Picking up my cell phone, I ignored the spreadsheet on my desktop screen and sent a text message I should have the day before. If I couldn't tell Grandpa, there was someone else I needed to have a conversation with. Someone younger, less hairy, and a hell of a lot nicer.

Me: You busy today?

It took ten minutes to get a response.

Luna: Nope. :] What's going on?

I shook my foot beneath the desk, thinking about what I needed to tell my best friend of the last eleven years.

Me: Nothing bad, but I need to tell you something, and it'll be easier in person.

That time there was only a one-minute delay in getting a reply.

Luna: Tell me now please.
Me: I didn't pee myself again, if that's what you're about to ask.

I only partially regretted telling her that I'd peed myself a month ago because I'd sneezed too hard after holding it in too long.

Only thirty seconds passed before I got another text.

Luna: I thought for sure that's what it was going to be!
Me: WTF is that exclamation mark for, bish? Don't sound so disappointed.
Luna: It's been a long day. A girl can dream.
Luna: I can come over tonight.
Me: [middle finger emoji]
Me: You okay?
Luna: [laughing emoji] I'll text you when Rip gets home so he can stay with my shortcake. I'm taking her to the doctor in an hour. She's been pulling at her ear and crying. I feel so guilty she's feeling bad is all.

The fact that we were talking about her baby, planning around a little thing named Ava, was just another reminder of how quickly life could change. Just two years ago, everything had been normal. Or at least what normal had been for us at that point. She'd had a guy in her life—not that her now-husband was a *guy*; he was a big hunk of a man—but things had changed.

Once upon a time, I had been a nineteen-year-old with maybe two friends who were girls, and Luna had been an eighteen-year-old who had smiled her way through a self-defense class that I had taught at Maio House for a little extra cash. I had asked her out to eat because I had liked how nice she had been to the other women in the class. I didn't like judgy-ass people, and that was why I had invited her. I was competitive enough, but I didn't give a fuck what other people did or didn't do, and Luna hadn't given me a single vibe that said she was anything but easygoing. And, as I learned, she really was about as laidback as you could get.

I fell in love with her within a month. She was kind, patient, optimistic, and was so chill, it relaxed me. Luna was a whole lot of shit that I wasn't. We spent the next eight years navigating through life together. Two girls with a lot in common but at the same time nothing in common, trying to survive and grow up. Then she got a boyfriend—and again, not that there was any *boy* in him—and right around that time, everything changed.

The next thing I knew, I was thirty-one years old, and the only thing in my life that was the same was my grandfather and Peter existing in it. Even my relationship with Luna had changed a little. I no longer knew who the hell this new person in my body and in my mind was. Not that it was bad or that I didn't like myself, but… I was just different. Everything was different. Circumstances had changed. *I* had changed. Everything about life had too. Like when you lose weight or gain it and aren't sure how you fit in your own skin anymore.

You aren't who you used to be.

And you aren't totally sure how it happened or when it happened, but it did.

And that was supposed to be okay. At least that was my grandpa's sage-ass advice. God knows he made up shit all the time, but it made sense… in a way. Like how, by the time every seven years rolls around, every cell in your body has been replaced by new ones. You're different. You're *supposed* to be. It's inevitable. It's natural.

Life keeps evolving whether you want it to or not.

And I wasn't about to whine about it.

Me: Okay. I'll text you when I get home, but it should be at the same time. Hope my goddaughter feels better, and chill out. It's not your fault she's sick.

I pushed all those thoughts aside: about needing to tell her the truth, about being different, about my worries, about my fucking regrets too, and cast one last look at the frame sitting on my desk. I focused back on the spreadsheet I needed to go through so I could send it off to the gym's accountant by the end of the week.

Jonah Collins was going to call, or he wasn't. He was going to come here, or he wasn't. There was nothing I could do to stop it other than calling someone in immigration and claiming he was smuggling drugs in his butthole. So....

I glanced at the picture on my desk then got back to work, turning the playlist on my phone on, which pushed it through a small Bluetooth speaker. Somewhere in the background, I heard the sound of voices coming back into the gym. Heard the sound of bodies colliding. I thought about whether I should go out on the floor and take advantage of Peter working on Brazilian jiu-jitsu skills today since my shoulder wasn't aching more than normal, unlike the day before. It had been at least a couple weeks since the last time I'd gotten on the mats with anyone, and even then, that had only been for about fifteen minutes to show one of the new girls how to do a submission choke she had been struggling with.

Meh.

Or maybe I'd just hop on an elliptical later and get a few miles of HIIT—high-intensity interval training—in to get my heart rate nice and elevated and burn some calories. Yeah, that sounded like a better idea.

I got back to work on cataloging expenses. Everything familiar and usual, or at least that was what I thought. I had my head full of numbers as I copied some expenses into the computer and was just lightly mumbling along to my 90s playlist when I heard the *knock, knock* on my opened door. Two lazy, light knocks.

Nothing special. Nothing to warn me.

"Come in," I called out, trying to hold back a sigh because, to be fair, it was nobody's fault I was in a shitty mood other than my own.

So when the footsteps treaded across the floor, I was still trying to tell myself to snap the hell out of it. Maybe I didn't need to be in a good mood, but I didn't need to be in a bad one either. Nobody deserved me being a bitch today. Not even my own body deserved that kind of stress.

Things were going to happen, or they weren't. It was that simple, and I knew it. I just couldn't convince the rest of me that that was the case.

So when the footsteps stopped and a throat was cleared, I took my sweet time looking away from my computer screen to take in the poor idiot who was being brave by coming into the office.

And that's when everything went to fucking shit.

At least that was what it felt like.

Like someone saw me living my life, minding my own business, trying my goddamn best, then decided to pick it up and throw it into a fire, just to watch it go up in flames.

I wasn't ready for the wide shoulders taking up the width of the hallway that separated the office from the rest of this part of the gym. I wasn't ready for the long, strong legs, that had led up to a body wrapped in nothing but layers of muscle, in my space. That body that out of so, so, so many I had seen over the years had done something to my internal organs—including my heart, if I was going to be honest.

I had seen so many half-naked men in my life that I had become desensitized to six-packs, ripped arms, and good-looking faces. I had never put any weight into physical beauty, honestly. I remember once, when I had been about fifteen or sixteen, telling Peter that I was worried about how much I didn't really care about boys. Or girls. I knew that some guys were attractive, but it didn't do anything to me. I hadn't found myself wishing for a fucking boyfriend. Most people I knew wanted to be in relationships, and I just hadn't given a fuck. Peter, though, had told me that there was nothing wrong with me.

You're perfect the way you are, he had said, like it was no big deal.

It hadn't been like I was lonely. I had friends. I had things to keep me busy. I had been a healthy teenager who got curious one night, put my hand over my underwear, and discovered that I really enjoyed masturbating. And that's what I did, frequently. But I'd never felt the urge back then to have someone else make me orgasm when I could do it myself pretty damn well.

I had enough nonsexual physical interactions with other people that it wasn't like I missed affection or any shit like that. When I usually thought about guys, I thought about how bad they smelled when their deodorants wore off and how bitchy they got when things went wrong, but that I enjoyed working with them because they were stronger than I was and helped me better prepare to compete against other females who weren't.

And if there had been a short period in there where I'd thought I might have had feelings for my friend, that was one thing, but I'd come to terms with that real quick, and I'd moved on from that idea just as fast.

As I got older, I hadn't been *hoping* to meet anyone. It wasn't something I thought about period. Not even for sex because I doubted anything could compare to my vibrators or my hand or my toss pillow that I kept hidden on a shelf in my closet.

I didn't have my first kiss until I was twenty. Only had sex at the same age because kissing had been all right and I was curious if sex was worth all the hype. I'd done it with a friend from college who had been a year younger than me and had been a virgin too. Sex had been like the time I took up rock climbing out of curiosity for a few months. Done and never repeated after those few times.

And then, I'd met *him*.

If I closed my eyes, I was 99 percent positive I could still picture those massive shoulders capped with rounded muscles. The biceps bigger than my head. The forearms that made my calves look puny. I'd never be able to forget how solid his pectorals had been in profile, or how perfect his flatly muscled abs were as they sloped into a waist that was so trim, most people would have a hard time believing just how much food it could pack away.

Most importantly though, there had been that damn smile. *That* had done it.

That dipshit… that fucker… had been an awakening that hit me out of nowhere the first time I saw him. Like those kids in videos who get hearing aids and can hear for the first time, and you get to witness their life changing. Or color-blind people who get glasses and can finally totally see all the fucking colors you take for granted because you can't appreciate having something that seems so natural.

That's what it had been like to look at him for the first time.

And if that wasn't enough, that two-hundred-and-fifty-pound body was connected to the face that had had me doing a double take. A forehead dotted with countless tiny scars on it, a nose that was still in great shape considering he had told me that it had been broken multiple times. Then there was the tanned skin stretched tight over high cheekbones, the lightest honey-colored eyes that were almost almond-shaped, and a mouth that was almost fake from how pink its lips were.

A year ago, when I'd been having a really bad night, I'd looked Jonah Ho-bag Collins up online, and in the process, found a list of the twenty-two sexiest rugby players in the world.

Of course, he'd been on it.

Maybe I hadn't known who he was when we met, but I'd been an exception. There had been no reason for me to recognize him. And as I took him in right then, in that moment, it struck me just how familiar his face seemed to me now. How familiar those features, especially those eyes and skin color, were. I had to hold my breath for a second it hit me so hard.

But this was a face that I hadn't seen in seventeen months. That mix of rugged yet handsome bones and bright eyes had disappeared on me. That mouth had never called me back.

The face looking back at me in my office hadn't liked me back as much as I had thought it did.

This face was on a person who had made me cry in fucking fury and disappointment. This face that was the second one to ever make me feel used and fucking stupid. I'd dreamed, literally *dreamed*, about punching the fucking face looking at me.

Stop.

I knew what was important. I knew what mattered. I knew what I had told myself I would do, even if it were hard as hell.

Most importantly though, I was no weak bitch.

It took a second, but I did it.

I focused, and I clung to it, but I accepted and processed the truth: this stupid face had given me joy… and love—and not a little bit, but a lot. So much that I wasn't going to instantly chuck my stapler at him like I really wanted to or scream "stranger danger" so someone else could beat him up for me.

I *had* gotten over the bone structure facing me. I didn't give a flying shit over the clear, honey-colored eyes that were set into those sockets below heavy, dark eyebrows. I felt nothing good for the man suddenly standing in my office in fitted jeans and an olive-green hoodie that hugged every part of an upper body that hadn't lost a single pound of muscle since the last time I had seen it.

I wasn't going to get mad. I wasn't going to cuss him out or do any other stupid shit. I was going to handle this.

I had promised myself that if this day ever came, I would do what I had to do. With some honor. With some pride.

But that didn't mean I had to be nice.

And it was because I didn't feel shit anymore for this specific person—because hating his guts didn't really count—that I didn't even raise my eyebrows at his random appearance after *seventeen fucking months*, even as some part of my brain freaked out at the fact that Peter had *literally* just told me about him yesterday. *Yesterday.* The same day I had just read about him not signing his contract.

He was *here*, in *Houston* of all places, when he had told me before he'd only been to the United States twice and both times had been for work.

God, I couldn't believe this fucker actually had the balls to be here.

I took a breath in through my nose and let it right back out. *Seventeen months. It has been seventeen months since the last time I've seen him,* I reminded myself.

I had this.

"Jonah." I let that sense of I-don't-give-a-shit-about-you flow over my arms and up into my throat, making it easier to say his name. To look at him.

There was nothing he could do that I couldn't fight. There was nothing he could say that would possibly hurt me. I had prepared for this. I'd warned myself it might happen… one day maybe ten years from now, when, hopefully, I might be hot as hell and living my best life, so I could rub it in his face that I was better than ever. That I hadn't missed or needed his ass for a second.

This asshole with those honey-colored eyes had the nerve to stand there, watching me, with all those muscles and that face and that green hoodie and those jeans and that closely cropped hair and smoothly shaved jaw, and say, all soft and almost shyly, *and in that fucking accent that had been the second thing to catch my attention,* "Hi, Lenny."

Hi, Lenny.

He'd *Hi, Lenny*-d me.

This fucking long and he was going to go with *"Hi, Lenny"* like we had seen each other a week ago at the grocery store?

I can do this, I repeated to myself.

If I could have reached my stress ball, I would have, but I couldn't, at least not without him noticing, and I wasn't going to give him the gift of seeing me squeezing my ball to keep my shit together in his presence.

This wasn't about me.

Asshole. Fucking *dickface.*

I didn't even look away because *fuck that*. This was *my* place, and I hadn't done anything wrong. He'd been the one who had lied when he'd kissed me seventeen months ago and promised to see me after his match.

"What the hell are you doing here?" I asked before I could stop myself.

The Asshole stood there, the fingers at his sides wiggling, fidgeting as he watched me. A moment went by, then another with us just staring at each other. *Why the hell was he finally here? Why now?*

I waited for a response but got nothing. Like always. Why would I expect differently?

All right. He didn't want to answer my question? He didn't want to own up to his actions? *Fine.* This was on him. I wasn't taking the lead anymore. I had promised myself I wouldn't. I could play dumb all day long too if that's what he wanted.

"If you're looking for Peter, he's in the building next door," I told him, keeping all my fingers tucked in and every curse word I knew in my mouth. Acting like it was no big deal he was here. No big deal that he had called *Peter.*

Goddamn it, I really wish I had my stress ball in my hand.

The Fucker's forehead scrunched; it was lined from years in the sun. Then that pink mouth formed an expression that wasn't a smile or a grimace but something in between. The next words that came out of his mouth—in the same quiet, soft voice that had cast some kind of voodoo magic on me once upon a time—tried their best to woo me over, again.

"I didn't come for Peter," Jonah Collins said, staring straight at me with that grimace slash smile on his face... like he couldn't be sure how he felt. Happy or nervous.

It took everything inside of me not to make a face at his bullshit.

What I did instead was sit there quietly and watch both of his dimples flash for one split second. Because of course he had a dimple in each tan cheek.

He didn't come for Peter.

Yeah *right*. Yeah, fucking right. *God.* I had to get through this as quickly as possible. *Now, now, now.*

I didn't break eye contact with those honey-colored irises as I looked at him. I could play this game. "I don't know what you know about Peter," I said, making sure to keep my features schooled, "but he isn't a personal trainer. If you want a tour of the gym, I can have the assistant manager show you around." He knew what Peter did at the gym. I had told him. He was a fucker, but he'd listened. I was sure of it. There was no way he had gotten that mixed up in his head.

But Jonah didn't say a word as he kept on standing there, so still it didn't even look like he was breathing.

What a prick.

If he wanted to talk about... things, it was on him. I'd wasted my last phone call and email on him eight months ago. I wasn't searching out shit in regard to him anymore.

"If you're looking for a trainer, I can get you in contact with someone who focuses on athletes like you," I said, hearing myself offering to find him a personal trainer and cringing inside. *Really? That's what I'm doing?* I was better than that. I could stand in front of him. I could speak to him. Of course, I could do this. Why had I thought I couldn't? I could look into his eyes and listen to his voice and ignore those memories of how much I had enjoyed those two things at one point. My mouth kept on going. "No one with any rugby experience, probably, but with football."

When I had first seen him, I had assumed he was a football player initially. Then, I'd really paid attention and noticed the differences. For his height, his body fat percentage had been too low for any positions he might have been able to play since he was so tall. The cauliflowering of his ears—a deformity, some called it, that made a person's ear lumpy—was more typical for boxers and the people who trained at Maio House than football players; they wore helmets, their ears were never directly impacted. Then, he'd opened his mouth and confirmed my suspicions.

"Lenny," Jonah Hema Collins—I had found out his whole name after he'd disappeared—said my name the same way he had before: all soft and nearly cheery and wrapped in his New Zealand accent.

But I wasn't falling for it. Not ever again. Nah.

"Have a heart," Jonah continued on like I wasn't sporting my I-don't-give-a-fuck face at him. That chest on his six-foot-five-inch body expanded as he pulled in a breath and held it. Those light eyes focused right on me, wide and nervous, and if he had been anyone else, I would have thought there was a trace of hope in them too. "Tell me how you've been."

I could feel my nostrils flare the entire time he spoke. Tell him how I'd been after so long? Was that what he wanted to hear?

Worried. Pissed off. Furious. Scared. Terrified. Moody. Tired. Exhausted. Angry. Resigned. Even more exhausted. Determined. All those things in every combination.

Tension blossomed in my shoulders and neck, like it was telling me to get my shit together before I did something I'd regret.

"Do you want me to get you a number for a trainer or not?" A trainer, I reasoned, he could have easily gotten back in France or New Zealand or South Africa, any other country in the world other than this one, my brain reasoned. Fucking Antarctica based on how his phone and email hadn't worked for so long.

He wasn't able to hide the way those big, tanned and scarred hands of his opened and closed at his sides. But Jonah Collins decided he had selective listening by the way he barreled over my question and asked another one. "Can't you tell me how you've been?"

He really wanted to know?

I smiled at him.

"I've been great. Is that what you want to hear? How I've been doesn't matter though, does it?" I even flashed my teeth at him with my next smile. "I need to get back to work. I'll write down phone numbers for two trainers, if that's why you're here"—doing God knows what, halfway across the world—"or if you still want a tour, I can get someone to give you one."

The brown-haired man, with hair just as closely cropped as it had been back in the day, watched me. His Adam's apple bobbed. His nostrils flared with a breath.

And I didn't like it.

I didn't like it either when one of his feet, which I remembered as being huge, brought him a step closer toward the desk. Toward me. Not hesitating exactly but wary.

Did he know that a massive part of me—a part I was trying to ignore—suddenly wanted to beat the shit out of him, and that's why he was trying to be all cautious and shit?

"Talk to me," he insisted, even if I had a feeling he was well aware of what I would do to him if I could. "Are you all right?"

The *now you want to talk* was there, in my throat, on my tongue. Just... there. And I didn't let it move. I didn't let it go anywhere.

Those golden honey-colored eyes searched and moved over me as I sat behind my desk, tension clenching everything between my chin down to my butt cheeks, and I wondered for just one split second what he saw. If I looked older. More tired.

If he could see how much sleep I had missed out on for a giant chunk of the time we had been... apart. I wondered what he thought about the weight I hadn't totally lost over the last few months but was still working on.

Then I reminded myself that I didn't care what he thought or what he saw.

"I'm fantastic." Hating the way my fingertips started tingling out of nowhere, I grabbed a pen from the cup on my desk and pulled one of my notepads over. I picked up my cell and started going through the contacts as I said sarcastically, "If you don't want a tour, *and* you want to keep on ignoring shit, I need to get back to work. I don't have time for this BS, but here are two numbers for trainers in case you need them while you're here. If you want a tour of the gym, just let Bianca at the front desk know, and she'll get you the manager. There's a really nice gym about twenty minutes away too if this one is too far."

Fucking fuckface.

I ripped the sheet off the pad and held it out to the man who was honestly just as tall and built as my memories tried to remind me. It was seriously unfair that he was better looking than I remembered. His skin was a richer shade from being out in the sun during the season, a gift from a dad he'd told me was a mixture of Samoan, Māori, and European. *Yeh, got my size from him,* he had told me once with a bashful smile, like he hadn't been able to help growing into that frame and it embarrassed him.

Asshole.

Jonah Hema Collins didn't say anything or take the paper, so I held it up even higher, giving it a shake. He wanted to stall? Fine. I could stall.

I met his gaze with hopefully the blankest expression I could muster. "Take it. And so you know, Peter knows about us."

That seemed like common sense, but... here was the last man I would ever expect to roll up to my family's gym and ask how I was doing and look at me like... like I didn't fucking know. Like he genuinely wanted to talk to me. Like he really cared about how I was and how I'd been.

Bullshit, bullshit, bullshit.

We both knew he didn't. His actions for so long had confirmed all that. I knew how nonexistent my place in his life was.

And if he was here for the reason I thought he was, *he* needed to take the next step forth. He just needed to know right now that whatever he was planning, I wasn't alone. I wasn't thousands of miles away from home anymore.

"I haven't said anything to anyone. Like I told you the last time I emailed you, I don't need or want anything from you. I don't know why you're here, but you don't need to pretend anything." I almost bit my lip but barely managed not to. "*We* don't need to pretend anything. But this place is my family—my home—and if you're an asshole, it won't end well, all right?"

It was on the second sentence that he flinched. This great, big frown came over that good-looking face that I couldn't ignore as much as I wanted to. He had been so fucking beautiful to me once, even though he had more in common with a villain than he did a hero, this man who could steamroll over other men like they were bowling pins, which was the last thing I would have expected with his soft voice, those eyes that I'd thought—wrongly—were kind, those freckles over his nose, and those damn dimples.

But he wasn't anymore though. Beautiful, I meant. He was just a reminder that appearances were only skin deep.

Beautiful people were *good*. They didn't do the kinds of things that he had. They didn't show up to rub salt on a wound that had healed, hoping to reopen it.

Because that's what his presence here was, regardless of what his reasons were.

Bullshit. It was all straight-up bullshit.

The nostrils on that nearly perfect nose flared, and those tiny, thin valleys across his forehead formed at the same time his frown did. "You think I would be an asshole to you?" he asked in that damn voice that had made me believe once that it was incapable of doing anything wrong.

He really didn't want me to answer that.

This man who had once made me smile and laugh said nothing. That broad chest rose and fell under his hoodie, and the lines across his forehead got even deeper. His jaw moved from side to side. For a moment, I watched him struggle with something, and then he stood up even straighter, like that was somehow fucking possible.

"Lenny... I never meant to hurt you," Jonah "Piece of Shit" Collins claimed, so carefully, I might have thought he was genuine if I hadn't known any better. "You have to believe me."

I couldn't help it then. I raised my eyebrows. The nerve of this asshole.

It only took a quick glance at the picture frame on my desk again to help me reel my shit in, reel in the ugly words and the sudden urge to throw my computer screen at him like it was a ninja star. My hand wanted to go up to my eyelid and hold it down to keep it from twitching, but I kept that sucker down. Making a fist, I stared at him, squinting while I did.

"How did you expect not to hurt me? When you didn't answer your phone once after I called you over and over again? Or when you didn't respond to a single one of the emails I sent you either? Because there were a lot of them."

I could see the tendons in his neck flex as he stood there, staring back at me with that grimace/frown/smile, and I was sure he was thinking of whatever excuse he'd made up in his head to justify what he'd done. But I only let him get out a single sentence. "I can explain."

The smile I gave him didn't feel as brittle as I figured it should have. And when I reached toward my mouse to prepare to get back to work, I didn't feel bad for how cold I knew my expression—my entire body language—was toward him. He deserved it. He deserved it and fucking more, and he had no idea how lucky he was that I didn't toss his ass out and tell him to fuck off until the end of time. He was so lucky I was over him and his shit and was more mature than I had been before.

"I don't care anymore, Jonah. Decide what you want and let me know. I don't care one way or the other. That's all that matters to me, and we can go from there," I said to him carefully, so fucking carefully, I would have high-fived myself for being so damn good at shooting him one last—fake—smile and then focusing back on my computer screen, ignoring him standing there in my office, in silence.

Because that was what he did. Stand there, looking at me. Whether he was cursing himself out or not, I had no idea. Whether he was cursing me out in his head, I had no clue either. All I knew was that he took his time there, totally still, facing me in his massive asshole glory, as I ignored him.

Two minutes later—minutes that I counted perfectly in my head as I randomly clicked around on the screen from time to time to make it seem like I really was working instead of trying to be cool—he exhaled deeply, stared some more, and before turning around, called out quietly, "I want to talk to you, Len. That's what I want." He paused, his gaze heavy. "I'm sorry."

He left then.

Because that was what he did: leave.

Then and only then did I grab my stress ball from my drawer, wishing I had another for my free hand because only one wasn't enough right then, and squeezed the fuck out of it, switching hands when the first one started to cramp. I was real grateful right then that I hadn't set myself up to be disappointed with how easily he left.

But it was right after I traded hands that my cell rang with Grandpa Gus's ringtone. I swore to God he was a witch. Only he could time this so perfectly.

We were going to need to talk. A lot sooner than I had hoped for.

I hit the answer button and didn't bother trying to hide the tension in my voice. "Grandpa."

"How's my favorite demon?" he answered like he always did when he was in a really good mood, and like always, it made me smile even though I didn't feel like it. I squeezed my eyes closed as I did it, feeling this knot swell up in my throat all of a sudden.

"Everybody is getting on my nerves today," I told him honestly, struggling to even get those words out as a mental picture of Jonah's face filled my head with those damn freckles and that grimace/frown/smile.

"Everybody is always getting on your nerves," he replied. "Want to get out of there and get some lunch?"

We needed to talk. Now, apparently. Shit. I knew I should have done this months ago… even a year ago… but…

I hadn't. I thought I'd have more time. My fault again.

"Are you in the mood for Pho Palace?" I asked. "I can meet you there in fifteen."

"Meet you there in thirty," he agreed a second before hanging up, not waiting for me to confirm thirty was good and not bothering to say bye. He never did. He said the b-word sounded too final.

That and I think he just liked hanging up on people.

Lowering my hand to the desk, I squeezed my eyes shut for another moment, shoved my chair back, and got to my feet. Fuck it. I had put myself in this mess, I was going to have to get myself out of it.

CHAPTER 4

"Jonah, it's Lenny again. I'm worried about you. Where the hell are you hiding?"

MY BEST FRIEND HADN'T SAID ANYTHING IN TWO WHOLE MINUTES.

In the first sixty seconds, she had narrowed her eyes, looked up at the ceiling, made a thoughtful face, looked back at me, narrowed her eyes some more, and then pressed her lips together, squinting so much that she probably couldn't see anything.

In that same amount of time, I had crossed my arms over my chest and waited for her to make a comment.

Over the course of the next minute, she had pulled her phone out of her purse, which had been sitting on top of my desk since she was in the chair across from me, and started pecking away at the screen. Luna didn't let me down as she finally loosened her lips, sat back in the chair, and took a deep breath. Her eyes went wide a moment before those green eyes flicked back in my direction as we sat there in my office the following morning.

Her index finger came up a second before she held up her

phone with her other hand and aimed the screen at me. "*This* is him?"

The image on the screen was of a deeply olive-skinned man with shorts halfway up his thighs, a green short-sleeved jersey stretched so tight across his chest it made you wonder how the hell he got it on and off, standing on a field with his arms loose at his sides. The man had biceps so big it looked like someone had shoved a ball under his skin, thighs wide and tight and lined with muscles that overlapped each other. The ultra-serious expression on his face, brows furrowed, mouth slightly parted, irritated the fuck out of me.

"Yeah, that's Jonah," I confirmed, looking back at Luna's face because I didn't want to look at his anymore than I needed to.

My best friend gaped, literally gaped, as she looked back at the screen. Her finger started pecking away at her phone again, and it didn't take a genius to guess she was scrolling through more pictures of him.

I sighed. "You're about to say something stupid, aren't you?"

Fucking Luna nodded before she made yet another face— still at her screen—and asked, in total fucking disbelief, "You *slept* with him?"

"No, we just played patty-cake," I answered her dryly.

Her phone went down, and I had her undivided attention again. Even her elbows went to her thighs as she leaned forward and asked way too carefully, "No, Lenny, for real. You. Had. Sex. With. Him?"

I blinked. I didn't need that reminder. "Yes."

"*Him?*"

I poked at my inner cheek with the tip of my tongue. "I'm not really feeling your tone of voice right now."

This bish looked back at the picture of Jonah Collins and shook her head again like she couldn't believe it. "I just... I mean..." She was stuttering. She was literally stuttering, and I just about rolled my fucking eyes at her.

I mean, yeah, I understood. Jonah was... a fucker, of course... a dipshit, dumbass, motherfucker... but he was beautiful. Handsome in a way that only few men could be, not feminine at all, but sculpted so perfectly from his perfect hairline to his roughly striking face... and then there was that body.

God, I hated his guts, no matter what I told myself about not feeling anything. Hatred. Hatred was a feeling. But it was also a verb sometimes.

"*Him?*" she asked *again* in disbelief.

"I think I might be starting to get a little offended by how surprised you sound, Luna," I told her, totally joking, because really, I did get it.

"I always... you never..." She kept stopping and starting with her words as she grew flustered. "You've never said anything about a guy before, Len. Not once in ten years. I just thought you were... asexual or something for the longest time." Her cheeks went pink as she whispered, "I thought you were a virgin until... you know."

I blinked at her again, knowing she had a point. "Yeah, no."

She gasped. "You never said anything! I thought for a while there you had something going on with that Noah guy, but then nothing ever happened, and I know you, if you really liked him, I bet you would have gone for it, and—*did you lose it to him?*"

My shady-ass past was finally coming to light. "I'm thirty-one. I didn't lose my virginity to Jonah, Luna. Jesus."

"*Who then?*"

There was a reason I'd never brought this up before: I just hadn't seen the point. On the other hand, Luna had given me some intimate details of her and the guys she'd dated before so... it was the least I owed her. "This one guy I was friends with when I started going to college. He was in a few of my classes." I shrugged, thinking about the guy that I had liked as a friend.

"Let me see a picture of him."

I rolled my eyes with a snort. "Stalker, much?"

"Does he look like him?" she asked, shaking her phone at me.

I slid her a look. "No. And stop looking so surprised. You might start hurting my feelings."

That had her groaning. "You know what I mean!"

I shrugged my good shoulder at her, honestly relieved that I had finally managed to tell her the entire story. At least 90 percent of it. Even though she was my best friend, she didn't need to hear the bad parts. No one did. I knew there were plenty of things she hadn't shared with me over the years. The same way I knew there were a handful of other things I had never told her either.

"So he's back?" she asked, focused back on her screen.

"Yeah."

Her green eyes went wide as she sat in the chair, eyes moving back to her phone while she processed my news. "What are you going to do?" she asked after a second.

"See what he says," I answered her simply. "I don't really have another choice." It wasn't like I could pick him up by his ankles and give him the shakedown over the side of a skyscraper so he'd tell me why he was here or what he wanted. Unfortunately.

"What does Grandpa Gus think?"

Fuck me. I straight-up grimaced at her.

That was what it took to get her to shove her phone back into her purse, drop her mouth wide, and gasp, *"You haven't told him?"*

I thought about lunch the day before and winced at how I'd talked myself out of telling him anything, even after he asked me if I was constipated from the faces I'd been making. "No..."

"Lenny!"

"I was going to, but he was in a good mood, and I didn't

want to ruin it," I explained, knowing it sounded about as lame of an excuse as it really was.

Luna's mouth was still open as she shook her head for about the tenth time in the last ten minutes. I couldn't blame her. I couldn't believe I'd been that much of a coward either. "You know, I never thought the day would come where I'd be the one calling you a chickenshit."

I rolled my eyes before glancing back down at the claim I had been in the middle of filing so I could get reimbursed for a faulty leg press that I'd had to pay to get repaired. "You know, I never thought the day would come where I would be calling you a smart-ass, Luna, but look at that, miracles do come true," I muttered in return... even though we both knew she was totally right.

I was being a chickenshit. A big one.

And she hadn't been the first one to call me out on it. Peter had too the night before after I'd told him about my surprise visitor, and that was because at this point, other than Luna, he was the only other person who knew what I was avoiding.

That was: telling Grandpa Gus something he should have known months ago.

The truth... not that I had ever technically lied to any of them. I just hadn't said anything, period. That was the only factor that worked in my favor: that none of them had known. Until now at least.

Grandpa was going to be even more pissed he was the last person to find out.

Luna had canceled on me the night before because her daughter hadn't been feeling well still, and we'd planned for her to come by the gym in the morning while her father-in-law watched her Ava, which was how and why we were here, in the office at the gym with the door closed, with her making crazy faces at me because I had sex with one of the most attractive rugby players in the world.

Luna Ripley, one of my top five favorite people in the entire world, gaped again before bursting out laughing. "Rip said something similar a few days ago, but what can I say? I've mastered my craft by learning from the best," she said, referring to her husband.

Her husband.

Jesus.

We were old enough to be married now, I remembered, deciding to focus on that for a second. Well, *she was* married. This was who we were now. Making and canceling plans because of *kids*. Real, human children.

Fuck, I still hadn't gotten used to that.

Her comment got a groan out of my throat as I shoved aside this thing with Grandpa Gus and Jonah that loomed over my head. "Bish, I know you're not talking about my pal Rip like that."

"Bish, we both know who I'm talking about," she claimed, bringing a smile onto my face as I signed my signature on the bold line of the form.

"Hey, don't talk about Grandpa like that either."

That got her laughing one more time. "I can't believe it though," she said after a moment. "How have you not *told* him? He always knows everything. He knew I was pregnant before I did, remember? Now that I think about, I'm surprised he didn't hire a private investigator or anything."

I'd forgotten that, but she was right. She'd been around the ageless vampire long enough to know how the man worked. And he hadn't hired a PI because I'd asked him very, very nicely.

It hit me then that he *had* let me get away with not telling him about Jonah.

"After he got mad, initially, he just never asked. Then last night, he left as soon as I got home because it was pickleball night, and I was in my room by the time he got back. This morning he was arguing with the tech people for our internet service, and we barely said two words to each other," I tried to explain, hearing my own bullshit and cringing at it.

Excuses, fucking excuses. I was a total chickenshit now. Seriously.

This person that was the closest thing I would ever have to a sister snorted across from me, thinking the same thing.

It was my turn to make a face at one of the best people in my life. "I don't know what the hell you're snorting about."

She was smiling—she was always fucking smiling—as she glanced at her ancient watch, then stood up and shook her blue-haired head, hand gripping the strap of her purse. "You know what I'm snorting at, Len." She smiled even wider. "I need to go. I'm meeting up with Rip for lunch, but text me later." The little shit wiggled her eyebrows. "You know, after you tell Grandpa G about you-know-who. Hehe."

I scowled as I got up and kissed her on the cheek, getting one back. "Tell him I said hi. Are we still on for lunch next week?"

"I will, and, yes, we're on." Luna slid me a smile and held her palm up between us, and I smacked it. "I know he's an asshole, but he's a really hot one, Len. Almost as hot as Rip. I'm so proud of you."

I groaned and waited until she was halfway down the short hall before I called out, "I love you, Luna!"

"Love you too, Len!"

I smiled to myself as I shoved my chair back and looked down at the claim form I'd just signed before grabbing it and heading out of the office. It didn't take more than a second to find Peter hanging over the top edge of the cage's walls, looking into it as two men, who I couldn't recognize from this far, circled each other.

On the way toward the gym next door, I waved at the small group of men and women on the mats, covered in sweat and breathing hard following whatever exercises they had just gone through.

It didn't take me long at all to leave the building and head toward the one next door. Inside, the ceilings opened up just as high, with row after row of equipment and machines lined up perfectly to maximize the space. I lifted a hand at all the people I recognized as I headed straight toward where the fax machine was at the front desk. It only took about three minutes to send the fax and get a confirmation back—because the company didn't believe in scanners—and I made a quick stop at the front desk slash juice bar to check on the two employees there and make sure they didn't need anything. They didn't. Bianca had bags under her eyes, but that wasn't saying much since I did too most days, and the other girl looked fine.

At least I had work stuff going for me without issues, I thought, as an image of Jonah's face filled my brain for all of a split second—specifically an image of Jonah's face after I'd told him that I didn't care about his excuses anymore. Just as quickly as that picture entered my head, fucking tiny little freckles on his nose and all, I shoved it away.

Seventeen months.

I had *nothing* to feel bad about. Nothing.

Back out to the training building, I managed five steps inside my office before coming to a stop.

Someone was sitting in the chair in front of my desk.

Someone with short hair so dark it could have been dark brown or black. Tall, based on how high up he sat in the seat, with wide, muscular shoulders, and a thick neck. Shit.

There were a couple other dark-haired men at Maio House but none of them had shoulders that size or trap muscles that bulky. The tallest man who trained in this part of the gym was six foot three. I took everyone's height and weight when they first joined. When they were finally forced to start cutting weight—which meant that right before they had a fight, they had to lose a few pounds to make it to their weight class because usually everyone was fifteen to twenty pounds heavier than they needed to be, and that was on the average side—I helped them keep track of it so that it wouldn't be too much that had to be cut in too short of a time period. I had known guys who had to drop out of fights because they had gone a little too crazy with sodium levels, and no one wanted to lose an opportunity, especially over something so stupid.

But that was all beside the point. Because it only took maybe a second for me to figure out who was sitting there. Think of the damn devil and he will appear, or whatever the saying was.

Jonah Hema Collins wasn't the devil, but I couldn't say he wasn't much further down the list than the red guy was on people I would rather never see.

How the hell had he gotten inside again?

I reminded myself for about the hundredth time over the last couple of days that there wasn't anything the Fucker could say or do that would hurt me. There was nothing that would change my life too much. There was nothing that could happen that I couldn't fight, because I would if I had to. I came from a long line of people who were really good at fighting. And that gene hadn't skipped a generation with me.

The man I'd known hadn't seemed like the kind of person to do something shitty… but everyone changes. That, and I wasn't sure I had even gotten to know him that well in the first place, from the way he'd turned out in the end. You know, like an asshole.

I was going to be an adult. I was going to keep *allllll* this shit to myself and punch my pillow when I got home. *That's* what I was going to do. Be an adult, even if a little part of me died from forcing myself to be decent since it wasn't like that came all that naturally to me.

If I couldn't make it until then, there were a couple bags right outside my office I had access to.

Seriously, who the hell had let him in?

"Good morning," the man sitting in the chair said as he turned his head to look at me over his shoulder, like he had either heard or sensed me coming in.

He could take his *morning* and shove it up his—

There went my speech. But I wasn't doing this for me, was I? Damn it.

"Hi," I told him, giving him my best Lurch impression.

I rounded the edge of the desk, knowing my hip was just a few inches away from his elbow as I did it. It wasn't a big room, but it wasn't that small either. It was just that he wasn't exactly what anyone would call a small man unless it was Andre the Giant we were talking about.

Jonah the Asshole didn't wait until I was seated to say, "I'd like to sign up for a membership."

Was he trying to piss me off? I wanted to ask him. I would have, if I had known I could get the question out of my mouth without going back on the promise I made myself. Because unlike some people I knew, when I said I would do something, I did it. I didn't disappear—

Stop.

If you don't have anything nice to say, you shouldn't say anything at all, Luna would tell me. But she had never warned me how fucking *hard* it was to live up to that. And I definitely didn't have a single nice thing to say about any of this. Especially not for this asshole in my office who was busy looking at me with a clear, guileless, totally earnest and open expression as he gazed at me over his shoulder.

And that just made me madder.

He wanted a membership *here*? Okay. Fine.

I pulled my chair out, lowered myself onto it carefully and then rolled it forward once more. Then and only then did I look up at him at the same time as I reached out between us, taking in that face that was almost model-gorgeous. *Almost.* Except he had been too busted up over the years to be something so... basic.

Fortunately for me, it didn't take much effort to remember that maybe I wasn't going to be a complete asshole, but that didn't mean I had to like him. Or that I had to be nice. Just...

polite. Out loud. The things I thought in my head were a different story.

Fuckface.

And it was with that thought that I watched as he scooted forward in the seat he had taken without permission or an invitation and reached out with that big, big hand. I watched in slow motion as his fingertips—long and with signs at the joints that said that nearly all of them had been broken at some point —brushed over the back of my hand so gently it might have been nice… if I didn't borderline hate him.

For the rest of my life, I was going to blame the fact that he genuinely surprised the shit out of me on why I didn't immediately slap his fingers away.

Jonah Collins took my hand with those strong fingers— while I sat there like a dumbass—flipping it over in the blink of an eye, so that my palm sat upward on my desk, and then set his own palm on top of it. His hand swallowed mine, making it seem a lot smaller than it actually was. The same way it had so long ago.

Before he'd left.

Before he'd changed my life for the better.

And also pissed me off in a way that was beyond fucking words.

I jerked my hand out from under his.

Fisting my hand, I set it on my thigh for a second before returning it to my desk because fuck it. I wasn't going to hide shit from him.

He was the one who did the hiding.

Those honey-colored eyes were still on me, and I could see the deep, drawn breath he took in. I didn't care if I hurt his feelings. He'd hurt mine enough. And he was real fucking lucky I was being this mature. That I was willing to *let* him be here in the first place.

But before I could say anything else, his shoulders pushed back and his chin went up again in that way I had only seen him do on the rugby field… pitch, whatever it was called. Like he was pumping himself up to deal with me. I ignored how that might have made me feel.

"Have lunch with me," the Fucker said softly in that accented voice that I wasn't attracted to anymore.

I said "no" instantly.

His shoulders stayed back as he tried again. "Brekkie?"

Breakfast? Why was he *doing this?* "What the hell do you want, Jonah?"

His Adam's apple bobbed. The man let his eyes drift over my face slowly, and I was pretty sure he held his breath. "I understand that you're mad—" That was as far as he got before I stopped him.

"Mad?" I snapped before I could remind myself that I needed to keep it cool. "You think I'm *mad?*"

If anything, the word *pissed* would be more accurate for how I'd felt a year ago. Months ago, even. But not now.

He sat up just a little, but just enough to make those big, flat muscles flex under the long-sleeved white T-shirt with a tiny Adidas logo that was gripping his shoulders for dear life. The asshole made sure he was making total eye contact with me, keeping that fucking face nice and even as he responded way too calmly, "Yes. I can see you are, Lenny. You have that face you make when you're bothered, squinty eyes and all," the man from New Zealand answered in that way that was so second nature to him, I couldn't believe I had liked the shit out of it in the past. "I want to talk to you about it. Explain."

Why the hell was he acting like… like… it was just a matter of talking? Like I'd want to pick back up on the way we had been with each other where we teased each other? This asshole was going to make me burst a fucking blood vessel.

Breathe, Lenny. This isn't about you. Be decent. You don't have to shit out sugarplums for this dipshit.

With a breath in through my nose and right back out, I managed not to bite down hard on my back teeth as I got my shit back together. Again. "Unless it's about something relating to Maio House," I told him carefully, "or about what you still haven't wanted to bring up on your own, there's no reason for us to talk, Jonah. I've said everything I needed to say already. I told you how I feel about anything you might want to explain." I paused. "I don't care."

His tongue poked at the inside of his cheek as he shifted his weight around. He fisted his hands again as he leaned forward, managing to keep his voice and features even, like this wasn't going downhill and I wasn't shooting down his bullshit. "I understand you don't want to hear it." Those eyes my favorite color in the world moved over my face again, slowly, so, so slowly it made me uncomfortable. "But I need to explain," he said, never blinking, or breaking eye contact or doing anything but laser-beaming that gaze on me. "I want to tell you what's happened." He swallowed. "I need to tell you."

To give him credit, everything about his body language, from the way the tendons at his neck were straining to what looked like anguish flicking within his eyes, said he was being genuine. He genuinely thought he wanted to talk to me. He wanted to tell me whatever it was that he felt he needed to say.

He believed his words.

But just because he believed them didn't mean that I did. Because I didn't. He'd had his chance. *Chances.* I had given him more than enough time to do something as simple as email or text me back, and he hadn't. Sure I blocked his number, blocked him on every social media website possible, but I hadn't blocked his emails… and they still hadn't shown up.

"I don't care about why or when or how anymore, Jonah. What I want is to know what you're doing here."

"I'm here to talk to you." He set that big hand back on the top of my desk, just inches away from my keyboard. "Give me a chance to explain. Please."

What was it that he wanted to explain? Why he had disappeared? Why he hadn't called me back? Why he hadn't wanted to be part of... my life? Why he'd decided to come back now?

Did he think I was a fucking mind reader? Because I wasn't. Of course I wasn't.

His fingers slid half an inch closer, his fingertips touching the edge of my keyboard. I couldn't help but take in those endless, brown fingers with their neat, short nails, and the scarred and forever slightly swollen knuckles. He slid it even closer to me. "I know I've made a mess of things, but I want to explain—"

I tore my eyes away from his fingers. "There are a lot of things I want that I know I'm never going to get. That's how things work sometimes." I shoved my chair forward even though I was already as close to my desk as I could get. "I have a phone call I need to take in a minute, so..." I glanced toward the door to give him a clue. *Get the fuck out.*

Jonah opened his mouth just as the phone literally started to ring—I didn't know who was calling, but whoever it was was my new favorite person—and then shut it. A breath later, he got to his feet, bringing him up, up, up so that he towered over my desk. And then he irritated me even more with his next words.

"This conversation isn't over, Lenny."

And before I could tell him that it sure as hell was—at least until he told me what the fuck it was that he wanted—he was gone.

But I hadn't missed the expression on his face or the tension in his shoulders as he walked out.

I couldn't stand him. I couldn't fucking stand him, I thought as I picked up the ringing office phone and brought it to my ear. "This is Lenny."

"This call is from the IRS. Don't hang up—"

I rolled my eyes and hung up, still feeling more than a little grateful. I wasn't ready. I didn't want to be ready to deal with him... but I wanted to know what was going on. I wanted to know what he was doing and what he was planning on doing.

What I did know right then, without looking at the clock, was that there was a conversation I desperately needed to have. One of the most important conversations of my life. Even if I was dreading it more than I had ever dreaded anything.

Then, after that talk, I really did need to get an answer from Jonah the Jackass about what the fuck he was doing.

I eyed the clock on my computer for a second and got to my feet. I couldn't put it off anymore. Now or never.

Fucking *shit*.

Grabbing my phone off the top of the desk, I dialed the number from memory as I headed around my desk and picked up my backpack from where I left it leaning against the coat rack that was older than I was. *I could do this.* The phone rang three times before the man on the other end picked up.

"Want to meet up for lunch again, child of the corn?"

"Hey, Grandpa. Yeah." I pulled my keys out of the backpack pocket and headed out of the office, wiggling a finger at the people standing at the edges of the mats while they waited for their turn to do whatever it was they were training. "I'd rather come home for lunch though. Do you want something specific?"

He made a funny little cooing noise that wasn't meant for me, telling me he wasn't totally paying attention before replying with, "Double of whatever you're bringing."

"Okay, I'll be there in thirty," I told him, shouldering the outside door open.

"What's wrong?" Grandpa Gus asked suddenly, and it didn't escape me the fact that he asked *what* was wrong, not asking *if* something was wrong.

He knew me too well.

And, God, he was going to lose his shit after we had our talk. Fuck.

Knowing that made it hard to keep toeing that line. "Nothing life-or-death. I'll see you in a little bit."

I didn't like the way he said "okay," but if I didn't like it, I deserved it.

Fuck!

~

THIRTY-FIVE MINUTES LATER, I OPENED THE DOOR TO THE HOUSE I had lived at on and off my entire life, holding a bag of burritos and tortilla chips in one hand.

And I was sweating my damn ass off despite the fact it was in the high forties outside.

But as I went through the back door connected to the kitchen that had been completely remodeled a few years ago and then through the hallway that led to the living room of the house that Grandpa had bought a thousand years before I'd been born, I listened.

Everything was quiet. Too quiet. Usually the television was on, or there was something playing over the speakers in the living room, or somebody was making some kind of noise, but there was none of that.

Hmm.

I kicked off my shoes and started creeping down the hallway, clutching the bag of burritos and hoping the paper bag wouldn't make too much noise.

Still, there was nothing.

I narrowed my eyes and peeked into the living room to find it empty. I held my breath and listened. And that was when I heard it. Just the slightest, most quiet little noise...

"I know you're there. I can hear you breathing," I called out with a snort.

Nothing.

I rolled my eyes and climbed up on the love seat, one of the two couches in the living room, and hung over the back of it. Then I reached down and smacked one of the two bony butt cheeks sticking up in the air. "Get up before you can't," I laughed at my grandfather, who was on his hands and knees. Hiding. To try and scare the shit out of me.

He grunted and looked up with a frown. "You heard me?"

"Your sinuses are acting up. Your nose is wheezing." I peeled my jacket off and dumped it on the armrest of the couch.

He muttered something like "damn it" under his breath as he struggled, just a little, to his knees and then up to his feet. At seventy-five years old, his bones only reminded him every once in a while that he was closer to a hundred than twenty now, but it wasn't enough to make me sad. He had barely slowed down over the years, and he sure didn't look his age. Grandpa was a vampire and would end up outliving me.

I got off the couch with a snicker and shook my head again as he came around. "How long have you been down there?"

"I heard you pull in," he replied, still frowning at being caught as one hand went down to rub a circle into his left knee.

Because this was our game.

Hiding and scaring the crap out of each other. Or at least trying to. We'd been doing it for so long that we could both usually pick up on signals that said something was up. Example: the silence.

With a snicker, I dropped the bag of burritos on the coffee table and spotted the paperback sitting on the surface. It wasn't just any book, but one with a bare-chested firefighter—or two—on the cover; I couldn't tell from this distance. And just like always, it fucking made me laugh even though my stomach was knotted up at why I was home.

Because my seventy-five-year-old, four-time world champion boxer of a grandfather loved the hell out of romance novels, and it tickled the shit out of me. It always had and always would. And it was a perfect example of what made up his personality: a mixture of a thousand *what-the-fucks*.

"How's the book?" I asked him, hearing the weirdness in my voice and pretending like I didn't, as he lowered himself to the couch and opened the bag of food. I didn't need to give him more reason to be suspicious.

"I just started it. It's about two firefighters right after 9-11. I'll let you read it before I return it."

Yeah, I wasn't sure that was going to happen after this upcoming conversation. "How long have you been down here?" I watched him pull out the container of guacamole and do a little shimmy in place.

Good. It was working. Guacamole always put him into a good mood. I'd bought it on purpose.

"Thirty minutes," he answered, setting his treat aside. "I think we've got ten or fifteen more max before 'The General' is up again."

The General.

Right.

I held my breath as he handed me over one of the burritos without glancing at my face, fortunately. I thought my plan was working. I thought I was buttering him up before I lit the firework that was his temper. I thought I knew what I was doing.

I didn't apparently.

Because he let me get as far as ripping the foil off from around my veggie burrito and get all of two bites in before he turned to me as he chewed, raised his graying light brown eyebrows lazily, and went straight for the kill.

"What's going on?"

Of course he'd known.

I wasn't a coward enough to slow down eating to drag out the time, so I swallowed what I had in my mouth as quickly as I could without being too obvious. I took a peek at him, planning on making eye contact, but he was looking at the guac. So I did it. Just like when I was a kid, I counted to three and went for it: one, two, *three*.

"Have you heard of Jonah Collins?"

I would never admit it to fucking anyone, but my heart

started beating faster as soon as I said his name out loud to my gramps.

He, on the other hand, didn't stop eating, but he did narrow his eyes as he chewed, his expression still on the guacamole. "No," he said after a moment, finally glancing at me in this squinty little way that confirmed he was getting wary. "Why?"

Yeah, he was on to me.

I didn't know how to answer his question without just blurting everything out, and that wouldn't be a good idea with Count Dracula next to me. I had to feed him information. Ease him into it. The guacamole he was currently dipping his chip into had been the lube to ease us into this just a little.

I dug through my purse and pulled out my phone and did a quick search, my fingers feeling heavier than normal as they moved. My heart was still beating too fast, but I ignored it. Once the search results came up, I held the phone out toward Grandpa Gus so he could look at the image on the screen.

He took the phone from me with his free hand and brought it closer to his face. "He's a soccer player? No. He's too big. Football? No. He's not wearing pads or a helmet—"

Shit. I had to do it.

"Look at his eyes," I cut him off, ignoring the nerves bubbling up in my stomach.

Grandpa stared at the picture for a few more moments, his chewing slowing, and I could *see* when something in him clicked. I knew when those gray irises shot to me for a moment before going back to the screen. This man who wasn't just my grandfather, my dad, my brother, and my best friend all rolled into one body, typed something on my phone with one hand, then started swiping at the glass. Over and over again.

I knew what he was doing. It was the same thing I would have been doing if our positions had been switched. It didn't help that I was too much of a chicken to say the words that needed to be said.

He recognized the eyes on the screen. I'd been counting on

it. He had seen them even more than I had. He had watched them change over the months from a greenish hazel to the lightest brown that reminded me of raw honey with its flecks of yellow and gold in them.

The most beautiful eyes in the world, I thought.

My favorite. Grandpa's favorite too, I would say. I wouldn't be surprised if they were Peter's too, now, even though he was partial to DeMaio gray.

"This is him?" Grandpa Gus asked after another moment in that tone I had only heard a handful of times in my life. Usually when he was furious. Which the last time that had been was… sixteen months ago. Yay.

I nodded, not that he saw it because he was staring at the phone. "Yeah, Grandpa. That's him," I confirmed, wincing at the squeakiness in my voice.

Lord, he was breathing in and out through his nose already. I needed to get this over with, quick, quick, quick. Now.

"I didn't think I would ever see him again," I started to explain. "I tried reaching out to him over and over again but never heard back. I just thought he didn't want to have anything to do with… us." Maybe that comment didn't help, but… it was the truth.

Jonah hadn't bothered trying to call, period. If he really wanted to get in contact with me, he would have found a way. He would have found someone to pass a message along. He could have called me from a different number. He could have set up a fake account and messaged me. There was always a fucking way if you needed or wanted something. *Always.*

And since reappearing, there had been breaks in his schedule. Bye-weeks. He'd had opportunities. But there had been fucking nothing.

Instead, all I had gotten were those four random postcards at first.

Grandpa's fingers flexed around my phone, and I watched

as his mouth opened to stretch his jaw and then closed. Fuck. I knew, *I knew*, he was seconds away from losing his shit.

"Who else knows?" Even his voice was hoarse. Just five minutes ago, he'd been hiding behind the couch, trying to scare the hell out of me, and now he was trying to sound like Batman. Before I could answer, he shot out another question. "Why are you telling me now?"

Now or never.

"Peter knows. I told Luna earlier. We talked about it—*no*. Calm down. Quit getting riled up. Your face is getting red, and you know it looks ugly when it gets red," I told him, hoping teasing him would work.

It didn't. I'd lost him. I could tell.

"And I'm telling you because he showed up at Maio House," I rushed, but it was useless.

The old man shot up to his feet, his face hitting tomato red. "He's not getting anywhere near—"

I sighed and grabbed the leg of his olive pants. "Calm. Down. Jesus, Grandpa—"

"*Calm down?*" he shouted, making me roll my eyes.

"Yeah, calm down. You're about to burst a blood vessel, and I'm not driving you to urgent care if you do."

Yeah, he wasn't calming down. He wasn't calming down at all. The redness was creeping down his throat. I knew I had to keep going. "And you know that's not fair for you to say that. I don't want him around either, but I'm not going to be the jerk here, and you're not either," I said to him, hoping he could hear the reason in my words because, surprisingly, saying those words hadn't been as hard as I would have expected.

They were the truth. They were a necessity. I had to keep going. "If he wants to be here and is going to be responsible and do what he should have been doing, then he has every right—"

All right, that sentence had been hard as hell, but not as hard as the choke Grandpa Gus let out.

The drama queen, who was red from his hairline down to his neck, threw his hands up over his head. "Right my—"

I had to set my burrito down, knowing I wasn't going to get any more in my belly anytime soon and curled my fingers tighter into his pant leg because I already knew he was about to start stomping around the room if I let him. "He *does,* and you know it. I don't like it any more than you do, but it is what it is," I tried to reason. "You know you'd be telling me the same thing right now if we were talking about anybody other than your best little buddy, and you know that."

His best little buddy and my best little buddy. The best thing in my life. The best thing, period.

Grandpa Gus started shaking his head the second the fourth word was out of my mouth. If I thought I was stubborn, this man was the original outbreak monkey. I should have brought him a cannoli too to blackmail him into behaving. Too late now.

"No. Stop shaking your head, nothing is changing. He's here, and he deserves to be. We can't force him to leave." I didn't want him to stay, but this wasn't about me either, was it? No, but…. "He can stay if he wants to do the right thing. If not…." I held my hands up at my sides and shrugged, even though he didn't see me do it because he was glaring at the ceiling.

The point was: nobody was getting forced to stay, much less asked to. No way. The ball was in Jonah's court. He had gotten himself here, he could decide when he was leaving, at least until I had an answer and a commitment… and he brought it up. Which he still hadn't.

Unfortunately, Grandpa hadn't stopped shaking his head; his fingers had started tapping against his thighs, and redness still covered just about everything I could see above his neckline. "But he left you!" the man who loved me like hell reminded me like I could have forgotten. "That chucklehead left you," he said it again, eyes bright.

One day, I'd be able to enjoy him calling someone a chuckle

head, but right then wasn't going to be the day. Not when my grandfather was huffing and puffing. Not when we were talking about something so important. Jonah Collins was important and always would be. Unfortunately.

Unless he died.

"He left *me*," I tried to tell him, struggling a whole hell of a lot with getting that reality out. Acknowledging it. Tasting it. But even if something seemed good, didn't mean it actually was. Saying it didn't make it any less abrasive... but maybe one day it would. Maybe. "But not *her*."

Me. Not her.

And I was fine with that.

Grandpa turned to give me his back as his hands went up to the top of his head, the red color deepening and making me want to roll my eyes even more. Those dark gray eyes were borderline crazy as he glared down at me like he didn't know who the fuck I was anymore. Like he couldn't *believe* I wasn't agreeing with him.

And, honestly, a part of me couldn't believe it either.

But I wasn't the same Lenny I'd been before.

Just part of her.

And maybe Grandpa Gus remembered that but didn't want to accept the fact that, for once, I wasn't ready to raise hell—but deep down inside, I knew that later on, he'd come to terms with why that was. "What then? What if he decides to stay? Can you look at him every day if he does?"

I sucked in a breath through my nose and shrugged as I looked up at him from where I was still sitting on the couch. "No, I don't know that I can." I leaned forward and planted my elbows on my knees, my fingers going to massage my brow bones. "I want to beat the shit out of him. I want to rip his balls off and squirt lemon juice on his open wound."

That got me a tiny, baby snort. And then I wondered where the hell I got being psycho from.

"But this isn't about me, Grandpa, and stop breathing like

that. You're being so dramatic. It's my turn today to lose my shit, all right?"

"He—" Grandpa Gus started to say just as we both heard it.

The one and only sound that would have stopped this blowout we were in the middle of.

Mo's little kitten cries.

The same kitten cries that melted my heart every time I heard them. Even when I was tired and crankier than hell. Even when I was worried and overwhelmed. Even when I was scared and didn't know how the hell I was still alive and who had been dumb enough to give me such a huge responsibility.

I stood up before Grandpa made a move to go to the stairs.

"I'll go get her. You calm down in the meantime and remember all the reasons why you would hate going to jail if you got caught committing a felony," I said before heading up to the second floor two steps at a time.

What a fucking mess.

Down the hall and two doors down, beside my bedroom, I walked right into the bright room and headed straight toward the crib. And as much as I was flustered, I couldn't help but grin as I peeked over the railing a second before I picked Mo up.

"Hey, chunky monkey," I said, smiling at the one thing in this world that scared the shit out of me more than everything and anything else ever had combined. I had cried a month straight when I had first seen the positive pregnancy test staring back at me. Then I had spent the next six months staying up at night, unable to sleep, because I'd been terrified that I didn't know what the hell I was getting myself into. That I had made the wrong decision.

She was my seven-pound, eight-ounce surprise when she'd been born. The instant love of my life. The best thing I ever did.

She was the sweetest, happiest baby in the world. And I'd heard from multiple people who weren't Grandpa Gus or Peter that she was the prettiest girl too, which I agreed with. Duh. She seriously cried like a kitten and now babbled all day. Was soft and sweet and smelled awesome, unless she'd shit her diaper. With dark brown hair and already fitting into eighteen-month-old clothes at eight months old, she was all chubby arms and legs that wiggled in the air as tiny little cries came out of her mouth.

But as perfect as she was, I focused in on my favorite part of her. Her honey-colored eyes with flecks of gold and brown in them. Big and already almond-shaped.

They were the eyes she'd inherited from her dad.

The same eyes Grandpa Gus had seen in the picture I'd showed him of Jonah.

CHAPTER 5

"It's me. Again. Lenny. If you wanted to run away, fine. But at least send a smoke signal to let the rest of us know that you're alive. You're pissing me off now. Call me back. Bye."

I LEFT GRANDPA GUS AND MO AT THE HOUSE WHEN I HEADED back to work, but my gut had known instinctively that neither one of them was going to stay there for long.

And that knowledge didn't help the damn stomachache that had nothing to do with the burrito I had wolfed down even with all the dirty looks I'd been getting slipped from the man who had wiped my ass a thousand times growing up.

I mean Grandpa's reaction wasn't a surprise. I would have been surprised if he'd taken it well. Plus, the way he'd been wasn't exactly overreacting if you really knew him, but it was close enough. It was exactly what any of his friends would expect.

The calm gestures he'd made and the smile he shot at baby Mo when I had come back downstairs with a hungry eight-month-old were all a lie. But to give him credit, he tried to be in a good mood every time she was close… which was all the time since he was her babysitter. That was why he'd settled for subtle sneers behind her back.

But that didn't mean that I couldn't picture him buckling Mo into her car seat soon and saying in a baby voice, "Grandpa Gus is gonna go kill somebody. You wanna come with me? You wanna help bury your daddy?"

So I tried to tell myself that him eventually showing up at Maio House wouldn't be the end of the world. It might actually be a good thing for Jonah Collins to see Mo if he came by—not that I knew if he would actually come back, especially after I'd run him off with my perfectly timed scammer call earlier.

If he hadn't left, was he going to be a father to Mo in some way?

Or was he going to see her, realize that this wasn't some part-time job, and decide to go back to whatever hole he had crawled out of and never come back again?

From the moment I had last emailed Jonah, three days after Mo had been born, and explained that I would never keep him apart from his daughter if he was going to genuinely try to be a part of her life, I had promised myself that I could put my pride aside and let him be there. I could stand there, imagining myself ripping off his balls and spitting them out with blood all over my face, but that was all I would do.

Live in my dreams. Where I could murder people without repercussions.

Anyway, the point was, from time to time, when I had been growing up, I had imagined my mom coming to see me. In my head, I had thought I could forgive her. You know, for giving me up, for not being around. I had thought that maybe we could have some kind of relationship.

But the older I got, and now that I had my own girl, I realized that that shit was never going to happen. There were some circumstances that would make sense, but it had been thirty years now, and she hadn't come back. That opening had closed a while ago.

I figured if she had wanted to find me, she could have. Any excuse she could have used to justify to herself leaving me with my grandfather immediately after my birth didn't hold any value anymore. It had been her choice to walk away, and back then, it would have been my choice to let her back in.

So I could give Mo that opportunity. Grandpa would have offered the same for me if she had tried to come back; I just knew it. So, yeah, if Jonah Collins wanted to be around... he could.

And if that made my head pound, nobody had told me to have some deadbeat, immature asshole's baby, did they?

I'd been so wrong about him; it made my throat ache with bitterness for a moment.

My best friend, Luna, had told me that when something was really bothering her and she knew there was no point in raging over it, or even thinking about it any longer than she needed to, that she would imagine balling it like a piece of paper and throwing it away. That was what I did right then: I threw it away.

Mo was here, and even though I had never, ever seen myself as a mom... and I had no idea what the hell I was doing seven-eighths of the time and was terrified because I didn't, she was *mine*. And I wasn't going to fuck up. I'd had the best example of a parent figure growing up, and I wasn't about to let her down.

Walking through the main gym first, I looked around at all the equipment to make sure things were up to standard. It was the middle of the week, and things were slow, but that was normal for the time of day. There were two personal trainers with their clients, and more random people spread around the floor doing various forms of exercise.

I took my sweet time using the covered path that led from one building to the other and wasn't at all surprised when I opened that door to the scene going on: a handful of guys training. Peter was there in the middle of it, along with two other assistant coaches.

Peter looked right over at me, and I didn't waste any time raising my hand and giving him a thumbs-down.

From the grimace he made, he knew what the hell that was for.

We'd talk about it later.

Or we wouldn't if Grandpa Gus came barging in like I expected him to.

He had never let me down, and he wasn't about to start now.

Twenty minutes later, while I was responding to an email from a small production company that wanted to film some scenes at Maio House, I heard the commotion outside that only happened when the old man dropped by. And five minutes later, when the "silver fox," like I'd overheard some blind women call my grandpa, headed straight into the office like he owned it—which he did—with Mo strapped to his chest, one of her diaper backpacks thrown over his shoulder, I wasn't even a little shocked.

"Is he here?" Grandpa Gus demanded as his hands went to Madeline—or as we all called her, Mo—to take her out of the carrier.

"Hey, Grandpa. I missed you too. Thanks." I got up and headed right over to put out the playpen I had stashed in a corner. "*No*. Did you see anyone out there that you don't know? And didn't I just tell you to leave it alone?"

The look he shot me literally said *and since when do I leave anything alone?*

Never, that was when, and we both knew it.

I groaned as Grandpa Gus handed the wide-awake baby over to me, brushing a kiss over the back of her head like he was rubbing it in that she was getting one and I wasn't.

There was a reason why I'd never wondered where I got my pettiness from.

I'm doing this for you, I thought as I took her weight and decided not to put her in the playpen yet. Bringing Mo up against my chest, I settled her there, backing up so I could sit in my chair and keep talking to Count Dracula while keeping an eye on him at the same time. It didn't look like he was carrying around pepper spray in his pockets, and a peek at his knuckles told me he hadn't busted out brass knuckles. I wouldn't put it past him, even though that wasn't really his style.

I should have been looking for a baseball bat, if anything. There was that one time he'd—

I stopped thinking about it. I wasn't even supposed to know about that.

I pinned him with a look when he just kept standing there looking way too passive-aggressive. I shook my head. "Seriously, Gramps, cut it out. Whatever you're planning on saying or doing, don't."

I held up Mo right off my lap. "Please. Do it for her. Look at those big brown eyes. I kept it a secret because I didn't want anyone here to know who her deadbeat dad is," I tried to plead with him, pressing my lips against the top of her full head of hair since she was already right there. She smelled just like the almond soap we used, even though it had been two days since the last bath I'd given her.

He didn't say anything but still just stood there looking way too broody in his olive-green khaki pants and button-down, long-sleeved shirt with a sweater pulled on over it as he finally peeled the carrier off. He called it his uniform for taking care of an eight-month-old baby, because it was important work. And you dressed for the job you wanted, he claimed.

Seriously, there was a reason we put up with his shit.

But if he wanted to be a pain in the ass, and he did, well, I could play dirty too.

"I didn't say anything because it's easier when the person who didn't want you doesn't feel like they actually exist."

He hesitated for a moment before folding the carrier and setting it on top of the chair where he'd set the baby bag. I could see his eyes narrowing again. His mouth moving.

But he settled for a sighed. "Are you trying to guilt trip me?"

I smirked as I rested my cheek on Mo's head as I set her back down on my lap. "Yeah." Who did he think he was talking to?

I was positive pride flashed across his eyes even as he made another face. And his answer confirmed it.

"Continue," he muttered.

I fucking laughed, brushing my mouth across the back of her soft head full of hair and soaking up her scent like a crackhead. I missed her so much while I was at work. If I didn't know without a doubt that she was in the best hands capable—better hands than my own—leaving for Maio House on a daily basis would have been the hardest thing in the world. "You know, I really wish I could go back in time to meet your mom and ask her if you came out special or if someone hurt you and made you like this."

His smart-ass expression didn't move, but I could see the hint of a smirk curl up the corner of his mouth. "Wonderful? Amazing?" He crossed his arms over a chest that hadn't lost too much of his muscle over the years. "A one of a kind?"

He was joking back with me. That was good.

"A one-of-a-kind something."

He sniffed, but I could tell he was thinking when he didn't give me any back talk.

Realistically, I knew he could and would stay mad. He was going to bring this up for the rest of my life, and I didn't expect any less. But I knew without a doubt that mad at me or not for keeping a secret, for telling him that he couldn't act a fool when the need ran so strongly in him, he was still going to do the right thing. Because that was what he'd taught me.

To do the right thing.

Most of the time at least.

So when he sighed in the middle of me sniffing Mo's neck while she giggled, I figured he'd come to some sort of decision. "We'll do this your way, *Elena*." He rolled his eyes just in case the sighing hadn't been enough.

I raised my eyebrows at him calling me my first name. Was he *that* mad? The side look he slid me said *yup*.

"Let me talk to Peter, and then The General and I will get out of here. I told her we'd go for a walk at the park today while you stay and work," he countered, rubbing it in that I was stuck here while they got to spend time together.

But I deserved it, and I'd take it.

I nodded. "All right."

He barely glanced at me as he headed back out onto the floor, really confirming just how mad he was. Oh well. It should have been a miracle he wasn't rallying his gang of Grandpas on Scooters to find out where Jonah was to go run his ass over.

Shit. He might be waiting to do that, knowing him. I needed to tell him not to do that either.

Figuring that could wait a few minutes, I sighed in my chair and set Mo to sit on my thigh. I smiled at her. She grinned at me right back, sitting there calmly and happily, bringing this sense of peace—even though I shouldn't feel peaceful at all with her dad somewhere around not telling me why he was here—that nothing and no one else was capable of doing for me. "Ma! Ma, ma, ma!"

She'd started calling me that a couple weeks ago, and it hadn't gotten old, and I hoped it never would. Ma. Me! I leaned forward and touched the tip of my nose to hers.

And Mo... Mo decided it was the right time to headbutt the fuck out of my face, but I reared out of the way at the last second.

I laughed. "Jesus Christ, short stuff, you trying to break my nose?"

She did a little squeal that I had a feeling meant *maybe*. She was mine after all. What else did I expect?

I laughed again. "Oh my *God*, I need to eat your face. Let me get a little bite," I whispered as she babbled back.

Brushing my fingers lightly into her side just enough to make her squeal again, I dipped my face close, blowing a bubble into her tiny almost nonexistent neck, getting a slightly louder squeal out of her. Her whole body shook with delight and something so pure, it was fucking priceless. It was something to think that I had *made this*. That she was mine and I was hers, and that there wasn't a single thing I wouldn't do for her.

"Ma!"

I lifted her chubby arms over her head and said, "Weighing in at eighteen pounds, the reigning champion of the baby weight division, Mo DeMaioooo!"

She shrieked in excitement like she always did and, oh my God, I loved it.

I clapped her fists together. "Yay!"

"Hi, Lenny," came the soft voice out of nowhere, making my head jerk up to find the figure standing just inside the office. "Oh. Who's this?"

But it wasn't just anybody. And I wasn't going to wonder right then how the fuck he'd gotten into the building again. Not when I was suddenly holding my damn breath.

I lowered Mo's arms and had to talk myself out of pulling her in even closer to my body as I watched Jonah take another step. And then one more. His eyes—Mo's eyes—bounced between the baby who had her back to him and... me.

Resentment, I knew it was resentment, made my stomach sour all of a sudden. Just about every ounce of joy I'd felt over Mo's presence disappeared in that instant as the big man kept coming into my office, one slow step after another after another. His feet didn't make a sound on the stained concrete, and I wasn't sure why I noticed that, but I did. Across from us, that tanned face was curious... but not at all guilty looking or nervous or any of the other shit that I might have expected him to experience as he approached his daughter for the first time ever.

What the hell was this fucker up to?

The question stayed in my head when he asked again, "Is she a friend?"

I loved this kid. I loved Mo so much there weren't words for how much. Which was funny considering how terrified and nervous I'd been before having her. I had worried my ass off that we wouldn't bond or that I would resent her for kicking my life off track… and, fortunately, all it had taken was hearing her fucking cry, feeling and seeing her in my arms, to make me instantly fall in love. Just seeing her wrinkled pink face had confirmed there wasn't anything I wouldn't do for the helpless little body that had lived inside of me for nine months.

So I didn't want to say her name. Because this fuckface didn't know it in the first place. Because he was an asshole who was looking like he hadn't missed his daughter's birth and the first eight months of her life and felt no shame over it.

But I said it anyway, because this wasn't about me. This was about her, and the fact that this shithead *was* here regardless of whether I wanted him to be or not. Because he was her father and there was no changing that.

"Mo."

His eyes went back to the small back facing him, and I watched the curiosity grow across his serious face. "It's a girl?"

If I'd had any more joy to lose, it would have been gone. How did this fucker not even know he had a daughter? Jesus Christ. *I had mentioned that in my last email.* He hadn't even had the balls to read it and make sure she'd been born alive and fine? Was this a motherfucking joke?

I was going to kill him and throw his ass in a swamp. That was it. I'd lived a good life. Grandpa Gus and Peter could raise her just fine. They'd come visit me in jail. Luna would be a great mother figure for her.

And then he kept going with the stupid questions.

"Babysitting, eh? I thought you didn't like wee ones?"

Babysitting?

Oh. *Oh.* He was going to get it for sure. For *fucking* sure.

I couldn't help it. I couldn't stop myself. If he wanted to play stupid, *okay.*

I looked at him, smiled sarcastically and said, "It's not babysitting if she's mine."

His normal expression had been there one second… and the very next it was gone.

Jonah's face instantly fell. The color in it doing the same, and I knew I didn't imagine him giving the slowest blink ever. Or that it took him a moment before he literally choked, "*Yours?*"

The sarcasm was stronger in me than usual today. "You want me to be specific? She's *ours*."

I was an idiot. How could I have been so *wrong* and *stupid* to have wasted months of my life getting to know him? How the hell had he been able to fool me so bad? I had honestly thought he was a good guy. A really good guy. A wonderful one. *Wonderful,* and I didn't throw that word around lightly.

But here he was—

He stopped breathing, his skin color going damn near almost white. I almost missed his croaked, "*Pardon me?*"

I blinked at him, ignoring the tone of his voice and the way he was blinking himself from across the table. I leaned forward and planted a kiss on her forehead in an apology for making this dipshit her dad. I'd make it up to her somehow. "She's ours, dumbass. Who else would she be?"

I remember hearing someone say once that time had, at one point, stopped for them, but it didn't seem like one of those things that was real. Like… your life flashing before your eyes when you think you're close to death. Once, when I had been younger, my godfather had snatched me out of the way of a moving car, and I hadn't thought of anything until I'd been on my back, wondering what the hell had just happened.

But as I sat there, I watched it happen. I watched Jonah suck in a breath through his almost perfect nose. I watched his head jerk…

Witnessed his mouth fall open.

And I saw that tall, solid body wobble in place for a second before his hands shot out to the back of the chair in front of him.

Those long, strong fingers wrapped over the top, becoming the only thing holding him up. If I thought his face had been pale thirty seconds ago, whatever color had been left, leeched out too.

And none of it, *none of it*, made any sense.

What he said next had *my* head jerking back.

"You're saying she's my daughter?"

CHAPTER 6

"Jonah, it's Lenny. Look, you really need to call me back. I'm not fucking with you. Seriously."

"WHY DIDN'T YOU TELL ME?"

He was lucky I had Mo in my arms when that stupid question came out of his mouth, because if I'd had my hands free, I would have been sliding over the desk like I was on *Dukes of Hazard* to choke the shit out of him.

I was pretty sure a lawyer somewhere would have let me plead Jonah's murder as a crime of passion. But unfortunately, I was never going to find out because of the kid sitting in my lap. Her simple existence was saving me from a life in prison and saving her dad—not that she knew he was her dad—from being murdered.

I could feel my face getting hot as I stared at him like I had never stared at anyone, not even someone I was competing against that I had beef with. His same stupid question rang in my ears all over again.

Why didn't you tell me?

Why the fuck didn't I tell him? Was he shitting me? Was he

delusional?

Yeah, my nostrils were flaring, my face was hot, and my eyelid suddenly felt like it was on the verge of exploding off my face as I took in the man clutching at a chair for dear life. Even his mouth hung open like all the life had been sucked out of him. I was pretty sure I wasn't imagining the fact that he looked on the verge of fainting either.

I kept my mouth shut though, at least while I had this booger on my lap. I didn't want her getting all flustered because she could sense me getting that way. She was sensitive, and if she'd sensed me even starting to get upset, whether it was sadness or anger, she'd immediately pick up on it and get fussy.

So, with all the strength I had inside of myself, I kept my voice nice and even, tried to will my eyelid to get its shit together and my face to quit being hot and my nostrils to go back to normal. I managed to put a smile on my face, even though part of me was making stabbing motions inside, and asked, *almost* sounding sweet, "Why didn't I *tell* you?"

God, the sarcasm was dripping off every word out of my mouth.

I bounced Mo on my thigh, earning a big toothless grin. We were pretty sure she was about to start teething soon, a little late but the pediatrician said not to worry, and from everything I'd heard, I wasn't exactly looking forward to it, but that wasn't for me to focus on right then. I had bigger things to stress over. Specifically six foot five inches and two hundred and fifty pounds of fuckface to focus on.

I kept my voice light…ish even though I gave him a bitchy bright smile. "What do you consider me calling you and calling you, and calling you some more? Me not trying to talk to you?"

He didn't answer, and whether that was because he border-line fainted or because he knew I was right, I had no fucking idea. Mostly because I didn't give him the chance to talk because I kept going.

"You never answered, *Jonah*. And I left you… oh, I don't

know… a dozen messages too. I did that until you stopped checking your voice mail and let it get full and stay full."

Jonah Collins brought both hands up to palm his forehead.

Why didn't I tell him? He was either a master liar, an asshole, or just… a jackass. I wasn't done though. "There were the texts too. It might have gotten old deleting every email I sent you, but I did try to contact you until right after she was born. So… I did try and tell you. Don't try and turn this around on me."

I thought about his words for a moment, watching his palms scrub over his forehead as he forced one loud, ragged breath after another.

Was he having a panic attack? He wasn't straight-up wheezing, but it wasn't much off. What a fucking *asshole.*

I stared at him, my anger rising. "Is that what you're trying to imply? That you either didn't care enough to listen to my voice mails, read my texts, or my emails? That you didn't *know?*" I told him on a whoosh, my stomach clenching up in pure fucking fury that almost made me want to throw up. On him.

Because it had pissed me off when I thought he didn't care enough to reply, but the possibility he hadn't listened or read a single fucking thing I'd sent him over nearly nine months, might have honestly been worse.

I wasn't going to overanalyze it and figure out what won because it didn't matter.

I didn't look at him, and because I didn't look at him, I didn't see his reactions.

The only thing of his that I did catch was probably the hoarse curse word he spit out. "Fuck."

He could say that again.

Why was he making it seem like he didn't know? I'd left him so many voice mails, emails, and texts. *So many.* And he wanted me to believe he had either not gotten them or ignored every single one?

Motherfucker.

Piece of shit.

Asshole.

Of course this would happen to me. The *one time* I picked out a guy who I felt comfortable with, who I was unbelievably attracted to, who I liked so much, who seemed like a decent human being... who wore a condom and everything... knocked me up during the two months of almost nightly sex we'd had. Then his life had gone to hell, and he'd disappeared.

Like some of the assholes in my life did. They just left me for other people to be there for me. Or for me to be there for myself.

And that was where my sad sob story ended.

So what, I had asked myself back then, once I'd made my decision to have Mo? So what if the baby's dad wasn't going to be in the picture? So what if I was going to raise this kid without him?

I was thirty, not sixteen, I had told myself. I had a grandpa, a Peter, a Luna, a sister of a Luna, a Ripley, a Cooper couple. I had friends.

I had been raised by a village, and my daughter was and would be too.

Everything had been going fine too, not counting that nonstop worrying and the fuckups.

Yet none of that made me feel any less pissed off toward this asshole having the nerve to look like he'd seen a ghost. Like he had any right to be mad or upset. Like I hadn't fucking tried telling him a hundred times he was going to be a dad.

He'd known.

He had to have known.

And on the tiniest, *tiniest* chance that maybe he'd been an extra prick and had ignored everything I had tried to tell him...

Well, I still couldn't believe that was possible. He was an athlete. He'd told me about having endorsements. He was a human being with family. There was no way he'd ignored all forms of communication. It was stupid for him to even try and pull that lie on me.

It had just been *me* he'd ignored.

Goddamn it, I hated his guts.

"You... you...," the mountain of a man stuttered, quietly, forcing me to take in his pale face. But at the same time, making me notice the way those huge shoulders had started to hunch too.

I stared steadily at him, leaning forward just enough to take another whiff of Mo's clean baby smell because I needed it for fuel to get through this ridiculous-ass conversation. "You what?"

Jonah reared up to that height that had been one of the first things I'd noticed about him, and he breathed out with wide honey-colored eyes that were bouncing back and forth between Mo's spine and myself. "I listened to the first two months of voice mails...."

Did he want a gold star or something?

I glared at him as Mo gave a wiggle warning me she was going to want to be put down soon. She was already rolling from her stomach to her back. I had a feeling it was going to be no time before she was crawling... or even fucking walking.

And really, what the hell was wrong with this asshole?

One of those big, hard hands went up to the top of his head, and I couldn't miss how it shook in the process. Fucking faker. "I broke my phone, but I didn't... I didn't...." He kept going, looking worse and worse with every word out of his mouth. Paler and paler, sick....

This was what he was trying to say? That he conveniently hadn't read any of my texts either? Just the ones at the beginning, and then he'd given up on the rest of them because he'd broken his little phone? *That's* where this was going?

Yeah, fucking right. I rolled my eyes. "*Okay,*" I told him, sarcastic as hell. How fucking convenient was that?

His shoulders dropped, and his fingers curved over his nearly buzz-cut head.

And then he pissed me off even more when he peered over

at me through his eyelashes, those honey-colored irises flashing. "You didn't say anything about being pregnant!" he suddenly exploded quietly on an exhale, color literally flooding his face. His tanned cheeks with faint honey freckles over the bridge of his nose and across his cheekbones went *pink*.

I didn't tell him I was pregnant? Was this bitch for real? Was he trying to turn this around on me? No. No, he couldn't be.

He was shaking, I could see he was shaking, but what-the-fuck ever.

"I'm sorry, Jonah, that you chose not to call me back or read my emails. I didn't know I was pregnant when I first started calling you and you were still listening to my messages, *supposedly*. I'm sorry that I was just contacting you because I was worried about you. I'm sorry that I didn't think to plan that you would only listen to my messages for the first... what? Two months or so, you said? Or that I waited until the last few months of my pregnancy to straight-up tell you over email." I rolled my eyes. "Dipshit."

Fury backed up my throat as I won the hardest match of my life and somehow managed to keep my tone cheerful even though I was literally ready to go to jail for the remainder of my life if I could beat him with a bat. Fuck it. "Are you going to pretend like I didn't blow you up for months? That you broke your phone and that's why I never heard back from you? Do you really want to make it seem like I'm the one who forced you to ignore me for so long?" I asked him, hoping that didn't come out as borderline hysterical as it felt in my chest and in my brain and in every goddamn part of my body.

But I wasn't done. Oh no. "I don't know about you, *Jonah*, but if someone were to leave me a ton of voice mails and text messages and notes on my apartment door, I would actually call them back. I wouldn't be a coward—"

"I haven't checked my email since then, Lenny," he said roughly, his accent coming out thicker, his voice cracking at the end even as the pink across his cheeks became deeper, stretching up to the tips of his ears. "Since I broke my phone. I swear!"

Did I look like an idiot?

I smiled at him again, and I knew he could see the smart-ass there. "If you want to play this *I had no idea* game, go for it, but I'm not an idiot. No smart, reasonable person would suddenly just disappear from the world and kill their career. You would have been communicating with someone. You just weren't communicating with *me*."

I was not mad. I was *not*.

The hand that wasn't already on his head went up to meet the other one, where he cupped the expanse of his scalp, breathing harder than I had ever, ever seen before, and that was saying something because I had seen him right after finishing a rugby game when he'd been exhausted and riled up and sweaty. I'd been in the stands and he'd come over and kissed me on the cheek—

God, I hated his guts.

"Lenny," he said, luckily ripping me out of that memory with the jagged quality of his voice, like it hurt him to speak. "I didn't know. *I didn't know* about… about…."

It was the strangest thing, seeing a human body imitate a balloon that had been pricked by a needle just small enough to make its ultimate death slow.

But that was what I saw.

And I wasn't sure what to think of it other than be suspicious.

This enormous asshole who weighed more than any other person in the building slowly sank to his knees behind the chair he'd been gripping onto for dear life minutes ago. If I hadn't been watching him so closely, I would have figured he fainted, but no, he'd just… dissolved. Both of his hands were all of a sudden gripping the back of the chair again, his body curled so that his forehead was pressed into the material in between his hands. And he was gasping for breath.

Was this a joke? Was he acting? I didn't see what he would get out of any of this but...

He was faking it. He had to be.

Jackass.

After a moment, his face lifted and his eyes moved back to Mo like... I wasn't sure how, honestly. Shocked, mostly. A little anger resided somewhere in there, but mostly... mostly it was surprise hidden in his eyes as he looked at the dark-haired baby on my lap.... with the same honey-colored eyes he saw in the mirror every day even though he didn't know it.

He was faking it.

"You...," he stuttered, those big hands still clinging to the chair with white knuckles. "The messages...."

In my lap, Mo started to fuss, and I knew I only had a few moments before I had to set her down.

"You're serious?"

I didn't even bother responding to that stupid-ass question.

"She's... she's my daughter?" Jonah Collins asked with all the speed of a damn turtle, each word basically whispered and gasped at the same time, making it really easy for a moment to reconcile him with the man I had known who had been sweeter and more easygoing than any other man I had ever known before.

But I forgot about him just as easily because *she's my daughter*?

I wasn't going to waste my time responding to stupid questions.

Then the man who was clinging to a chair and watching me with glassy eyes, went there, softly, but he still fucking went there. "Are you sure?"

I'd taken four different pregnancy tests when I missed my period because I hadn't wanted to believe it was possible, that this was happening to me. I'd asked the doctor to test me twice when I had gotten around to going to a physician in France.

Since I'd been fifteen, my period had been like clockwork. It was more reliable than my first car had been.

Hadn't I told this fucker *multiple times* I could count the number of times I'd had sex on two hands?

"You can say I'm sure that you and I were together a lot exactly nine months before Mo was born. And I'm sure that she has the same eyes and hair as you do," I told him coolly, but really stabbing him in the throat in my head.

He didn't say anything. What he did do was squeeze his eyes closed. Gulp.

I felt myself sneer. "Why are you looking like you're going to be sick?" I demanded, even though I didn't want to, but I was pissed, and him looking like that just made me even madder. He had no right.

Jonah lowered his forehead until it was back to resting on the chair in front of him, and I could barely hear him as he mumbled, "Because it feels like I am."

I narrowed my eyes and started to lift Mo up to wobble on feet that weren't ready to walk, when her squirming got worse. She was going to need to go in the playpen sooner than later, but I was feeling real damn clingy right then.

The Fucker tipped his face back up to the ceiling, eyes closed, and took so many deep breaths in through his nose and out of his mouth that I lost count.

"She's really…. She's mine?" Jonah Hema Collins stammered at some point.

I glared the fuck out of him, annoyed he was asking the same damn questions again. But I saw the same things that I'd been seeing. The white-knuckled grip. The unsteady body. I could hear what might have sounded like anguish in that voice that had pulled an Ariel in *The Little Mermaid* on me.

And I had to fucking think about it.

If anyone else was trying to claim this bullshit to someone I knew, I would tell them they were full of it. That there was no way it was possible for someone to just disconnect like that.

And I wanted to believe that, I really did. But Jonah didn't look right.

The fact was, his hands had been shaking. His mouth and skin were pale again. Unless he'd been practicing in the mirror for the last year and a half, what were the chances he could make himself look like he'd been kicked in the balls repeatedly?

But still... if something seemed too good to be true, it's because it was.

Like he had been.

Too nice. Too easygoing. Too humble. Too good-looking. Too perfect.

Too interested in me.

The fact was... it didn't matter who he had seemed to be and who he hadn't. It was this man in front of me I was going to have to deal with... potentially for the rest of my life if I didn't kill him first. And all it took was a quiet stream of gibberish from the kid in my hands to remind me I'd do anything for her.

Even put up with and get past this asshole. Set aside all the shit and just... deal. Handle it.

"I don't want to talk in circles around this; if you knew, if you didn't know, it doesn't matter anymore." I was mostly lying, but not totally. "I thought that's why you were here. To see her. To talk about her. The only thing that matters now is if you're going to stay. If you're going to be part of her life or not. Like I said, I don't actually give a fuck about your excuses anymore, Jonah. I just want to know what you plan on doing."

I stopped talking because he dropped his hands.

And because it almost made me feel sick that I was going to have to put up with his dumbass for who knew how long.

This massive, intimidating man who tackled men just as big as him for a living without pads, with just the sheer size and strength of himself, lifted his head and eyed the kid I was bouncing up and down on my lap... and me. And I couldn't miss how he looked more like a popped balloon than ever. How... defeated or something. Sick.

His shoulders went up, and I'd swear he sniffed.

He fucking sniffed and my arms bubbled up with goose bumps.

And I hated myself for how my heart dropped as I watched him. Maybe because I'd seen grown men in all stages of despair before: after lost fights when they were disappointed in themselves, after fights when they thought their lives and worlds were over. I'd seen men and women when life was just taking a massive shit on them and they weren't sure how the hell to get out from under the weight of all that crap.

But I had never, ever seen someone so big look so small.

And I didn't like it. I didn't like that I felt bad. It wasn't my fault.

Mostly though, I was pretty sure I didn't like the way he looked or that it affected me.

"Are you about to cry?" I asked him, hearing the horror in my voice, but it was only because I didn't know what the fuck to do with it. With him.

His answer was another sniff.

And then his fucking eyes went and got glassy.

I narrowed mine even more, ignoring the tightening in my chest as his tanned hand went up to his temple. And in that way that reminded me of the man I thought I had gotten to know, he answered, "I may, Len."

Did he have to answer that honestly? Goddamn it. Was I that annoying too when I told people the truth even when they didn't want to hear it?

"Her name is Mo?" that voice with its New Zealand tones to it, asked on the end of another sniff that made the hair on the back of my neck prickle.

I pressed my lips together, ignoring those fucking sniffs and the way they made my head, and other parts of my body, feel. "Did you think I was going to name her Jonah?" I griped, still watching him, trying to pick up on his body language. "Her name is Madeline. I saw it was popular in New Zealand," I explained honestly, because that was exactly why I had done it. "But we call her Mo."

That first-base-sized hand went to his chest just as his eyes closed, and he took in this breath that seemed so rattled, it might have hurt me if I still gave a single fuck about him.

Jonah's head tipped toward the ceiling, and he wiped at his cheek with one of his tan fingers as his Adam's apple bobbed— and nope, I didn't feel shit. I didn't feel a thing while he wiped at his olive cheek, leaving behind just the slightest glitter behind. "I... need a minute, Lenny. I came back to apologize. To try and talk to you again after this morning. I wasn't expecting...," he said so quietly I had to strain to hear. I blinked. "I need more than a minute to think about this. Is that all right with you?"

No. I wanted to give him a middle finger and a kick to the fucking balls, *that* would be all right with me. But what he actually got was silence. He could do with that whatever he wanted.

Dickface.

I didn't say anything as he opened his eyes, cast another long look at Mo's back... glanced at me for another moment, and then seemed to nod to himself. I was pretty positive his eyes were even glassier too. I watched him turn around and walk right out after another exhale, shoulders slumped, everything about his arms and shoulders and even his neck and chest were just... suspicious.

I wasn't sure what to think about what the hell he'd just said and done. Wasn't sure how I felt because obviously I was confused because I'd felt bad at how upset he seemed to be. And that irritated me.

With a sigh, I looked down at Mo and blew out a breath. Her bright brown eyes were zeroed in on me, like she wasn't sure how I was feeling. Then she smiled and grabbed the collar of my shirt and tried to tug it toward her, choking me a little in the process.

It was then I remembered why I was here. Why I'd just gone

through this conversation. How the hell this child made me a weak bitch and a stronger bitch at the same time was beyond me.

"Well, that didn't go the way I thought it would," I told her quietly as I peeled her fingers off my shirt before she really did choke me out.

I didn't think she cared about how it had gone down, honestly, because she just kept on smiling at me… and clinging to my collar for dear life.

With another kiss and finally succeeding in extracting myself from her grip, I opened up her playpen while she sat on the floor and then set her in it. I pulled out a few toys from the cabinet beside my desk and set them in there too. Then I picked up my phone from the top of my desk and opened my messages so I could shoot one off to Luna, who was the only reasonable person I could bring this up to right then.

Me: My baby daddy was just here.

I bit my lip and sent off another message.

Me: He made it seem like he had no idea who Mo was. He tried to say that he'd stopped checking his voice mails and texts, and that he broke his phone, and that he hadn't read an email in his account since before he "took off." I don't know what the hell is going on, but he just left. He seemed pretty upset.

Luna wrote me back immediately.

Luna: He's there???!!!
Luna: Wait.
Luna: If he didn't know about Mo, then why was he there in the first place?

Wasn't that the million-dollar question?

I set my phone back on the desktop and stared at it.

I stared at it for a long time, not knowing how the hell to answer.

~

"So, what are you going to do?"

I sighed to myself as I finished washing off the pureed lentils that were all over my hands from Mo's dinner. She didn't mind being fed with a spoon, but she liked me putting a dab in her hand and then trying to hoover it herself even more. The girl was all about eating. Luna's baby was a fussy eater, but Mo scarfed everything down. She got that from me. You didn't come between us and food. The only thing she regularly tried to spit out was peas, and I couldn't blame her. I hated peas too.

But that wasn't at all related to the question that Peter had just shot me.

I was actually surprised that Grandpa Gus hadn't brought anything up while I fed Mo—and tried to sneak my own bites in—as they ate dinner. Grandpa had come back into the office maybe ten minutes after Jonah had left and seen the look on my face. He'd made his own face, swallowed his comment, even though it had to have been hard, then grumbled out his and Mo's plans for the rest of the day, settling for giving me a slanted, pissy look before they disappeared, leaving me all alone to think about my decisions in life.

It wasn't my fault he hadn't been in the building when Jonah had come by.

Grabbing the dishtowel from the hook on the cabinet to my left, I turned around to face the two men sitting around the kitchen island and shrugged. We all knew what Peter was asking. "I don't know."

"You don't know?" the smart-ass, Grandpa, asked before raising his eyebrows and bringing his after-dinner decaf coffee up to his mouth to take the smallest sip in history.

"No." I shot him his own special look that said *I know you, old man.* "He came into the office and made it seem like he had no idea Her Majesty existed. He acted like he was...." An image of Jonah's devastated face filled my head, tears in his eyes and all. "He looked really upset after I told him." Why the hell I didn't mention him tearing up was beyond me, but I kept my mouth shut. "Then he walked out of the office because he said he needed to think."

Grandpa hmphed from behind his coffee cup, and it made me wonder what Peter had said to him to make him be so... subdued. Because he had to have said something. Nothing I suggested would sure as hell be enough to keep him from making comments. Peter was Grandpa's voice of reason and was usually the only thing in the world that would get him to think rationally.

I was going to have to thank him later for whatever he'd said or done.

Luckily, it was Peter who kept up the questions... confirming that he had gotten my grandfather to bite his tongue on the topic of Jonah and Mo.

Jonah and Mo.

I'd never had an ulcer before, but I suddenly wondered if that weird feeling in my stomach was a sign I might be getting one even though I didn't eat anything, usually, that would cause one. But weirder shit had happened. Like me even meeting the Shithead in the first place. I hadn't decided that I was even going to take a three-month teaching position at the judo club until weeks before. My friend had bailed on me at the last minute for that trip to Versailles. And Jonah wasn't even supposed to be on the same tour I had been assigned to. If he'd gone on the original tour he was going to be on, or if I hadn't decided to get a sandwich right at that moment...

I wouldn't have had a reason to talk to him.

I would have just checked him out and left him alone. Maybe. Who the fuck knew?

But he had been on the same tour, and I had gotten in line behind him and overheard him and his friend struggling to communicate with the cashier. That was all it had taken. And here we were.

"Do you believe him?" Peter asked in a careful voice as he tapped a finger against the lip of his coffee mug.

Leaning back against the counter, I shrugged. It wasn't like I hadn't asked myself the same thing since he'd walked out of the office. "No. But at the same time, I don't think he could be that good of an actor." I was going to have to finally explain part of the story, wasn't I? "None of it makes sense, but at the same time, it does. I guess."

Bringing the towel to my face, I scrubbed it downward, trying to get my thoughts together. Grandpa was staring at me with his beady, evil little eyes, and Peter just sat there, his attention on Mo who was in her own little world, babbling away her own story, living her best baby life with a full belly after a day of fun.

Fuck.

They needed to know the whole story now. Well, most of it, anyway.

"He was a professional rugby player in France when we met right after I got there. He had just started playing for a team in Paris," I told them, trying to keep my voice and story impartial. "He had a game one day… or a match, whatever they call it, with a team in another city." I knew exactly what team and city, but my pride wouldn't let me admit it was burned into me. "He ruptured his Achilles during the game and fractured his orbital bone." The rupture had been one thing. As he stumbled away, he got elbowed in the face by a man that had looked like a giant even in comparison to Jonah, but that wasn't relevant to the story. I didn't give them those details. "I didn't hear from him again after that," I kept going. "He sent a few postcards to where I was living in Paris, but that was it."

He'd cut me out of his life almost cold turkey. We had gone

from texting each other throughout the day, making plans to see each other almost every night when I didn't have to coach in the evening or when he had to wake up early the next day, or he didn't have a game somewhere else, to… nothing. Just nothing except for those postcards that didn't say anything. He'd been a surgeon about it. In there one moment and out the next.

Well, mostly out the next. It took me a month to figure out that he'd left me a going-away present. Fuckface.

Grandpa let out a breath through his nose that sounded like he was blowing a raspberry, and it snapped me back into focus. I had to tell them the rest.

"I tried almost everything to get in contact with him. The guys I knew that he played with told me that he'd had surgery in Paris, but that they hadn't seen or heard from him since that game. No one knew where he went, and if they did, they wouldn't tell me. All I knew was that he'd ruptured his Achilles, he had a broken bone in his face, and that he was going to be out for twelve months, if he even came back. I guess he'd had another Achilles injury before."

This part was getting harder and harder for me, but it just took one glance at Mo to help me calm down. She was busy making noises and playing with a squeaky toy in her chair, oblivious to how loud she was being and that it made me have to raise my voice. That fucking girl.

Maybe everything *had* happened for a reason.

But here was the only moment where I had felt shame. Because I had thought *yeah, right, bish,* when an ex-girlfriend or ex-fuck buddy showed up at the gym trying to reconnect with one of the guys. I had felt embarrassed for them and how they'd been ghosted and thought how sad it was that they were trying to hold on to these men who didn't want them anymore. I had pitied them.

And then I had been put into their shoes, and it wasn't a party. It wasn't nice. It made me angry. It made me feel ashamed… of myself.

I had tried so hard my entire life to not ever be embarrassed by anything I did. Whatever I did, I did for a reason, with no regrets, even the shady shit. Yet, I had been there. Because of a guy.

Because of a man who had grinned, blushed, and told me cheers after I'd helped him.

"I even tried contacting his brothers and sisters, but they must have thought I was a stalker or delusional or something," was as far as I told Peter and Grandpa, not wanting to go into details. "I never heard back from any of them. Or him, obviously. Or his teammates. You know most of the rest of the story after that. I found out about Mo when I was there, came home. I gave him one last chance when she was born, and then I stopped trying to contact him. A few months later, articles popped up that he was coming back to finish his contract with the Paris team…. And he still never reached out.

"All I know is that he's here now, and he's pretending like he didn't read a single one of my texts."

Bitch.

"Or hear a single one of the voice mails I left him."

Double bitch. He was lucky I knew it was possible to delete all of your messages without actually listening to them. Even if that possibility was pretty far-fetched.

"Or wasn't a professional athlete with endorsements and under contract and try to claim he didn't check his email. Or maybe it was just my emails he didn't want to read," I finished, thinking *fucking bitch* again. "So I don't know what to believe."

Grandpa's fingers had already been pinching the bridge of his nose before he started talking. "He can *believe* I'm going to—"

All Peter had to do was glance at him, and that had Grandpa instantly pressing his mouth together and literally hunching over, hand still in place between his eyes.

That had me raising my eyebrows, and when Peter glanced at me, the slightest hint of a smile crossed his mouth. Oh yeah, I was going to have to ask him what he'd said to get him to chill out. It was impressive.

"I don't need you going back to your coven of vampires or your Grandpas Gone Wild clique and getting them all riled up —" I started to say before the sound of a phone vibrating on the counter had all of us looking around. It was Peter who frowned down at his cell, which I guess had been resting on his thigh or something, because he got up and walked out of the room before answering it.

Grandpa slid a look toward the door my other dad had just walked out of before saying, in a strangled voice that said how much self-control he was using, "I made a couple of calls and got Big Mike to give me the number to the lawyer he used to get custody of his girls."

It was no wonder I loved the shit out of this man.

"I started looking some up online today, but I couldn't really find any information on what would happen since he's not a U.S. citizen or even a resident, so that was a good idea," I said, sensing the heaviness coming back into my stomach and chest. "I've tried not to worry about it too much because I know that I haven't done anything wrong. I have proof I tried to reach out to him, and that there's no way I would lose Mo if he tries to… be active in her life. Between all of us, I know that we've got this. And I know that I should be happy that, if he was going to come back, it's now, before she gets older or starts asking questions I don't know how to answer."

I watched Grandpa's eyes drift toward Mo again, who was busy chewing on her teething ring. I saw love soften his features for a moment and couldn't miss the way the edge fell off his voice as he asked, like he didn't want to but was forcing himself to, "You want him to be part of her life then?"

It wasn't until right then that it hit me how my gramps might feel about some random man coming in and taking over the duties he had taken over effortlessly with Mo. The same duties he'd had with me… even though there were less. With me, it had only been him until Peter had shown up when I was three. Mo had three of us from the start.

But the point was, I wouldn't be surprised if he didn't want some guy coming in to usurp his duties as one of the men in Mo's life. Then again, he'd been totally fine with the relationship I'd always had with Peter. So maybe I was just overthinking it.

"If he wants to be, yeah. As long as he's dedicated to being in it," I answered, watching him closely to see if anything spelled out him being worried or if he was just angry in our honor for being dumped. "I know I had a couple of dreams here and there that I had a mom that came looking for me, Grandpa, and at one point, I would have been excited for that to happen. So I'm not going to take that away from her. But I'm not going to let him disappear later on if he thinks it's too hard to be around, or if he isn't planning on giving it his best, either. He needs to know I'll hunt him down if he doesn't commit to her."

Grandpa leaned back in his seat, seeming to think over what I'd just said.

Jonah Collins lived in a different country. A different continent. But I wasn't going to make that a deal breaker. When you wanted something to work, you made it work.

This wasn't about me anymore.

This was about the baby chewing away at a toy in a way that made my nipples have PTSD from when I had breastfed her before she'd decided she was done with my boobs.

If he wasn't lying, then he'd just found out he had a daughter, and that wasn't like... he'd found a twenty-dollar bill in his pocket. It was the biggest kind of news possible. It was a fucking *daughter*. The best one ever, I thought. Or at least she was tied with Luna's too.

I heard Peter before I saw him pushing open the door into the kitchen holding his hand out. He looked tense. That was never a good thing.

"It's him. He wants to speak to you."

CHAPTER 7

"It's me. Lenny. I really need to talk to you, so stop being a prick. I'm going back to Houston soon, and we need to talk. We don't have to see each other. Just a call. Text. Whatever. I don't give a shit. Please."

I WASN'T EVEN A LITTLE SURPRISED THAT WHEN THE DOORBELL rang, everyone was in the living room, watching television. Or at least pretending to.

But it wasn't like I would have expected any different. And it wasn't like I wanted them to be any different than the way they were: nosey and loyal. If anything, the only thing I was surprised by was that Grandpa hadn't called Luna to invite her in on the action.

It *almost* let me down.

I'd have to text her tomorrow to give her an update.

Rolling onto my feet from where I'd been lying on the floor with Mo as she shook the toys in her hands from side to side pretty violently, I headed toward the front door and unlocked it, swinging it wide, not even bothering to look through the peephole.

I stared at the Fucker. The Still an Asshole who was in the same clothes he'd been in earlier: a long-sleeved shirt that was almost a size too big and dark jeans. The only thing different were his eyes. They looked suspiciously puffy and tired instead of stricken and surprised. Mostly hidden in his big hand was a small stuffed bear he seemed to be holding onto tightly.

Whatever.

I still didn't even bother with a "hi." I settled for waving him and that enormous body in. "Come on, we can talk in the kitchen." Which was just far enough away and had a nice swinging door, where the rest of the house couldn't easily eavesdrop. Not that I honestly thought that would stop my gramps.

He didn't say a word as I closed the door behind us and waved him again to follow me down the long hallway. I didn't glance over my shoulder to see if he looked into the living room, where my two favorite men and my favorite girl were still hanging out, like the nosey asses they were. And if he slowed down to look at the baby playing with her toys on the floor, I had no idea either.

It wasn't like it mattered.

He was here, trying to talk to me, and that's what we needed to do.

Only seventeen months late.

I waited until the swinging door shut before I gestured toward the stools around the island. Then I went for it. "You said you had questions. Ask."

I could have said that a little nicer, but... I didn't feel like it. Not when this uncomfortable feeling settled in my chest as I confirmed that his eyes *were* puffy. I still couldn't stand him.

The Prick straightened in the stool he'd taken, his chest expanding with a deep breath before he set the stuffed animal down on the counter, laced those long, solid fingers together and set them on the island in front of him. The damn bear had on a tiny T-shirt that said HOUSTON on it, and I had to force myself to stop looking at it. Those eyes, which were beautiful regardless of how hard I'd punch him in the kidneys if our lives weren't so entwined, met mine and he asked, very, very calmly, very, very quietly in that way I had liked when I had first met him, "Who did you reach out to? To tell me."

We had already covered this, I thought. But okay. Here we went again.

"I reached out to your brothers and your sisters to get in contact with you. None of them responded to me, even though I sent them each a couple of the pictures I had with you." I kept going. "I can pull up phone records if you want. I got a new phone six months ago, but I can still turn on my old one if you want to see the messages I sent. I didn't delete them. I tried contacting you. Maybe not as hard as I could have, but I did try. I reached out to Arnie and Akira, and they promised to pass my message along to you but...." I tipped my head to the side.

Jonah visibly winced, and I sure as hell didn't imagine the way he swallowed hard before saying, "Akira played for Japan this past season, and Arnie went back to Dunedin. They boxed my things and left them at the team's office. I haven't seen either of them since."

Since his Achilles shit? I pressed my lips together and raised my eyebrows. "That's convenient. But you can ask them if you want. I'm not lying about any of it. Maybe your brothers and sisters remember my passive-aggressive private messages on Picturegram."

"Yeah, nah," he replied quietly, his palm already centering over the middle of his forehead. "I believe you."

That's why he'd asked again? *Okay.*

"How old is she?" he asked after a minute.

"Eight months old." She'd been conceived toward the end of when we'd known each other.

He must have had his questions ready in his head because he shot one out right after the other with only a bob of his throat. "What day was she born?"

"May 2nd."

If he was trying to figure out the dates in his head, I wasn't going to overthink it. I mean, I would ask too if our roles were reversed. I already thought he was a dickhead.

"Her full name?"

"Madeline Hema DeMaio."

That he reacted to. I could see it by the way his fingers flexed and by the way those round, wide eyes flicked to me in surprise. "Hema?"

If he hadn't come here, and the day came that she asked whom her dad was, I would have told her. I wouldn't have hidden his name from her, or the fact she shared it. It was just everyone else that I was keeping that secret from. "She's yours," I explained, only barely managed not to add "dipshit" to my answer.

The hand he'd had on his forehead fell away. "Not Collins?"

"You weren't around. If you decide you want to be part of her life, I'm not opposed to changing it. She's a DeMaio regardless of what's on her birth certificate," I told him, hearing the gruffness in my voice, the question: *but are you staying or are you going?*

Jonah eyed me seriously… cautiously, and I kind of liked it. "You'd consider it?"

"Yeah. You are her dad," I answered. "All I wanted was for her to know she's loved. That she belongs. I didn't want her to feel any different just in case we were all she ever knew. And if you wouldn't have shown up, I never would have told anyone you were her dad, at least until she asked." I swallowed around the lump in my throat and the ball of anger that was there too. "Like I said, nobody knew about you, not even my grandpa or Peter. Not Luna. Well, no one but my roommate back in Paris, but she wouldn't say anything to anyone. We've barely even talked since then."

He watched me. The problem was, I wasn't sure what his silence meant. What I did realize though was that it didn't matter what it meant; what mattered was what was going to happen from here on out.

"I don't know why you're here," I told him. "You said you didn't know about Mo, and I don't know why else you would have come, but I need you to make a decision at some point, sooner or later. If you're right and you did up and disappear because of whatever reasons"—*you're still an asshole*, I thought but didn't say—"then I'm sure this is a shock to you. You can't make a decision about whether you want to be a dad or not in just a couple hours, and I don't expect you to."

Even though he should since this was involving a child's life. His child's life. Anyone who wasn't a deadbeat would already know what they were going to do, but maybe I was being unfair. Hadn't I had to do some serious thinking in the weeks after I'd taken those tests? Yeah, I had, and I wasn't enough of a hypocrite to claim otherwise.

I kept going. "But she needs you to make a choice. If you want to be a part of her life, then do it. I know we don't live down the street from each other, and this is going to be complicated, but I'm not worried about that. I just need to know if you even want to make the effort in the first place." *Or if you're a piece of shit and don't.*

I made sure to pin him down with a look, but it was totally unnecessary. He was 1000 percent focused on me. Everything about him was. Jonah was thinking big time.

So I didn't stop.

"If you don't think you can make her a priority in your life, every day until you die, then we're going to need you to go. She's little now, but she isn't going to stay little, so you have to decide because it's going to be a lifetime commitment. I don't want her to ever feel like she's not important. She's going to have enough people who try to make her feel that way when she's older. But I'm not going to let a father figure do that too."

I held my breath and met his eyes, giving him what my old coach had called my Michael Myers face. Because that's what I would turn into if he fucked with my chunky monkey. She wasn't *ours* yet. He didn't have the protection of being family to me or Grandpa until he made a choice, and we would both do some sketchy shit without question if we had to. "If you break her heart, I will make you regret ever thinking about playing rugby. So I want you to understand that before you make a decision because there aren't any take-backs or refunds.

"I will never, ever ask you for a cent if you don't want to be a part of her life. I won't ask anything of you. I don't need anything from you. You're free to go if you want to go, but you have to make that choice, and it's a final one unless she decides she wants you around when she's older," I finished telling him, fisting my hands at my sides because I could feel them start to get tingly. "You have to go in ready for this, living in another hemisphere and all." I raised my eyebrows at him. "When you want something to work, you make it work. You're in or you're out, Jonah. I just need to know sooner than later. Once you've had a chance to think about it."

You're in or you're out. Bam.

We stared at each other. Eye to eye. My dark gray ones trying to burn into his honey-colored browns. Like we were having a competition. A competition that I sure as hell wasn't going to lose at. Not when Mo was at stake.

Grandpa Gus had been a great white shark for me. Peter a fucking hippo that killed more people on the down-low than a lion. And they had raised me to believe in myself. To defend myself. I'd been called Lenny the Lion for half my life for a reason. I'd turn into Freddy Kruger if I had to. I had no problem being someone's worst nightmare.

So when his gaze didn't stray for even a second... I had to narrow my eyes.

And shit got even more real when he kept on looking at me as he let out a deep exhale and spoke in a voice I had never heard from him before. A voice that didn't belong to the smiling, soft-spoken man I had met who hadn't known any French and had basically blushed when I had translated for him.

Jonah Collins said, gaze unflinching, "There's no choice, sweetheart."

It was my turn to swallow, and it had nothing to do with that dumbass term of endearment he'd used.

"If you say she's my daughter, she's my daughter."

Something hard thumped inside my chest. Something I didn't want to look at too closely.

"I'm sorry, Lenny," Jonah said. "I'm sorry I didn't know."

My ears started to buzz like they were debating whether or not to believe what he was saying.

As if he knew what I was thinking, he continued on. "I'm sorry I'm just now getting here, but I know now. There's nothing for me to consider. I'll be a part of her life, if you'll let me," he ended in a voice that had, word by word, started to sound more like him… the intensity in his eyes didn't waver for a moment. Like we were back at this game, and he was intent on not losing either.

If he was trying to get on my good side… it wasn't working.

I knew why he was here, and that was the last bond left between us. So I wasn't going to think about that. Nope.

"There's quite a bit we need to talk about, I know, but I'd like to start with seeing…." Jonah swallowed, and those nearly almond-shaped eyes widened again. "Seeing my daughter." He took a breath. "My Mo… if that's all right."

Seeing his Mo. His daughter.

I hated his accent. I really did. Him too. More than ever especially when my heart went *whack* with the way he said those words.

His voice had definitely wobbled, and I told my chest it better not be a bitch and wuss out on me. So he was getting emotional. He wouldn't be getting emotional if he had just called me back.

If he hadn't been such an ass.

What I wouldn't have given to hear those words out of him while I'd been pregnant, even if he didn't want to be together. I would have settled for that. I would have been okay with just *knowing* he would be there, instead of leaving this weight around my shoulders that had made me angry and rejected. It wasn't like we had actually been boyfriend and girlfriend... officially... back in France. We had been together, but I'd never thrown around a title, and neither had he. I would have understood if we'd drifted apart eventually. But at least he wouldn't have been cut cold turkey from my life.

I wasn't going to think about that.

"Of course you can see her, but I'm not joking. I need you to be committed to her if you're planning on being a part of her life. You're not buying a car you can trade in later on," I repeated, needing him to understand.

I would kill him myself, and if I didn't, I knew people who knew people.

And Grandpa Gus was a straight thug sometimes, and I didn't want to know the people he knew.

But Jonah didn't hesitate. "I am," he confirmed with a tip of his chin.

Well....

I wasn't going to hold my breath that he wouldn't change his mind. As much as I wouldn't have minded insulting him by reminding him that he didn't have the greatest track record, I kept that to myself. At least for now. He could have that much.

This was about Mo. She *was* young, and if he bounced in the next few weeks, she would never remember. I was fine with giving him a shot now. Better now than later. Because he wasn't going to get another one if he fucked up, and I'd warned him.

"Come on," I said, thinking we needed to go ahead and get over him meeting Grandpa Gus.

I wasn't sure how it was going to go but... tough shit.

He nodded as he got up, following me as we headed back to the living room. All three of them were still there, except Peter had made his way to sit on the floor where I had been, and he was watching her roll from her back onto her stomach and bouncing her butt, hands slapping the floor. She was going to crawl any day now, I could feel it. And that made me smile, even though the silence was stifling.

There was no way I was the only one who sensed the tension in the room.

But there was a reason why I loved Peter and thought the world of his morals and, unfortunately, a reason why I had liked Jonah so much.

"Mo! Say hi!" Peter said. "Hi!"

I could see Mo's eyes widen either at Peter's tone or at the man who was then standing right next to me as she moved her head to look in our direction.

I wanted to keep looking at her but decided to focus on the dumbass who had participated in creating this beautiful, perfect child. This child who was going to take ten years off my life but that I loved so much. So fucking much.

Jonah's eyes went wide, which didn't surprise me. But the hard swallow he had to take sent something I wasn't going to inspect too closely straight to my gut. If that wasn't an emotional gulp, I didn't know what was. I noticed right then that he was carrying the little stuffed bear and holding it against his thigh.

But the Still an Asshole swallowed hard again as he asked, "Can I... can I touch her?"

I had to settle for answering him with a nod since I didn't trust myself.

Jonah was still staring at the baby who had stopped trying to roll over to watch him instead, as his voice's volume took a nosedive, and he said something that had me side-eyeing the fuck out of him. "It's been a bit since I've held a baby, but I suppose it can't be too difficult to remember, eh?"

Ugh. It wasn't going to work. This innocent bullshit.

"It's not that hard," Peter responded to him. I was pretty

sure he was side-eyeing him discreetly too. Measuring him up or something.

I held my breath and forced myself to be decent. For Mo. Damn it.

"I'm sure Grandpa Gus dropped me on the head a few times while he figured things out again, and I turned out all right," I got myself to say, but only Peter looked over with a smirk that was still tense.

Grandpa Gus grunted though—not taking the bait he would have been all over normally over me being dropped—his eyes glued to the man I still hadn't introduced him to standing in his living room.

Peter lifted Mo up, and I could only watch as Jonah set the bear he'd brought on the side table, took a step forward and then another, before those big hands went to that not-so-small but still growing and fragile and soft body, and he took her. Hands curled under her little armpits as her feet dangled in the air, looking smaller than usual in comparison to the biceps barely flexing as they held her up for inspection.

Ten fingers. Ten toes. Dark haired. Adorable as fucking shit. I'd wiped her down after speaking to Jonah on the phone and put her in her pajamas: a long-sleeved onesie with the Cookie Monster on the chest.

Jonah took Mo... his *daughter*... and he said, very softly, very gently, and with just the slightest hint of a tremble in his voice, "Hello, Mo."

The happiest baby in the world smiled before she replied in her own language.

~

SHE PASSED OUT IN JONAH'S ARMS.

I wasn't overthinking it. Mo didn't know a stranger. She loved being fawned over and didn't give much of a fuck who paid her attention as long as someone did, which according to

Grandpa Gus was exactly the opposite of how I'd been. He claimed I came out of the womb bitch-facing people and had clung to him for dear life like someone was going to try and steal me away. It was only Peter that I had taken to immediately.

But my little nugget had passed right out in her father's arms thirty minutes after meeting him. Totally and completely *out*. Peter had taken her then, settling her right back down when she started to fuss at being moved, and headed up to her bedroom. To give me a chance to talk to this dipshit, I guessed.

"When can I see her again?" Jonah asked me as we stood at the bottom of the stairs, watching Peter go up, slowly, *shh-shh-shhing* the entire time.

It only hurt me a little to answer that. "Whenever you want."

He nodded, and I could hear the deep breath he took before he turned and lowered his gaze to me. I was five foot eight, but he was still a lot taller than I was.

Not that it mattered. I didn't know shit about tackling, but I had a purple belt in jiu-jitsu. I had learned a long time ago not to be intimidated by people bigger than me. I wasn't about to start now. To be fair, his expression as he looked at me was probably almost as intense as the one I'd given him when he first showed up, but I didn't even think about getting all meek or anything.

He didn't either apparently. "We need to talk."

I didn't want to talk to him, but I nodded. If he was committing, that was one thing. It didn't change the fact we were going to have to figure out the details of making this work as we went along.

"Have lunch with me tomorrow."

No.

But for my girl, I would, so I nodded.

"What time are you available?"

I shrugged and heard the distance in my voice. "Whenever."

His eyes moved back toward the living room, where my grandfather was sitting, more than likely shooting daggers dipped in poison at him with his eyeballs. To give him credit, after Mo had smiled at him, Jonah Collins had shaken Peter's hand and officially introduced himself. Peter had been polite, but I could tell it was just manners and compromising. For us.

But Grandpa…

He'd taken one look at the hand that Jonah had extended toward him and didn't move an inch to take it, despite the blatant-ass cough that Peter had aimed at him. Jonah had tucked his hand back in after realizing he wasn't going to get a handshake and still told him it was nice to meet him with a nod. Grandpa didn't say a fucking word.

All in all, for my gramps, that hadn't been so bad.

"Thank you for letting me see her," Jonah Collins said, still watching me with those clear light brown eyes that were so striking on his tanned face.

I wanted to dislike him, I really did. I wanted to think he was full of shit, but honestly, I didn't know what to think about his reactions all day. Maybe he was telling the truth or maybe he wasn't. I was willing to put it aside and just steep in that in private. But at the same time… fuck him. Obviously he didn't feel that guilty over shit, so why should I spend the rest of my life bitter over someone who hadn't cared about my feelings in the first place?

Once I thought about it like that… well, since when did I give anybody that kind of power? I was going to live my best life for me, not for somebody else. It made me mad just to think that I'd do otherwise.

I was not going to waste my life being pissed off at someone. I had better shit to do. People didn't give enough credit to what not giving a fuck could do for you. It was freedom.

"Uh-huh." I bit the inside of my cheek. "I'm off tomorrow. If you aren't here by one, I'm not going to wait to eat."

He nodded tightly.

We made it to the door before he called out over his shoulder, "Lenny."

"What?" I asked, reaching around his hip to undo the lock and ignoring the side of the tight, high butt inches from my forearm as I did it.

"I'm not going anywhere."

My hand froze for a second before I brought it back to my side. "Okay."

He turned around then, aiming that annoyingly intense face at me, looking down in a way that had me wishing for maybe the first time in my life that I was taller. That he didn't have the ability to have that tiny advantage over me. Once upon a time, I had liked how jacked he was.

But that had been once upon a time.

And I remembered now that I had never been crazy about fairy tales in the first place.

And even with those thoughts, I still wasn't prepared for all that size and mass focused solely on me as he said in a voice that had lost all traces of uncertainty and choking emotion, "I didn't mean to leave like that. I swear. I didn't know."

I didn't say a word. I wasn't going to brush this off and make it seem like him leaving or not knowing was not a big deal. But I didn't need to bring it up every three seconds either, I realized. You didn't help an injury by aggravating it constantly. And it wasn't like I was ever going to forget what happened.

Maybe he knew that… maybe he knew it was the best thing to let me keep my silence… because he opened the door then and stepped out. It wasn't until he turned around and reached inside to grab the handle while I stood there that he said it again, "I'm not leaving, Lenny."

I wasn't holding my breath, and I was pretty sure he knew that.

CHAPTER 8

"You are genuinely pissing me off now. I made it back to Houston, not that you give a shit, but I still need to talk to you. (pause) It's Lenny."

I WOKE UP THE WAY I HATED THE MOST: JOLTING MYSELF AWAKE.

One minute, I'd been totally out, and the next second, *bam!* I was wide awake, staring straight up at the ceiling and *listening*.

Based on how much sun was coming in through the windows, it had to be at least nine in the morning. Three hours later than I usually woke up. Well, it was more accurate to say it was three hours later than General Mo, the Hungriest Baby in the World, woke me up to feed her. Rolling my head to the side, I peeked at the baby monitor that lived on my nightstand, even though I didn't need it. Mo might not cry often, but when she was hungry, she was *hangry*.

She got it from me.

There was no ignoring her or mistaking her usual kitten cries for *you better feed me now, lady*.

But the baby monitor wasn't on the nightstand where I knew without a doubt I had left it. That in itself wasn't weird.

Peter and my gramps would creep into my room while I was sleeping to take it sometimes. I never slept with my door closed anymore. Neither did they, at least not all night.

It didn't take me long to go to the bathroom, do my business, and then drag myself down the stairs, passing by the empty bedrooms in the pajama shirt I had been able to start wearing again since Mo wasn't breastfeeding anymore and I didn't have to whip out a boob on call. As comfortable as nursing bras were, I'd been wearing sports bras for so long that nothing else compared to the comfort they brought me. I'd missed them. It wasn't until I reached the bottom of the stairs with a giant yawn that I knew something was different.

There were noises coming from the living room, which on Sunday was totally normal. Sunday breakfast was the only time we all managed to eat together in the morning. Peter was usually at Maio House by six, and Grandpa tried to sleep in while I got Mo ready for the day and spent some solo time with her. He usually didn't crawl out of his coffin until after seven.

But it was the familiar but unfamiliar voice I could hear speaking in the living room that had me pausing.

I didn't have to look at my phone to know it was nine-fifteen in the morning, and I didn't need a DNA test to know the voice I could hear belonged to the fuckface.

What the hell was he doing here?

We'd agreed to lunch, but I figured that would be around noon.

Four steps later, I stopped at the edge of the wide opening that led into the living room and peeked.

On the floor, two brown-haired men, one with more salt than pepper in it and the other with a fade cut, were kneeling, surrounding a baby kicking two chubby bare legs in the air but also somehow trying to roll over at the same time. A baby that wasn't wearing a diaper. Beside her, was the stuffed animal that Jonah had brought over the night before but hadn't gotten around to giving her.

"It's easy, but you have to be fast now that's she rolling over." It was Peter, the smaller one of the two, who spoke as he pulled a diaper out of nowhere like a magician. "You lift her bottom—" He held two feet together and lifted said butt in the air an inch before sliding the opened diaper beneath the bare butt. "—spread it out, fold the front over, and put the tabs back down, and you're done."

Jonah, I couldn't help but notice, was watching him like a hawk as he kneeled beside what looked like two balled-up baby wipes right by his right knee.

"She's eating real food now. That gets messy, but it's still simple," Peter said as he helped Mo sit up.

"How did you learn? With Lenny?"

"No, she was using the bathroom on her own by the time we met." I watched Peter's nearly black eyes flick toward the man beside him and saw the protectiveness hidden in them even from across the room. "We took a class and watched some videos to learn how to do everything."

Jonah made a subtle startled face. "Videos?"

"Yes," Peter confirmed, stealing another quick glance at the other man before looking back down with a frown. "Len couldn't sleep much at the end—in the last trimester. We looked up everything then to be ready. We learned together."

Something flashed across Jonah's face as he gazed down at the baby. Regret? He might have been faking that too. How the hell would I know?

Peter kept talking though, his gaze shifting back to Mo so that he couldn't see what I was seeing. But that fiercely protective look on his face didn't lighten up. It didn't go anywhere, and it made my heart grow a few sizes. Maybe this other idiot hadn't liked me enough to even keep being my friend, but Peter would always have my back. *Our* backs. Always.

"If you're planning on staying," Peter said, "you'll figure it all out. It's easy. Madeline won't get mad if you do something wrong. She doesn't have anything to compare to, and she doesn't know a bad mood unless she's hungry. She's a good girl. She's tied with her mom for being the best two girls in the world... aren't you, Mo? Aren't you good and special and smart? Just like your mama."

"I didn't know Lenny was... pregnant. If I had, I wouldn't...." He swallowed and seemed to struggle for a second to find the right words... or the right lies. "I would have been here. Or maybe... maybe Lenny would have been with me, I don't know." He shook his head. "I still can't believe she... exists."

Me be with him. Ha. Something that could have been anger or sadness swirled around in my chest.

He continued talking quietly to Peter. "I've missed out on heaps. I know it doesn't change much, but I want you to know that I wasn't avoiding my... her... Mo." He closed his eyes for a moment before gluing them back down on the figure on the blanket. His expression startled and nervous and just... heavy. "Wish I could take back the mistakes I've made."

I had no right to let those words make me feel nauseous. I knew that.

I had no right to imagine what those mistakes were—him disappearing for months and having sex with a ton of women, him doing drugs, having another child somewhere, getting married, getting involved with the wrong people—but I ran through all those possibilities in my head anyway.

I hadn't looked him up in months. The only information I had been caught up on was how his rugby team had been doing over the season, and that was only because of the articles that every so often popped up on my home screen page... from all the previous stalking I'd done before Mo.

I had no idea what he'd been doing with his life. Because it wasn't any of my business. Because I wasn't going to look it up.

Jonah and I hadn't exactly been in a relationship. We had been friends. Who liked each other a lot. Who were attracted to each other, at least I had thought.

But I hadn't been his girlfriend. I had never been anyone's girlfriend.

If he had done something after we'd gone our separate ways, it wasn't like he had cheated on me.

For the most part, I'd always thought I was a logical person. But if I was going to be totally honest with myself, when I had been super pregnant, I would lie in bed and cry over the idea of him being with someone else while I gained weight and my boobs hurt and I couldn't poop and got irritated by everything even more than usual. I had thought about him spending every night with someone different... even if he had told me before we'd done it that he rarely had sex too. *Can't trust anyone, sweetheart. Hope I don't bugger this up,* he had laughed while he'd taken my clothes off that first time, slowly, letting those big hands linger in all the bare places he came across. And I had laughed and told him *I hope you don't either.* And we had both laughed some more after that.

There had been a reason it had been him. Because he had seemed so nice and fresh and honest and good and not at all like the horny assholes I had known who slept with everyone. Or the guys I knew too well to be attracted to. There were good guys out there; of course I knew that. But most of them had girl-friends, and the ones who didn't were like Jonah—except I felt nothing for them. They knew who they were, they weren't addicted to sex, and they were particular about who they let into their lives and their beds. And there was nothing there for me.

Some of the most successful men I knew were almost absti-nent. Because they knew what it was like for people to want them for all the wrong reasons. You didn't find real things by looking, usually.

And that's why I hadn't second-guessed too much Jonah's insistence that he was out of practice. He had seemed too real. Too himself. For a while there, he had given me the idea that maybe he could have been mine if we had been together long enough.

That wasn't how it had worked out, but it's how I thought it might have. If we'd had time. If he hadn't been derailed with his injury. If he had liked me more, I guessed.

But that unreasonable part of me that was connected straight to hormones reared its ugly, no-reason-to-be-possessive-but-I-was-going-to-be-a-possessive-psycho-anyway head and made me want to kick the Asshole's ass all over again for being off living his life, forgetting about me, probably making out with a different woman every week, while I'd been at home, substituting coffee for a hot mushroom drink, missing food I craved out of nowhere that Grandpa wouldn't let me have either, while my skin stretched and my organs moved with the life I'd been carrying inside of me.

I was a jealous motherfucker, even when I hadn't had a boyfriend. God knew I had wanted to kill Noah every time I saw him with a different girl while I'd thought I'd been in love with him when I'd been younger. The bitch.

Just thinking about Noah right then made me want to kick his ass too while I was at it, but for a completely different reason.

Keep it together and quit being a psycho.

The fact was, I could be with whomever I wanted to be with. I hadn't been abstinent because I was pining over the dumbass in the room or because of the one I had thought I liked as a teenager. I'd had more guys flirt with me while pregnant than when I hadn't been for some reason.

Thinking that eased the tension in my chest a little more. It made the crazy take a step back and see that I'd always had options too. I had done what I wanted to.

But by the time I managed to zone back into the conversation that Jonah and Peter were having, I had missed part of it. I figured I had skulked around long enough while eavesdropping. Fortunately, Peter saw me out of the corner of his eye right as I stepped into his line of view so I didn't have to speak first.

"Morning," my second dad greeted me. "General Mo has been keeping me company this morning. We agreed we'd let you sleep in." He gave the baby a tickle.

"Aren't you two the best?" I asked as I took a couple steps into the room, finally conscious I was just wearing a long T-shirt in front of Jonah. Whatever.

Mo made a happy squeal and a "Ma!" at the sound of my voice, lighting up my entire life with every little, joyous sound she made. Glancing at Jonah, who was still on his knees, I slid him a blank look before scooping her up for a hug.

"Hi, Jonah."

At nine in the morning, his eyes were clear and wide awake, everything from his white and black pullover hoodie to his jeans clean and fresh looking, and his bristly facial hair hugged the shape of his annoyingly almost-perfect face. But it was the easygoing, pleasant expression he wore that got on my nerves the most. Like nothing was wrong and it didn't bother him that I couldn't stand him. "Good morning, Lenny."

I wanted to grumble, but I didn't. Instead, I gave Mo kisses on each cheek and pretended I was going to eat her hand while she babbled before saying, "I thought we were meeting in the afternoon."

"Yeh." He flashed me another little smile that was a little too friendly for how crabby I was feeling at him being here unexpectedly, looking all nice and shit. "Couldn't sleep much last night." His attention flicked from me to the baby and back before he added quickly, "You said I could see her whenever I wanted. Hope it's all right."

It wasn't, but that was Asshole Lenny speaking. I had said those words, and I'd meant them, but I guess I hadn't expected him to show up early in the morning the next day, either. He had me there. "It's all right." I switched her to one arm as she tried to stick her finger in my nose and focused on Peter, attempting at the same time to will the grumpiness away because I had put myself into this situation. "Did you eat breakfast already?"

"Not yet. It's Gus's turn, and he was still cooking when our visitor arrived."

Our visitor.

Luna would tell me to be a better person, but that wasn't so easy. Still though, I grabbed what I had to work with—just the tiniest bit of understanding and patience—and dragged my gaze back to the biggest person in the room even though I didn't really want to.

He was here for Mo, and this was the rest of my life.

"Jonah," his name in my throat was irritating, but I hoped it would get easier with time "would you like to eat breakfast with us since you're here? It's vegetarian."

Those brown eyes flashed with surprise… and then he nodded.

∾

INVITING JONAH TO BREAKFAST WASN'T THE WORST IDEA I'D EVER had. It wasn't even in the top twenty or possibly even fifty things, but it was fucking up there.

Because if I could have taken a picture of Grandpa's face when I walked into the kitchen following Peter, with the Dickwad trailing behind, I could have found at least fifty people who would have paid for the image. That shit was *priceless*. Grandpa's mouth had dropped a quarter open, his eyes had gone pretty squinty, and it was just… something.

But whatever magic Peter had worked on him was carrying over because he pressed his lips together after a heartbeat, flared his nostrils, and gritted out, "Four for breakfast?"

Luckily it was Peter who answered with laughter in his voice because he was probably thinking the same thing about the face my grandpa had made—you know, about it being priceless. "Yes, Gus, four of us today."

The smile that had come over Grandpa's face was so brittle I was surprised it didn't break into pieces. To give him credit, he kept whatever was on his tongue to himself as he turned around and faced the stove again. His shoulders were stiff, and I didn't need to see him to know he was making faces down at the stove. Knowing him, he was probably whispering to himself in a whiny, high-pitched voice.

Luckily, I hadn't expected it to get better as we ate, because it didn't. Not when I was being quiet and grumpy as I fed Mo and myself. Peter was being himself, eating, talking to Mo, nudging Grandpa from time to time, and sending me these looks I wasn't totally sure what the hell they meant. Meanwhile, Grandpa Gus stabbed at his roasted potatoes like they had tried to kill him.

That was when the questions started.

And I didn't stop them. Because I had compromised with myself: they were going to happen sooner or later, and unless he got ugly, I wouldn't step in. But if Jonah was going to be in Mo's life, he was going to be in the rest of ours too.

"So…," Grandpa muttered as he started attacking a piece of pineapple with his fork. "Edward—"

I was 100 percent sure he knew damn well that wasn't his name. Knowing my grandfather, he probably knew everything about him by then. Birthday, height, weight, every team he'd ever played for, the names of every member of his family. Everything his stalker self could find on the internet.

"Where are you from? Australia?"

All right. This was where he was going with this. Being a pain in the ass was what came the most naturally to him. I eyed Jonah as I tried to spoon a little bit of extra mushy oatmeal into Mo's mouth.

He chewed, eyes on my grandfather. "Auckland. New Zealand, Mr. DeMaio."

Mr. DeMaio? Somebody was laying it on thick. I made a face at my girl who responded by grinning.

"New Zealand," my grandfather echoed with an ornery tone that only those who knew him really well would recognize. "Is that where your parents are from?"

"Yes. My great-great-grandparents on my mum's side immigrated there around the 1870s from Scotland and Norway," Jonah explained, glancing up and focusing on Mo. He took a breath and exhaled out another smile as his eyes slid to meet mine. "My other granddad is Samoan, and my nan's got some Māori and Samoan. Some Pakeha too."

That had all three of us looking over at him blankly.

"European." He paused. "White."

I just realized I had never asked him that. Honestly, I had never really thought much about where he got those—stupid—crazy looks from. I had met two of his teammates who were Māori, both of whom had a richer skin tone than he did. And as I looked at his features right then, I realized he didn't look… one thing or another. He really was a perfect mix of heritages, from his bone structure to his skin color… everything.

He really was a handsome asshole.

But a lame one.

Grandpa huffed a second before he backstabbed me. "Lenny has always liked her… Europeans."

I didn't think twice about flinging Mo's spoon right at my grandfather, and it was his good luck he had reflexes like a retired cat because he lunged out of the way at the last minute, avoiding getting hit in the shoulder.

"It's your eyeball next time. You don't really need both," I warned him, shaking my head at his betrayal. *Always liked her Europeans.* I didn't even know how the hell he still managed to surprise me.

Grandpa, though, fucking laughed for the first time.

I slid him a look as I got up and grabbed another baby spoon from the drawer. Fortunately none of us said much the rest of the breakfast besides Peter bringing up comments about a couple of the guys he was training, with me and Grandpa Gus commenting on it. After we all finished, Peter stood up and headed straight toward the coffeemaker. "Jonah, would you like some coffee?"

I was in the middle of trying to spoon the last of Mo's oatmeal into her mouth when he answered.

"I'd take a cup of tea if you have any."

I forgot about how much he liked tea, I thought randomly, annoyed I remembered that detail.

"We don't have any," I answered, sounding bitchy, even though it was the truth.

"It's all good," Jonah responded, not sounding at all put-out.

Peter glanced at me over his shoulder after refilling two mugs. As he and my gramps grudgingly left the kitchen, he mouthed *go do something.*

Shit.

I guess we could skip lunch and go straight into our talk to avoid spending more time with Salty Britches in the house and on edge.

"Would you like to go for a walk around the neighborhood with Mo and me?" I made myself ask as I licked the rest of what she didn't eat off the spoon.

His "yeh" was so instant I had to glance at him.

Did he have to sound so excited? Suck-up. I nodded more to myself than anything before I turned around, setting the towel aside. "Okay. If you don't mind watching her for a second, I'll go get dressed."

His eyes widened, but he nodded, his gaze immediately straying to our supreme leader who was sitting in her high chair, chewing on a teething ring.

I forgot that according to what I'd overheard, he hadn't seemed to have a whole lot of experience with babies.

Well, it wasn't like I had either. He'd learn. If he wanted to.

If he knew what was good for him.

"She's not going to try and swan dive off the seat or blow anything up," I tried to assure him, suddenly remembering how Grandpa had told me the same thing at least twenty times after she had been born. It had been one thing when Luna had shoved her baby at me the first time, like I had known what the fuck I was doing. But it was a totally different thing to have my best friend, who did have experience with babies, standing three feet away making sure I didn't do anything wrong.

It was a totally different thing when the tiny thing in my arms was *my* responsibility to keep alive.

My responsibility for the rest of my life. Because with my luck, she would end up the way I'd ended up with Grandpa Gus: a life clinger.

Plus, according to Grandpa Gus, it was *really hard to break a baby*. At least that's what he'd said over and over again when he smelled the terror coming off me. I had stared at him for a long time after he said that, wondering what the hell kind of shenanigans he had gotten us into before my memories became solid. It was probably better that I couldn't remember.

"I'll be right back. You'll be fine," I told him.

What I got was a mostly determined nod in return.

Well, maybe he was nervous, but he wasn't a total chicken-shit. I'd give him that. I'd brought Mo around enough of the guys at the gym, and plenty of them hadn't even wanted to hold her in the first place. Not even now.

And I had been the same way when someone had tried to get me to hold their baby. *No, thank you*. So… good for him. I guess.

It didn't take me long at all to put on real clothes and brush my teeth. It might have only been ten minutes later that I opened the door to the kitchen with my palm and called out, "You ready to go?"

Jonah turned from where he was sitting beside Mo's chair, that muscular body facing her, and nodded.

I kept my mouth shut as I watched him figure out how to

take her out. I didn't miss how steady his hands were then, the same as when he was running full speed clutching a white ball to his side while dodging men trying to tackle him. Like those times when he was fully concentrated and completely in control.

Instead, in this case, here he was. With calm hands, a determined glint in his eye as he cradled an eight-month-old to his chest like she was a bomb ready to go off.

Holding the door open, they passed into the hallway ahead of me, with Mo babbling in the process, totally fucking fine. The jogging stroller we used to take her out was already right by the door, and it only took a moment to get it all set up. I showed him how to set Mo down and then strapped her in. Wordlessly, we carried the stroller down the steps of the house between the two of us, and I asked, sounding just the tiniest bit grumpy, "Do you want to push it?"

If he said no….

Those honey-colored eyes flicked down to the stroller, his hands going to the front of his jeans to wipe down the material that was *almost* clinging to his thighs because those things were so big—not that I was paying that much attention.

But he dipped his chin a moment before saying, "I'll push the pram," as he got behind the handle and started doing just that.

I couldn't help but eye him as we passed one house and then another on our walk. In the low seventies, it was a rare warm day at the end of January, thankfully. It had been eighty-four degrees on Christmas Day; two days later, it had dropped into the forties. Texas weather had a mind of its own. The sky was a grayish shade of blue, and luckily, the neighborhood was an old one, with massive trees that lined the streets, the weeping branches giving plenty of shade.

It was just a nice Sunday out on a walk with my girl and… her dad.

I eyed the tall brown-haired man again and wondered if he was being honest about not knowing.

Fucker.

"Your granddad hates me," Jonah said out of nowhere.

He was sweeping one side of the street to the other with his eyes, his knuckles pale over the handle of the stroller, like he was gripping the hell out of it in case it suddenly decided to run off on its own.

If he was looking at me to lie to him, he was shit out of luck. "Yeah, he does," I agreed, because it was the truth. Grandpa Gus did hate him.

What surprised the hell out of me was the snort that ripped through Jonah's nose at my response. It triggered, for one second, memories of him doing the same thing when we'd known each other. What I didn't let myself remember was how much I'd liked it.

"Can't say I blame him much," the fucker accepted, while I made myself stop thinking about his snort.

All I could manage to do was grunt out a "humph." I got a side-eye in return. A tight expression came over Jonah's face as we briefly made eye contact.

"Lenny—" he started almost immediately before I cut him off.

I had a feeling I knew where this was going and didn't want to go there. "I don't care what happened or what your reasons were, Jonah. I don't want to talk about it anymore." I had before, and I wanted him to know that. But I didn't now. Not anymore.

That was a lie, and my heart knew it and my brain did too. A tiny part of me wanted to hear what he had to say. But nothing he said or did changed a thing.

He told me he would call me.

He got hurt.

He disappeared.

For. Seventeen. Months.

He had reappeared into the world a year after I'd last seen him, and over the next few months, he didn't make a single effort to contact me.

Motherfucker.

I mean it didn't matter. It didn't need to be brought up anymore. It really didn't, and I had to focus on that. We were here, and we were going to be in this together, some way, some-how, and that was the important part. And if we needed to do this for a long time, then I needed to not get pissed off and become irrational.

I wasn't spending the rest of my life being bitter toward him. I could passively hate him. That worked.

"All that needs to matter at this point is our relationship with Mo. I don't want to talk about... then." I squeezed my hands into fists. It was the truth. It *was*. "If you're going to be part of the rest of her life, that is."

The look he sent me though....

I wasn't sure what to think of the way his eyebrows knit together or the clench in his cheek. I wasn't sure what to think of the words that came out of his mouth next either. "I'd like to explain, Lenny," he said carefully, dousing me with that accent of his that made everything out of his mouth instantly sound prettier than everything out of mine, even though I still wanted to trip him near a flight of stairs. "Need to, really. I'm not going anywhere."

"It's easy to say things. It's not as easy to do them."

I didn't mean for my words to come out so bitchy, but it wasn't like I could take them back after they were out. Maybe he didn't remember how he had stood in front of me the day before his game—match, whatever—held my face in between those big hands, and said, *We should go to the catacombs when I get back from Toulouse, yeh?*

We never made it to the catacombs.

I had never made it to the catacombs.

"I deserved that," he replied, and not for the first time, it hit me that he didn't fight back, or that he didn't get mad or try and deflect. Jonah looked down at the ground, that wide jaw working.

His fucking throat started to go pink, and I almost felt guilty. Almost.

But Jonah kept going, his throat bobbing as he owned my borderline bitchy comment. "If that's what you want, I won't say anything, but know I want to." One bright brown eye focused on me. "We can talk about our girl, then?"

We passed by one of my favorite historic houses in the Heights. A massive white and purple home that reminded me of my best friend's much smaller house, but I had my mind on other things. *Our girl.* He'd gone with that, huh? Fine.

"Sure," I told him, training my eyes on the house as we walked by.

"I'm going to contact my lawyer—"

I stopped moving at the same time as a car honked from behind where we were walking. Clenching my fist and holding my breath, I glanced over my shoulder just as a familiar voice hollered, "Hey, Lenny! Hi, Mo!"

What were the fucking chances? I wondered as I faced the minivan that pulled up beside me. "Hi, Mrs. Polanski," I said to the graying blonde woman in the driver's seat who was waving.

"I'm heading to church, but drop by the house this week so I can get my hands on that baby," the woman who was about the closest thing to a mother figure I'd ever had called out with another wave. "Love you!"

"I will. Love you too!" I yelled back at her with another wave that was only partially half-assed while I processed what the fuck had just come out of this asshole's mouth before Mrs. Polanski of all people had rolled up.

Contact his lawyer?

Jonah had stopped too at the honk, and he instantly held up a hand the second I turned back to him. "Not like that. Listen to me. I'd like to be put on Mo's birth certificate. She would have dual citizenship, I think, as well. And I owe you—"

Was he trying to give me a heart attack? Fuck me. "You don't owe me anything."

The Asswipe frowned. "I owe you. Children are expensive. I don't know much about them, but I know that," he kept going. "You don't have to look at me in that way. I don't want to fight you for rights, but I think she should know where I come from. I want her to know me."

I could feel my lip curling up like it wanted to snarl, and I tamped it down, keeping my face even.

"I suppose we'll have to do a paternity test, but I'll find out, see what needs to be done." He blinked, as if something finally hit him. But just as quickly as he stopped to do that, he refocused, like he was on top of the situation all over again. "Once I talk to my agent and lawyer."

He didn't look away from me, and all those features got even more determined, and I didn't know what to think about it. "I meant what I said about wanting to be around. I want to do right by her." I didn't want to see the earnestness that moved over his face. "I *need* to do right by her."

I swallowed and watched him gesture toward the stroller he was pushing around.

"If I would have known...." He lifted up a brawny shoulder. "I want to do the right thing. I want to do what I should have from the beginning. If I could go back in time and do things differently, I would, but I can't, Len. You don't owe me anything, and I know that. I appreciate you being willing to let me see her and be a part of her life."

His hands flexed around the handle, and he continued. "I know you don't care for me much now, and it must not be easy, but I appreciate what you're doing. You're right about how saying something is different than actually doing it, but I'm not going to leave like that again. I'm going to be a part of her life... of your life."

Did he have to look at me like that as he said those words? What game was he on? And did his eyes have to be so shiny and direct?

"I want to earn your trust again. Want to raise her with you."

I wished right then I had my stress ball in my pocket.

"You'll have to help me, I'm sure, but I can promise I'll try my best to not mess it up heaps," he said in that calm, collected voice that shouldn't have ever gotten under my skin, but it did every single time. Maybe it was because I'd been raised around so many loudmouths, but that was one of the things I had liked the most about Jonah as I'd gotten to know him. He was just himself.

I had thought for a long time that his quiet confidence had been his most attractive trait. More than his body. More than his smile. More than his face and how cheery he'd been.

But I'd learned the hard way that he hadn't been as confident as I had expected. Otherwise he wouldn't have just... fallen off the face of the earth after his injury. I'd been injured countless times and didn't wallow in my own bullshit for long.

But, to be fair, at least he was here now. I could give him that. For Mo.

"We can do this together, yeah? Be on... the Mo League, if you want to call it," he asked. "I can do better, Lenny, if you give me the chance. I can promise you that. I will do better."

I still said nothing.

The Mo League?

I fucking hated how much I liked it. Hated how reasonable and even sweet he was attempting to be. Hated that I was even in this position in the first place. Not having a kid, but not having her with someone who I could fully trust. Someone I loved, even. That would have been nice.

But this was what I had so....

A hand with short, trimmed nails wrapped itself around my wrist, and I looked up into those honey-colored eyes that popped so much on his tanned skin and held my breath. "There's so much we have to work out, but I'm more than willing to. I won't give you a reason to regret it."

Regret was a weird thing. It was the one topic that Grandpa Gus had drilled into my head over and over and over again when I'd gotten nervous while I'd been growing up. You did something and you could regret it, or you could not do something and regret it. You never knew which way it would go. Everything in life is a gamble.

But I knew what I would regret the most. I knew it deep inside my bones, deep inside my soul, deep inside everywhere.

I looked at the man standing with me on a quiet residential street at ten-thirty in the morning on a Sunday and thought of the words he had already used both in my presence and out of it.

He claimed he wanted to be around for Mo. He'd said it without thinking about it too much, which I wasn't completely sure was a good thing. But… he couldn't fuck up if I didn't give him a chance to.

Jonah couldn't be a dad if I didn't give him the opportunity.

I didn't need to look at the sweet little booger with big honey-colored eyes to know there was nothing I wouldn't do for her, and spending time with a man who'd hurt my feelings… being obligated to be in contact with that man for the rest of her life—of *my* life—well, I could do it. I *would* do it. The way Mo had come to exist was in the past already. But her future was up to us.

I could only hope this might be the easiest thing I ever had to suck up to do.

Being a mom wasn't for weak asses, that was for sure.

So, I flashed him a grimace that I hoped was at least part of a smile. "Fine. Welcome to the Mo League. You can be the vice president if you're willing to fight Grandpa Gus for the spot, but he fights dirty, so you're probably better off being the secretary, I guess."

CHAPTER 9

9:08 p.m

Your voicemail is full.

In case you deleted my number,

this is Lenny.

Call or text me. Please.

WHEN I WALKED INTO MAIO HOUSE ON TUESDAY MORNING AND *felt* the awkwardness in the air, I knew something was up.

And I had a feeling it was because of a bubblehead from New Zealand.

He had come over multiple times by that point. Of course they'd seen him, he was massive and an unknown. They hadn't been aware of *why* he was coming in. It wasn't unheard of for people to drop by the office to talk about training or marketing stuff or different programs. Managers for the athletes came into the office to talk about one thing or another from time to time. Some of the guys dropped by for advice or to talk... a lot less now than before, but it still happened. Sometimes. Rarely, really. And that kind of made me sad.

Most of my real friends had stopped training MMA over the

last few years for one reason or another, mostly from injuries and some because of relationships and families. Priorities changed, and I was the last person to not understand that, especially now. During the last big hurricane, a lot of them had moved away when our old facility had been destroyed by floodwater and mold. And they hadn't come back.

But whatever.

Where I'd gone from knowing everyone and being friends with them all, now… at most I was someone they kind of knew. I didn't work with them on the floor much, and if I did, it wasn't for hours on end like before. Hell, even with Luna, we had to work a lot more at our friendship than we'd had to in the past. We had to schedule lunches every other week to see each other.

Anyway, thinking about that felt like an enormous bummer on my soul, and I focused back on the important stuff.

Men had come into the office when Grandpa Gus had worked there, and they came in now with me. For business purposes. But it wasn't every day that a six-foot-five-inch man built like a tank came into Maio House and headed straight into the office. It was something worth noticing. Especially when there were so many nosey eyes and ears.

I knew these people, and they wouldn't avoid looking at me directly unless they were talking about me.

It wouldn't be the first time it happened.

Fuck it. I had nothing to hide or any explanations I needed to make to anyone.

The old me would have asked them *you got something to say?* But now… now I just walked into my office and waited until no one could see me to turn around and give the floor in general the middle finger. Both middle fingers. Fuckers.

Half an hour later, I had my computer on and a cup of matcha tea sitting on my desk. I had side-eyed the guys and girls once more on my walk to and from the break room in the other building. I had settled in to go through the voice mails that had the red light on my office phone blinking. There were five new ones.

The first one was nothing special. One of the fighter's managers wanted to schedule a time for a photographer to come in and take pictures of him while he trained. No big deal.

The second one though had me hitting the delete button like I wanted to break it. *"It's Noah. Call me."* The fact he had called the work phone instead of my cell phone said enough. I had to open my mouth to stretch my jaw after that.

The third call was from a blogger who wanted to talk to Peter, the fourth was some vague message from a woman who just said, *"This is Rafaela Smith. I'm looking for Gus DeMaio. I'd appreciate it if—"* That name didn't ring a bell, and she didn't say what she wanted, so no thanks on that return phone call, and the fifth was from the repairman who came in to fix the gym equipment. He was the first one I called back.

We had just barely hung up when the phone rang.

"Maio House," I answered, moving the mouse so I could access my email. "This is Lenny."

All it took was a simple "Hey" to piss me off.

If I could kick half the members out, I would. I really would. I'd kick all of them out if their dues didn't pay the bills. Fucking bigmouths.

I knew it was petty, but I didn't give a shit. "Who is this?" I asked, even though I knew exactly who it was.

Noah sighed. "Noah, Lenny."

"Oh."

He had to know how lucky he was I had gone with that instead of *what do you want, person who I've known since I was three, who left me when I needed him.*

"How you doing?" he had the nerve to ask like it hadn't been months since the last time we had talked.

"I'm fine, you?" I asked him like I was petty and held grudges, because I did. But Noah knew that, yet he'd still decided to call me twice within twenty-four hours.

And, apparently, he did know that because he didn't even bother sighing or getting his feelings hurt by how detached I was speaking to him. "I've been better," Noah responded like I genuinely cared.

I didn't *want* to waste my time rolling my eyes, but I did anyway because *was he fucking for real?* "Do you need something? Peter's busy right now, but I can get him to call you back when he's done in an hour." Not that he actually would.

"I don't need to talk to Peter," my childhood best friend said, his tone weird and annoying as hell. "I heard something interesting."

I closed both my eyes, grabbed my stress ball from the drawer, and squeezed the fucking shit out of it as he kept talking.

"Who's the guy that's been showing up to the gym?" he asked casually in the time it took me to do that.

Noah had been my best friend. We'd grown up together. We'd studied judo together at the same club for fifteen years.

And for a couple months, I had *thought* I'd been more than half in love with someone who couldn't see me as more than what I had been to him: the girl who he'd grown up with. His kind-of sister. His friend.

Then one random day, I had taken a look at him and decided *yeah, no.*

It might have been the day after I overheard him bragging about having sex with one of my friends, but it happened. Just, *nope.* Nah. And as I'd gotten older, I had realized that I hadn't loved him. Not like that. It had just been… a lapse of judgment. Hormones maybe.

But I had stuck around after I'd come to my senses. Because maybe he could be a douchebag, but he'd been my friend. He'd known me back then better than just about anyone other than Peter and my gramps. He'd been my *friend.*

Or so I thought.

Then, many years later, after we had both grown up, I got pregnant, and he suddenly lost his shit and left.

And now he was here. Calling me, asking about something that had nothing to do with him. Not anymore.

I "hmmed" into the receiver, forcing my index finger to click the mouse so I could open the most recent email I had gotten. "Pretty sure that's none of your business. Was there something else you needed or...?" *Can you fuck off now?* I wanted to ask but barely managed not to.

"Lenny."

I blinked and moved my tongue across my upper teeth, telling myself again that I wasn't going to let this bullshit-ass call bother me.

"Who is he?"

I squeezed my stress ball. "I don't feel like talking to you anymore, Noah, but if there's something else you need, or if this new gym that you're at has questions about anything, they can give me a call," I told him, hearing the sarcasm dripping from my voice.

"Don't be like that."

I rolled my eyes. "Have fun in Albuquerque." Then I hung up.

All righty, I could have done without that.

Shoving my chair back, the fucking hint of a tension headache creeping up on me right between the eyebrows, I got up and headed to the doorway. I stopped there, clapping my hands as obnoxiously loud as I physically could. Under normal circumstances, I would never, ever interrupt anyone training.

But I wasn't fucking playing around.

The trainers could get mad at me if they wanted, but I didn't care.

Just as I expected, just about every head in the gym turned toward me as everyone stopped what they were doing.

"I don't know which one of you snitched, but whoever comes in and out of here is none of your business. It isn't anyone else's either," I said in a voice just slightly louder than my speaking voice. The room projected everything perfectly like I knew it would. "Got it?"

Silence replied to me at first.

And there was only one person who vocally replied. "Wasn't me. I can't stand Noah."

The fact he even knew I was referring to Noah confirmed what I had expected.

No one else had anything to say. I did see one guy turn to look at the man next to him—Carlos, it was Carlos— and I knew what his kind of body language meant. My gut said that fucker was the one who had told Noah. It didn't surprise me. Before he'd left, he'd spent a lot of time with Carlos.

I sent that guy a long, deadeye stare, the kind I'd perfected over the years.

The kind that said he better watch his tires because having to be a role model now wouldn't stop me from doing certain things.

I almost slammed the door shut behind me on the way back in, but I just barely managed to close it softly. I didn't want me slamming it to come across as me being pissed off that Noah knew because I was hung up over him leaving. Everyone knew why he'd bounced.

God, I hoped someone kicked his ass again sooner than later. I was glad he'd lost his last fight. He'd deserved to lose.

I had barely closed the door when the work phone started ringing again.

"Maio House," I answered, mentally preparing myself for the possibility it might be Noah again but being pretty sure it wasn't. He wasn't the kind of person who would call back after getting hung up on.

"Good morning, Lenny."

Jonah. I wasn't sure if it was slightly better than it being Noah or the same. "Hi."

There was a pause. "Is this a bad time?"

I blew out a breath and reached for my stress ball again. "No," I told him, hearing the aggravation in my tone. I let out another breath, attempting to relax. I tried again. "Do you need something?"

There was another brief pause. "Oi. I can give you a ring at a better time."

Oi.

I shouldn't have started smiling at it, but I did because it was just that kind of day where he'd be the lesser shithead. I squeezed my stress ball and sighed. "No. Now is fine. Did you want to go see Mo? She's at daycare right now. My grandpa dropped her off this morning."

"She doesn't have a nanny?"

I squeezed the ball in my hand tight, the smile he'd started to cause melting off. Did this bitch have any idea how much a *nanny* cost? "Grandpa Gus is her nanny. No one can or will take better care of her than he will," I explained, choking the nonexistent life out of my small gift.

We hadn't really talked much on the rest of the walk on Sunday. Plus, I hadn't missed his comment about needing to call his manager or lawyer. I shouldn't be surprised he hadn't told anyone about Mo. Had he by now though, or was he still... waiting?

"Twice a week he drops her off at daycare for a few hours. Sometimes my friend's father-in-law keeps her for part of the day too. She comes to the gym a couple times a week too. It changes. We wing it."

"Oh."

I blew out a breath away from the receiver before reaching up to pinch the bridge of my nose for a moment at the sudden sting there. "So did you want to go see her?"

"Yeh, but I was asking because I called about the paternity test. It isn't much notice, but they can see us this afternoon if you can get away. Next available time they can fit us in is two weeks from now."

"At what time?" I asked, even though I damn well knew I could leave whatever time I needed to.

"One."

I let go of my nose. Now, or two weeks from now, or months from now? *At least he wasn't waiting.* "Yeah, sure. I can get away. What's the name of the place?"

I SAW THE BIG BROWN-HAIRED MAN THE SECOND I PULLED INTO THE parking lot. Jonah was leaning against the wall beside the two glass doors, arms crossed over his chest, taking advantage of the shade from the building. He must have recognized my car from his visit to Grandpa's house because he stood straight up just as I pulled into a spot.

By the time I was slamming the driver's side door shut, he was only a few feet away.

He smiled at me.

I didn't smile back.

And I wasn't going to overthink what it said about him that my nonreaction didn't do anything to his. "Glad you could come," he said, sounding genuinely pleased.

In the time we had known each other, I hadn't seen him in a bad mood. I wondered what got the job done. Maybe it was just injuries that made him lose his shit and turn into a dick.

Or maybe he had used his injury as an excuse for not coming back.

Okay, that was far-fetched, and I could admit it. I hated reasoning that out. He really had gone a year without posting anything on his social media accounts. From the moment he had been injured, he literally had wiped himself off the face of the planet like a missing person. There had been articles written about him just removing himself from any and every kind of spotlight, and if it hadn't been for his agent claiming that he had heard from him, everyone might have thought he was dead. That article with his quote had hurt, but I hadn't believed for a second after that first month that something bad had happened to him. He'd left of his own free will.

I'd stopped looking him up by the time he'd rejoined his team. I'd only known he had because of the article that had come up under news on my homepage. Like he'd been reborn out of the ashes or something.

"It's one of the benefits of working for my grandpa," I told him after a second, hearing my grumpiness, as I beat him to opening up the rear passenger door and ducked inside. Mo was wide awake as I unfastened all the little straps holding her in her car seat, giving her cheek and forehead a couple quick kisses in the process as she babbled away.

I smiled at her. "I don't want to do this either, Mo Peep, but we kind of have to, okay?"

Based on what she replied with, I don't think she believed me.

Thankfully, I managed not to bang my head as I backed out, holding her to me as I snagged her bag with my free hand. I was pretty much a fucking magician as I moved out of the way just enough to hip check the door and close it, holding a heavy baby in one arm, a backpack in another, and holding my keys in my hand at the same time.

Jonah was still smiling when I looked at him.

I still didn't smile back.

He held out his hand. "I'll take the bag."

The baby was heavier, but I nodded and handed it over.

"Choice," he noted as he slung one of the straps over his shoulder. "Keeps your arms and hands free, eh?"

Mo's backpack *had* been a good idea. I had tried using a regular diaper bag for about a week before I'd gotten annoyed and shifted everything to a backpack. But I didn't tell Jonah any of that. I just shrugged.

Jonah's smile stayed in place as his eyes moved from the

baby who was giving him wide identical eyes, to my face, and back to Mo.

Little Mo Peep reached a fist out toward him with a happy smile and a "Ba!"

He took it and gave it a shake. "Nice to see you again, wee one."

I cleared my throat.

"Right then, I found the office," he said as we walked beside each other following the handshake that had rattled me just a little. "They wouldn't let me register until you arrived."

Up ahead, one of the two glass doors that he'd been standing beside opened and a tall brunette came out, her phone held to her face. Jonah kept right on talking as he lunged forward to take the door just as the woman let go of it, her eyes locked on him.

"Shouldn't take but a minute or two, I would think. It's on the second floor," the Still a Shithead kept talking, his eyes on me over the head of the woman who was basically staring at him with a dreamy expression on her face, still holding the phone up. "The lift is right here."

Jonah wasn't just one of the tallest men I had ever met, he was built as one of the biggest too. Muscles on top of muscles on top of muscles. And with that trimmed facial hair that became a beard halfway through the day and that perfectly shaped head...

Well, there was a reason this lady was probably pulling a muscle in her neck looking over her shoulder.

He was all fun and games to look at. But that was about it.

"Okay," I told him as he let the door shut behind him, and we loaded into the elevator.

Once upstairs, one of those big hands gestured to the left of the hallway. We went that way before he pointed at the first door on the left. It was nondescript and the name of the business didn't exactly scream DON'T KNOW YOUR DAD? DON'T KNOW YOUR MOM? WE CAN HELP! Thankfully.

It didn't take Jonah long at all to go speak to the receptionist behind the desk and come back with a small stack of paperwork on a clipboard. "If you trust me to hold her while you fill it out, I'll take her."

I didn't trust him to text me back, but hold Mo? I nodded, telling myself not to feel irritated and failing.

He didn't say a word as we traded the clipboard for the baby. His hands were mostly steady as he lifted her up and brought her against his chest, fitting her there tightly as Mo still looked up at him with these eyes like she didn't know what the hell to think of him... but she was trying to figure it out. And not exactly having a terrible time while she did from her wide-eyed expression and those grabby little hands clutching his shirt.

That was a good thing. I guess.

The paperwork only took a few minutes, and I turned it back into a receptionist with a smile and took the same seat, with Jonah still standing there, holding Mo and doing something that might have resembled the slightest bounce I'd ever seen. But that wasn't what caught my attention. They were both looking at each other... but she had a hand on the tip of his nose, was mumbling who the hell knew what, and he was smiling at her from under her grip and asking, "Yeah? Is that what you think?"

That was what she thought because she kept on going.

Once Mo was done telling him her life story, I decided to be decent and try my best to be a good person.

Okay, at least a decent one.

"Were you waiting for long?" I made myself ask, even as I told myself that I didn't really care how long he'd been waiting.

"Yeah, nah." His eyes flicked down toward me, but his head didn't actually move. After all, Mo was still holding on to his nose even though she was staring at something over his shoulder.

"Did you drive here?" I suddenly thought about how I

hadn't actually seen him getting in or out of a car at any point. Now that I thought about it... I couldn't remember seeing a parked car outside of the house on Sunday when he had come over either. Or Saturday night when he'd left. I'd taken Monday off and not seen him.

Jonah was busy still looking at Mo as he lowered himself into the seat beside me, knees going wide to plant her on the thigh furthest from me... the side of his opposite leg touching my knee. "An Uber brought me," he explained. "I do need to look into a hire car company though."

A hire car company? Like a rental company?

"I wasn't sure how long I would be here." He glanced at me with those honey-colored eyes, lingering on my face for a second too long. "At first."

It was a miracle I didn't scoff.

"But I have my IDP," he rattled on, like I'd asked, moving his attention back to probably the nicest person in the room. She was definitely the cutest person. I watched as one of Jonah's cheeks went higher than the other and his fingers touched her red stretchy pant-covered lower leg. "I'll get a ute for the rest of my holiday soon."

His holiday.

That got me thinking about our time frames again. How he would have to leave. For work. For rugby. Because his life was elsewhere. I didn't know where. But the point was: he would be gone for a long time, regardless of what continent or country he was in. Would he actually come back?

I really wasn't sure how we were going to make this all function, but... we couldn't be the first dumbasses to put ourselves in this kind of situation. One person living and working on one continent, and another living and working on another.

If you want something to work, you find a way to make it, my fucking brain attempted to remind me right then.

Damn it, I hated when my conscious made me feel guilty. If

Jonah had been a friend, I wouldn't have hesitated to offer him help. Yet here I was.

I glanced at the Fucker and found him smiling gently at Mo who had half her fist shoved into her mouth as she stared at the ceiling tiles.

Jesus, I was going to need to tell Luna about this. Someone was going to need to fawn over me being a decent human being toward someone I legit wanted to kick in the ass.

"If you need to borrow a car before you rent one…" I started to say, feeling only slightly bad that I was struggling so much to get the words out. I was a decent person. Just with people who I didn't have beef with, is all. He was my girl's dad, and I was going to be stuck with him, I tried to reason. And mostly, I'd just fucking promised myself that I wasn't about to make my life more miserable because of him. I wasn't going to be the crazy shit non-ex. I was going to be the cool one that thought she'd dodged a bullet by not being still together. "You can borrow mine."

Jonah blinked, and I would swear even Mo looked at me like she didn't know who I was.

"Thank you," he replied after a second, clearing his throat. "But I wouldn't want you to be without a car. I can hire one, it's no problem at all."

Mo's hand moved to Jonah's ear, and I watched his gaze follow the movement. His nostrils flared, and the cheek I could see twitched. Then he reached down to tap her own ear in return, earning him the cutest, sweetest little giggle.

They were going to make me throw up.

"If you change your mind, just let me know," I pretty much mumbled. He was still a fucker.

The smile he aimed was at the baby. "It's all good. No worries."

Uh-huh. I had a good idea of how much money he made. I had done my crazy-person research right after he'd gotten injured, when I wanted to find him. I bet he was all good.

Thinking that then made me flash back to the microscopic apartment he had lived in in Paris. Real estate was expensive in France; it had made me never take for granted what I had in Houston. Jonah's place—an apartment he had shared with two teammates—had been smaller than Grandpa's bedroom, bathroom, and closet.

I doubted Jonah knew anything about designer clothes. His tennis shoes were nothing that couldn't be bought at a mall. He had never been flashy about his money or his belongings. He had a watch on his wrist, and I couldn't read the name on the face of it, but I'd swear it was a Casio or a Timex. It wasn't a new one either.

Jesus knew I didn't care about material things. I didn't spend more than ten dollars on a shirt nine times out of ten, but I'd upgrade to guacamole any and every time I had the option. Those were where my priorities lay.

The receptionist came back to the window then and called us around to the back while I was watching Jonah and wondering what the hell he did with all the money he made.

Neither one of us said much as we went through a door and on down a hallway, following a tech. We hadn't gone very far when my phone rang. I pulled it out of my pocket and took a look at the screen.

"Grandpa, let me call you back," I answered, knowing damn well I couldn't form that sentence into a question without him turning it around on me.

He ignored me. "Where are you?"

I lowered my voice when Jonah glanced over his shoulder as he continued down the hall. "I texted you. We're about to do Mo's paternity test. I'll call you when we're done."

He sucked in his breath over the line. *"What? Jasper doesn't believe you?"*

I made a face and tried my fucking hardest not to laugh at him calling Jonah Jasper on purpose. "He does," I insisted, not exactly whispering, "but we have to do it anyway, I'm sure, for legal shit, Grandpa. I'll call you back."

"Has he *looked* at her?"

"That's not how it works, and you know it. Calm your titties."

Jonah stopped walking and turned around, a hint of a smile making the right side of his mouth creep up. It made his dimple pop. Ugh.

I couldn't help but smirk at him, shrugging a shoulder that felt a lot friendlier than it should have. But then again, I guess we *were* talking about him. And our kid. So...

On the receiver, Grandpa choked. "I don't have *titties*, Lenny. They're still flat, and you know I work hard to keep them that way. And you know what? I don't know where I went wrong with you. I swear, I don't know—"

I laughed. "I'll call you back when I get out of here. Go finish reading that firefighter book or take some Ensure or some A positive blood in the meantime, okay?"

"Ensure?"

"Love you, *bye.*" I laughed again and hit End, pulling a Grandpa Gus on him with the hanging up. Only he would get upset over Ensure. The blood thing didn't even faze him. He took it as a compliment.

I fucking loved that crazy-ass old man, I really did.

I was still laughing when I glanced up to find that Jonah and Mo had stopped outside of an opened door, but it was Jonah who was looking at me. Mo was too busy looking at the man holding her, clutching the collar of his shirt, stretching it and trying to put it in her mouth. Jonah was smiling.

At me.

I almost stopped smiling but then got myself to drop that shitty idea. What was I going to do? Give up my happiness for somebody else? Hell no. How many times was I going to need to go over this? I could hate him passively. *I could hate him in the deepest little corners of my heart and not waste any energy doing so.*

I raised my eyebrows instead, set my phone on airplane mode, and slipped it back into my pocket.

We filed into the small room, the technician pulling out whatever it was that she needed. I had barely stepped inside when the Shithead held her out toward me. I made a face at him as I took her.

To be fair, his expression was somewhere between embarrassed and sheepish. "She'll want you if she cries." His smile faltered. "To her, I'm still some bloke."

I pressed my lips together and told myself there was nothing to feel bad about. But when those lids slid over his honey-colored eyes slowly *and* I saw his Adam's apple bob, I opened my mouth to tell him that wouldn't always be the case.

But he beat me to it.

"Not for too long though, yeh?" he asked me, or Mo, or maybe both of us.

Since I was the only one who could answer, he was lucky I nodded.

Fortunately, the buccal swabs didn't take long at all, and even more luckily, Mo didn't fuss. She was too busy pulling on my hair, and I was too busy telling her "No, no, no" to pay that much attention either.

Jonah stood right at my elbow the whole time, a physical eclipse of·muscle blocking the overhead lights, as he'd burned a hole into the technician helping us.

"This won't hurt her, will it?" the kinda-new dad had asked, hands shoved into the pockets of his jeans.

The woman gave him a knowing smile. "Not at all."

Then we were out of there with promises that we would be contacted with the results. The formal results at least. I was positive that the Fucker trusted I wasn't lying about him being the father.

It wasn't until we were walking down the hall to head out of the building that my stomach grumbled, and literally a split second later, I heard his grumble too. I remembered that from back in France. We'd had that in common—we were both always hungry.

This was the rest of my life.

And I wasn't going to fucking ruin an hour of it, even if he did deserve a twenty-four-hour case of the shits.

Fuck it.

"I haven't had any lunch," I told him, even though I didn't want to. But I knew I had to practice being decent to him. Not nice, just… okay. "You?"

He held the door open for us. "I had second brekkie about ten."

Second breakfast had been my favorite thing back when I'd been trying to compete in a higher weight class. I missed those days of eating even more than I usually did and knowing it was for a good cause. "Want to go get some? I can probably drop you off at your hotel afterward if it isn't too far. I need to get back to the gym." I really didn't, but he didn't need to know that.

I could hear him directly behind me as we approached my car. "I'd love to. The hotel isn't too far of a drive from here, if you wouldn't mind."

"All right." I was doing this for Mo. *I was doing this for Mo.*

After we were all buckled in, I took my phone off airplane mode and found three voice mails from Grandpa Gus. Turning on the engine, I made sure the car's Bluetooth didn't pick it up and blast him over the speaker, and then called him back. He picked up immediately.

"Where are you?" he answered before I could make a sarcastic comment about being a stalker.

"We just got done at the lab…." I trailed off, hoping he wasn't going to go on another rant about Jonah.

Grandpa mumbled something under his breath before asking in a stilted voice, "Can you take your time coming back?"

I frowned down at the steering wheel. Take my time going back to the gym? "Why?"

There was another pause, then, "Because."

Because? Uh. "No promises?" I offered him as my brain took his tone and his question and ran with it. What the fuck was going on that he didn't want me to see?

"Okay," he replied before hanging up again.

What the hell was that about? Of course now I was going to drop by. He couldn't say something like that and expect my red flags not to go up. What the hell was happening? I wondered as I put the car into reverse and said, "I have to run by the gym for a second. We can eat afterward, and I'll drive you back to your hotel then." Or I'd call him an Uber. Whatever. We could see what happened. If he got on my nerves, he could walk.

"Sure," he agreed as I set the car into drive.

I wondered what the hell was going on with Grandpa Gus, and I kept on wondering as I drove us out of the parking lot with a quiet Jonah and a quietly babbling Mo in the car talking to her imaginary friend. She was such a talker; I loved it.

"Everything all right?" he asked after a little while.

It wasn't until I started trying to extend my fingers from around the steering wheel that I realized I was gripping on to it really tight. "My grandfather just asked me not to stop by the gym, and I don't know why," I explained, unable to hide the instinct that said something was wrong.

He "hmmed" his response, at least initially. "He's a bit aggro I'm with you. Maybe that's it?"

"Aggro? Aggravated?"

Out of the corner of my eye, I saw him nod.

So I shook mine right back, focusing on the road. "I mean, yeah, but that's not it. He's petty, but he would have said that if that were the case."

He "hmmed" again before, "So you manage the gym now?"

"Yes."

"You were only working there part of the time before," he

stated for some reason, like he wanted me to know he'd listened… at least sometimes.

I pressed my lips together for a second. "Yes."

"When did you start?"

"Six weeks after I had Mo." I thought about leaving it at that but changed my mind. "Daycare facilities here are really expensive. It was Grandpa Gus's idea that I take over managing it, and that he would stay home with her instead. It made the most sense." I had always known it was inevitable. I was pretty sure I had told him that too at some point.

But back then I had thought it was going to be years before the day came.

I flexed my fingers around the steering wheel and kept explaining so that way I wouldn't have to bring this up later. "The good thing is, those two love and adore each other. I told you, he takes her to daycare once or twice a week in the morning for a few hours, so that she can get used to being around other kids. Sometimes, my best friend's father-in-law watches her if Grandpa has something to do. She comes to see me and hang out in the office too pretty often."

He looked at me, but I didn't return his gaze.

"I'll write it down for you, so you know where she's at all the time. I know you aren't… working while you're here." He was on vacation. On holiday. On his off-season, I reminded myself again. *Not permanent.* "I'm sure I can talk Grandpa into splitting babysitting duties with you so you can take advantage of your time while you're here, if you want." I had no idea what the fuck he was doing during the day, and I wasn't going to ask because it wasn't my business, and I didn't care. "But he might end up making you pay a rental fee or something for him to give up Mo," I told him, with a snicker even though I didn't mean to.

"A rental fee?" he asked with a familiar-sounding soft laugh that irritated me. "It wouldn't be babysitting though, would it? More like… parenting, no?"

I swung my head to look at him again. Not babysitting. *Parenting.*

Asshole.

The small smile he sent me when he caught me looking at him had me wondering for a split second if he didn't know exactly what he was doing; saying all the right things that I wanted to hear to trust him again. Hadn't he said that? That he wanted to regain my trust?

Fucker.

"Yeah," I replied after a second, facing forward again. "It's not babysitting if she's yours. And she is. And luckily Grandpa Gus thinks Mo is his. Peter thinks the same. She's our community baby."

Jonah's damn smile grew wider, I just knew it. "That's awesome. No such thing as too much love."

Ugh.

"I'd like to spend as much time with her as I can while I'm here."

While he was here.

"There's so much I don't know about babies." His hand went up to slide over the top of his head, back and forth, from what I could see. "If you could put up with me for a while, I would appreciate it if you taught me everything I've missed." He paused, and I could sense him burning a fucking hole into my face. "I've been coached all my life, you know, and I bet you're good at teaching too."

I flexed my hands around the steering wheel. *Stand strong.* I could survive this man and his eternally cheerful attitude and his politeness and his voice and all his smiles. I could.

And that's why I didn't say shit.

And Mr. Understanding and Patient didn't let my negative ass stop his chatter.

"Reckon your grandfather could show me too if he ever stops hating me," Jonah finished brightly.

My nose betrayed me with a snort. "Yeah, even if he didn't

hate you, you wouldn't want him to show you how to do anything, trust me."

"Is it that bad?"

I snorted again even though I didn't want to. "The worst. When I was a kid, he tried to…." *What the fuck was I doing?* I shut up.

Out of the corner of my eye I could see him shift that big body in his seat as much as he could in my small SUV. "Lenny, you can tell me anything you want, you know."

How could I tell him that I didn't want to? Well, easily, that's how, but…

Through the rearview mirror, I glanced at the car seat.

That was the relationship that really mattered, even if it hurt me a little to settle for it. She was more important than me and my feelings.

"Anyway, you're right. It's not that hard taking care of her. But it is scary. I still am, scared I mean, but not about the same things. Like not holding her head and neck correctly or holding her too tight or not feeding her enough. But I'll show you what I know. If you want to learn."

The Asshole didn't waste a second. "I want to."

I squeezed the steering wheel again, trying to find the right words. "Okay. You'd just have to… put up with me until you're comfortable enough to be around her by yourself."

He made a soft sound with his nose. "That wouldn't exactly be a hardship, would it?" he replied. "Cheers for offering, Len. I accept."

I should probably call Noah back so he could piss me off and remind me of what a douchebag was. That would be exactly what I would need to keep this meh-train going with Jonah. I was the conductor, and I wasn't ready to retire.

I cast another glance at that handsome-as-hell face beside me and kept my damn mouth closed.

That big body shifted in the seat again, legs and shoulders moving one way and then the other. Then he went for it. "Are you seeing anyone?" he asked like he wanted to know what fucking time it was.

I didn't see how that was any of his business but… fine. I guess it kind of was. I'd want to make sure, if he was in a relationship, that the woman wasn't some kind of psycho. And if my chest felt a little weird at the idea of him being in a relationship with someone, I wasn't going to linger on it. I hadn't looked at his Picturegram account in forever, and I wasn't about to start now. Maybe there was someone. Maybe there wasn't.

I wondered then if he'd taken down the two pictures of us he'd put up there so long ago. One had been of us at Versailles, the first day we'd met. It had surprised the hell out of me when he'd shown me he'd posted it, hours after meeting. He'd started following me immediately after.

The second picture had been of us at Sacré-Coeur with the city sprawled out behind us on a beautiful day. I had really liked that picture. That one had been taken a month before his injury.

"No," I answered him, ignoring the tingle in my stomach that felt an awful lot like disgust. "Are you?"

The second it took him to answer felt like it weighed a thousand pounds.

"No, there's no one," he replied slowly. There was another pause. "There hasn't been."

Hasn't been? Since when? Last week? Last month? Six months ago?

It was none of my fucking business. I wasn't going to ask, and I wasn't going to look to find out either.

I kept my eyes forward as I said, "Okay." I tried to make the feeling that had moved from my stomach to my chest go away, but it didn't want to go anywhere. It was going to happen. The dating. I was thirty-one. He was thirty. Now or never. "We should probably talk about that then while we're on the topic, so we know what to do if—*when*—the situation rises. You know, when I decide to start dating again—" His head swiveled toward me, but I didn't see what his expression was because I didn't look at him. "—or when you do, so that way we're on the same page. I think it might be best to wait to introduce new people into Mo's life until we're sure that they're going to be around."

His "all right" took a moment or ten longer than I would have expected. And it sounded a lot rougher than it needed to as well. It came out hesitantly, if I wasn't imagining it.

My hand shot out before I could think twice about it. "You sure? Deal?"

That big hand that was a lot more calloused than I remembered, settled over mine before I had a chance to take it back, his fingers sliding over my own, giving them and my palm a warm squeeze that lingered longer than necessary.

Well, I'd been doing that for a low-five, but… okay. That seemed even more permanent. All right.

I wouldn't be doing that again anytime soon.

I swallowed and pulled my hand away, returning it to the steering wheel.

We had a whole lot more to settle, but suddenly, I really didn't feel like asking any more of the hundred questions we had to discuss. Not when we were so close to Maio House, and I was still unsure what the hell my gramps's weird call had been all about. Luckily, in no time at all, I was steering the car into one of the three reserved spots—one for Peter, Grandpa Gus, and myself.

As I was putting the car into park, I asked, "Do you want to come inside?" Then immediately fucking regretted it.

Shit. I imagined the looks the assholes inside were going to be giving if and when he came in with Mo and me. As soon as I thought that, I wanted to punch myself.

What the hell was I doing? Worrying about what they would think or say? They could all suck it. I wasn't hiding anything.

"It might be a while," I let him know, irritated with myself for worrying over what other people would think or say if I walked in with him.

He was Mo's dad.

And he might be a dipshit, but it wasn't like anyone else knew that.

Fuck it. They could think whatever they wanted to think. It was more than likely going to be true anyway.

Oblivious, Jonah nodded as he unbuckled his seat belt, reaching for the door with his other hand.

I got Mo out, Jonah grabbing the diaper backpack in the process. But it was just as I was standing straight again that I realized what was happening. I held Mo out to him and raised my eyebrows. "Take her. The more you hold her, the more comfortable you'll feel with her."

His "all right" sounded pretty dubious to me, but I could appreciate him not trying to get out of it. I guessed.

He kept the diaper bag over his shoulder as he pulled her in real close to his chest, eyes widening the slightest. "We're going to get along just fine, aren't we, Mo?" Jonah asked as he gazed down at the girl with his same eyes.

Mo answered by grabbing his nose and pinching it with a quick burst of animated commentary.

He grinned right back at her.

All right. Enough of that. I was glad I wasn't the jealous type.

I turned around and headed toward the entrance to the training facility, Jonah and Mo trailing behind me. I punched in the code then opened the door. I held it wide and watched the corner of his lips arch upward as he headed into the building first, stopping just inside.

He really was a big son of a bitch, I thought as he brushed by me.

Gesturing him toward the office like he didn't know where it was, I stopped almost immediately at the sight of Grandpa Gus, a woman, and Peter standing right outside the office door.

But it was Grandpa's posture that had me pausing. He had his arms crossed over his chest, and the look on his face was one I hadn't seen, ever. Not even when he mean-mugged Jonah the other day during breakfast.

But even Peter, who was pretty damn easygoing, looked tense.

Taking in the woman, who had to be somewhere around my height, she had to easily be in her sixties or early seventies. Slim without looking exactly frail. Her hair was all white and was cut in a chin-length bob. She had on a dressy blouse and white pants.

She was… elegant.

And I had no clue who the hell she was, but I already knew I wasn't going to like her because of Grandpa Gus and Peter's body language.

If I had thought I was imagining that something was going on, it would have been confirmed when Grandpa Gus spotted me and winced.

This was the man who had given me the puberty talk complete with visuals and a book. Who had bought me pads and tampons without flinching dozens of times. Who had shaved his own calf to teach me how to shave my legs. This was the same man who had given me a very serious sex talk before blatantly asking if I needed him to take me to get on birth control, even though I'd never said anything that would give him the impression I was interested in boys. This was the same man who had gestured toward my boobs a hundred times while helping me train and growled, "Do something with them!" when they were halfway popping out of my sports bras back before I'd gotten smart and started doubling up on them.

This was the same man who had left a box of condoms on my bed eight weeks after I'd had Mo.

Grandpa Gus and I didn't do awkward. We never had. So the fact that he was sucking in a breath, making a face that said he was dreading whatever was about to happen…

I already didn't like it. I didn't like it at all.

And I knew somehow that it wasn't because of the man with me.

And I got that reconfirmation to listen to my gut instinct not even two minutes later.

"Elena," Grandpa Gus greeted me tensely, making that dread grow even bigger.

This person here wasn't a friend. She wasn't someone to be trusted. That's what that name meant.

I braced myself, trying to rack my brain for whatever the hell this lady could mean. Who was she? "Grandpa," I said as I stopped beside him, giving him a kiss on the cheek and then going up to my toes to give Peter one too, right as Jonah stood beside me. Really, he shouldn't be surprised I'd shown up. He'd basically asked for it by being so weird and cryptic. He *knew* me better than that.

"Peter, Mr. DeMaio," Jonah said, extending a hand toward Peter first, shaking it, and then doing the same toward my grandpa.

Honest to God, even I was impressed right then that he'd taken the initiative to be the bigger person and try shaking his hand again. I was going to have to think about that later.

Something was off because Grandpa Gus decided this woman was the greater threat because he shook Jonah's hand after a moment of hesitation, when I damn well knew that if things were normal, he would have just stared at it until things got uncomfortable.

That was how we rolled.

Usually.

I turned my attention to the woman standing there, holding a pale pink leather purse in her hand. A hand that had a huge diamond ring on it. And something weird happened when I took in her face. It looked familiar…. I couldn't think about when I had possibly seen it before, but it was really, *really* familiar looking.

"Hello," the woman said in a careful, lightly accented Texan drawl. A brief smile flashed across a very nice face that had taken the years and rolled with them. She really was beautiful in a fancy kind of way.

I was narrowing my eyes as Grandpa Gus's hand moved in my peripheral vision as he gestured to the woman. "Elena," he said again, reminding me that I could go another thirty years before he ever called me by my name again. A name he had passed down to me from his own mom, who I had never met.

I waited, glancing at Jonah who was looking totally calm… because he didn't know the weird shit Grandpa was saying and doing that was setting off my own inner alarm.

"This is Rafaela," Grandpa Gus said in a tight, unwelcoming voice.

Was he… uncomfortable?

I didn't smile or extend my hand. I did frown though and stare at him, trying to pick up more hints.

Grandpa stared, something about his face… apologetic? "This is…."

Since when the hell did this man struggle for words? I glanced at Peter and saw even more how uncomfortable he must have felt right then. I wasn't sure I had ever seen this man feeling weird. Defensiveness rose up inside of me.

The woman coughed discreetly, looking awkward too. Then she thrust out her hand toward me and said, "I'm your grand-mother, Elena."

I stared at the hand in the circle between us and asked very slowly, my ears starting to ring as I asked, like I had heard wrong, "Who?"

Peter blew out a breath, but it was Grandpa Gus who replied. "Your dad's mom."

That had me looking up at the beloved face to my right, raising my eyebrows, my ears buzzing louder, and still ignoring the hand that was holding steady in the middle of the air. "Your ex-wife?"

He grimaced but nodded. Not even bothering to say the words out loud. The simple *yes* being too much.

I glanced at Peter who was busy looking up at the rafters, peeked at Jonah, who looked really confused, and then at the woman herself. At *Rafaela*. My dad's mom. My *grandmother*.

Grandpa Gus was already watching me when my eyes met his, and I couldn't help but smile. And then I kept right on smiling because I couldn't help it. Grandpa closed his eyes just as I started laughing and sliding my hand through the woman's.

Fucking *shit*.

"It's nice to meet you, Grandma."

CHAPTER 10

11:55 p.m
> I'm getting real sick of your shit now.
> Can you please,
> PLEASE, call me back?

11:57 p.m.
> You know what?
> Fuck it. I take back my please:
> Just call me back.
> It's the least you could do.

11:58 p.m.
> It's Lenny.

"IF YOU TWO ARE DONE STARING AT EACH OTHER, I'M GOING upstairs to grab a jacket so we can get going, Lenny," Peter said in the same grown-up voice I heard him use most often with the guys at the gym.

He was still tense after the encounter with *Rafaela*.

I poked at my small bowl of nice cream—blended frozen

bananas, maple syrup, vanilla extract, and cocoa powder—and kept on staring at the older man who hadn't said a word since I had gotten home over an hour ago.

I knew what he was doing. Like he knew what I was doing. And Peter, of course, was well aware of what we were both doing.

Being assholes.

Because neither one of us thought we were wrong.

Except in this case, I wasn't being stubborn, and Grandpa Gus really had been wrong for what he'd done earlier.

Peter just sighed when neither one of us responded, sneaking through the swinging door with a shake of his head.

Mo, who was sitting in her high chair, did her own thing as she shoved tiny handfuls of mushy cereal into her mouth... and over her cheeks... and the rolls of her neck... and all over the front of her shirt. She'd already eaten more than enough and still needed another bottle before going to bed. She could have fun. I was too busy not breaking eye contact with my seventy-five-year-old grandfather to watch her finish painting her food masterpiece. I wasn't going to look away first, not this time.

This really was on him, and he knew it.

It was him who finally broke the silence that Peter left us in. And the way he broke the silence was the exact way I would have expected. "Surprise?" he offered, even throwing a hand, palm up, at his side.

I glared at him.

He sighed all exaggerated and had the nerve to roll his eyes, like he hadn't gotten on my case when I'd been a teenager the three times I had done the same to him. "*Fine*, but you could have handled it better."

I flipped the spoon upside down in my mouth and left it there as I raised an eyebrow at him. "Yeah? You think so?"

The truth was... he was right. I could have handled it better. The entire thing, I could have handled better.

If I'd been a totally different person.

The expression Grandpa Gus gave me in return in that moment said he knew I was right. But he could have handled it better too. I hadn't told him to choke after I'd called the woman I'd met *Grandma*.

Grandma had stood there afterward, her eyes slowly narrowing, either at me calling her that or at the fact I was laughing. Probably both though. "Is there something funny that I'm missing?" she had asked in a tone that was bordering on chilly, as Grandpa tried to hide his choke by clearing his throat.

"Oh, no," I had responded to her, feeling my body shake as I kept on laughing, somewhere in between this-is-fucking-hilarious and this-is-fucking-bullshit.

She had narrowed her eyes even more, and for one tiny moment, I wondered if maybe that's why I had thought she looked familiar. Because we looked alike. I guessed. A little. If you closed an eye and imagined me with better fashion sense and a slimmer bone structure.

I had slipped my hand out of hers, shook my head as I blinked back tears that had popped up out of nowhere, and then taken a step back. "It was nice to meet you. This is your great-granddaughter, Mo, and her dad." I had dipped my head toward the muscular bicep by my cheek on my left. "I will try my best to pencil you in for another visit thirty years from now if that works for you." I had turned to the other direction then. "Grandpa, Pete, I'm going to get some lunch, and I'll be back later." I pivoted on my heel, flashed the Still an Asshole the biggest smile I might have ever given him because *come the fuck on*, this situation? Stupid. "Are you ready to go eat?"

His eyes had been wide in surprise, but he answered anyway. "Yes."

And we had left. The entire thing had taken... what? Two minutes? Less? It wasn't like I had given her a chance to talk. Mostly because I didn't think there was anything she could have said to make me stay.

The grandmother I had never known had finally and

randomly shown up, and I couldn't have given a single fuck. Was that harsh? Maybe. But it was harsher, I thought, to not exist for thirty years and then finally make an appearance without a warning—except I guess that had been her who had left a message that morning, but that didn't count for shit—and in the process stress out two of the people I loved the most in the entire world. Two people who had clearly not wanted me to meet her. For a reason.

So, yeah, could I have handled it better? Sure. If I were my best friend, I would have been gracious and understanding. But I wasn't Luna.

I had no interest in this woman I had never met before. A woman who Grandpa Gus had maybe mentioned three times in my entire life. The things I knew about her could be counted on one hand.

She and Grandpa had been married for exactly six years before she filed for divorce. *But I shouldn't have married her in the first place,* he had told me in his way so that I wouldn't hate her, I guessed now.

After being separated, she moved to San Francisco and had been living there as far as I knew.

She had remarried some real estate guy or something and had three children with him.

I hadn't even known her *name* until today. Grandpa Gus had always just been... Grandpa Gus. This other lady who had given birth to Grandpa Gus's one and only son had left them together. Eventually, when my dad would have been twenty-five, I had been born, and the rest was the story of Lenny and Grandpa Gus. The greatest story of all time.

He had always been such a big figure in my life, this all-consuming force that was my friend, my brother, my cousin, my dad, grandfather, and very sun. He had been all I had ever needed. And then Peter had showed up, and even more than before, I hadn't wanted for anything. There had never been a void in my life, and if my mind had sometimes wandered over to thinking about people who hadn't been around, it had solely been my biological mom and my biological dad.

A *grandma*? Never.

"What was she doing here?" I asked.

His features lost some of their sourness, but I didn't exactly like what replaced them. "She wanted some advice about a chain of gyms her husband is considering buying."

Gyms? Oh.

"She showed up, asked Bianca to give me a call—"

"And she called you?"

"Only after Rafi said she was my ex-wife," he defended the sweet receptionist that I did like, but I wouldn't have liked her any longer if she'd called Grandpa G for no reason like that. It should have been me she called under any other circumstance.

"And then?"

"I got to Maio House and she was asking me about the chain when you showed up," he stated, crossing his arms over his chest. Watching me too carefully, like he was expecting me to do something.

Something that wasn't hurt snuck under my ribs, but that was as far as I let it go as I asked, "Is this the first time she'd reached out to you?"

He shot me a look like *what do you think*, eyes steady and solemn. "The last time I spoke to her was before you were born. I never told her if you were a girl or a boy or what your name was. All I said was that Marcus's girlfriend was having his child."

Grandpa Gus didn't actually say the words he was hinting at, but he didn't have to. I knew him well enough to understand what he was implying.

She hadn't called back to check thirty-one years ago. She hadn't known about me. She hadn't cared to know about me. She hadn't come here to get to know me. He hadn't wanted me to go to the gym because he'd wanted to spare me from meeting someone who should have cared I'd existed… and hadn't.

It didn't hurt my feelings. Or surprise me.

"Lenny, you had nothing to do with her not being around. It's me she couldn't stand to see again, do you understand?"

I nodded and clamped those words somewhere else. "There was a voice mail at the Maio House this morning." I made a face as I finally stood up, making my way toward the sink so I could rinse out my bowl and set it in the dishwasher. "Well, hopefully me telling her I'll see her again in thirty years got across to her because I have about 0 percent interest in ever seeing her again."

"You're not the only one," he muttered, still sounding strained. "It's been thirty-eight years for me, and I could go another thirty-eight again."

I turned around as I wiped my hands on a towel. "You haven't seen her since Marcus"—that had been my biological dad's name—"was eighteen?"

Grandpa nodded, eyeing Mo for a moment before blowing a bunch of kisses at her. The little nut cooed, calling him "Baba." He didn't bother looking at me as he answered, "Not since his high school graduation."

"She didn't go to his funeral?"

He made a sharp, bitter noise in his throat. "No."

What a bitch.

"She said she couldn't get away, but that he was *in her heart*," he whimpered sarcastically, even bringing up his hands over his heart. Grandpa rolled his eyes. "Marcus wouldn't have cared, kiddo. I didn't raise him to be anti his mom. He never liked her in the first place, and I'm not putting that blame on myself. I never said a bad word about her. I didn't give him a reason to think that I didn't like her. It was my fault she left, and I made sure he knew that. We shouldn't have gotten married in the first place, but I thought I could be someone else," he said carefully, shifting his gaze toward me. "I took years of her life away by not being upfront. I can't hold too many grudges. I ended up with him, and then you, and now I've got my new best friend right here. Life is good."

Life was good.

Even if I didn't know or trust this person who had reappeared. This person who had still, after so long, not given enough of a fuck to see me, but had only come around for business purposes. The kind of woman who wouldn't go to her own son's funeral because *he was in her fucking heart* like that meant anything. It was one thing if she didn't have money to travel or had been too sick to or something, but that bullshit wasn't an excuse or an equivalent.

Bitch.

Just as I opened my mouth to ask him another question about her, the doorbell rang.

"I'll get it. You wipe her off. I'll change her shirt in a minute," Grandpa said, already up on his feet before I could get the door myself.

By the time I had dampened the towel I'd used to wipe my hands off on and scrubbed it over my girl's face as she tried to get away and fight me with her fists—showing she was her great-grandfather's granddaughter, the door to the kitchen swung open again. Except this time, it wasn't just Grandpa Gus. There was someone behind him. That someone being eight inches taller, a whole hell of a lot broader, and nicer. But still an asshole.

It was Jonah.

"I wanted to call," he stated like Grandpa wasn't scowling at the world in general in front of him. "But I can't reach your mobile number, and Peter's went straight to voice mail."

He—

Jonah kept going as he stood there in the kitchen, one long arm loose at his side, the other… was holding a children's book? I was pretty sure it had an illustrated cover. "I was hoping to spend some time with Mo. Start some of my lessons if that's all right with you."

Did he have to give me that small, shy smile as he asked that fucking question?

I curled my fingers into a fist and had to fight the urge to flare my nostrils. "I'm sorry, but I'm leaving in a minute."

Jonah straight-up frowned, but I ignored it as this terrible idea settled into my brain—revenge, it was revenge because I was a petty shit—and it took everything inside of me not to smile at it.

"But," I continued on, "Grandpa is staying. You can stay with him if you don't mind him shooting ugly faces at you and being sarcastic and a little rude."

The look the old man sent me would have me rolling in private later on when he couldn't see me losing it.

I wasn't sure what it said about Jonah when he thought about it for all of a second and then ducked his stubble-covered chin. "If he'll have me, sure."

"He will not—" Grandpa Gus started to say before I cut him off.

"It would be his pleasure," I finished, shooting Grandpa a smug smile before eyeing the book in Jonah's hand again for a second.

He knew firsthand payback was a bitch. Just as well as I knew that he was going to scare the living shit out of me in revenge when I was least expecting it. But whatever. Then I'd scare him back, and our vicious cycle would continue.

"Lenny, are you ready to—" Peter started to call out as he ducked his head into the kitchen before blinking. "Oh. Hello, Jonah."

"Peter," the biggest man greeted him.

Peter's eyes slid to me. "Change of plans?"

"Nope. Jonah is staying with Lestat here."

Peter pressed his lips together, and his eyebrows arched up a little too.

"You're going with Peter?" Jonah asked.

I lifted a shoulder.

His shoulders dropped maybe a quarter of an inch and his mouth made a little O for a moment before he said, "If you made plans, you should go."

I agreed. You shouldn't go back on your word. Plus, I hadn't thought about canceling on Peter period.

"If you're sure..." Peter trailed off, warning me it was a bad idea that we were leaving these three alone, but it amused him anyway, and he was trying to not show it. "Ready?"

Grandpa puffed out his cheeks, confirming yet again that Peter had said something to get him to calm down on the comments.

"I'm ready," I told him, before dipping down to give Mo a kiss on each cheek and one on her forehead. "I love you. I'll be right back, booger. Be good."

Her answering babble probably claimed she was always good. That, or she was telling me to fuck off because she knew what she was doing.

I made a face I wouldn't call a smile at Jonah, even though he gave me a real one, and gave my grumpy grandfather a kiss on the cheek. "Good luck and behave. Mo and I won't go visit you in jail."

I didn't miss Grandpa Gus's snicker as I followed Peter out the side door and around his car. We had barely gotten buckled in when he burst out laughing, tossing his head against the headrest. "That was cold, Lenny."

"That's what he gets."

He snorted as he held his palm out to me, and I smacked it.

"HE'S NOT COMFORTABLE ENOUGH STANDING," I TOLD PETER ON our way back home two and a half hours later.

My father/uncle/friend figure nodded as he steered us down the street that would spit us out closer to our neighborhood. "I know. I've talked to him about it over and over again.

I've talked to his striking coach too, but they aren't working on it enough. He's relying too much on takedowns when he isn't consistent enough with them either. His submissions are weak. He relies too much on brute strength and doesn't think enough. I might ask Gus to come see what he thinks."

It sucked when fighters from our gym lost. I felt like I lost when they did, and I hated losing. It happened. It was a part of life, but it still sucked.

Yet, I could safely say that we knew a minute into the amateur MMA fight that Carlos, who I was fairly certain had ratted me out to Noah, was going to lose. All the yelling Peter and I had both done—so much that my throat felt raw and his sounded hoarse—had been ignored. Every "Elbow!", "Watch the arm!", "Grab the leg!", and "Level changes!" had been ignored. Every. Single. One.

I almost felt bad for the kid. Peter was going to rip him a new one tomorrow for not *listening*. I knew some fighters totally zoned out everything going on around them, but in MMA especially, you had to keep an ear out. At least it was the smartest thing you could do if you were in a pickle. Someone might give you some advice you could actually use. They could also piss you off, but you had to let things slide off your back sometimes.

"Maybe he needs a new striking coach," I suggested as the car turned onto a familiar street. Grandpa wouldn't be interested in doing more than giving Peter advice on what to do. Carlos didn't have the personality that my grandfather would want to work with.

"He needs something, but I don't know if a new coach will be enough. He's too cocky."

I couldn't argue with that. He was right. "Speaking of needing things...." I trailed off. "Grandpa didn't finish telling me what happened with that lady after I left." I called her *that lady* on purpose. She wasn't really my grandma.

Peter made the slightest face, which was really the equivalent of a huge gesture coming from anyone else. "Not much.

She asked why you laughed at her, didn't like what he told her, and then she left."

I hummed and crossed my ankles, sneaking another glance at him. He was still making a weird expression. "Are you okay with her showing up?"

"I wish she hadn't. If it were up to me, you would've gone the rest of your life without meeting her, but—" He glanced over with those dark, dark eyes. "—Lenny, you know it's Gus who kept her away, don't you?"

I was an adult, and these two men I loved so much were still trying to protect me. And they always would, I knew. Always.

But even knowing that it was her divorce from my grandpa, and the reasons behind it, that had kept her away, didn't change shit. If Mo had a daughter, there was nothing that would keep me away from her. Nothing.

So I told him the truth, most of it at least. "I know, and I wish she hadn't come either. I don't want her to cause either of you any problems."

I didn't know what to think of the silence that followed afterward as he parked the car and we headed inside. I knew her appearance worried him and my grandfather. For multiple reasons.

And as much as I didn't want to make this about me, it was hard not to. She'd shown up to talk to Grandpa. Not to see me. That hadn't even been in the plan.

So fine. Fuck her. Shoving *Rafaela* aside, I followed Peter into the house.

All the lights downstairs were still on, which wasn't surprising. But not for the first time since we'd left, I wondered how it had gone between Jonah and Grandpa Gus. I kind of regretted we didn't have a camera set up in the house so we could spy on them.

But at least, if Jonah had fucked up, Grandpa Gus would give me a play-by-play on what happened.

The first thing I heard was the sound of the television on

softly in the living room. I peeked inside, unsure if someone was going to be hiding or just sitting there. But Grandpa wasn't trying to scare the shit out of me yet. He wasn't alone either.

On the floor, Jonah was stretched out beside Mo—eight times her length, it seemed like—who was sitting up, smashing colorful blocks together.

The thing that struck me the most was the little smile on his face as he spent his time looking at her instead of the replay of a boxing event playing on the television. He looked... happy? Did he already really like her? He should. She was amazing, but....

Grandpa Gus, on the other hand, was sitting in the middle of the couch, arms stretched out to both sides, eyes straight on the television.

"We're home," I called out as I took a step forward and stopped being a stalker.

Two sets of adult-sized eyes moved, and Mo shrieked.

I had read in a book that right around her age she might start getting clingy with people coming and going, but she hadn't. She was still so happy to be reunited after some time with me and Grandpa Gus. It killed me a little and made me feel guilty for leaving her alone so much.

At least she was always with someone who loved and cared for her. That's what I told myself.

But if I had any doubts that someone was still holding a grudge that I had left him with a visitor, the expression Grandpa Gus shot me would have confirmed it. It almost made me laugh, but I figured he was already going to make me pay for it without making it worse. It would still be worth anything he put me through, though, even if I pissed my pants.

"How'd it go?" he asked grudgingly as Peter stepped up behind me.

We looked at each other.

"He lost," Peter answered with disappointment.

I walked over to the other side of Mo, got down on my

hands and knees and blew a raspberry on her upper arm before aiming for each of her cheeks so I could ask, using every bit of strength inside of me not to laugh, "How'd it go here?"

I glanced up to find Grandpa shooting me the same face.

Yeah, someone was going to scare the fuck out of me at the very least.

"Well, I think. Changed my first dirty nappy." Jonah glanced at me with a slight smile on his face. "It was… something special. It didn't smell like I thought it would."

I looked down at my girl so he wouldn't see me grin at what he'd gone through. He didn't need to sound so happy about it either. "Did it get out of her diaper and go all over her back?"

Out of my peripheral vision, I saw his head tip up. And when I glanced back at him, his expression was serious as hell, and his voice was stunned and slow as he asked, "Is that possible?"

From the couch, Grandpa snickered, and I couldn't fucking help but snicker too as I nodded at the beautiful man. "Yeah." I cupped my hands and made an exploding gesture with them.

His blink made me laugh.

The things this man would learn. Honestly, part of me couldn't wait to see his hands full of shit for the first time. Maybe Mo would throw up on him at least once. That would definitely make my day.

Jonah laughed, and I highly doubted it was my imagination that it sounded a little nervous. "I know what to expect now, I suppose. I never would have guessed someone so small could do such a thing. Is every child that… capable?"

"She takes after *somebody*, so it isn't surprising," my hater-ass grandpa threw in on a mumble, eyes back on the screen, and a smirk on his face.

I pulled the elastic out of my ponytail, not caring it was going to leave my hair a mess, and shot it at Grandpa. It hit him right on the chest. He had the nerve to throw his hand over the spot and shoot me a face that was *way* too dramatic for how much that only slightly stung.

A deep chuckle escaped the brown-haired man as he started to move one of those long, muscular legs that were taking up a ton of floor space. "Thank you for allowing me over," Jonah said as he got to his knees and thrust a hand toward the man sitting on the couch.

Grandpa Gus's nostrils flared for a moment before he took it, looking just as put out as I would have expected, but he gave it a shake anyway. He didn't say anything in response though, and he did make a suspicious face.

With his hand back, Jonah paused and tipped his chin down. That same big hand moved toward the baby's face, and one single finger—his index—touched a chubby Mo cheek before lightly giving the round little belly covered in a soft lilac onesie a tap. "Goodnight, Mo," he said in that voice that was somehow laced with just enough kindness to sound sweet.

Mo waved her whole hand in the air, earning her another little tap of a finger against her tummy.

And in a way that I could have admired on any other person his size, Jonah got to his feet lightly and quietly, meeting my eyes as soon as he was up. "Thank you again, Lenny."

It ate at my heart to say "You're welcome" because I was an asshole.

His smile made me feel worse.

I almost sighed but got to my feet, scooping Mo up just as her dad made it to the hallway that would lead him to the front door. "Do you want me to give you a ride to your hotel?" I basically gritted out after him.

Over his shoulder, those intense honey-colored eyes lingered on my face. "It's late. You should stay. Shouldn't take too long for the driver to arrive if you don't mind me sitting outside until they do."

Was I being that much of a jerk that he thought I was going

to pitch a fit over him waiting on the porch? He had fucked up, but he was here. I wasn't *that* petty.

There were millions of people in the world who fucked up too and wouldn't even think about facing their mistakes.

Like the woman who had showed up today.

That thought had just entered my head when my gaze landed on a brand-new book sitting on the coffee table. *Where the Wild Things Are.* Something nudged at my gut as I took in the cover and the fact this dickface had brought it for Mo.

He unlocked the door and opened it before I could get out. "We'll wait with you."

Grabbing Mo's jacket, I slipped it on her as I watched him dip his head and step out, closing the door once she was ready. He settled on the top step, all the way over so he was inches away from whacking his elbow on one of the pillars straddling the stairs as his fingers moved across the screen of his cell phone. I sat down as far as I could on the same step to the left, balancing my girl on my thigh, with her back supported by my upper arm and chest. I tugged the hoodie part of her jacket over her ears just as she began grabbing at my sweater, trying to stick it in her mouth.

Down the street, I could hear kids playing even though the temperature had started dropping a little to bring a chill. Blended into those noises were car doors opening and closing. They were all familiar, comforting sounds of being surrounded with the mostly historic homes on our street.

I glanced at Jonah when he set his cell phone on his thigh and aimed his upper body toward us, an open expression on his broadly boned face. His gaze flicked down to Mo, and a small, but tender smile replaced it.

I only had to think about it for a moment, still relishing her weight and her smell, but knowing damn well I would have it after he left. "Do you want to hold her while your ride comes?"

He sucked in a nervous breath and reached over with those massive hands, meeting my eyes briefly with that smile on his face, before plucking her gently off my lap and settling her down on one muscular thigh. "So small," he murmured as he held her, both sets of fingers stretched out wide in case Mo decided to go for a nosedive.

"She's pretty big for her age," I found myself telling him, as I thought about how he'd assumed I wouldn't want him on the porch. I was all for being an asshole… but only when it was necessary.

"Is she?" Jonah asked, attention downward. He dipped his face close to hers, eyes going big. "She must get that from you."

Mo answered with "Ba" like *yup*.

I peeked at his shoulders alone.

He flashed me a quick grin before focusing back down on his daughter. *Our daughter.* "I was a skinny kid until sixteen."

I made a disbelieving face at him that got me another grin.

"I'm not joking. Even my own mum had given up on me growing. In one year, I grew… sixteen, seventeen centimeters. The next year I grew another eight. Bit of a crap two years. My knees hurt the whole time."

Holy shit. What was that? A foot in two years?

He changed the conversation around back to me. "You've always been tall?"

I curled my hands over my shins as I watched his index finger brush the bottom of a tiny foot. "I'm not tall, but yeah, I —"*I had to try*, I reminded myself. I was going to have this man in my life for a long time, and he was being awfully fucking decent so far. So… I could be decent back. It was less work than flipping him off every chance I had. "I was taller than most of the boys and almost all the girls for a long time. Now, I just kind of wish I was shorter."

"Why?"

"It's hard to find pants that fit," I told him honestly. I was an inch too tall. It was a curse.

His chuckle made the dimple closest to me pop. "Yeh, I

know what that's like. It's a bit of a pain in the ass, isn't it? I've got, maybe, five pants that fit me well."

I snorted and only slightly regretted it when he shifted those honey-colored eyes at me, giving me a glimpse of both his dimples as he smiled sweetly.

"Would you like to talk about your grandmother?" he asked out of nowhere.

That caught me off-guard, but luckily there was only one answer to give, and I didn't hesitate to share it. "No." I didn't want to waste any more time thinking about her and her mysterious reappearance, much less talking about her, especially with Jonah. There were a few too many holes there I wouldn't be able to jump over if I tried explaining the situation.

He'd heard enough to have an idea of just how absentee she'd been. Which was 100 percent.

There was that and... I just didn't want to talk about her.

He nodded in understanding and smiled some more, his teeth very white against his tan face, a gentle reminder to me of how he'd been in France. Of why I had liked him so much. Of why I had looked for him and waited for him and been so disappointed when he hadn't come.

That familiar question floated around in my head, and even though I knew I had no business asking it, knew I wasn't going to like his answer or still might not believe it, the fucking question was there. Wanting to be asked.

I glanced down at my hands still covering my shins. What did I have to lose? Nothing, that was what. I'd made a commitment to get along with him, and I was going to stick to it until he went total dickhead on me and earned me being a bitch back.

So I just fucking asked, "Did you really not know I was pregnant?"

I watched him glance at me with alarm. Or maybe it was surprise. But it was something.

"I'm not going to kill you or anything if you did. Nothing will change between you and Mo. I just want to know," I told him, knowing it was the truth. "You're here now. Your relationship with her is what matters to me, but... I don't want to wonder about it. I just want to know the truth." I squeezed my shins and tried to give him a smile that felt pretty damn grimace-like. "I won't get any madder than I've already been. Promise. I don't think I could ever get that mad again, anyway."

All right. Maybe I didn't need to throw that last part in, but it was the fucking truth. I couldn't get any more pissed off than I'd been back then.

He should be so fucking lucky he hadn't seen me there at the end.

Jonah took a long and steady breath that made me feel better instantly. In my experience, the people who were the most passionate when accused were always the biggest lying sacks of shit. Another slow smile that wasn't all happiness and joy crossed over his mouth. It was a bittersweet expression.

Actually, no, I realized after a second. There was no sweetness in it. It was pained.

"What's that saying?" Jonah asked gently, taking hold of our girl's foot in his big hand and swallowing it up with those long fingers. "I cross my... heart? Is that it? I cross my heart, Lenny." He lifted his head and looked right into my eyes with that heartbreaking face. "*I didn't know.* Not until I got here and you told me. I had no clue."

I watched his face. I watched his face so damn carefully....

"I would have been here in a wheelchair if I had known," he claimed, steadily, quietly. "On crutches. On my hands and knees, I would have been here."

It was a lot harder than I would have assumed to process that thought. *If I had known you were having my baby, I would have come. But if I hadn't known, I still would have waited because you weren't important enough.* God, when the hell had I become this person?

This has nothing to do with you, I reminded myself, even if it was uncomfortable.

Even if it hurt. Just a little. Stung more than hurt, I'd say. And even that idea had me shifting on the step, from one butt cheek to the other. But I could focus on the positive part of what he was trying to say.

He would have been around for her, at least. And that was what mattered. What would always matter.

How he felt about me was the last thing I needed to keep carrying around so close to my heart. It needed to be somewhere around my damn colon for me to hate him passively, and that's what I'd agreed with myself on. That I wouldn't hold on to it. *I wouldn't.*

"I got your first messages," Jonah continued. "I told you. I saved them. Even the angry ones."

The ugly feeling made my stomach churn. "Look, I just wanted to know if you were being honest about knowing or not. I don't need to know what—"

The hand that wasn't holding Mo's foot reached out, cool fingertips touching the top of my hand over my shins. "No offense, love, but I don't care whether you want to know or not. I know I said I wouldn't bring it up, but I can't do that. I don't want you thinking for any longer than you already have that I left because of you."

That fucking ugly feeling in my stomach churned again, crawling up my esophagus and wanting this conversation to be over with. "Jonah—"

The Asshole shook his head. "No, Lenny, you have to hear me out. Please." His hand closed over the top of mine, and I didn't move it. I wasn't retreating. That wasn't me. "It's no excuse, I know, but I was in a crap state of mind then." He winced. "I shut myself off from everyone. Everything, really. My family. My mates. My team. Physios. Everyone."

His hand squeezed over mine, but I couldn't move it.

"You."

Me. He remembered he'd left me hanging. How about that?

Jonah kept going. "It was stupid and reckless, and I'll regret it for the rest of my bloody life. I thought my life was over. All the work, the sacrifices...." The fingers over mine jerked so slightly I thought I might have imagined it.

But I didn't.

And I still didn't move my hand away.

"I had to get away, even from myself. I stopped listening to the voice mails altogether. The calls never stopped, you understand. I deleted them at first but stopped doing that too. I was tired of the calls to see how I was doing, to tell me how sorry they were. I thought... I thought it was over," he explained softly. "I slipped one night getting off the recliner, and I broke my phone out of frustration.

"I'm ashamed that it all got to me—the people ruling me out from coming back, saying I was done because it was my second Achilles injury. I couldn't bear to read it. To hear it. That's when I stopped checking my emails, because of all the messages too, and I hadn't seen them. Not since then. Not until you told me about your emails. I've read them all now. It took me a bit to get the right password."

Now, almost a year later.

"I stopped getting online around then too. The media...." He trailed off.

I squeezed my shins again, his own hand staying exactly where it was over mine.

I had never... I had never been so down over an injury that I had felt like my life was over. But I had seen so many of my friends go through that. The grief. Because that was what it was. Grief over losing your identity. Or at least at the idea of losing it. At the overwhelming possibility of it.

The anger. The bone-deep sadness. Some people never got over it, and I should know. I had seen that happen to a lot of people I had known who went from being competitive athletes one second, to losing it all in another. I had known after my first surgery, that I ran the risk of hurting myself so badly that the next time might be my last. That each injury and surgery took me one step closer to losing it all. So I was mentally prepared to a certain extent.

But most people weren't.

And not everyone could accept that something they had worked for their entire lives might be gone in the blink of an eye.

"Thinking I was done, Lenny… not of my own choice… it hurt. That… that anger and grief…." I blinked at how he'd picked that one word out of so many others he might have used. "I had to talk to someone about it, understand? It made me make heaps of decisions I regret now. The biggest being that I was so lost in thinking my life was over then, that I made it that way. I lost all my endorsements. Nearly lost my agent if it hadn't been for my grandmother calling to give him updates. I was almost dropped by my team for what I did.

"I didn't have the nerve to get back to you or anyone. And later, once I was back, once I knew I still had footy, I had to wait to come here. To find you again. You blocked me on everything, and I doubted you'd communicate with me unless I came," he finished on an exhale, his hand moving over mine, molding itself over mine even more. "To apologize and explain that what I did was my fault and had nothing to do with you."

I stared at the step beneath my feet, and then I swallowed as hard as I ever had, trying my hardest to ignore the warm skin on me.

I had always trusted my gut. My instincts had never failed me. Not ever.

And those instincts right then were telling me…

That this fucker was being honest. That he had gotten hurt, panicked, became… depressed. He had been hurting back then. And if I were anyone else, I might have not understood how dark of a place that could be… but I did.

And I knew without a doubt that it couldn't be easy for him to admit this to me. It couldn't have been easy to do something about it, even if it had taken him months to *go talk to someone* as he'd put it. Everything in me said he was being truthful.

Asshole.

I had to glance at that open face of his, and I couldn't wrap my head around him being in the slums. I really couldn't. At least not by looking at him and seeing all the brightness he carried around in his smiles and even in his damn eyes.

And… I knew exactly what it was like to think that your life was over. That everything you had hoped and dreamed for was gone, just like that.

I thought I was pretty fucking tough, but all that toughness hadn't been enough to keep me from sobbing into my pillows when no one could hear me because I was never going to compete in judo again and my life was never going to be the same again.

Because I had made a choice that hadn't been easy, but that I hadn't been able to find it in me to regret.

Maybe if I hadn't been injured so much in the past…. If the chances of becoming reinjured weren't so great, I could have still continued competing. But the risks outweighed everything, and I had a whole lifetime ahead of me to do things with my girl that I wasn't willing to possibly lose because I'd already pushed my body to the limits so many times.

So… yeah, I understood. I understood very, very well.

Except I hadn't been a little bitch about it. I had cried into my pillow, but I hadn't gone off the deep end. I hadn't run away and hidden.

But I knew one thing, and I knew it well.

If Jonah Collins had tried to feed me some other excuse, I would have thought he was full of shit.

But he hadn't fed me anything but what my gut honestly believed was the truth, damn it.

What did it say about me that it annoyed some part of me that he wasn't the total douche I had been thinking he was for the last year? He was just… a human being who thought he had lost the thing he loved the most in this world. He'd lost his shit and didn't want to be around anything or anyone.

I would never do anything like that, but then again, I wasn't that sensitive. For me, getting mad made me want to get even with whoever had pissed me off. Anger and grief were an accelerant for me; those things didn't douse shit in my brain. They made me want to attack. To continue on and persevere.

Yet here he was, this Maybe Not a Douche who claimed he had waited too long to come here, where I lived, to explain why he'd left.

Who knew I'd blocked him.

While it wasn't exactly relief that I felt at his admission, it did feel like a weight had been lifted off my shoulders. Off my chest. Even a little off my heart and soul.

There were still a thousand questions I had that I would be willing to ask, but... not then.

Not when it was hard enough to talk about going through a dark period in your life in the first place. I didn't kick people who were already down. I wasn't going to start now. One thing at a time.

Sitting straight up, I slid my hand out from under his and then reached over to pluck his phone off his knee.

He gave me a curious look as I exited the app he had open, the one that showed his ride would be at my house in two minutes and took in the default background image on his screen. By the time the SUV had pulled up to the front of my house, I had just finished hitting the Save button.

"I added Grandpa Gus's phone number to your contacts since you already have Peter's," I told him as we both got to our feet. "I saw you still have my number. I'll unblock you when I get inside so your calls can start coming through again."

He didn't move as I took Mo from him, sucking up her warmth and weight and giving her some of my body heat even though she felt nice and toasty, probably from her dad's body heat.

"Monday, Wednesday, and Friday, I get to work at seven in the morning. I stay at the gym, and then leave work at four unless I have to stay for some reason. Most Tuesdays and Thursdays I work from nine until six, and every once in a while I might stay later, but it's rare now. I usually work every other weekend and take Monday and Tuesday off on those days. Each of those Saturdays I teach a self-defense class at eight in the morning," I told him carefully. "You can call me anytime."

He blinked. And by the next blink, he was nodding. "Ta."

I didn't know what the fuck "ta" meant, but I'd look it up inside. I took two steps backward and stopped. "Jonah."

Even in the darkness without the porch light on, I knew he was listening.

"You aren't the first person to get injured and think the world was over. I would have understood. I get why you left, but it still fucking sucks that you did that. I thought I knew you, and it hurt that I didn't because I never would have expected for you to just... leave like that." I hugged Mo a little closer. "Don't fuck this up, all right? Don't make me regret this."

I know I didn't imagine the way his shoulders rolled backward, his spine straightening, and his entire body seemed to just... come to life. He grew in front of my eyes. From a six-foot-five monster to one that would give the Hulk a reason to pause.

And he said in that beautiful voice, "I won't."

CHAPTER 11

8:30 p.m

Fucking Christ,

you fucking asshole,

text me back.

JUST TEXT ME BACK.

We need to talk.

I don't care if you don't want to.

Don't be a bitch.

There's something important

you need to know

"THAT'S A STUPID DEAL AND A STUPID FIGHT," I SAID INTO MY CELL phone as I turned around and backed into the door, opening it with my butt.

The man on the other end of the line said the same thing he'd been trying to sell me on for the last five minutes. "It's a start—"

"A worthless one. He's not going to take it, and you're wasting his time and my time by bringing it up again. It isn't enough money, and I'll tell you right now his offer with *other organizations* is a lot better," I cut him off, looking around the gym floor as I headed toward the juice bar counter.

"Lenny," the man on the line groaned.

"Sorry, but you know I'm not going to tell him to take it," I kept going, taking in the members working out, living their own lives. It only reminded me that I had woken up late, hadn't meditated, and Mo had peed all over me—and her crib—before seven in the morning. I needed to squeeze in some time on the bike or the Stairmaster today, at least. Maybe during my lunch break. Fifteen minutes of high-intensity cardio was better than nothing. "Offer him more. I know you can."

My eyes narrowed in on an impressively tall figure standing at the juice counter, chin tucked in, gaze focused downward. That height looked awfully familiar. So did those shoulders, and that haircut and color.

What the hell was he doing here?

The man on the other end groaned and moaned without actually using words, eating up the time it took me to make it to the bar, still holding my phone to my face, while I stopped directly to the side of the man I knew. A little too well. It was Jonah.

He was pulling bills out of his wallet with a funny look on his face.

"Look, do it or don't do it, but I told you what's going on," I said into the phone, the familiar head instantly turning in my direction.

Jonah gave me one of his endless little smiles. I held up a finger.

"I need to go. Call me back if you can do better. Bye," I said, not bothering to wait for him to say "bye." It was one of the most important intimidation tactics that Grandpa Gus had taught me over the years. If you wanted something, you could get it using sugar, but if you used a little vinegar too, sometimes it worked better.

But I wasn't worried about him or the deal. I was just doing a favor for a member who had asked Peter for some advice. Then Peter had come to me to help him out.

What I was busy focusing on was the man holding five twenty-dollar bills in his hand the night after he'd left my house.

I flicked my gaze toward the employee behind the counter, who doubled making juices if they were busy enough. She smiled innocently. I really liked Bianca. I smiled back at her but saved the words for the man. I had already told her good morning earlier.

"What are you doing?"

"Good morning, Lenny," he said in that voice I was planning on surviving through for the next eighteen years of my life. "How ya goin'?"

"Fine," I confirmed, glancing at his wallet and his money again. "You?"

He flashed me that little smile again. "I came over to see about a membership, if that's all right. You've got a flash facility here. I like it."

Flash…. Flash…. Fancy?

I'd looked up "ta" the night before, and apparently it was slang for thanks.

"He's doing a month-by-month membership," Bianca chirped up politely. "That's what you asked for, isn't it, Mr. Collins?"

Jonah's smile fell off as he looked at the receptionist and nodded tightly, back to looking weird.

What the fuck was that about? I wondered before a more important idea filled my head. I still had no clue how long he was going to be here for. Or where he was going. I figured that was something I should know, wasn't it?

I'd ask him later. Or sometime in the near future at least. One thing at a time.

"Activate a card for him, but default it as a manager special, please, Bianca. He's family."

Her blink said more than I wanted it to. *He was family.* I had just fucking confirmed *something*. The next few words out of her mouth did the same. "What's a manager's special?"

"It's on the house."

She blinked again. "Um, I haven't done that in the system before." She lowered her voice. "How do you want me to do it?"

"That's not necessary," Jonah butted in, speaking to me as he sidestepped so that his outer left biceps brushed my shoulder.

I slid him a look before rattling off instructions to my employee, at the last minute throwing in access to the other building too.

"You don't need to do that." He decided not to drop it, his arm touching mine again. "The gym at my hotel isn't much, and I liked the look of this place. I wasn't expecting a thing by coming here."

If he was trying to suck up to me by complimenting Maio House, it was working. But I didn't want it to.

Grandpa Gus and I had spent a lot of time going over the floor plan when he'd decided to rebuild. I had loved Maio House back when it had been a hole-in-the-wall boxing gym. Now it was all sleek and clean and brightly lit—both buildings were—and I loved them. I took a lot of pride in this place. How could I not when it had my last name tied to it?

"I'm sure you didn't," I assured him. "But you are family, and you don't have to pay to work out here. So quit arguing with me. You're making it weird."

I could feel Bianca's gaze on me, and I wondered if the nosey asses in the other building had started whispering over in this building too about who they thought Jonah might be. To give her credit though, her fingers flew across her keyboard, and she scanned one of the laminated keychains with a barcode on it.

Glancing up at Jonah again, I found him with his attention

already down on me. I gave him a small smile, and he raised his eyebrows like it was me he was exasperated with.

"What?"

"You don't need to do this," he said, angling his body some more so that his arm was fully pressed against mine, his thigh right there too.

Well, unfortunately for his ass, I didn't have any personal space issues. He could press that arm and that leg against me as much as he wanted, and it was never going to bother me. I'd had strangers' feet literally on my face countless times. Mo had thrown up in my open mouth before. I'd licked her poop by accident.

There weren't even a handful of things that grossed me out, and that arm and leg right there and those honey-colored eyes nearly glaring into mine weren't going to get him more than a blink and a raise of my eyebrows right back.

"No offense, but I don't really care what you think I need to do or not," I whispered back to him, using those same words he'd thrown at me the night before when I had tried to tell him not to give me his excuses.

And what I got as a reply were his dark eyebrows knitting together.

And then that slow fucking smile crawled across his mouth —and even his fucking eyes somehow—and he nodded, still smiling, as he said, "It's going to be like that, is it?"

I fucking hated him. I really did. And that was why I kept myself from smiling at him, at least totally smiling, and shrugged my good shoulder. "Yeah, it is."

This microscopic douchebag laughed.

"Just as saucy as I remember," he muttered, with that laugh that was just as bright and cheerful as his smile was. It was so annoying.

The memory of him sitting next to me on the bus the day we'd met and laughing then too, *You're a bit saucy, eh,* hit me straight in the chest like a dull ache. I'd teased him over... I couldn't remember what anymore. But I'd been teasing him, I knew that much.

We had hit it off.

And now we were here.

"Would you like me to get Deandre to give him a tour?" Bianca asked, cutting into my thoughts, as she handed him his new laminated keycard.

I only had to linger over his words from the night before for a second before I reminded myself of my decision. Eighteen years. I might as well make the best out of it. I wasn't about to start being my own worst enemy now. We *did* get along. A little too well.

At least he wasn't Noah.

"I can do it," I told the receptionist. I didn't double-check with Jonah if that was fine, because what if it wasn't? I wouldn't get over him preferring a stranger to me even though I knew I should. "I'll show you around real quick."

He nodded back before bending over to grab a duffel bag I hadn't noticed until right then that he had sitting between his feet. It was navy blue with lighter electric blue accents on it. And it was then, as I looked down at his bag, that my eyes finally noticed something else.

Jonah was wearing shorts. And not just any shorts. His rugby shorts.

They were navy blue and about as loose as thighs the size of Jonah Collins's could let shorts be, which wasn't that loose at all, especially not higher up on his legs. Looking at the seams for a split second, I was pretty positive he'd had to tug the material apart *hard* to give it a little more of a stretch to not be so tight.

And yeah, there was a tiny split at the bottom of each leg like he'd taken scissors to them for just a little more room.

And speaking of his thighs, they were just as big, if not bigger, than I remembered. Considering I had grown up around men who babied and pampered their bodies, I was pretty nonchalant about looks and muscles. But his were something else completely. He had the kind of thighs that no bodybuilder, light heavyweight, or even heavyweight MMA champion was capable of. Sprinting legs. *Massive*. Bulging muscles that my hands briefly remembered were rock hard.

And those damn shorts started about five or seven inches above his knee, showing way more leg than any of the guys around the gym showed, except for the handful in on the MMA side who favored tiny compression shorts.

But none of them, as fit as they were, were any comparison to Tall, Dark, Less of an Asshole Than Yesterday, and Handsome.

And just like I remembered, he wasn't the slightest bit self-conscious about it.

Or his long white socks that set off the dark curly hair of his legs.

No big deal. I had seen them, and I could move on with my life now. There were plenty of other rugby players in the world who probably had the same build.

I sniffed and shot him a pleasant expression as I raised my eyes. This funny shape came over his mouth, but he didn't say anything about whether he knew exactly what I was looking at or thinking about. Good. "Come on, I'll show you around," I told him, tipping my head to the side.

He followed me, his own head swinging from one direction to the other, soaking up the rows and rows of machines and equipment.

I started pointing. "This is the cardio section. There's everything from treadmills to stationary bikes, a couple of Stairmasters and elliptical machines." I gestured to the other side of the walkway that cut through the center of the gym and swept out into another line crossing it. "The machines are set up by muscle group. The ab and glute machines are all in the front."

I highly doubted he used those.

"Biceps and triceps in the middle and the last row over there has all the back and chest machines, for doing rows and pull-downs." He knew what I meant. There was no way he didn't know his way around a gym.

Jonah nodded as we walked, but I knew that most of that part of the floor would be unused by him. It was the other section that I'd bet he would be working in. "There are dumbbells all along the wall by the mirrors. Squat racks are on the left. Bench presses, from what you can see, are in the middle. There are a few barbells in the corners, but you can steal the ones off the squat racks or bench presses too. The Smith machines are on the right wall."

"How old is all this?" he asked all of a sudden. "When you told me your grandfather owned a gym, this wasn't what I pictured."

I wasn't totally sure how to answer that. I waved him to follow me toward the door that led to the walkway between the buildings. He was already familiar with this door, obviously, since it was the same one he had somehow managed to sneak in through before. "We had a building that was a lot smaller before. The same one my great-grandfather owned, where he started Maio House as a boxing gym. A few years ago, though, a major hurricane hit, and it was devastating for the area. Neighborhoods and parts of the city that hadn't been in flood zones in a hundred years, flooded. And that building was in one of those areas, and it destroyed everything. But we were one of the lucky ones, because Grandpa's paranoid and had gotten flood insurance before I was born, even though everyone else told him it was unnecessary.

"Anyway, it took a while, but the policy came through. The land that the original building had been on was really valuable, and he sold it. It was too small to rebuild on, and it wouldn't be the same. About ten years ago, he had bought this plot of land because he had thought about expanding and setting up another satellite branch, and it was cheap then, but never got around to it. So, he decided to rebuild here. This place opened a month after Mo was born, so it's brand new."

He had stopped to watch me as I told him the story, and a frown had slowly formed over that dark pink mouth. "It was in the news, the storm."

"Yeah. Grandpa rented out a place temporarily, but it was tiny and only fit a cage and a few mats. That's why I went to France."

"It makes sense now. You didn't have work here."

I nodded. "And my other job was just part-time. That's why I left."

"You had another job?" he asked, surprised.

"Yeah. I only worked here twenty-hours a week. Grandpa never let me work full-time until a few months ago, and it wasn't like he paid me a lot hourly. I just worked the front desk." I shrugged. "I worked in the mornings at a retirement home."

"A retirement home?"

"Yeah," I confirmed. I guess we'd never gotten around to talking about that before. "I was there for seven years as an aide."

"You never said anything about the flooding," Jonah commented after a second, thoughtfully.

"It was awful, and a lot of people had it a lot worse than we did."

He nodded like he understood, and I'd bet he did. "What did you do for work when you… got back?"

When I got back knocked up? I gave him a funny face, pushing down that rising anger at the fact he didn't know what I'd done after I got back from Paris. Because of our lack of communication. "I went back to the retirement home and worked the front desk. I was there until Mo came."

And he hadn't been around.

I changed the subject before he asked anything else about that time and pissed me off in the process. "Anyway, I know you've already seen the other building, but let me show you where everything is in case you want to work out there. It's a little quieter and more private, and there's more space for certain exercises," I told him moving to open the door out, but his long arm beat me to it.

That big, muscular bicep was inches from my head as he swung the door wide, and I ignored how close the front of him got to my back as he did it. Just as I was about to rush ahead to open the next door so that he wouldn't, I changed my mind. Fuck it. What did I have to prove? He could open the door if he wanted to. And if I was going to like it, it was only because all these rude asses I spent time with hardly ever did.

Probably because they knew I could do it my own damn self.

I led him in, feeling the heat from his body directly behind me as I showed him—like he couldn't see—the section to the right covered in high-quality fake turf. "There are tractor tires down on the far end, if you can see. In the shelves all the way on the wall over there are ropes and different things that you can use."

The thought barely entered my mind that if he worked out here, I would see him more.

Oh well.

"But you have access to everything. The only time this part is used is usually really early in the morning or after five when everyone is off. But there aren't that many people who have the middle membership that gives them access to this building, so you'll be left alone most of the time," I let him know. I hooked my thumb behind me. "I'll be in the office usually if you need me. I doubt anyone will give you a hard time, but if they do, let me know."

His eyebrows furrowed. "You reckon someone will say something?"

I mean, I guessed he probably hadn't had anyone give him a hard time since he'd hit his growth spurt. At least no sober person would. All you had to do was look at the wall that was his upper body to know it would be a dumb idea.

I could say that from a professional and clinical point of view. I sized up guys for a partial living. Kind of.

"I don't think so, but—" An image of Noah's face flashed before my eyes, but I shook it off. "—people are weird, and you're bigger than they are. Just let me know though. Everyone is mostly really nice."

He made a funny face that I knew was my fault for being so vague. "Does anyone know now that...."

"You're Mo's dad?"

"Yeh."

"No."

Something in his eyes dimmed, but I couldn't and wouldn't feel bad about it.

"I told you I hadn't told anyone. It's only been a few days since you got here. The only people I've told have been my grandpa, Peter, and my best friend. It's no one else's business but ours. We still have a lot to figure out first anyway."

His expression got even more grave. "You don't want anyone to know?"

"That's not it. I just don't think I need to announce it." I paused as a thought entered my head. "Why? Do you want to keep Mo a secret?"

Because my girl wasn't going to be a secret. If he wanted to protect her privacy, that was one thing, but if he didn't want people to know he had her in the first place, that was a totally different situation. So.

Luckily he answered with his own head jerking back as he frowned. "No. Not at all. I have family and some mates to tell first. My agent. I just wanted a bit of time to have this for myself, is all. Once I tell one person, it will get out, and I'd like to enjoy it while I can, Len, if that's all right. Without having to answer questions."

Oh.

Okay then.

"I'm not going to try and keep it a secret or anything, but if they figure out you're her dad… then they figure it out. I'm not going to announce it or send out a newsletter or anything." I rocked back on my heels. "It's just nobody's business but ours, and I've never shared my private life around. At least not in a long time." Not since I'd been young and everyone had been a parent or brother figure to me.

Now… all those people had moved on with their lives, and there wasn't a single person at Maio House anymore that I had that kind of bond with. Except Peter.

And goddamn did that make me a little sad now that I thought about it.

Time didn't stop for anyone or anything.

I really didn't have any true friends here left.

Jonah looked like he wanted to say something, but he didn't.

I was over talking about this anyway. I kept going with my tour. "There are locker rooms in both buildings, but there are always fewer people in the one here. You can use either, but you'll need a lock."

"I'll pick one up tomorrow," he said.

Apparently I was wearing my nice pants today because I offered, "You can just leave your stuff in the office in the meantime if you want. Or I have a lock you can borrow too."

Did he need to look so surprised again? "Whatever would be easier for you."

I tipped my head toward my door and didn't wait for him to follow me over, but he did. Flicking on the lights, I went to my desk and opened the drawer where I left the lock I let the guys borrow from time to time.

Jonah stood halfway into the office, honey-colored eyes glued to his right where Grandpa Gus and I had put up a wall of picture frames. Somehow, I could tell which picture he was looking at. It was one of a much younger me standing between Grandpa Gus and Peter, pointing at my crotch. Not my crotch actually, but at the belt around my waist, over my gi, the traditional white practice clothing you wore in judo.

"My first black belt," I explained.

He didn't look back at me, but I could tell his eyes moved to another picture to the side of it. Jonah tilted his head to the side, leaning in even closer. "This belt is different than the other," he noted.

"Some people don't know that there are different… levels. That was right after the Olympic trials."

His head jerked back, and he blinked. "You didn't tell me you competed in the Olympics."

I shook my head. "I didn't. I fractured my ribs two weeks before."

He made the same face everyone did when I told them about the timing on my damn ribs. "Training?"

"No." I lifted a shoulder. I had been pissed off back then. Most people had figured I would have been devastated, but, no, I'd been mad. At myself. At Noah for asking me to help him out one day when his kickboxing coach had called in sick, when he had decided to go for a leg kick instead of a punch and side-stepped too much, connecting with the corner of the strike shield I'd been holding for protection—and connecting with my ribs.

I shouldn't have left the training facility for the weekend to go back home. I should have said no to Noah in the first place, but I couldn't take it back. It just felt like a really dumb decision now that I couldn't go back in time. I wasn't mad about it anymore.

Those honey-colored eyes flicked over my face in confusion.

"Four years before that, I broke my wrist the day of the opening ceremony. The janitor in the bathroom didn't put up a sign that the floor had been mopped, and… I busted my fucking face because I hadn't been paying attention and didn't react fast enough to not lose my balance. It just wasn't meant to be for me, I guess." I shrugged again. "Anyway…."

I stopped talking at the facial expression he was making. "What?"

The expression eased off a little but not enough.

"What?" I asked again.

He shook his head, the corners of his mouth going up a hair. "You said that like… there was nothing special about it."

"I didn't even get to walk in the ceremony."

"It isn't special because you didn't walk in the ceremony? All right. That makes sense."

Was he being sarcastic?

I didn't know how I felt about that. It reminded me of how he'd been… before.

He watched me for a moment longer before dipping his head down and plucking the lock and key out of my hand, his fingertips brushing my wrists lightly as he did it. "Is it possible for me to see Mo this evening?"

"Yeah," I answered. "I'll be home too, so you don't have to be stuck with Grandpa Grumpy."

His mouth went up just a little higher, his eyes doing this thing that said he was amused. "He's only being protective. Can't blame him. He doesn't know me yet."

Something inside of me shuttered closed, and I took a step back. "I hope you'll stick around for Mo to get to know you at least. She's the important one."

Jonah lifted a hand and rubbed it over the center of his chest, seeming to hesitate for a moment before changing his mind. "Len, you said last night that you thought you knew me."

Was he asking or was he telling me?

"But you did know me," he said, intensely. "I'd like you to get to know me again. Not just Mo. I want you to know who I am too."

Okay. I didn't know what the fuck to do with that at all.

And so I said just about the dumbest shit I could have. "Okay." Okay? And then I kept going with the dumb shit. "I should get back to work. Have a good workout."

Those eyes watched me for a moment. Then he nodded, strain in his gaze, and took his own retreating footstep. "Thanks again. I'm grateful."

"It's nothing. Don't thank me," I said, knowing I should stop there but not. Why the fuck did he have to say that and make it awkward? "I'll probably have more people sign up once they see you walking around in those shorts."

He glanced down. "Something wrong with them?"

I shrugged my good shoulder. "I'm just messing with you. I didn't know what to say with you telling me that you want me to get to know you again, and it just kind of came out."

His eyebrows lifted, and he smiled slowly. I watched him lift both toes of his sneakers up as he rocked back on his heels to take in his clothing... and I fought off the tiny little lap of tenderness that reached me. I should have kept my mouth shut about all of that. I shouldn't have given him the damn membership either, damn it.

Those eyes flicked up for a moment, and he flashed me an even bigger smile like he had some reason to be pleased. "Cheers."

This was a really stupid idea, I thought to myself the second he left.

A really, really stupid idea.

∼

THREE HOURS LATER, THE ALARM ON MY PHONE WENT OFF RIGHT while I was wrapping up a conversation that had me closing my eyes a minute into it.

I rubbed at the spot between my eyebrows after silencing it. "Grandpa, they're going to check your ID when you register for the tournament. You can't sign up for a younger age bracket—and I can't even believe they have a bracket for people your age anyway. Aren't they scared someone will break a hip?"

He huffed. "They have insurance for things like that... and you really think they'll check my ID?"

Only my grandfather would try to fucking cheat in a basketball tournament by lying and attempting to play with men younger than him. "Don't they always check?"

That got me a grumble. "Yes." Did he have to sound so bummed out? No, but he did. "I can keep Mo here that day, so don't worry about trying to lie and play earlier. Maybe Jonah will take her."

That got me a grunt. "I still don't know about that Edward."

I fucking laughed. "Stop calling him the wrong name!"

"I will when you stop laughing over it."

I laughed even harder, and my cheek started hurting when he started chuckling too. "You're the worst, Grandpa. I swear you're the worst."

"You're confusing worst with fun. Funnest. Best."

There were tears in my eyes by then. "I don't think funnest is a word."

"It should be," the old vampire argued.

Fucking hell. "Go pee before your prostrate exam. I need to go get Mo now."

My gramps snorted. "I hope he uses enough lube this time. Call me later."

I was definitely fucking crying by the time I pulled myself out of the chair with his comment about lube ringing heavily in my head. There was something wrong with him. I'd swear. All that boxing. All those hits. It explained everything. It really did.

I was still cracking up as I pulled a drawer open and got my wallet and keys out. Edging my way around the desk, I finally focused in on what I had to do... and what I should do. I hadn't seen Jonah again all morning. Slipping my phone and wallet into the back pockets of my jeans and grabbing my backpack, I headed right out the door and stopped.

There was a broad kneecap connected to a heavy and hairy thigh right there.

"You okay?" I asked the freshly showered man sitting cross-legged beside my door with his bag sitting next to him.

"Yeh," he answered with a happy expression. "Figured I'd wait for you to finish."

Why though? I kept the question to myself. "I was about to see if you were still here," I told him. "I have to go pick up Mo from the daycare before noon so they don't charge me for the whole day. Grandpa Gus had an appointment this morning and has another one right now, and he'll get her afterward from his friend's house. Do you want to come with me?" I paused. "You don't have to if you would rather see her tonight."

He was already getting to his feet. "I'll come. Tonight, too, if that's not a problem."

If there were such a thing as a right answer, that would have been it. I tried not to let it show on my face though. Unfortunately, he took it the wrong way and kept talking, like I would tell him no.

"The more time I spend with her the better. I need to make the most of it while I'm here."

I hated him. I really did, and I didn't trust a word to come out of my mouth right then when he was saying all these... things that were nice but too nice. Too perfect.

But the *while he was here* hung there, and the Still a Tiny Bit of an Asshole raised his eyebrows in return.

"Of course you can see her tonight. Let's go," I muttered, figuring we could talk about his plans later.

"What's that face for?" he asked when we had gotten about halfway to the door leading outside.

I kept my gaze forward and didn't even bother lying. "I don't know what to think of you."

He waited until he was pulling the door open. "Nice thoughts?"

I snorted, and I sure as fuck didn't look at him. I didn't need to see him smile at my sarcasm.

"Would you like to know what I think about you?" he asked teasingly.

"Sure," I said as he caught up behind me, telling myself not to take him playing around to heart.

"You didn't even think about it."

I glanced at him over my shoulder and gave him a face. Like there was something he could say that would hurt my feelings. Ha. He hadn't gone to a private Catholic girl school for a year with a buncha bitches.

Jonah lifted up one of those shoulders. "All right. You're brave—"

That had me coughing. "Brave?" Where the hell did he get that from?

Jonah's arm brushed mine as we walked side by side. "Yeah. You didn't hesitate to say yes, did you? I'm not sure I'd want to know what you think of me." He paused. "Actually, I wouldn't want to know."

He probably didn't, and I was only going to feel *slightly* bad about that. "It's not all bad," I mumbled, reluctantly.

He chuckled. "Well, as long as it's not all bad…."

I rolled my eyes and kept my mouth shut to not egg him on.

Or make him do something that would make me really smile.

What he did do was brush his forearm against mine again.

Luckily, he waited until I was backing out of the parking spot to talk again. "How ya goin'?"

"Fine. You?"

"Great," he replied.

"The gym is working out okay?" I was feeling friendly today apparently.

"Oh, yeh, it's nice," he replied as he shifted around in his seat, one hand wedging itself between the door and his thigh. He hadn't needed to move backward. He was the last person to ride in the front seat. "Has everything I need and more while I'm here."

While he was here were the keywords there. I really did need to ask him eventually what he was doing and where he was going. I hadn't gotten another notification on my home screen with news on him switching teams, so I could only guess he still hadn't made a decision. I was pondering that over when he asked a question, and I had to ask him to repeat himself.

"Do you have an idea where I might be able to get jandals?"

I hesitated. "Jan—what?"

"Jandals… Thongs?"

I blinked, an image of that body in a thong filling my brain for a second. Well, it was something else being stuffed into a thong that I imagined. That was a mental picture I needed to live without.

"Sandals?" he offered, hopefully not being able to read what I'd just imagined.

Oh. *Oh.* "I thought you meant"—I looked at him, but he looked totally and completely innocent—"—thong underwear."

He looked at me for a split second. Then that deep, deep laugh trickled out, filling the car. "Nah, sweetheart. That'd be a sight, wouldn't it?"

It would be a sight. If I was still into that.

I had dug myself into this hole by bringing up his underwear, so now I had to get myself out of it. I got back on topic. "What size shoe do you wear?"

"Fourteen in En Zed," he replied. "Don't know about here though."

I thought about it. "Let me text someone. I don't know if they carry size fourteens around in normal stores, but you can order some online, worst case. Order them today and you can get them in two days. I'll find out for you when we park."

"You're a sweetheart, Lenny."

That had me snickering at the windshield.

"What's that laugh for?"

I shook my head. "Just about every single person I know would laugh if they heard you call me that."

His attention was outside the windshield too when I glanced at him. "Can't speak for them, but you've been bloody good to me so far. Heaps better than most would in the same position."

I side-eyed him. "I'm being all right to you because you're here and I can tell that you're trying," I told him honestly.

Some of his smile dropped off, but he clung to that shit, and it was him trying to keep it that made me keep going. Because I didn't want to make him feel bad, even though he deserved it. He *was* trying. I'd never tear him down for being responsible.

"Look, I'm real good at holding grudges, but only if they're called for, and I'm not going to make my life miserable by being mean to you if you're trying your best," I finished, facing forward again. "I'm good at a lot of things, Jonah, and getting along with people, especially men, is one of those things." I pressed my lips together and made a face at the windshield. "Except you've seen me naked unlike them, but whatever."

He choked so deeply I glanced at him and smiled a little. I really was in a good mood. He was so easy to fuck with, and it just made me want to do it more.

So that's what I did. "And I've seen your winky. And we've had sex."

It wasn't like Mo had been immaculately conceived.

Jonah's face was already pink and, from the looks of it, escalating to a special shade of red, and it just egged me on.

"But I've seen a lot of little breakfast sausages at the gym, so don't get all shy," I told him evenly, secretly eating up the color at his cheeks and the choking sound he made again. Heh. I'd forgotten he was such a prude. And that brought me joy.

"Why?" he got out after a second.

"Why what?"

"At the gym?"

"When the guys drop weight, they get on the scale naked, and half of them don't have enough modesty to put on a towel when they do it. I don't go over to them and hold up a magnifying glass to inspect their sweaty, hairy little chicken eggs or anything. They're just... there. Like overripe, sad little bananas sometimes."

Out of the corner of my eye, I could see a big hand go to his face, and I could barely hear him as he repeated, "Sad little bananas?"

"You forgot overripe."

His groan filled the car, and I couldn't fucking help but laugh at goody two-shoes.

How the hell had I forgotten that? I remembered I'd referred to a penis as a willy right after we'd met, and he'd cracked up big-time. Then I'd called it a pee-pee to fuck with him, and he'd had tears in his eyes.

Fortunately, we rolled up to the daycare soon afterward, where Mo spent some time at twice a week. Since most of the parents who dropped off their kids worked "normal" full-time hours, there was no one parked out front. Jonah and I got out at the same time. He did what I had started growing to expect from him: he opened the front door for me, making eye contact as I passed him.

I kept my own expression nice and even as I did it.

And half of his mouth tipped up, that fucking dimple popping.

"Hey, Lenny," a familiar voice called out from the office directly in front of the double doors.

I tore my attention away from the man who stopped directly beside me, his forearm and the back of his hand brushing my upper arm and elbow like there wasn't enough space in the entrance so he had to stand so close to me. "Hey," I greeted the older woman who came to a stop in the doorway, keeping my arm exactly where it was. "How's it going?"

The director of the daycare moaned. "Fine except for this monster cold I've got. I've got to stay away from the children for the time being." Slowly, her eyes swiveled to the man literally standing right beside me, and I could *see* her eyeballs widen just a little but just enough.

That was my cue. "Rachel, this is Jonah. He's Mo's dad. I was going to ask you if you could add him to the list of people who can pick up my little monster."

Her eyes widened even more, and I couldn't say that I blamed her.

I tipped my head up to look at Jonah and gave him a little smile. "You have your license, right?"

That bottom lip was pulled into his mouth with his teeth right before he nodded. He glanced at the woman and said, in a voice quieter than I had ever heard before, "I have my New Zealand license. I can bring my passport if you need something else."

I frowned. What the hell was he whispering for? He didn't speak very loudly in the first place but....

Poor Rachel, on the other hand, was too busy trying her best to keep it professional, to wonder why Jonah was talking like he was Stuart Little. But I knew what she was thinking. *How the fuck had Lenny had a child with brown-haired Thor?*

I wouldn't have known how to answer. I still didn't totally get it either. I wasn't the most attractive woman in the world, but we'd... gotten along. Or at least, he'd thought my sense of humor was awesome, and he'd been charmed by my foul fucking mouth.

"Sure, sure," she agreed while I was still wondering why Jonah had been whispering. "Let me get that from you, and Lenny, I'll need you to sign a form stating that you're giving permission to do this...." She trailed off an explanation that I mostly listened to as I watched Jonah fish his license out of his worn, slim wallet and hand it over.

Ten minutes later, Rachel was buzzing us through the door after making us squirt hand sanitizer on our hands. The doorway would lead into the main part of the building where the kids were split up. Grandpa Gus and I had picked this exact daycare because they focused on babies. There were eight kids in Mo's "class," which, as of two months ago, consisted of the six-month-olds and up. There was another class with the really young ones, six weeks to two months. Three months to six. A fourth class had one-year-olds to two-year-olds. It was small, clean, and pretty exclusive because of the size of their groups. Plus, they had an app that let us see what she was doing via cameras in the rooms the kids were in.

If it hadn't been for Grandpa Gus pulling out the big guns and winking and over-the-top flirting with Rachel, I was pretty sure they wouldn't have accepted us.

Then I'd seen their rates and wished they hadn't.

Jonah followed me in, his head swinging around the room we had been let into, a room with the one to two-year-olds. A teacher and an assistant were busy collecting toys.

"One more room over," I told him.

"You said she comes twice a week?"

I pushed open the Dutch door that led into Mo's room. "Yeah, but on the same days every week." It was the only time they had been able to fit us in around the other kids' schedules.

"So your granddad can have a break?"

"No, to spend some time with other kids. He'd keep her all the time if I asked, but I don't want to put that on him. It gives him time to do the things he likes that he hadn't before." Oooh, I could see Mo already on a mat made up of individual squares with letters on each by herself, with a set of what looked like stackable, colorful cups. "Being an only child, not having any kids to play with, sucks sometimes. And I want her to know how to share."

"Know from experience?"

"You're damn right I do." I smiled as I lifted a hand toward Mo's teacher a moment before dropping to my knees beside my girl, soaking up her cheery shrieks of babble when I ducked my head into her vision as she reached her arms toward me.

"I'm so happy to see you too, booger," I told her. My heart swelled so big, I was pretty sure it might explode. Words flew out of my mouth as I kissed her cheeks. *Hi* and *Iloveyousomuch* and *Imissedyousomuch* and *Howwasschool*? Her reply was to pull on my hair that had fallen out of my ponytail and landed on her face.

And it was then after all those words that I sat back on my heels to give Jonah room. Jonah had crouched down beside us at some point, elbows tucked into his sides. His eyes flicked from me to Mo and back again, and the smile that came over his face was more genuine than I ever could have hoped for. Slow and steady, and so white and bright and earnest, I felt bad for regretting there for a while that it was him I had created her with.

He wasn't a bad guy, for the most part. He was still a little bit of an asshole for what he'd done to me, even if I did understand I'd been the last thing on his mind when he'd thought he'd lost his true love. But there was hope for him, at least where Mo was concerned.

That was enough.

"Hello, Mo," he said quietly, reaching one of those big hands out, letting those small fingers wrap around one of his.

"Say hi to your dad, da-da-da," I told her, holding the toes of a foot covered in a soft-soled shoe.

The smile on Jonah's face grew brighter but more wistful too. His throat bobbed. "How's my wee girl?" he asked, reaching across with his other hand to touch what I knew was the softest little cheek. Then he did the same to the other one with a deep, deep sigh.

I totally knew where the hell he was coming from with that sigh.

Maybe he didn't love her yet, but I could tell the possibility of it was there. It would be no time. With those big brown eyes and that gummy grin and the soft skin and all that fucking potential she had in her tiny little bones... Mo gave me hope that I didn't know I was capable of. Hope for... life. Or something. She had her whole life ahead of her. She could do anything.

"Is this normal?" Jonah asked quietly.

"What?" I was pretty sure I knew what he was referring to, but I wanted to make sure.

Two shiny light brown eyes moved to me before moving back down to Mo, and I couldn't help but smile.

"Is it normal to think she's awesome? I think so. I remember they put her into my arms, and the first thing I told my grandpa was that I didn't know I could love someone I'd just met so much." I touched the growing foot again. Even thinking about that swell of emotion almost a year later, still felt like a miracle. It had been, and was, the most unexpected thing I had ever felt.

I felt his sigh.

"As soon as you told me she was mine... *my daughter...* something happened. I don't know how to explain it. The more I see her, the more...." He exhaled again, and somehow it came out thoughtful. "It's strange and wonderful to think she's mine. This person who has no idea who I am yet." His free fingers touched her other foot. "But she will. She'll know she's mine. She'll never doubt it."

I watched some big emotion swallow his features, staining them pink again. An emotion I wasn't sure I was capable of handling or interpreting. But I knew what I thought of it.

I understood how it made me feel.

Protective of him too. This big man with his quiet voice and infinite patience. Someone who felt the weight of a life on his heart and wasn't trying to run away from it. But had instead instantly stepped into it.

I wasn't sure how we were going to make this work. Wasn't sure how often he would really be able to see her. But I knew he would, and I knew we would find a way. Something told me he would see her every second he could.

Jonah Hema Collins was no deadbeat.

Those honey-colored eyes flicked to me for a moment at the end of my thoughts, and the open vulnerability in them shot straight into my heart. "She'll know, won't she?"

A frog magically appeared in my throat, and there was no way I could ever lie to him about that answer. "Yeah. She will, Jonah. She'll know. We'll make sure."

The last thing I expected was the hand that moved from a small cheek to the hand I had resting on the top of my thigh. Warm, rough fingers slid over my own like it was totally normal. I'd remember the next words out of his mouth every day of my life. I would remember them each time I thought I had no idea what I was doing being a mom. Jonah Collins squeezed my hand. That muscular shoulder rolled upward, and he said, in a rough voice, gripping my fingers tight, "What a gift you've given me, Lenny."

CHAPTER 12

1:55 p.m.

Wow, seriously.

Wow: Three months now?

TEXT ME BACK.

It's really important, dipshit.

Your voice mailbox is still full.

"WHAT THE FUCK IS HE DOING?" I ASKED PETER, WHO WAS standing beside me on the outside of the cage, peering at the two fighters in the center too. "Watch his arm, Carlos!"

"I don't know," Peter replied to me a moment before yelling again. "Grab the leg! *Grab the leg!*"

He didn't grab his leg. Or watch his arm.

I glanced down at my cellphone. Thirty seconds were left before the timer went off, signaling the end of the second round for Carlos's training session with a fighter who had come to train with Peter for the winter. The guy was a light heavyweight named Sven Andersson from Iceland.

And he was kicking Carlos's ass as Peter and I watched him make one stupid mistake after another.

Rookie mistakes, really. They weren't even the kinds of mistakes that a person made when they were cocky. He was rushing and being impulsive. They weren't fighting full-strength, but half or three-quarters could still cause a lot of damage. He was being straight-up *stupid*.

"Jesus Christ," Peter muttered as the Sven guy landed a snap kick to Carlos's face. He was wearing head protection, but we both jerked our heads back and winced at the sight of his skull taking that kind of impact. He was a douche for ratting me out to Noah—I was pretty sure it was him—but I didn't want him to get his ass kicked during practice either. Peter and I had made faces at each other over the gap in their weight classes and skill levels, but we'd kept our mouths shut when both of them had insisted they wanted to spar.

I held my breath as Sven went for a really hard combo that left Carlos off-balance for a moment before they clashed together, grabbing one another. I glanced down at my phone again. Ten seconds left. "He's not defending against the clinch at all," I told Peter. "Keep your chin down!"

He didn't keep his chin down, and Peter didn't argue with me. Instead, Sven backed off, and Carlos rocked back on his heels as the other man landed a few more punches that I could tell were lighter than they had been before. Sven knew without a doubt he was winning… and had been the whole time.

The buzzing on my phone had me elbowing Peter who blew the buzzer we had to call time, and the two men in the cage separated.

I met Peter's eyes, and we both made a face. Again.

He pressed his fingertip between his eyebrows.

I knew what he was going to ask me to do, and I was going to make him ask for it.

He still had his finger between his eyebrows as he aimed a dark brown iris at me. "Help him, please."

It would be my pleasure and he knew it, so I just nodded at him and kicked my flip-flops off. I made my way up the steps and into the cage, watching Carlos as he crouched, trying to catch his breath. He looked exhausted.

But mostly, he looked pissed.

He'd lost his last fight a few days ago, and he was doing even shittier now. I'd be pissed too if I were him.

"Yoo-hoo," I said quietly, ignoring the Sven guy sitting a few feet away, trying to catch his breath too.

Carlos glanced up immediately and panted out, "Yeah?"

I motioned for him to get up, and thankfully, he did, breathing hard the whole time. "What's going on? What's got you so distracted?" I asked as I crept forward.

He didn't look even a little wary at my approach; he just looked irritated. I didn't enjoy embarrassing people, but being hard was sometimes the only way to get across to someone. Especially when that someone had an ego and needed to see that they weren't listening.

"Your technique has been shit, but being fast and aggressive usually makes up for it. But you know it isn't always going to," I told him bluntly.

The younger guy frowned. "My technique is shit now?"

"Your listening skills are shit. Your technique isn't much better. There were at least three opportunities, that if you would have listened, you could have easily gotten him into a rear-naked choke or an armbar, but you didn't listen when Peter and I were yelling. You were too focused on forcing the offensive instead of doing a little defense and then sneaking in there to get him." I motioned toward the fence just behind him. "Back up real quick. Let me show you."

He listened, fortunately, and went to stand so his back was to it. I stopped right in front of him and then took it even closer so that we were literally pressed completely together with one of my knees wedged in between both of his. I wasn't wearing the stretchiest pants I owned, but I could still move in them. I always did a few squats before I bought bottoms to make sure they weren't too constricting. I never knew when someone might ask me for help, or when I'd feel up for it.

"Right here," I told him. "I'm you. You had him against the fence, you could have lifted your knee"—I showed him —"swiveled your hip"—I showed him that too—"and then…."

And then I threw him. Over my hip, quick as lightning, I threw him when he least expected it and scrambled back onto the floor before he realized what was happening. I grabbed his arm while he was still confused, wrapped my feet and legs around it like I had done it a thousand times before—because I had done it at least ten thousand times—and then *pulled*.

He tapped out so fast I'd swear I heard Peter snicker. And just as quickly as he slammed his palm across the surface of the cage, I let him go. I wasn't there to hurt him.

Even though I *had* pulled more than a handful of shoulders out of sockets in my day.

Hurting people because they didn't want to tap out wasn't something I got a fucking kick out of, unlike some people I had known. Feeling ligaments and tendons being torn, especially with my history, was just… not for me. I liked to win but not by genuinely causing someone pain.

So I'd give it to Carlos for tapping as fast as he did.

Somewhere deep down inside, he still was thinking at least.

I squeezed his shoulder before getting up, taking in his wide-eyed stare at the rafters of the ceiling. "You know better. That shouldn't have been so easy. Clear your head. Focus. Listen. You can do this. Just think." And with that, I squeezed his shoulder one more time then walked back out, raising my eyebrows at Peter as playfully as possible once I was totally out. "I'm going to get water while you talk to your boy. Do you want some?" I asked Peter as I slid my flip-flops back on.

Peter was trying to hide a grin, but I knew it was there as his mouth pinched together and he shook his head and started over toward the steps I had just come down. Just as he was beside me on his way into the cage, he grinned and patted me on the shoulder. "You still got it, Len."

Damn right, I did.

It was hard not to smile at his comment, because… it did make me feel good. Maybe I didn't regret giving up judo for Mo —and for my fucking self—but it was nice to know I could still hang in there if I wanted to risk it. Not that what I'd done had been a risk because I had been in control, and I'd used my good shoulder.

I was still trying not to smile when I lifted my head and spotted the figure standing at the far end of the room closest to the entrance. I knew that haircut, but it was the height and that damn body that really struck me.

It was Jonah.

I had seen him every single day over the last four. At the gym either during or after his workout. He would come by my office if I didn't see him on a trip to the main building. Just yesterday he had gone with me to Mo's daycare again to pick her up and drop her off with Mr. Cooper, a family friend who babysat his granddaughter just like my own gramps did. And every single night, he would get to the house right around six— when I got home—and stay until Mo passed out.

I wanted to dislike him, I really did. Every single day we were together, I would look at him and some asshole part of me yearned to be mad, to tell him that I didn't need or want him in my life. I wanted to tell him that he'd hurt me by disappearing, regardless of the fact I now understood why he had. I wanted to ask him if he hadn't liked me enough once we had time and distance apart, and that's why the postcards had stopped. Then again, he'd come here without knowing about Mo, so that didn't make sense.

But…

He had already made his reasons clear. That was all I should have needed or wanted. There was no point in finding out more details. He smiled so fucking much and was so damn polite to my grandpa who was still treating him worse than people treated those with leprosy.

Fuck me, I couldn't hate him even a little bit, and that was the truth. It was probably the single most annoying thing to ever happen in my life: not being able to hate his ass.

Most importantly, Jonah was so into Mo, how could I?

He never took a night off from seeing her. I'd seen how thoughtful his face became when I told him things: how to dress her, bathe her, tricks that worked about 50 percent of the time for feeding her. And Jonah *listened*.

All that patience and commitment and how good-natured he was....

It was so bad that Grandpa had whispered to me over dinner one night, sounding bitter as fuck, "You couldn't have picked a shithead?"

I shot him a look that had him rolling his eyes like he blamed me for him not being a total dumbass we could hate on.

So far, that had been all of our stories where it came to Jonah Collins.

Annoying.

And the annoyingly-not-annoying man was over in the fake turf area that morning, hands on his hips, a belt around his waist, facing the cage. I headed over to him, taking in his shorts and the bulge of muscle directly above his knees, branching out to the stacked muscles that made up his upper thighs. The belt around his waist, I saw, was connected to four forty-five-pound weights stacked on top of each other. Sweat covered the cutoff T-shirt that showed off those massive arms.

I didn't have to look at footage to know he'd been running from one end of the turf to the other with one hundred and eighty pounds trailing behind him.

"Hey, Lenny," he greeted me.

"Morning," I replied, standing just off to the side of his workout area. "How's it going?"

"All right. Getting started with my warm-ups."

Warm-ups?

"Got a bit of conditioning left, I'm thinking. Eventful morning?" he asked with a cock of his eyebrow.

"It's more of a pain in the ass morning."

His hand went to the side of his head, and his smile was slow as he squinted an eye and asked, "D'ya really throw him or did I imagine that?"

I couldn't help but smile finally, just a little. "You saw that?"

Those white teeth flashed. "*Yeah,* I reckon everyone did."

My smile grew a little, and I shrugged. "He's distracted, and Peter wanted me to show him he was."

He fucking beamed at me, following it up with a chuckle, surprised and, I was pretty sure, impressed. "It was *awesome.*"

My half-dead heart thumped once at his compliment.

But before I could process it more, he went on. "You picked him up like he weighed nothing and…." He did this thing where he leaned forward a little and then angled his body to the side like he was showing me a stunted version of what I'd done.

Awesome.

Well, fuck me.

"He's about a hundred and fifty," I told him, feeling even nicer with this bonus on top of Peter's compliment. "I can still pick him up, and it doesn't bother me too much."

That wiped the smile off him, replacing it with a frown. "Because of the shoulder you're always pretending doesn't hurt?"

What? It was my turn to frown. "I'm not always pretending like it doesn't hurt."

His face was a little too smug and knowing.

"I'm not."

One honey-colored eye squinted at me. "You sure?"

I scoffed. "Yeah, maybe sometimes, but not all the time. And it doesn't bother me as much as it used to since I don't use it the way I did before. Thank you." I wasn't over here watching how he ran to see if his Achilles was as good as it used to be, was I?

Which reminded me I hadn't once asked him how it was doing. He didn't seem to favor it at all, but you never knew. I'd known players with genuinely fucked-up knees—knees they could barely stand on—who still competed, adjusting their fights to not leave themselves too defenseless by staying on their feet.

"Sure," he agreed way too fucking easily, still looking smug, but his eyes were curious. "Been like that for a bit, hasn't it?"

So he had noticed. Before. "I guess we never did talk about that?" I asked him, earning a shake of his head. "But yeah, my shoulder has been shot for a long time. One more injury and I might never be able to lift my arm up over my head, is what the doctors said the last time." It still hurt to say that sentence out loud. Less, but the ache was still there. "It's why I don't do judo anymore."

Jonah froze, the lines across his forehead deepening again. "Not at all?"

I shook my head.

His already soft voice got even quieter. "Why?"

"I've had five surgeries on just one of my shoulders. Each time they said I was done, and I didn't listen or give a shit. But now I've got someone who needs me, and I'm not going to risk doing something irreparable to it anymore." I shot him a smile that was still tighter than I would have wanted. I was okay with my decision. Mostly. I had gotten used to the idea. It wasn't like I hadn't known the day would come eventually.

I just hadn't known it would be so soon. Judo was brutal on a person's body. At the international level, everything was harder. It required more power, more strength, and at some point, your body just couldn't handle taking the beating or even inflicting it. We all wanted to win, and that meant doing what you had to do to ensure you were the winner.

But...

Well, it still sucked. Eighteen years were gone.

But my life wasn't over.

"It was my choice, and I would make the same one if I had

to," I told him honestly. It hadn't been easy, but it had been right. That was fucking life sometimes, wasn't it?

He watched me with those honey-colored eyes and nodded, but I could see the tightness at his jaw. It made me wonder if he thought he had lost everything, but he hadn't actually. He just hadn't known it from the start.

I'd had my dream ended too, and maybe I had been in the literal dumps, but here I was. These people I loved wouldn't let me mourn and wade in my heartbreak and pity for too long. They would never let me forget what really mattered.

When life throws bad shit at you, you dodge it and throw whatever you can right back.

At least that was how Grandpa Gus had tried to raise me.

"Why? You want me to show you how to do the same so you can start doing that to other players if they tackle you too hard?"

That got me one of those deep laughs that made his face light up even more than his smiles did. "That wouldn't be a bad idea." He grinned. "Could you do it to me?"

I felt my eyebrows go up, felt my brain tell the rest of me to go back into the office. To leave right now and quit playing around. We weren't enemies, but we weren't friends either.

We were a team. In a way. Because a team worked toward a greater good, and our greater good was eighteen pounds and six ounces.

My subconscious tried to remind me I'd never really been a big fan of team sports. I didn't like the idea of leaving my future in the hands of someone else who might not give as much of a fuck as I did. It's why I'd been a good swimmer, a pretty good gymnast, and I hadn't been a big fan of cross-country running, but I'd been all right at that too. The one and only time Grandpa had enrolled me in a season of basketball when I'd been ten, I'd been asked to leave the team because I hadn't been a good team player.

And yet knowing all that…

I ignored those instincts that asked me to walk away. "You?" I asked him, to be sure he was suggesting what I thought he was suggesting.

Jonah dipped his chin.

I knew what the answer was going to be, but I didn't want to kill his sketchy dreams so quickly. "How much do you think you weigh right now?"

"One-hundred and thirteen kilos, usually. Might be a bit more or a bit less," he answered.

Yeah, that settled it. "That's going to be a negative then. Five years ago, I would have tried, but even then I could only lift Mount Denali, not"—I waved my hand toward his body —"Everest. I *could* get you on the ground without throwing you though."

For once, I didn't like his laugh.

"You don't think I can?"

Those cheeks tipped up, and he had the nerve to tip his head to the side like he was trying to be adorable. "I was joking when I asked, I mean."

I slipped out of my flip-flops and walked over to him.

"I'm sure you could easily have taken a Denali before your last surgery..." He trailed off, watching me too carefully. "I'm an Everest though, eh? Sweet as."

I ignored his NZ slang that I had started getting the hang of and grinned, actually feeling a little excited. "Are you going to be upset if you get the breath knocked out of you?"

He tipped his head to the other side a little, narrowing those honey-colored eyes. "No…?"

"Are you sure?"

Jonah's face got warily cheerful again. "Lenny, love, I've been getting tackled since I was—"

All right. He'd said it.

I stopped directly in front of him, reached out as quickly as I could, grabbed him by the collar and swept his legs out from under him.

He fell like a beautiful, ancient Redwood tree. The sound of him hitting the turf *loud*. I mean, literally, it was a boom. The floor wasn't padded and wasn't built to cushion falling bodies.

I pressed my lips together as I looked down at him slightly, half expecting him to be pissed, maybe a little shocked even if he *was* used to being tackled by men bigger than me. But all I got were wide, shocked eyes. He sucked in a breath and then gasped.

Maybe that hadn't been my best idea ever. He was worth a lot of money when he was healthy. Shit.

"Jonah, I'm sorry—"

This fool fucking burst out laughing. "Bloody hell, Lenny, how'd you do that?"

I'd had a lot of guys react in different ways to getting thrown around, but never, ever had one of them fucking *laughed*. Never. Not even close.

And as Jonah cracked up from his spot on the floor, knees up, feet flat on the floor, arms loose, looking shocked… something inside of me kind of… cracked.

More than it already had, it felt, and I didn't know what the hell to do with it.

"You aren't the first big guy I've foot-swept before," I answered him, smiling back and not able to help it, or regret it either. "But you're probably the heaviest, and now everything from my knee down is probably going to hurt because I'm a show-off, so don't get butthurt I got you."

This idiot just went on laughing.

And I couldn't help but keep smiling down at him.

The rest of my life.

I thrust my hand out at him, and he met mine halfway, wrapping those fingers around me, before I kind-of sort-of helped heft him back onto his feet, even though his own muscles did most of the job.

I huffed, practically sitting down on the ground to get enough leverage. "If we were hiking in the woods and you broke a leg, you would die. You'd be left there, for real," I joked, knowing damn well I shouldn't but unable to stop when I was feeling in this good of a mood.

"You wouldn't try to help me hike out?" He chuckled as he slipped his thumbs into the waistband of his shorts and adjusted them.

"So the bear could get us both when it smells your blood and comes looking for you? I don't think so."

Another big, booming laugh came out of him, and that shit went straight to my spine. "I thought it was sharks that will hunt down something bleeding."

I could feel the corner of my mouth pull up in a smirk. "Well then, you better hope we aren't on a boat in the ocean together if you start bleeding, because I wouldn't be able to lift you back on the boat either."

"In that case, we'll make sure Mo is around since you have all these plans to let me die if things get tough. I couldn't see there being anything the two of you couldn't do together if she's anything like you."

I hated him. I really did. And myself, because I had no business joking around with him, but I couldn't regret it too much either. Damn it.

"I'm not scared of *trying* to pull you in, but I've torn both rotator cuffs. You should just know what to expect. It's not my fault you're heavy." I tried not to smirk but failed. "But if it makes you feel any better, we'll be able to pull you back into the imaginary boat between the two of us," I joked, unable to stop myself.

"Good thing I'm a great swimmer," he countered playfully. "I'll make sure to keep my fitness up so you and Mo don't have to worry if you're the ones bleeding in the water."

Me and Mo.

Well, I'd hope he'd try to save the mother of his kid. At least for that reason alone. That's why he was still here, after all, wasn't it? Because of her?

Something that wasn't exactly a knot tried to form in my throat, and all I could do was manage a half-assed smile that had his grin melting into a long, loaded look.

I was worthy of love. I *was* loved. Just because he hadn't....

I was fine. Great. We could be friendly. It would be easier if we were.

Jonah was watching me, and his Adam's apple bobbed before he said, "Have lunch with me, Lenny."

What? "I'm not going to see Mo for lunch today. Grandpa Gus is taking her to the Children's Museum."

Those honey-colored eyes stayed steady on my face. "I know. I heard him last night," he said just as the door to the building swung open. "We can just talk about Mo if that's what it takes to get you to come."

It was second nature to glance over and see who was coming in, but as soon as my brain processed the face, a sigh built up in my chest.

It was a guy I'd kicked out of the gym two months ago.

"Hold on a second," I told Jonah while focusing in on the man-child, who had apparently immediately spotted me too based on the way his feet seemed to stutter as he walked in. "One sec," I said again, before turning to head a few feet closer to the door. I was already shaking my head at him. "No, man."

Shawn's nostrils flared. "Listen, Lenny—"

"Nope," I cut him off. "Turn around and walk back out. It's not happening. You've got another three and a half months before you can come back." I had *specifically* told him the exact date he could rejoin the gym when I'd had to suspend him for repeatedly elbowing another fighter in the spine while they'd been sparring, even after Peter had told him to stop.

The guy, who hadn't even been a member of Maio House for that long in the first place, dropped his head back, and I watched his hand tighten around the strap of the bag he had over his shoulder. "Come on—"

I wasn't going to waste either of our times by letting him

spout off some bullshit he thought would let him get away with being here. Even if it was really good bullshit, it wasn't going to happen. "No."

"It's been almost *three months*, Lenny. Give me a break."

I shrugged. "It's been two months and sixteen days. You should have thought about that before you broke the rules." I knew better than to say I was sorry. I was sorry he was missing out on valuable training, but no one had told him to do something stupid over and over again.

Actions had consequences. Everyone knew that, and if they didn't, they should.

"I regret what I did."

So did I.

When I didn't respond, he managed to get out, "Can I *please* come back?"

"No."

He dropped his head back again. "I said please."

I couldn't even feel that much remorse in me as I replied, "And I said not yet. You've got three months and fourteen days to go."

"Oh, come on!"

Was he raising his voice at me? My silence was his response, and it wasn't what he was looking for. I could wait him out.

He definitely did raise his voice then. "Are you *fucking serious?* I've got a fight in three weeks. This is bullshit!"

I raised my eyebrows at him because I knew he wasn't fucking talking to me like that. "I get that you're pissed off," I told him calmly, keeping my voice *just* level *just* barely, "but don't talk to me like that." Not if he wanted to keep all his teeth in his mouth.

"This is bullshit!"

Was it? Just as I opened my mouth to tell him to calm down, a big figure stepped right next to me and said in a voice I had never heard out of him before, "Mate, you keep raising your voice, and we're going to have a problem."

It was like he hadn't seen him behind me or something, because the moment Shawn's eyes flicked behind me to find who was speaking, he took a step backward. And that was the last thing I noticed then because I was too busy looking over my shoulder as well.

Jonah was staring straight through this moron with these intense eyes that I had only seen once or twice in my life, which said a lot because of who I had grown up around. What I had grown up around.

But Jonah's expression was something else completely. Maybe because he was usually so easygoing and self-contained. I had seen him, from a distance, stare down opposing players during their games—matches, tests, whatever they called it—but this one....

I had to look away from him. I didn't miss the way Shawn shuffled back another step before flushing red and basically mumbling, "Please, Lenny. I said I was sorry. I won't use my elbows on anyone again."

I didn't need to look over to feel the intensity radiating from the man at my side, and it took a whole lot of self-control not to glance at Jonah but instead focus on this other imbecile. "Three and a half months and don't ever step up to me like that again or use that tone of voice. You were warned, Shawn. You were told to stop, and you didn't. So it's three months and fourteen days. Are we clear?"

A big forearm brushed my arm, and I could hear Jonah breathing steadily.

Shawn gritted his teeth together, shook his head, and then he turned around and walked back out the way he'd come.

I glanced back at the Not Really a Fucker without trying to move my head so I wouldn't get caught. I didn't trust my facial muscles then. I didn't trust myself, period, honestly.

Jonah was too busy watching Shawn leave to notice what I was doing. Those crazy focused eyes followed him until the door slammed shut. Only then did he speak again. "Is there anyone else here who talks to you like that?"

I was too busy taking in his mean-ass expression to reply with more than, "No."

Jonah lowered his gaze, eyebrows still knit together; that mouth of his hard, eyes slightly narrowed, and I really hoped more than anything that my own eyes didn't widen at the sight of his pissed-off face. But when his mean face immediately fell off—and I didn't feel disappointed by it, not a lot anyway—those features turned into the ones I was familiar with. Normal, good Jonah. The one who had turned pink a few days ago when I called penises sad bananas.

Normal Jonah looked at me with only a hint of tightness at his jaw. "I didn't mean to use that tone around you."

I blinked up at him, still hearing the voice he'd used in my head. "Where did that come from?" I asked slowly, hoping that didn't sound anything close to dreamy. Because I wasn't... feeling that way. I wasn't feeling any kind of way. Surprised. Impressed a little. That was it.

Okay, maybe even a little pleased he had stepped up beside me. *Maybe*. A little.

I couldn't remember the last time anyone had done that. Now that I thought about it, I wasn't sure anyone ever had. If I needed someone or something, I knew they were there. And I could sure as hell defend myself.

Huh.

The puff of a laugh out of him almost erased the memory of Mr. Deep-Voice a moment ago. "From footy." His right dimple popped. "I didn't like the look or the sound of him. He had no right to talk to you like that. You sure you don't deal with arse-holes like that regularly?"

I wished he didn't suddenly sound so concerned, especially when that tone he'd used and that face he'd made were still so fresh in my head. "Not often. Every once in a while."

He didn't exactly look like he believed me.

But I still couldn't help but eye him as my bitch-ass ovaries decided to stretch out right then and remind me they were there. Awake. Listening. Paying way too much attention.

Ah, fuck it.

"I don't know how to tell you this without it coming out wrong...."

"All right...." He trailed off too, beginning to give me a smile that seemed nervous and wary and curious at the same time. "Should I be worried?"

I shook my head, still fucking eyeballing his face, seeing the cheeks slowly, slowly turning pink on their own. "Here I'd been thinking this whole time that you were so nice and sweet and too good to be true, and now you just used that I'm-gonna-kill-you voice, and you were looking at him like you might hurt him, and...." Honest to God, I sighed as his eyebrows went up and that mouth tipped up a little higher in reaction. "You've got a little bit of an alpha thing going on in that polite-ass body, buster."

His face *definitely* went pink then, but his voice remained playful. "Only a little?"

"Is there more in there? Because I don't think I'm ready for more anytime soon. I'm still in shock." I rocked back on my heels, peering at him and all that tan skin and white scars and sun lines and that blushing fucking face that shouldn't have belonged on that body.

His palm went up to scrub at the cheek that was already beginning to get bristly this early in the morning, and I could barely hear him as he coughed, sounding almost fucking shy or maybe embarrassed, "I'd like to think so."

I snickered and couldn't help but smile at Blushing Pants. "I think I'm going to have to start watching your rugby games again if that's when Jonah with a capital J comes out."

That palm went over his face again as he tipped it back, and I could see him press his lips together. I was pretty sure I heard him snort before replying, "I suppose you should. I don't want you thinking I'm Jonah with a small j all the time."

I laughed.

A sense of longing hit me, reminding me of the friendship we had built up so quickly. The friendship that had turned into something more just as quickly. I had liked this man. I had liked him a lot.

This was the asshole I had missed. The one who had given me a reason to be so pissed off when he'd left. I had missed that guy.

"I like Jonah with a little j too," I told him honestly, letting that easiness of how well we got along fill my heart and remind me yet again that I had done the right thing letting him be here. "I knew there was a reason you're the one I had a baby with, Jonah with a capital J." And then I took a step back, because it was easy being friends with him, but I didn't need to confuse the rest of me by feeling things that could change that. "Thank you for scaring him. You're the first person to stand up for me like that in about twenty years. It was nice, and I appreciate it."

He blinked and the very tall man, who I had mistakenly thought was all teddy bear but really had some honey badger DNA in him apparently, smiled at me with that gentle, sweet smile that I really did like a little too much. More than the serial killer one, if I had to pick. "Anything for you, Len."

And there he went.

I took another step back and didn't totally have to force my next smile. What was the last thing he'd said? About having lunch? "I need to go get Peter some water. Come get me if you want to eat later... if you still want to have lunch with me without Mo around. I brought my food, but it'll be good tomorrow."

He nodded, and I was only a few feet away when he called out, "I wasn't inviting you to eat to see Mo, Len."

I fought a smile as I went to the break room and filled up a bottle of water before heading back to the cage. Sure enough, by the time I was back at Peter's side, he was the first one to turn very slowly to look at me, and ask, way too casually, "Everything okay with Shawn?"

I unscrewed the lid, not looking at him. "Yeah."

Peter went "hmm."

Then I went "hmm."

And he asked, "Did your friend say something to him?"

My friend.

I took a sip and held the bottle toward him. He took it. "Yeah, he did. It almost made me feel like a lady or something."

Peter smiled with the bottle against his lips.

I couldn't stop myself from glancing over my shoulder to find Jonah carrying two more forty-five-pound weights across the part of the floor he was on. I could see the pop of his triceps from all the way over here. He slowly lowered the weights to the ground and, when he stood back up again, readjusted the band of his shorts. Then he moved toward a corner and picked up what looked like a mini-notebook and started writing something down in it.

I'd bet he was just keeping track of his reps so he had something to compare to next time. He tapped the end of it against his forehead for a moment before jotting something else down in it.

I went up to my tiptoes and pressed my lips together for a second. "I like him more than I should, Peter. I don't like it."

Peter, though, didn't respond.

"He laughed when I swept him. Can you believe that?"

This man I knew as equal parts my father and friend was watching me carefully, thinking, and he took his time giving me a slow smile at the same time he set his hand on my shoulder. "He's a good person, Len, but he has no idea what he's gotten himself into."

I smiled.

Peter bumped his elbow against mine. I did it right back to him.

"Would you mind getting my jacket from the office?" he asked.

I nodded, kicked off my flip-flops *again* and jogged across the mats to my office. Flicking on the lights, I headed toward the coat rack where seven different coats in different sizes hung. Six medium-sized jackets and sweaters, and one tiny baby jacket. I grabbed a hoodie from the top hook and turned to my desk. I dropped the mail I was still holding on top of it and, for some reason, pulled my phone out of my pocket just to check if I'd gotten something.

There were four texts, but when I went to my messages it instantly took me to the last messages I'd been replying to. Grandpa Gus's.

Two of the four were from him, which were pictures of Mo at the zoo with drool all over her face and a big smile too. According to his messages, the day was so nice, he'd changed his mind about going to the museum. I saved those to my gallery and texted him back.

Me: Tell her I love her.

Then I went back to my messages and was torn between being annoyed and… something else.

I went with opening the annoying one first.

It was from Noah.

Noah: Call me when you get a chance.

Like that was going to fucking happen.

With that over, I opened up the next message.

I read it, read it again, typed a response, and then I grabbed my damn stress ball from the top drawer and walked back out.

CHAPTER 13

2:23 p.m

You're a real fuck head.

GOD, I FUCKING HATED PEOPLE, I THOUGHT AN HOUR LATER AS I rewound the video footage for the camera facing the front desk.

I'd forgotten that Grandpa and I had compromised with the security cameras in the main building. He'd wanted the bare minimum our insurance required, and I'd wanted one in every corner and multiple dome cameras every ten feet, and we'd settled for somewhere in the middle. Luckily, *luckily*, there had been cameras aimed in the right places for what I was looking for.

And what I was looking for was the dickwad who had stolen Bianca's cell phone. Literally, from what I understood, they reached over the front desk counter while she'd been busy and plucked it from where she had left it beside the keyboard while she'd helped another member who had dropped her purse and gotten her stuff strewn all over the floor.

So now I was going through the footage before we called the cops and reported the incident.

Once we figured out who'd done it, it would save time.

I wasn't complaining too much. She'd called about thirty minutes after I'd gotten the text message that had forced me to squeeze my stress ball for a solid three minutes.

I grabbed my glass water bottle and chugged down half of it before focusing back on the footage. I rewound three minutes further back than originally and hit play.

I was in the middle of switching from one camera to another when there was a knock on the door, and I hit pause just as I called out "What?" like a fucking asshole as I rubbed at a spot between my eyebrows.

There was a pause and then, "It's Jonah," the deep voice answered.

Oh.

I got up, flipped the lock, and cracked it open, finding the familiar face standing right there. I grabbed him by his sweat-shirt, yanked him in, and peeked back out through the crack.

Kicking the door closed, I flipped the lock and turned around to face the man standing literally inches away, a surprised but amused expression on his face. He was holding an orange smoothie in one hand. "Is there something I should worry about?"

"No." I brushed his hip as I wedged myself by him and sat back down in the chair. "I don't want anyone else to see me in here. I told Bianca she could tell you and Peter where I was, but that was it."

"What are you up to in here? Spy work on the side?" He moved to my elbow, bending over at the hips to peek at the computer screen. He set the smoothie on the surface of the desk and nudged it toward me. "For you."

I looked at him. "For me?"

Jonah nodded.

Huh.

I gave him a little smile and pulled it toward me, taking a sip. It was my favorite, Orange Sunshine. "Thanks."

He just smiled.

I eyed him one more time then hit play. "Someone stole Bianca's cell—that's the girl at the front desk, the one who signed you up. I'm looking through the footage right now to find out who I'm going to have to kill for being an asshole."

One day, years from then, I'd look back and think about how easily he'd replied with, "Oh, is that what you're going to do?"

"Uh-huh," I replied, staring at the screen. "Ooh, wait, wait, wait…."

I skipped forward a few seconds and squinted, watching a figure hovering by the desk before Bianca had even moved away from it. Then it happened, she ran around it, disappearing from the view of the camera I was watching on and into the view of the one I'd seen right before. I waited, four seconds went by, five, six, seven—

Warm breath hit my ear, and I held my breath as I glanced out of the corner of my eye to find Jonah's face directly next to mine, his cheek moving into place *right there….*

Did his skin have to be so clear? I could tell that he'd shaved that morning, but hair had already started growing back in with a vengeance, the stubble thick and full. His lips were slightly parted.

I flicked my gaze back to the screen.

I kept my eyes on it and then leaned back two seconds later and shook my head.

"Bingo, ho," I whispered to myself as I wrote down the shirt and hair color of the asshole. Not that I totally needed it, I had a clear view of his face. Dumbass.

Now all I needed to do was fast forward through the camera facing the doors and find out when he walked through so I could time it with when he scanned his card. Or better yet, it might be faster to just show Bianca the footage and see if she recognized him off the top of her head. Yeah, that would be better. Might as well try that first. I took a screenshot of the dumbass's face and couldn't help but cackle to myself. *Busted.*

The snort beside my ear had me glancing over to find Jonah with a big dumb grin on his face.

"What?"

His big dumb grin got even bigger. "I like it when you laugh evilly to yourself."

I blinked. Well, that wasn't anywhere near what I'd expected, and I couldn't stop the way my cheek went up in a half-grin. Grandpa Gus had told me the same thing more than once before.

"What are you going to do now?"

I spun the chair around to face him fully. "I'm going to show her his picture and see if she recognizes him. If she doesn't, I'll look through more footage and figure out what his name is before I call the cops."

"You're going to call the police?"

I nodded. "Yeah. Cell phones are expensive, and it wasn't an accident. Unless Bianca decides she doesn't want me to, but I hope she does." I sighed. "Are you done for the morning?"

"I am," he answered. "I wanted to bring you a snack and see if you wanted to have lunch."

That wasn't disappointment I felt. Jonah was just here for Mo, I reminded myself. That was all that mattered. Plus, he'd brought me a smoothie. "I need to stay here and deal with this."

"Dinner then?"

Alone? Or… with Mo? Uh….

"Actually, I have something I need to do tonight."

His eyes bounced from one of mine to the other, mouth going flat and pressed. "Oh."

"I was thinking about taking Mo with me too, sorry."

Well, that instantly changed his expression. He even let out an exhale I didn't totally get what to think of. All he said was another "Oh."

For the first time, I thought about how he was here, alone, with no one else. As far as I knew, he woke up early, had breakfast, squeezed in a long run of cardio, had a second breakfast.

Then he went to the gym and trained for three or four hours, had lunch, played patty cake at his hotel for hours and then came over every night. I hadn't seen him even talk to another person other than my family, except for his weird little whispering sessions I forced him into.

What was he going to do tonight by himself?

And why did I care and feel guilty?

And why the hell did I invite him? "Do you want… to come with us?"

The fact he instantly said "Sure" was a spear straight into my stupid-ass heart.

"It isn't anything fun," I warned him, watching that handsome face.

This big, beautiful man ticked his head to the side. "It's all good. I'm not particular about what we do." One of his dimples popped. "I'd do anything with you."

That fucking spear went in just a little deeper.

And I left it there as I eyed him. "It's my old sensei's sixtieth birthday today, and they're throwing him a little party thing. He asked if I could come by and help with the white belts—today it's the little kids—before." Something I wasn't going to consider to be anxiety poked at my stomach for a second as I thought about the request again. And how I couldn't say no.

"All right," he agreed just as easily.

I pasted a smile on my face. "Okay. You'd just have to sit there with Mo. It shouldn't take more than an hour or two. The class is an hour long, and his cake is right after that. We don't have to stay long."

Yeah, that wasn't nerves or dread I was feeling.

That was a lie. It was. I forced another smile on my face, hoping he couldn't see through it.

If he did or he didn't, Jonah didn't comment on it. He just said, "Whatever you need."

CHAPTER 14

6:21 a.m

> You are a fuck face,
> but I really do need to
> speak with you.
> I don't need anything from you
> but that. Promise.

"LENNY, HAVE YOU SEEN MY YELLOW—WHERE ARE YOU GOING?"

I paused for a second in the middle of tying my tennis shoes before finishing the knot and saying over my shoulder, "It's Sensei Kenji's birthday, and he asked me to come by tonight and help with the white belts." I switched feet and started tying the other shoe. "And I washed your Hawaiian print shirt yesterday. I hung it on the rack in the laundry room so it wouldn't wrinkle."

Grandpa Gus didn't let me down as he leaned against the doorway and watched me tie my other shoe. "What? I didn't get an invitation."

"Maybe because you called him a lazy knucklehead the last time you were in a room together?" I stood up and flashed him a grin. "Or because you gave him a bad review on Google just to be petty after I quit?"

He scrunched up his nose, but his mouth stretched into a flat line before becoming a smile. "He is a knucklehead, and he deserved that review."

I shook my head. "Come with us if you want. It's not like not being invited has ever stopped you before."

"I've got better things to do."

"I'm taking Jonah and Mo with me."

That got me a blink. "Emmett is going with you?"

I knew I shouldn't egg him on by groaning, but I did anyway. I hoped this never got old. "Would you quit calling him the wrong name?" I definitely shouldn't have laughed either, but apparently, I was going to be that mom one day who laughed when her kids did bad things and then struggled to be serious. I really was.

And it didn't help that he laughed too.

What I didn't miss was that he didn't agree he was going to stop, and I knew better than to assume he would. At least until he was ready, and knowing him—and I did fucking know him —it wasn't going to be anytime soon. It was a good thing Jonah was patient.

"Yes, he's coming with me. We're going to eat dinner first and then head over."

What wasn't a good thing was how well my grandfather knew me, especially when the next question he asked was "Are you nervous?"

I totally knew snorting was the worst physical reaction I could have, but I did it anyway. Because we both knew I was… not necessarily nervous, but maybe something close to it. Very close to it.

He slid me a look that was way too knowing. "You know you don't have anything to worry about, demon child. It's past time you went, and you know it."

I did know it, but that didn't make it any easier to collect my things and kid, and head over to pick up Jonah.

~

JONAH HAD ONLY BEEN IN THE PASSENGER SEAT FOR MAYBE FIVE minutes when I asked, "Are you sure you don't mind coming?"

"Yeh. I'm sure," he agreed, fingertips bouncing on his thigh. "I've been looking forward to seeing you in action."

In action. With the little kids. At the club I had spent so much of my life at.

Before I'd told them bye and never gone back.

There were very few things I regretted, but how I'd handled leaving was one of them.

"About that—" I started to say before I forced my mouth closed. The smell came out of fucking nowhere, stealing the words out of my mouth.

Pungent. Rabid. *Fucking disgusting.*

What the *fuck?*

I coughed and looked to my right at the man who hadn't moved an inch and was still looking out the window with a tight jaw. Even the veins along his forearms were popping more than usual, but I let that thought go in one ear and right back out the other. I had more pressing matters. "Jonah, please tell me you pooted."

He was still looking out the windshield when he answered. "Are you asking if I passed gas?"

I took another tentative sniff and coughed, shooting his profile a horrified face at the fucking awful smell. What was wrong with him? What the hell had he eaten for dinner? "Yes," I gasped. Good God, I rolled down the window and leaned over to the side like that would make the smell any better.

It didn't.

"Is there something dying in you?" I wheezed, trying to hold my breath in as much as possible and failing. "I don't care if you do, but roll down the window if there's some Agent Orange type shit coming out of you. Whoa. God. I can taste it."

That had him glancing over at me, a remote expression on his face that I might have sucked up in any other circumstances. His forehead furrowed, his mouth a line as his nostrils flared. "It wasn't me. I didn't do anything," he defended himself. "I can't smell a thing."

How could he not smell that?

I coughed and sucked in the exhaust smell from the surrounding cars instead of the goddamn bomb that had gone off in the car. "It wasn't me."

Jonah clearly tried to take a whiff, but all he did was shake his head. "No, Lenny, I don't smell anything."

I slid him another horrified glance, but that damn smell didn't go *anywhere.*

And then it hit me.

Like a cold finger along my spine, the knowledge—and the heavy feeling of dread—ran down me.

Fuck.

I glanced in the rearview mirror as I got to a stoplight and looked at the car seat holding a quiet little body I couldn't see.

"Oh no," I whispered more to myself than Jonah, my mind already racing with what needed to be done.

"What's happened?" he asked, finally sounding worried. "Was it you?"

"No." I eyed the car seat warily. "Mo just shit herself."

He took another sniff, and I could see him shake his head. "I don't smell anything."

I sucked in another little breath through the opened window and rushed out, "Your septum's deviated then because she shit herself." Which meant I needed to pull over because there was no way I was going to survive the thirty-minute drive, and neither was my kid if she had a loaded diaper.

Because her diapers were one thing when she pooped herself, but I knew that damn smell when it got that bad. I guess my brain had just blocked it out in a sense of self-preservation from the last time she'd done the same thing. How the hell could I ever forget retching as I cleaned her butt from how awful it had smelled?

Worse: I knew exactly what color was going to be in her diaper.

What the fuck had Grandpa fed her? Fucking *fuck.*

I accidentally sucked in a breath and gagged.

How the *hell* did something so small smell so goddamn *awful?*

I retched and heard Jonah laugh like an asshole. "I can't smell a thing."

I held my breath as I turned the wheel into the first parking lot on the right-hand side, pulling into a small strip mall with a pharmacy and gas station. I barely managed to throw the door open, leaving the car running when I sucked in another big breath through my mouth. Where the hell was a respirator when I needed one?

"Are you all right?" my girl's dad asked a moment before a hand landed on my upper back and he slapped me lightly three times, sounding totally back to himself, thankfully, even though I wasn't worried about that anymore.

"Mm-hmm," I groaned, shaking my head and trying to clear my nostrils.

What had to be his hand stroked up and down the center of my back slowly. "All right, take a breath. I'll see what's going on, yeah?"

Did he expect me to plead with him not to?

And *what the fuck was going on with his nose that he couldn't smell death in the air?*

When he opened the door, I took a step away and watched as he gave me a brave little smile before ducking inside the back seat.

I held my breath as I watched through the window as he unbuckled Mo from her seat, whispering who the hell knew what to her—probably how smart she was and how she was never going to need a man other than her daddy—and still Jonah didn't flinch or slow down as those big fingers worked at her straps. Those big hands then went under her armpits, and he was talking away at her, making happy faces like that wasn't radiation in the air as he lifted her up.

And I sucked in another breath, planning on holding it and letting this boss handle Poopy Pants since he had no olfactory senses. How many times exactly had he had his nose broken? Fuck.

I watched as Jonah took a step back and began to straighten, bringing a wide-eyed squirming and babbling Mo to that wide chest. "I don't know what you—"

His mouth shut. Those lips of his pressed down into a firm line that made the corners of it go white. He shot up to a complete standing position, and I watched his own honey-colored eyes go wide.

His lips parted, and then they parted some more until they were open half an inch.

Mostly, there was no way to miss the way he gulped and asked very, very cautiously, "Lenny?"

"Yeah?"

His Adam's apple bobbed as his arms began to extend outward, moving Mo slowly away from him as he asked in the most hesitant voice he'd yet to use with me, "What is that?"

I knew it! "I told you she smelled!"

He shook his head quickly, blinking rapidly all of a sudden. "No." Those big feet moved so that his whole body did too in a counterclockwise motion, stopping only when Mo's back was facing me.

My eyes went wide and my own mouth parted before I managed to whisper, "Oh fuck."

His voice was *just* slightly higher than normal. "Oh fuck what?"

One of my feet slid back on the concrete. "Oh dear God."

Mo's body went two inches higher, two inches farther away from her dad; his voice even sharper than a second ago as he asked, "Oh dear God what?"

I blew out my cheeks, slapped my hand over my mouth, and gagged. It was honestly a fucking miracle I didn't throw up, and I knew it. I could handle feet on my face. I could handle touching them. Sweaty armpits on my cheek or forehead were nothing. Blood? No big deal. Pee? Whatever.

But....

Jonah held her even higher up and asked in a voice that was definitely fucking higher, *"What is on her back?"*

I gagged again.

"What is on her back?" he demanded in that Jonah with a capital J voice.

I pinched my nose, closed my eyes, and shook my head, hoping, fucking willing myself not to actually fucking throw up... and not totally sure I could pull it off when my stomach did a damn somersault.

"Lenny, *what is on her back?"* he asked breathlessly, holding his daughter—our daughter—about as far away from his body as he could get. *"Why is her back wet? What is all over my fingers?"*

The only thing I could do was press my eyes closed, shake my head, and dry heave with a balled-up hand over my mouth.

"Why is her back so warm?" Jonah gasped. *"What am I touching?"*

Shit.

Literally.

"Lenny."

My hand was still over my mouth when I whispered one word and one word only.

"Diarrhea."

The breath he let out was a whisper. "Tell me it doesn't go all the way up to her neck."

I couldn't lie.

So I didn't say a word.

It went all the way up to her neck.

And into her hair.

From what I could see, the poop went all the way closer to her tiny, little ears.

It was slow motion as Jonah gulped, and those hands holding that baby started raising her even higher… and higher… and higher… until her butt was straight over his head and he was looking up at that pants, onesie, and diaper-covered bottom… eyes widening by the millisecond as the rest of his face joined together to make a horrified expression. I could only guess he wanted to confirm with his own eyes what was going on.

And that was when it happened.

When that butt was up high… two or three feet over his head… eyes up and wide… mouth open too in a frozen mask of terror…

And at least for me, I'd remember that shit—literally—for the rest of my life.

I'd remember something that looked like a teaspoon of mustard-colored blob fall like a gruesome, mutated drop of oatmeal rain… on Jonah's fucking cheek.

We both gasped at the same time.

Mo laughed a second before she said, "Ba, da!"

The moment hung in the air in the time it took me to let my mouth drop totally wide open in shock and disbelief.

"Lenny, what was that?" Jonah whispered.

HOLY FUCK.

"What just fell on my face?"

HOLY SHIT.

"What is that smell?"

I took a step back.

"Why are you stepping away? What fell on my face? What is that smell?" he demanded, sounding so fucking desperate. Jonah dry heaved as he lowered his arms, Mo kicking her legs, and he

shook his head. *"Please tell me that was a bird dropping on my face,"* he whispered.

I took a half step back, clutching my fingers to my chest... and I lied. "It was a bird dropping," I whispered too.

My girl was held parallel to the ground again, giving me a clear, clear view of a horrified handsome face... with a clump of Mo poop on a cheek.

On Jonah's cheek.

I managed to keep my lips pressed together for about two seconds before I lost it.

I bent over and burst out fucking laughing as Jonah thrust her away from him as far as possible again... and gagged.

"ARE YOU STILL MAD AT ME?" I ASKED AN HOUR AND A HALF LATER as I drove us down the street after... everything.

Jonah's laugh was more of a puff when he answered with, "No, love. I was never mad."

I bit the inside of my cheek and forced myself to keep my eyes straight on the road. "You weren't mad when I was crying laughing then?"

Because I'd been crying laughing a lot. Especially after Mo's poop had landed on his face. And while he'd been cleaning it off with a baby wipe afterward. And when he'd carried her into his hotel room, holding her away from his body as he let out a dry heave here and there.

I'd also been crying laughing when I'd wiped her off as best as I could with baby wipes, when I'd jumped into the shower with her, and again when I'd gone back down to the parking lot and found him arranging the newly cleaned car seat cover. I didn't even want to know how much it had to have cost him to get that thing washed and dried in record time while Mo and I had gotten cleaned up.

The whole fucking thing had been hilarious in a fucked-up way.

To give him credit, he'd only been serious at first.

But still.

He'd gotten shit on his face.

Dreams did come true sometimes.

That big body angled itself in the seat better, and I didn't need to look at him to know that he was more than likely making a face at me. "No."

I pressed my lips together for a second before asking, "Do your hands still smell?"

His groan made both of us laugh.

"How often does that happen?"

"Coming out of her diaper or onto the seat?" I snorted.

Jonah groaned again. "Forget I asked. I'd rather be surprised, I suppose."

That probably was the best choice, but I still couldn't help but snort again, the memory of the poop of his hands and all over her and her thighs and back so fresh.

It made my fucking month. I'd bet Grandpa Gus was going to ask if I'd gotten pictures of the incident.

I'd gotten her showered and dressed as fast as I could, but we'd lost all of the time I'd set aside for having dinner before heading over. He'd bought four sandwiches, two apples, and two bottles of water that we'd scarfed down in record time in the hotel lobby before leaving once more. Luckily, Mo had eaten right before we'd left my house and hadn't been too grumpy about her early bath and adventure.

An image of her crap hitting his face filled my head yet again.

Oh. That child, giving priceless memories to cherish for the rest of my life. I already wanted to start laughing.

"Welcome to fatherhood." I snickered as I finally turned the car onto the street that I had driven on, and been driven to, thousands of times.

Fucking fuck.

I had no reason to be nervous. I knew that. It wasn't like they were going to stone me or anything.

Maybe just boo. It wouldn't be the first I'd been booed.

I didn't glance at him as I pulled my car into the parking lot of the still-familiar strip mall and found a spot in the back. There were just as many cars as I remembered there being for this specific night. "We're here," I told him. But when I got a chance to take him in again, I had to pause.

"What's that face for?"

He was frowning. "Why were you gripping the steering wheel that hard?"

Why?

I opened and closed my hands, feeling the stiffness in them. All right. I guess I had been gripping the shit out of it. Taking a peek at Jonah's frown, I tried to think of an excuse to give him.

Nothing came to mind though but the truth.

I didn't want to admit it even to myself.

Fuck it.

"This is the first time I'm coming to my old club since I quit," I admitted.

Those beautiful bright eyes just slightly widened before he asked carefully, "Before Mo?"

I nodded.

That had his eyelids lowering into a slow, slow blink. "How long did you study here for?"

My finger wanted to scratch my nose, but I kept my hand on my lap... in a fist. I cleared my throat. "About twenty years."

His cute mouth opened in a small O.

Yeah, exactly. I blew out a breath. "I came to tell them in person I was retiring and just never came back." That sounded just as shitty out loud as it did in my head.

"They were upset with you?"

"No." I shook my head. "Not at all." Not even a little bit. When I'd dropped the news, they had been surprised—of course they had been surprised; it hadn't been a secret I'd claimed I was never going to have kids—but all the people who had known me had given me a hug and wished me the best.

Yet none of that had helped ease my guilt over leaving.

Or over staying away for so long when none of them had given me an actual reason to cut them out cold turkey.

Like a hypocrite, my conscious tried to say. Fuck. I rarely thought about it so that I wouldn't feel guilty. That thought had me almost squirming.

"What are you worried for then?" the man in the seat beside me asked.

I didn't want to answer that specific question, so I didn't. "Jonah," I said carefully. "Make me feel better. What's the worst thing you've ever done?"

The answer came out of his mouth like a missile, without hesitation, without a second thought. "Leaving you and not being brave enough to call you for almost two years."

I stopped breathing.

And then I swallowed those words down for later, needing to inspect them and the way he had that answer on his soul so readily accessible. I was honest, but not like that. Why'd he have to go and drop that on me right now, just like that with no warning or anything? Why the hell hadn't he thought about that some more?

Scratching at the corner of my eye, I tried again. "That's not what I meant. I meant more along the lines of borrowing your parents' car in the middle of the night and sneaking out."

"I never did that."

I had to keep from smiling. "Yeah, me neither. You haven't… stolen anything?"

He frowned and shook his head.

"Never?"

"No."

"Beat someone up?"

That got me another shake of his head and a frown. "The

older boys tried to beat me up," he clarified, reminding me of his comment about being short and skinny for so long.

It touched me, it still seriously touched me. And made me mad he'd been picked on. "Your brothers saved you?" I asked.

"My sisters." One of his cheeks hitched up. "A few times."

More like all the time, I bet, since he'd said he'd never beat anyone up. I loved that his sisters were the ones to save him too. I focused again. "Did you ever toilet paper someone's house? Thrown eggs at someone's car?"

No and no, with horrified looks each response.

I was fishing now. "Trespassed?"

That got him to tilt his head to the side. "I did jump into the neighbor's yard once or twice to get a ball when we'd toss it over the fence. But I let them know afterward."

Something that felt an awful lot like hot chocolate poured down the center of my chest. Tenderness, it was tenderness for this innocent, good soul. He had to be protected at all costs. He really did.

And I couldn't help but smile at him even though I tried my hardest to press my lips together and stop from doing it.

And then this idiot had to turn it up a notch by grinning at me. "What? Have you done those things?"

"I've never beat anyone up for fun or stolen anything," I explained, eyeing two cars that pulled into the lot and parked. Little kids in their gis climbed out, followed by a parent or two. They looked so excited. I had been the same way back then.

Actually, I had usually been that way.

Jonah's next question had me glancing back at him. "Lenny, which of those things you mentioned have you done? The toilet paper and eggs?"

I nodded. More than once. I didn't want to tell him how many times either if I didn't have to.

An eyebrow went up. "Trespassing?"

Okay, that question wasn't so bad. "Yes, but for good reasons."

His face said *tell me*, but it made me hesitate.

Should I?

One three-second-long glance at his face gave me my answer. "We're family now, right?" I got myself to ask, trying to ease into this.

The "yes" that came out of his mouth was as immediate as his "sure."

My chest ached for a second, and I hoped I didn't regret this. "I'm inducting you into the first circle of trust," I told him carefully.

"Okay...," the man I'd had a child with agreed, a little carefully.

His tone had me glancing up at him, and honestly, I felt a little annoyed that he wasn't immediately jumping for joy at being inducted even further into my good graces. "Never mind," I muttered quickly. "It's not that interesting of a story."

Lines crossed his forehead as he frowned. "I didn't say to kick me out of the circle two seconds after bringing me into it, did I?"

I pressed my lips together, processing that.

"You asked me if we were family, I agreed. Then you got this look in your eye and said something about a circle of trust, and I'm still over here struggling with you referring to us as family," he explained, still frowning. "Then, you looked like I kicked you, and that wasn't my intention when all I was doing was thinking that sounded nice."

His frown melted effortlessly into an unsure smile. "I know how strong that word is to you. It seemed like you kicked me right in the—" He motioned toward his waist. "—when you used it."

Oh.

And that was exactly what I said. "Oh." My shoulders dropped so suddenly I had no idea they had even been up in the first place. "I thought you didn't want to be part of the circle of trust."

The lines on his forehead got even deeper as he frowned and smiled at the same time. "Yeah, nah, that's not the case. You surprised me is all." His eyebrows went up. "Made my day, eh."

I held my breath for a second, keeping my cheeks from totally coming up, and it was a lot harder than I would have imagined. "I'm sorry for jumping to conclusions," I admitted.

That got me a blink of long, thick, black lashes. "You're sorry?"

"Yeah." What the fuck was he frowning for? "I know how to apologize when I'm wrong."

His face went blank way too fast. And I didn't like the way he blinked again either.

"I do," I insisted before smirking. "Quit being a pain in the ass."

One of those slow, deep laughs came out of him.

Whatever. "If you're willing to be in the first circle of trust—"

"Hold on a moment. How many of these circles are there?"

I had to think about the things he didn't know. The things I wasn't willing to tell him yet. There was only one big thing, but I couldn't exactly make it that obvious. "Three," I threw out randomly to throw him off because two didn't seem that impressive.

That must have been an answer he could live with because he nodded, so I kept going.

He was family, I reminded myself. Whether we wanted him to be or not. And he hadn't done anything to make me feel like he'd change his mind about being in that position.

"As a member of the first circle of trust, you're assuring me that you won't be calling the cops on me, right?"

To give him credit, he agreed immediately. "Not even if they paid me."

I tried not to smile but failed. Then I went for it. "My best friend's cousin broke into her house a few years ago, and he tore her place up, bad. I found out where he lived, and Grandpa Gus and I went and did the same thing to his shitty house," I told him with a grimace. "It's kind of a felony, so please don't tell anyone." He stared at me from across the darkened car for so long that I added without meaning to, "She's family. Someone had to do it."

His smile was small but bright.

"What? Do you think I'm a bad person?"

Jonah shook his head. "No. But you have me wondering how one goes about becoming your best friend. I could use that kind of loyalty in my life." He reached over and took my hand. "You do whatever you have to do for the people you love, eh?"

You do whatever you have to do for the people you love.

And that was why he'd forgotten about me so easily, I thought, and instantly sucked in a breath and tried to straighten.

But Jonah didn't let me.

His features went serious. "What did I say?" he barely managed to ask before he closed his eyes and shook his head. "Lenny." He reopened them, his face even more grave. "I never forgot about you."

It was my turn to shake my head. "No, it's fine—"

"It's not fine and don't tell me it is. I never forgot about you. I swear. Not a day went by that I didn't think about you."

My heart kicked up into a gallop even though I didn't want it to. I didn't want to have this conversation. Not ever, but especially not right in that moment.

"Listen to me, Len. I liked you heaps, *heaps,* do you hear me?" I could feel his gaze like a laser burning holes into the side of my face as I looked out the window. "I ruined this, and I know that, and I want to make it up to you. I'm trying to, slowly. But you have to know: I left because I was a fucking arsehole. I hated myself. Honest, hate for being such a damn fool and not avoiding that tackle. I didn't think anyone would understand, but I see now that you would have, and I'm sorry, love. I'm so damn sorry I left the way I did. If I could take anything back, it would be that. If I could make it up to you somehow, I would, but I know that I can't, and I still want to try anyway."

The fingers on my hand tightened, and Jonah edged over as much as he could in his seat. "I'm trying my best here, and I'll keep on trying my best, do you understand? I want you to get to know me again. I want you to be my friend again. I want to be more than that—"

"Jonah, stop." My voice was shaky, and I felt like my chest had been cracked open more than any time in the past.

"No." His forehead came to rest against the side of mine, and I didn't let myself close my eyes. I made myself keep them open and aimed out the windshield. "I came back here for you."

I couldn't help but roll my eyes and try to lean away… but he wouldn't let me. His hand curled over my neck, keeping me in place. "Why are you doing this?"

"What? Why am I telling you this?"

"Yeah," I told him, speaking around the knot that had taken up space in my throat. "You didn't come back for me."

His gaze didn't move off mine for a second. "No? You think I know so many people in Houston, Texas?"

I wanted to look away, I really did, but I didn't. I looked right into his eyes, and he did the same in return, this hurt, this… this… sense of how he'd just *left* me because he hadn't cared about me enough, set up shop right in the center of my damn heart, stealing the air from my lungs, the pride from my spine. "It was seventeen months, Jonah."

"Yeh, it was," he replied, hotly. "Seventeen months of me being miserable and then thinking of you and how much fun we'd had before I'd fucked up my life in one moment."

But he'd still *left*. For so long.

"I didn't cheat on you, is that what this is about?"

I didn't mean to hold my breath, but it happened. I didn't

want to do this, I knew I didn't want to, but... "It wouldn't have been cheating because we weren't together."

"We weren't together?" he taunted me in another whisper, that hand on my neck inching up to cup my jaw as I continued resisting looking in his direction. "Is that what you've been telling yourself? From the second we met, we were only apart when I had to train or I was gone with the team, or when you had to coach. We slept in the same bed together more than we did apart after those first two weeks," he told me, like I hadn't been there. Like I didn't *know*.

How could I forget? And when I went to suck in a breath, it was harder than normal. So much fucking harder.

"I still sleep on the left side of the bed even without you, Lenny."

Some primal part of my brain that knew all about survival didn't want to believe what he was implying. Saying. It wanted to cry bullshit.

But an even bigger part of me, the reasonable, practical part, thought she knew Jonah well enough to tell the rest of me that he wouldn't lie. Not about that. Why would he? I had told him he was under no obligation to me. I wasn't and hadn't been trying to reel him back in. I'd enjoyed his friendship. I'd enjoyed *him*.

He wasn't lying, and I wasn't going to insult him by claiming he didn't know his own thoughts and feelings.

That didn't mean it made it any easier for me to handle what he was implying. Maybe it was easier to think that he hadn't wanted me as much as I'd wanted him. Maybe it was a hell of a lot easier to not dream that he'd made a huge mistake and that he had felt the same way.

None of that meant I was anywhere near being ready for it or wanting to do anything about it.

"I don't ask you to lunch because I want to just see Mo. I want to see you too. I want to be your friend again. I want to be more than your friend. I want to be more than any other friend you've ever had before or ever will."

Well.

I gulped as I looked into his eyes and saw a million different things reflected in them.

And not a single one of those things were bad.

I still hadn't taken a breath as I told him in a voice that only wobbled a little bit, because apparently today was the day for me to face shit, "Are you sure about that?"

The hand on my jaw cupped my cheek then, and his voice was soft and strong somehow as he answered, "Oh yeah."

I finally turned to look at him. We stared at each other. We stared at each other and stared at each other.

Finally, he broke the silence, quietly. "I'm willing to prove it. If the children try and hurt you inside, you can use me as a human shield."

I didn't say anything for so long that Jonah flashed those dimples at me and had me shaking my head and setting all those things I wasn't sure I wanted to face yet aside. "You're an idiot."

He smiled even wider, but I could see something in his eyes that was an awful lot like regret. And I kind of hated it. "Yeh, my sisters would agree with you, eh," he told me.

"It's good to know they're smart," I replied, trying to file away his words and his offer for later.

Sneaky ass, my stupid weak-ass heart whispered.

Jonah leaned forward, rested his head against mine, and took his time with his next words, setting each one down carefully like it was an egg. "Going back to the subject of you and best friends and family…" The hand on my arm loosened, and his gaze was intense. "You'll have to tell me what all the requirements are. I want to nominate myself."

That thing inside of me that had broken when we had been at the daycare with Mo cracked open even wider, leaving me with this intuition that nothing was ever going to be able to glue those pieces back together. And honestly, if I sat back and thought about it, I wasn't sure I would want them to. I wasn't sure what the hell I wanted anymore.

Or at least, I wasn't being totally honest with myself that that was even the truth.

"It's easy." I sniffed and straightened, raising my own hand up to pat his prickly cheek with my fingers. "If you're my ride or die, you don't ask questions, and you do exactly what I say all the time."

His eyes went wide, and he grinned and then started laughing right in my face. "Is that all?"

One of my cheeks went up into a partial smile as I nodded.

Jonah's smile grew just that much more. "In that case, I feel like we should cuddle on it."

Cuddle? "A handshake?"

"No. This is family business. Best friend business. A cuddle is appropriate."

I maybe sat there for a second before I thought *fuck it.*

Then, before I talked myself out of it, I slid my seat back and got up to my knees as fucking Jonah moved his own seat backward... and then opened his arms as wide as he could in my car. I crawled into his lap without a second thought. He drew me into the wide chest I hadn't been up close with in a long, long time as my butt settled onto his thigh.

Jonah hugging me was the second to last thing I expected, followed only by me actually taking what he offered. A cuddle. Fuck me.

I just went right in and let him hold me as I pressed my forehead against the side of his neck as I thought about what it was he'd said. Those big arms wrapped around me and held me.

His voice was a whisper as he said, "I know we need to go in, but let me cuddle you a minute, yeh?"

What was I going to say? No?

And so Jonah cuddled me—hugged me—a minute.

When we finally climbed out of my car, we pulled a talkative

Mo out of her car seat, grabbed my bag out of the trunk, and headed toward our destination.

The nervous apprehension of how I'd be welcomed after so long was still there.

These people had mattered to me for years, and while I might not give a fuck what 99 percent of people thought... this reception might actually hurt.

Jonah grabbed ahold of my hand halfway through the parking lot, and I didn't even think about taking it away and losing the contact.

"No worries, Len," he whispered right before opening the door for Mo and me, her backpack over one shoulder and my own bag over his other one.

Her scent reassured me that I had done the right thing when I'd left this place, and whatever happened, I could handle it. It had been worth it. It would always be worth it.

And when the door slammed closed behind us and a group of people turned to look at us...

I wasn't expecting them to yell, "Lenny!"

I definitely didn't expect to be bombarded by hugs either while Jonah stood right next to me the whole time.

CHAPTER 15

8:55 a.m.

Call me back, you dickwad.

8:56 a.m:

Or text me back. I don't care.

It was almost a week later, and I was having a pretty good day considering all the small, shitty little things that had been building up since the night before.

Mo had been fussy all night, and I was worried she was getting sick. I'd gotten into an argument with the HVAC company that we usually worked with within an hour after getting to work, and then Bianca had told me the inventory for the juice bar was off. By a lot. I'd had to spend three hours looking through footage to see what happened and had been more than a little disappointed when I'd caught an employee, who had been at Maio House for eight months, giving out what I counted was eight different smoothies for free.

Firing people was the closest thing to feeling guilty I ever felt. Not exactly guilty-guilty or *bad*, but... something similar. I was waiting for him to show up tomorrow so I could talk to him in person.

So when my phone beeped with the light flashing with a call coming from the front desk, I mentally prepared myself for some other small problem to pop up since it was that kind of day.

"Yeah?" I answered before pulling the receiver away from my face so that I could yawn.

"I'm sorry to bother you again, Lenny," she apologized immediately.

"You're not bothering me, Bianca. What's up?"

"Oh, okay," she said with a tight little laugh. "Umm, there's a woman here—"

Grandpa's ex-wife? *Again?* She hadn't called since that other day or tried to communicate in any way, and I wasn't even a little surprised. I'd never been worthy of being worth her attention in the first place, why would I be now?

"—looking for Mr. Collins—"

Oh.

Why did that instantly make me feel nauseous? Who was looking for Jonah? Why was a woman looking for him? He'd said something along the lines of there not being someone else. I wasn't imagining it.

Just four days ago, he'd clearly stated that he hadn't cheated on me.

Even though we hadn't actually been together, as I'd been telling myself. Even though he had been telling himself something different, and I wasn't sure how I felt about that.

Okay, I was sure, I just wasn't going to think about it.

"—and I've explained to her that he's not here, but even if he was here that he doesn't *work* here so I wouldn't know where he was. And, umm, she's refusing to leave. What should I do?" she asked, and I could already picture her wringing her hands.

Nausea flared up in my stomach and more than a little anger

because if this fucker had lied about having a girlfriend or a wife, I wasn't just going to kick him out of the first circle of trust, but I was going to beat his ass too. It was just a little harder than it should have been for me to ask, "Is she young or old?"

"Eh… older?" Her voice dropped and she whispered, "I think it might be his mom. She has the same accent, I think, even though he's only said about five words to me."

How about that?

That shouldn't have felt like such a relief, I accepted. And then my negative ass picked up on a stray thought… or *his sugar mama*? I'd known a couple guys who trained here who had some cougars they spent some time with. You know, good for those ladies.

But that doesn't mean this lady is here for that, my brain tried to be reasonable.

I made a quick decision. "Just leave her there. I'll go talk to her." After I contacted The Not Really an Asshole at All first.

"Okay, I will. Thanks," Bianca agreed quickly before ending the conversation.

I didn't waste a fucking second picking my cell up and finding the number I had saved for him, then dialing it. He picked up on the third ring.

"Hello, Lenny."

I was going to shove that Lenny up his ass if this was bad. "Hi," I told him, hearing just a tiny hint of aggression in my voice. "There's a woman here asking for you."

"Who?" he asked, sounding genuinely surprised. The sound of a voice coming over what I could assume was a loudspeaker blared in the background. Where was he?

"I don't know. I wouldn't be calling you if I did." All right, that came out totally bitchy. "My receptionist said someone was asking for you, and I'm heading out there to tell her that you don't work here, so why should I know where you are." I got up as I talked, heading out of the office and through the building, pushing the door outside open with my hip. I didn't hesitate to ask, "Where are you?"

"Hiring a car finally," he answered, his voice still sounding confused. "I don't know who it might be. The only women who would be looking for me are you, my sisters, my nan, and my mum." He cut off abruptly, and I was pretty sure he whispered something under his breath that might have been a curse word.

"What?"

There seemed to be a short hesitation before he answered with, "I'll be there as soon as I can."

I didn't like how that sounded, and I had to know. "Jonah, are you secretly married or have a girlfriend or something that you didn't tell me about?" AKA that you lied to me over?

There was a pause.

And then he let out that deep laugh that didn't sound like he was genuinely all that amused. Honestly, he sounded more than a little on edge as he did it, and I definitely didn't like that either. "No."

I just bit the inside of my cheek and then ground my molars together for a second before punching the code at the door to the gym part of the facility and yanking the door open pretty freaking hard.

"I'll be there soon," Jonah said, and then he hung up like Grandpa Gus had been rubbing off on him too.

I swear to God. *I swear to God....*

I took a deep breath in, let a deep one out, and told myself that I wasn't going to be fucking pissy. Not over Mo's dad. Not over the man who said he'd come back to Houston... for me. Not over the man who said he'd been crazy about me and wanted to be my—newest—best friend and asked what prerequisites he needed to get the position.

Nope.

And I kept right on telling myself that as I walked through the building, calling out a grumpy "hey" at a few people who I knew as I headed toward the front desk. At first, all I saw was

Bianca standing behind it, doing something on the computer with her back to me. It wasn't until I was pretty much at the tall counter that I spotted the woman sitting on one of the three benches in front of the giant glass windows that just a little bit of my blood pressure regulated.

The woman waiting around, in dark black slacks and a silky yellow shirt, was 100 percent related to him. There was something so similar about their faces... and she was definitely old enough to be his mom. And as she sat there with her ankles crossed, I could see that she wasn't in the best mood of her life. She was tapping her fingers on the back of her opposite hand and would press her lips together for a second, pucker them, and start that cycle all over again.

Huh.

If this was Jonah's mom, why would she be here and he not know? If I had thought about it, I would have picked up on the fact that he had only ever mentioned her in passing before. He had briefly talked about his dad a few times. Two sisters and three brothers too. Both sets of grandparents too. But not his mom.

Fuck it.

I rapped my fingers against the counter and said, "Hey, Bianca."

The younger girl turned around and grinned at me. "Hi." She discreetly tipped her head to the side as she said, "The package I was telling you about is here."

I flicked my eyes in the direction of the woman. "Oh yeah?"

She nodded so slowly I couldn't help but smile at her and her code words.

"Thanks for telling me."

I put one foot in front of the other until I stopped just a few feet away from the woman burning a hole into the wall while flexing one foot and then the other.

The new shorter distance between us didn't confirm any of my suspicions. She didn't exactly look like Jonah. She was several inches shorter, over a hundred pounds lighter and didn't have any facial hair. I eyed the designer purse with its two letters stamped all over it and waited the two seconds it took the woman to slowly move her gaze over to me, looking up at me through her eyelashes with her lips flattening.

This was going to go well, I could just tell.

"Hi," I told her as professionally as I could, which mostly just meant I kept as much attitude out of my tone as I could. "I was told you were asking for Jonah. Can I help you?"

The same honey-colored eyes that Mo had, and Jonah too, looked up at me through at least two layers of mascara, and I could *see* and *feel* the way she flicked her gaze down from my face to the black Polo shirt I had on with Maio House stitched onto the breast, to my black pants and low black boots.

I'd gotten slow looks like the one this woman was giving me countless times in my life. Before and during high school. Sometimes when I met fighters' girlfriends.

It was measuring and calculating and not thinking much of me.

Luckily, I didn't give a single shit what people I didn't know thought.

I didn't even care enough to look her up and down right back. I just stared at her as I crossed my arms over my chest and waited. I had all day.

There were only a few people in this universe who could out-stubborn me. Jonah's maybe-mom could try her best. I'd been dealing with Grandpa Gus for thirty years. If anything, I'd be impressed if she ended up getting under my skin even a little.

Luckily, or maybe not so luckily, she only did one more sweep of me, pursed her lips, and went with being direct. "Is he here now?"

Yeah, there was the accent.

And *oh, hi to you too.* I blinked once. "No. We're not in the business of keeping track of our members, so I'm wondering if there's something I can help you with."

It wasn't my imagination that one of those familiar honey-colored eyes went a little funny for a second before one hand—perfectly manicured—slipped into the purse at her side. In the blink of an eye, a matching wallet was pulled out, and in another blink of the eye, she was handing over a card. Her license.

"I'm looking for my son. I would like to speak to him," she said, sounding like just telling me this information was a hassle.

It took me a second to process the information on it. Sure enough, Collins was on the license along with a first name of Sarah. The date of birth on the license too showed a year that would have made sense to go along with the thirty-year-old I had gotten off the phone with. Huh.

Why wasn't Jonah answering her calls? Every impression he'd given me was that he was close to his family, at least some of them. It didn't exactly make sense.

He'd obviously told her where he was at some point. Given her enough information to come to the gym to look for him, but not the name of his hotel or anything else like that. This wasn't totally adding up.

"If it isn't an *issue*, I have no problem waiting here until he arrives," the woman, Sarah, said in a snooty voice that didn't hit me anywhere near the way her maybe-son's did. Mostly because he didn't talk like he thought he was better than me.

I handed her back her license. "I don't have a problem with you waiting here if you want, but it might be a better idea to find him at his hotel." Maybe I should have said something different, but I didn't. Fucking attitude.

And then this woman gave it right back. "I would go to his hotel if I knew where it was."

Was that my fault?

I smiled at her, and it wasn't anything like the smiles that my best friend—and Jonah, now that I thought about it—

handed out like they were candy on Halloween. "I was under the impression that if someone wanted to see you, they would tell you where they were staying."

Shots fired.

I felt a little bad right after the words were out, but only a little. All right, not really. If this *was* Jonah's mom... well. That meant she was Mo's grandma. Which meant that even if I didn't like her, she was still her grandma. Which meant that she was family. I had seen enough friends have shitty family members to know how that game went. It had made me grateful on a lot of occasions for how lucky I was that my family was tiny and I liked and loved everyone in it.

Her eye did that funny thing again as she lightly dropped her wallet back into what might have been a three-thousand-dollar purse. "May I speak to the manager?"

"That's me," I explained, letting my asshole smile dissolve. The *grandma, grandma, grandma* chant in my head went nowhere.

There.

The woman who my baby girl may or may not be related to, opened her mouth like she was going to say something else, but another voice beat her to speaking.

A voice with the same accent that Jonah and his maybe-mom had. "Still no Hema?" A woman's voice.

I glanced to the side to find a woman walking over.

A really pretty woman with long, dark brown hair, an oval-face, and blue eyes.

Why the fuck did I feel on the edge of blacking out with rage?

"No," Sarah Collins answered, still using that snooty-ass tone that had put me on edge.

The other woman pouted. Okay, it was more of a frown, but it sent my blood pressure soaring either way. And my eyelid....

I had literally just asked him about a secret marriage or a girlfriend, and he'd said there was none of that. He wouldn't lie to me. She could be anyone. There was no reason for my eyelid to start jumping all over the place and for me to assume my vision was about to go dark. No way.

I needed to get the fuck out of here.

Sliding my palms over my thighs, I faced the older woman and said, "You're more than welcome to wait. There are a few water fountains and a juice bar straight ahead if you want something. Let us know if there's anything else you need."

And like the chickenshit I apparently was now, I turned around and headed back the way I had come.

Fucking shit. *Fuck.*

A part of me genuinely hoped that this woman really wasn't related to Jonah, but my sixth sense said she was. That was just my luck. If I could take the exchange back, I wouldn't. She'd been a bitch and so had I, but what was I going to do? Bend over and take it?

Yeah fucking right.

And then there was the woman with her. Shorter than me, slim, really fucking pretty. Asking about *Hema*. Who was she and why did I care so much?

I was losing it. I really was.

I needed to cool it. I needed to breathe, and I could tell meditation wasn't going to do the trick. Not when I was this riled up.

Luckily, the solution came to me instantly.

Peter was on the floor when I got into the building, working with a small group. I kicked my boots off inside my office, sending both of them flying toward my desk. Today was his day with the lesser-experienced amateur fighters. What that meant was that they weren't good at fighting both standing up and being on the ground. But they weren't total noobs. The eight guys and three girls were on the mats. From the look of what Peter was trying to demonstrate, they were going to be working on handstand rolls, which meant that they were lined up in three rows and would go from a standing position to a handstand, then allowing themselves to roll out of it to get back into a standing position.

It was a lot of balance and control.

I had done it a ton in judo. Most fighters did it a ton, period. You had no idea how many muscles it took to stand up without using your hands. You also had no idea how important it was to be able to get up without using them either. The faster the better.

"Need some help?" I asked him, knowing what answer he would give me.

He eyed my pants for a second then smiled. "Show them how it's done."

I hoped I didn't regret this.

I eyed the floor for a second, wondered for another second when the last time I had done a handstand was—not since I had started showing while I'd been pregnant—and decided, *fuck it*. I'd done these a hundred thousand times in my life. If I lost my balance, so what? They were still learning how to do them.

I tucked my shirt into my pants and went into a handstand that wasn't as steady as they once were, but at the same time my muscles said *I remember this*, and let the memory of it kick in.

I did them over and over and over again, until I was sweaty and my collared shirt was damp and had fallen out of where I'd tucked it into my pants and rolled into my neck each time I went into one, until eventually, Peter and I were helping one person at a time work on their handstands against the wall furthest to the back, bodies leaning against the wall until arms and shoulders shook, until sweat dripped off faces and made tiny little watery pools all over the blue surfaces. I was catching my breath when I noticed someone with a right arm that was giving out on them and stepped forward to help them out of it.

That was when, out of the corner of my eye, I saw a big figure making his way across the floor in our group's direction. The biggest man at the gym now. The biggest man in my life.

"Lenny," Jonah Collins called out like I didn't know it was me he wanted.

Behind him, closer to the door he'd just come in through, were the two women. The older one and the younger one. And they were looking back at me but speaking to each other. The younger one was making faces too.

"Jonah." *He didn't owe me anything.*

I forced myself to look away and glance at one of the women as she tapped her heel against the wall as she tried to push off of it and hold her balance on her own.

Mo's dad stopped directly beside me, looking at me, and not the people still in position and said, "Could we have a moment?"

Always so polite.

I wasn't dumb enough to ask Peter if he could handle this without me. Of course he could. He hadn't needed me in the first place, but I still patted him on the back after I nodded at Jonah and went toward him. The second I was in front of him on the edge of the mats, his hand went to my elbow.

I didn't say a word.

That stupid handsome and rugged face was aimed at me, and he let out just about the deepest exhale I had ever heard from his body… and that was saying something because he'd let out a pretty big one the day he'd found out he was a dad.

"You okay?" I asked him, trying to remind myself that he wasn't a fucking liar.

He'd told me he didn't have a girlfriend or a wife.

He hadn't "cheated" even though there had been nothing to cheat on.

He had told me.

Those light brown eyes didn't flicker away as he told me the truth. Like I had a feeling he always did. "I was better before you called." His expression was tight. "Better now that I'm here talking to you."

This was the man I thought I knew. I swallowed and gave him a little smile. Then I reached up to squeeze his forearm with my free hand, the skin smooth and warm over all that fucking muscle just there. I was relieved, and I hated that I was.

The pressure around my own elbow tightened lightly, and he said following another exhale, "My mum is here."

Great.

The fact he didn't exactly look happy about her visit didn't reassure me.

"I didn't know she was coming. Didn't know she would bring my sister either."

That was relief that went down my spine at *my sister*.

Had she grown out her hair? Was that why I hadn't recognized her? Or had I just gotten pissed off before I'd even bothered to try and figure it out? I felt just a little ashamed of myself for jumping to conclusions. *Just* a little.

"It's a bit of a story, Lenny," he explained, oblivious to how close he'd been to finally losing his balls as he gave me a smile so tight that his dimples didn't come out. "A long one. I didn't tell her about Mo until a few minutes ago."

"You still hadn't told your mom about her?"

He shook his head gravely. "I haven't told anyone, but not because I didn't want them to know. I just... didn't want them to know yet." His dimple finally popped then. "It's selfish, yeah, but I wanted you both to myself for a bit longer, and if it got me out of answering some questions that aren't going to be comfortable, that was a nice bonus."

Oh.

"She knows now, and so does my sister, and in a matter of minutes, my entire family will as well. I'll have to call my agent as soon as I can to break the news to him too before he finds out from my brothers. He's their agent too, and he's still upset with me over what I did before. He's not going to be happy to find out I have a daughter I didn't tell him about."

I bet he wasn't.

I had a decent idea of how much shit he'd gotten after his

injury. And unless someone knew the whole story—at least his pieces of it—it didn't look that great for him. And as far as I knew, he hadn't signed a new contract with a new team. It could and would, more than likely, look really bad for him.

Jonah's expression went tight but hopeful, and all it made me want to do was whatever I could so that this wouldn't back-fire on him. "Will you come eat with us? Mum is in a foul mood, I'm sorry, but she would like to meet our girl. My sister would too."

I swallowed that *our girl.*

"If you don't want to, or can't, it isn't an issue," he clarified. "I just thought…."

I looked from one eyeball to the other. "Why weren't you answering your mom's calls before? Is there something wrong with her?"

The fact that it took him a second to snort said everything. Then his words after that were super liar, liar, pants on fire. "Yeh, nah," he tried to say even as his cheeks went pink. "She's a bit intense is all."

Intense? More like bish level 100. But I kept that to myself to share it with Grandpa later.

"Liar." I smiled at him. "You should probably know that I didn't exactly get off to the best start with her." *And I was worried your sister was really your secret girlfriend,* I thought but didn't say either.

"It's all right."

Something told me most people didn't get along with his mom, but my goal was to find out firsthand why he didn't answer her calls.

And now that I thought about it, I'd never even heard his phone ring around me. Not ever. Not even at night when he was at the house for hours. Even my phone was constantly bing-bing-binging, and that's why I set it on vibrate.

I wasn't that fucking popular.

But he was.

I'd ask him about it later.

"Are you sure you want me to go with you? Because you can go get Mo by yourself if you want, since you've got your own car and everything now."

If I was surprised by how easily the offer popped into my head, then Jonah was just as surprised to hear it. Those light-colored eyes just bore right into me before bouncing from one of mine to the other and back again. And even with his pink cheeks and the lies in his eyes about not being worried about his mom, he was still too cute. Handsome. Just fucking handsome.

"I want you to come," he said, looking right into my eyes.

He wanted me to really meet his mom? AKA spend time with her?

I made myself not glance at her because that would have been weak as hell, and instead did the same thing to his eyes that he'd done to me: like I was searching for something in them that said *bullshit, bitch*.

But there was nothing there even close to that. Not a single thing.

He wanted me to meet his mom. And sister. Wanted us to spend time together.

Fuck it.

"Okay," I agreed. "I want you to tell me the whole story later." Because I had questions. A few of them.

"I will," he agreed easily.

I hated how much I liked him. "Okay, I'll go with you."

He gave me that tiny little smile.

I smirked back at him. "Why do you look so relieved?"

"I'm just glad you're coming," he replied. "Let me introduce you, eh. I've got my ute—"

I tried to process that.

He caught it. "My car." He flashed me that trademark smile. "I told you I was hiring a car. We can go together to get Mo, or if you'd like, we can meet somewhere instead."

I felt like a pussy considering option B, but I took it. "We can meet somewhere. That'll give you some one-on-one time with your mom and sister." Poor sucker.

The smile he gave me didn't make it clear whether he knew why I'd chosen that option or not, but he didn't tease me over it. Jonah tugged me forward, and I went along willingly, noticing that his palm slid down my arm as we turned, and he gave my wrist a light hold for a second before dropping away.

He really was a good guy.

And as we headed toward his mom, and I took in the look on her face, I could tell that I wasn't going to be saying the same thing about her cranky ass.

In three seconds we were in front of the two women, and Jonah's hand was at the base of my spine, his palm halfway on my jeans and halfway over my shirt, which I *knew* was crazy sweaty, and he was saying, "Mum, Natia, I'd like you to meet Lenny, my girl's mum."

Somewhere inside, I flinched. Not his friend. Not... anything else. His girl's mom.

That's what I was, I guessed. My most important title. It wasn't like that should be a surprise.

And I had no reason to feel disappointed.

"Lenny, this is my mum, Sarah, and my middle sister, Natia."

Yeah. From the look his mom was giving me, she wasn't exactly going to be joining the Lenny DeMaio Fan Club anytime soon. That was for sure. And ask me how many fucks I gave? Zero, that was how many.

But one glance at the younger woman had me pausing.

She was grinning wide, and her hands were laced together under her chin.

Okay then. I thrust my hand out toward his mom first, keeping any excuses or lies to myself. I wasn't that glad to meet her. I wasn't sorry for how I'd spoken to her either. So I went with the most basic shit: "Hi."

Those eyes that she had given her son, who had then given them to my daughter, flicked from my hand to my face to Jonah's and then back to my hand.

Yep. Kind of a bitch. She wanted to make it awkward, we could play.

I wiggled my fingers just as the man beside me started to grumble, "Mum."

I wasn't dumb or blind, and I watched her force herself to take my hand, giving it a shake that wasn't anything close to a limp fish. I could respect that. I could at least respect that a whole hell of a lot more than her making it seem like I had cooties.

No part of me was surprised when she said in that cultured —and pained—voice "Hello" like she couldn't bear to have a conversation with me.

I could respect that too. A lot more than her forcing out a "pleasure to meet you" or some fake shit like that. We both knew neither one of us was all that pleased right then.

Fine by me.

Jonah let out a sigh that wasn't one that belonged to a man who was all that relieved. I'd think about what that meant later. In the meantime, I stuck my hand out toward his smiling sister, and fortunately, she didn't make me wait at all to take mine.

Or to pull me into her with surprising strength and throw her arms around me with a "It's awesome to meet you!"

All right, I hadn't been expecting that.

I snorted and hugged her right back. "It's nice to meet you too." She squeezed me even closer, and I thought *okay* and returned it.

I must have not been the only one thinking the same thing, because when I pulled back, Jonah's big smile had taken over his face while I'd been hugging his sister.

His sister.

I still didn't want to think too much about how much of a relief that knowledge had been. Later on, when no one could catch me, maybe I'd creep on her Picturegram account and see why I hadn't recognized her. It was bugging me. I was usually good with faces and names.

"Off to lunch then?" he asked, still cautiously, and I was pretty sure I wasn't imagining his wary expression as he kept an eye on the space between his mom and me like we were going to fight each other.

"Ooh, I'd love some lunch. Mum made us come straight here," Natia complained with a roll of her eyes.

"I'll go get Mo and meet up with you then?" I asked him.

"My granddaughter's name is Mo?" Sarah, Mrs. Collins, asked with dismay. She didn't look all that excited about it. Like I had chosen that name because it was short and I didn't know how to spell anything longer? Uh-huh.

I took a breath in through my nose and reminded myself that my own grandpa was a pain in the fucking ass. That thought made me feel a lot better. It gave me hope. This lady didn't know me. She didn't know, more than likely, what had happened between her son and me. "It's her nickname," I answered, specifically leaving out what her real name was to be a shit.

The look Jonah gave his mom was one Grandpa Gus and I had given each other a lot over the years. *You need to calm down* face. Because crazy knew crazy.

"Can we meet at the café we've gone to before?" the Tiny Bit of an Asshole said at the tail end of the look he gave the other woman.

Panera. He was talking about Panera. I nodded.

One corner of Jonah's mouth went up, like he was trying to hold on to what he could so that he wouldn't get mad or upset or whatever it was that was stewing there between him and his mom. "How long do you suppose it'll take? Thirty minutes?"

"Give or take," I agreed. Looking at Sarah again, seeing her gripping the strap of her purse like she was trying to choke the life out of it from how white her fingers were getting. His sister just stood there with a smirk on her face, looking back and forth between the two of them.

This kind of tension wasn't new. I could tell that real easy.

I wasn't expecting the warm fingertips that lightly brushed over my forearm. Just for a second, but enough to have me snapping my eyes up to that face so close. "See you there then, love," he told me quietly, and I heard the tiny, quiet noise his mom made when he said it.

Fuck her.

Tugging on the bottom of my shirt, I was thankful I had extra clothes in my office at all times. "See you there."

The rest of Jonah's smile fell off as his gaze flicked to his mom.

"Look, I don't know how this is going to go down, okay? Hopefully it'll be fine, and she'll be nice once she sees that you're the cutest and sweetest baby on the face of the planet, but you don't have anything to be worried about, all right? If she's mean, we'll leave and you'll only have to see her if your dad forces you, but I think your dad already knows how cool you are, and he'll keep her in check. But if he doesn't, you know I will. You know I'll cut her if I have to, right?"

I glanced into the rearview mirror to eye the back of her car seat.

I snorted. "Right. I knew you'd agree, Mo."

Obviously she was so worried.

She'd shouted at the top of her lungs when I'd gotten to Mr. Cooper's house—that was my best friend's father-in-law who watched Mo every once in a while—to pick her up. Apparently Grandpa Gus had been invited to play a pickup game of basketball and had dropped her off an hour ago. Luckily, Mr. Cooper's house wasn't too, too far from the gym. I'd known him my whole life, and he was the nicest man.

With one more turn of the wheel, I spotted the big sign for Panera coming up just on the left and turned in. I pulled into the first spot closest to the door that I could find and parked. I had left the gym first, with Jonah, his mom, and sister busy still talking just outside my office in some hushed tones, so I had no idea what kind of car he was driving, much less what rental car she might have had, if she had one in the first place.

But I had barely opened my door when I spotted, in the side mirror, a very familiar body stepping off the curb and heading over. By the time I slammed the door shut and opened the rear door, Jonah was there, pulling out Mo's diaper backpack from the passenger seat and handing it over to me.

One look at his face confirmed he was tense as hell.

"You all right?" I asked, watching through the glass as those big fingers fiddled with the straps almost clumsily.

He made some kind of response.

"Jonah?"

"Yeh," he answered, distractedly. Then he sighed. "Nah. My mum is in a mood, and I'm sorry, Len. I'll tell you everything later, but I hope you'll give me a chance to explain tonight."

He was still fumbling around with the straps as I watched him and thought about what he said. "Is she being mean to you or something?"

Jonah's laugh was dry, and I didn't like it. "Some of it's deserved, but some of it isn't. I'm used to it."

Used to it?

For all the shit Grandpa Gus had given me over the course of my life, there was nothing to be... *used to*. I had always known all his shit-talking was love. I rarely took anything he said to heart because I knew he loved me as much as I loved him. I knew he thought I was a champ, even when I wasn't. He'd never cared whether I won or lost as long as I had tried my best.

But this? This tone he was using, the apologies he was making? It didn't sound similar at all. Then again, I had apologized to him for Grandpa being a pain in the ass toward him, so I wasn't sure how he should take that.

"I promise I'll explain later," he said before muttering, "bloody finally" as the latch on the straps finally unbuckled themselves and he managed to get two arms out before the rest of that baby body followed, Mo streaming out some really important shit as she gripped his sweater in her hands.

I couldn't help but smile at the smile on Mo's face or at the animation in her voice as she babbled to him. She'd been watching Jonah the entire time as she rambled on, with that curious and open expression on her face, like she was all about this person and wanted to tell him exactly what was on her mind. It was nice.

I fucking loved her. So, so much.

"Don't worry about it," I told him, figuring after that last debate that I really wasn't in any position to say shit about his mom.

Grandpa Gus was still calling him by the wrong name every opportunity he had. Just the night before, he'd called him Carlisle. Three days before that, he'd chosen Emmett. God help me.

"How ya goin'?" Jonah whispered to Mo as he pulled her right up against that massive chest, a big, white smile crossing over the closely bearded face. "How's my sweet girl?"

Mo, in response, was watching his face with those big eyes like she was staring into some kind of mysterious universe that had her completely in awe. Whatever it was that she said, she said slowly and in a voice that sounded pretty close to awe as well. They really were going to make me throw up one of these days.

I was too busy looking at her cute little face to see one of those tiny hands reach up, quick like lightning—like me, I wanted to think—and wrap its fingers into the short-trimmed hair on the face in front of her and yank at it.

Jonah blinked in surprise—and I was sure in more than a

little pain—as I said, "No, Mo, no," and went to undo one tiny finger at a time from that crazy strong grasp. Which I also liked to think she got from me.

"Oww, Mo, oww," Jonah said with a minor wince as I pulled the last finger off from its death grip. "Please, no."

My little psycho just laughed. *Our* little psycho just laughed. And clapped her hands.

I snorted, and Jonah shot me a smirk.

"You look so pleased with her."

"I am," I agreed with a laugh. "Where's your mom anyway? Inside?" I asked him as I closed the back door, tossing the backpack over my shoulder.

The lightheartedness in his voice disappeared. "Inside."

I didn't like how he sounded, and it made me frown at his back. Before I could think about it too much, I reached forward, slipped a finger through the belt loop directly in the center of his back, and tugged at it. "Is she mad at you because of Mo?"

He stopped walking immediately, his chin coming up to rest on his shoulder. Conflict moved beneath his eyes. There was my answer.

I knew what that was like. But I also knew that Grandpa Gus hadn't been pissed at me for getting pregnant. He'd been pissed at me for keeping it a secret so long. He'd been pissed at me, initially, for refusing to tell him who her sperm donor had been. He'd been mad at me for crying over it.

He hated when I cried.

But he hated it even more when I forgot the lessons he'd taught me. The important one then being that actions had consequences, and I couldn't blame anyone else for my own mistakes. Which was what I'd done to be fair, for a while.

I'd blamed Jonah's super sperm for kicking my life off track when it really had been fifty-fifty.

So his mom being pissed at him?

"We're adults, the last time I checked. What's she going to do? Call her a mistake? Say we screwed up? Because she's not a mistake—at least I don't think she is," I told him, sounding defensive.

Jonah turned all the way around to face me, forcing me to drop my hand. But his free one, the one he wasn't using to hold up the baby, grabbed mine unexpectedly, and he said, watching me carefully, his voice serious as hell, "She's not a mistake."

Now that really did make me smile at him genuinely. "Good. Because I'd kick your ass if you thought she was."

His laugh was rough as the hand on mine gave one more squeeze before dropping away. He shook his head all the way inside. It was then, as he stopped to open the door for me, Mo balanced in one arm, that he gave me another tight smile that honestly just irritated me. Not toward him, but toward his mom.

He was warning me. I knew it.

Because I knew what dealing with a drama queen was like. At least what it was like for me. Because Grandpa Gus was too much, but I thought it was hilarious and it always amused the hell out of me. Not once had he embarrassed me with how over the top he could be. I had never *dreaded* it. But based on the look that Jonah was sporting, it didn't seem like that was the same in this case.

And why didn't she know where he was? Or why hadn't he answered her calls? Why didn't his phone ever ring?

And *also,* who the fuck flew all the way from what may or may not have been New Zealand on a whim?

I needed to figure this shit out. And also make sure that Sarah, *Mrs.* Collins, didn't upset her son too much, because I liked him happy and easygoing. I dealt with enough drama and egos; she wasn't taking this away from me. At least not if I had anything to say about it.

Jonah waited by my side as I placed my order on the screen to avoid the line, and I didn't say a word when he batted my elbow away when I started to pull my little wallet out of my back pocket and paid.

He wasn't hurting for money. Plus, I'd carried giant-ass Mo around inside of me for nine months and four days. It wasn't my fault Jonah had passed along his size-gigantean genes to her, regardless of what he said about being a skinny little turd back in the day. If he wanted to pay for my food, I wasn't going to stop him.

Jonah's hand landed on my lower back with the gentlest of pressure after I filled my drink, steering me toward the corner of the restaurant. I couldn't help but notice all the men and women who stared at him as we passed by, also noticing that he didn't pay them any attention. It was like he didn't see he was the object of any attention.

When I snickered, he glanced at me and tipped his chin up, asking what that noise was for.

I smirked. "Five bucks says someone comes over and gets you confused with a football player."

He didn't break his stride as he wrinkled his nose. "American football?"

Reaching over his shoulder, I touched my fingers to the little hand Mo had on his neck, just to get a little taste, and snorted. "If I need to offend you in the future, I know how now. Thanks."

He faced forward again, shaking his head as he did so, confirming my suspicion that he really was offended by that idea. "Nothing against American football players, but…."

The fact he trailed off said everything, and it just made me snort, catching sight of *another* person in the restaurant gazing at Jonah like he was trying to figure out where he had seen him before. "Well, if it matters any, I think rugby is a lot more entertaining than football from what I've watched. Not that I really know much about it still."

He stopped walking for a second, giving me a view of his mom at a table possibly five feet away, glaring in our direction with eyes that honestly reminded me a little too much of Grandpa Gus when he was being a shit. Ha.

"American football," he corrected me.

"American football," I conceded. "Smart-ass."

The smile he gave me was one of the smaller ones, and I wondered again what the hell was up his mom's ass to make him so hesitant. He wasn't even this bad when he'd first shown up to talk to me, I was pretty sure.

With one last lingering look I wasn't going to overanalyze, he turned that enormously muscular body forward again and cut the rest of the distance that separated us from his mom and his sister, who was busy hunched over her cell phone, tapping away at the screen. To give Mrs. Collins credit, she stood up, her eyes going wide, and even her mouth opened. I was pretty sure she gasped.

And I was definitely sure that her eyes went glassy instantly as Jonah stopped to the side of the wall where she had been seated at a bench and held Mo up even higher on his chest as he said in that ridiculous, lovely voice, "Mum, this is Mo." He did that thing where he lowered his forehead until it rested against the much smaller one—her hands grabbing the T-shirt Jonah had on under his open sweater—and he finished in an even deeper, more charged voice, "Mo, this is your grandmother. Your gram-my," he enunciated carefully.

"Oh, Jonah," the other woman whispered, her voice pretty damn wobbly. "You could've been twins."

"Hema," Natia gasped, dropping her phone onto the surface of the counter and standing up too.

The next thing I knew, Mrs. Collins was crying, and his sister looked pretty damn close to it too. There were tears rolling down Jonah's mom's cheeks, and she wasn't even trying to wipe them up. Huh. I guess she wasn't as awful as she'd seemed. At least not toward Mo, and she was the one who mattered. She didn't have to like me, but she did have to like her.

The older woman's fingers came up to cover her mouth for a moment, and in the next, she was holding them in front of the center of her body, her voice just as shaky as it had been before when she sniffed and then asked, "May I hold her?"

The gold-brown eyes on the biggest head around me flicked to my direction, glassy, so damn glassy, but asking.

Hadn't I made it clear that we let everybody hold her as long as they weren't shitheads? And didn't he know that she was half his too? He didn't have to ask me for permission. I just raised my eyebrows at him like *duh*.

And as Jonah turned his body just enough so that our girl could get a good look at the woman who had a pretty impressive part in her existence, she still wasn't able to tear her eyes away from the man holding her. The little fingers she had on his shirt dug in and said, "Da, ba?"

Did she know? I wondered. Did she know somehow that this was her dad?

She looked at Grandpa Gus like he was an eclipse, but she looked at Jonah like he was a once-every-five-hundred-years meteor.

She knew, some part of me recognized. She had to know. Somehow. Some way. She was easygoing but not like this.

"Baby Mo," the most handsome man I had ever known said quietly, tenderness hugging every syllable. "This is your grand-mother, your gran, look, darling. Look."

He'd called her his darling.

And I was not going to fucking tear up in the middle of Panera over it.

Mo didn't look anywhere else though. Her little fingers just wrapped themselves even tighter in the shirt her dad was wear-ing, her body leaning toward him like she was preparing for him to try and hand her off, and she wasn't about to have it. I watched Jonah swallow hard—a gulp, it was a gulp—and smile this wonky smile before he laughed a watery laugh and hugged her to him, swallowing up this baby in those enormous arms so that the only way I knew there was someone in them was because I had seen her disappear inside the cocoon of muscle he'd created.

Jonah laughed again, the tone low and full of... something. Joy. Love. Like he didn't expect it and it shocked the fuck out of him.

I was not going to fucking cry, damn it. But I did swallow hard and sniff once and glance at the woman who was grabbing a napkin off the table and dabbing at her eyes with it. Beside her, Natia was scrambling for her phone, trying to take pictures with shaky hands and saying, "She's so *cute*, Hema. I want to hold her too. *Please*."

"You can hold her later. I think she wants me now," Jonah murmured, letting the arm he had around Mo fall away.

But she kept on leaning into him, those little hands not loosening their grip at all.

I wanted some of that baby too—that warm, soft weight against me—but I couldn't imagine going eight months without my little monster. And for being an only child... I knew how to share. I was pretty good at it.

"I'll go get a high chair for her," I told the new dad and the new grandma and aunt.

"I'll get it," he offered, but I gave him a look before ignoring him.

By the time I came back, Jonah was sitting at the end, and his mom was on the bench across from him. I set the chair on their end and watched as Jonah stood and settled Mo into it with only a little bit of trouble, as she kicked her legs around, being difficult.

Heh.

"Ma!" Mo shriek-shouted once she was sitting.

"Good job, booger." I bent over and gave her kisses on the neck, getting a couple more squeals out of her that made me smile and another stream of babble.

I took a seat beside Jonah, figuring I'd let him handle her if he wanted. I pulled out a couple of baby wipes and handed them over. He took them, thought about it for a second, and wiped off the little tray once with each one. Next I handed him a container from the backpack with cubed cheese in it that Grandpa had left with Mr. Cooper. He unscrewed the lid and peeked inside of it, eyebrows going up. And my child, in a move that was all me, grabbed a chunk of cheese and instantly tried to munch on it with her razorblade gums.

That was my girl.

Beside me, Jonah chuckled that low laugh. "Reminds me of you," he whispered, like his mom couldn't hear. Of course she could.

I still snorted. "I was just thinking the same thing." Wait. "What the hell is that supposed to mean?"

The big shithead just chuckled some more, thinking he was hilarious as he looked at me playfully from under his eyelashes.

Playfully. Ugh. I kind of wished he was back to being an asshole.

That was a lie. I didn't wish that at all. What I did wish for….

Well, it didn't matter what I wished for. So I wouldn't wish for shit.

Across the table, the woman sighed, and it didn't take a genius to know why she was doing it, but I still glanced at her anyway. Mrs. Collins had her gaze set on Mo, who was still too busy staring at Jonah while smacking all over her softened cheese to acknowledge that there was someone brand-new around. Two new someones.

"I think she's in love with him already," I told Mrs. Collins when her expression turned as dreamy as her resting bitch face allowed. "She doesn't stop staring at him, but she'll let you hold her. She's only met one person she didn't like."

"Who?" Jonah was the one who asked.

I scooted my chair toward the table a little closer. "My best friend's sister, but I'm not a fan of her either. She cried every time that sister held her."

"How many times did you try?" Sarah, Jonah's mom, asked, interrupting us, her gaze still on the dark-haired golden-eyed baby.

I had to think about it as I pulled a reusable stainless-steel straw from Mo's backpack and dropped it into my fresh lemonade. "Twice."

She hmphed, and I narrowed my eyes at her, not even bothering to try to hide it.

"We thought the first time was a fluke, so we tried again another day, and didn't try after that," I explained, trying not to get bent out of shape by her thinking I was causing my kid emotional distress or anything.

One of her eyebrows went up a little, and I could tell that still wasn't good enough for her. Or maybe I was being a bitch and looking too much into it. I doubted it though.

Our source of entertainment grabbed another block and shoved it into her mouth, sucking on it, loudly, pulling it out of her mouth, staring at it, and then putting it back inside.

"Jonah said she's eight months," the woman said after a moment.

I gave my lemonade a stir. "Yeah. Her birthday is May 2nd."

"Is she your only child?"

I stopped stirring and stared across the table.

Shut the fuck up, Lenny. It's not worth it. Just shut the hell up.

And… I couldn't. When the hell did I ever give shit up? Never?

I gave my lemonade another stir, slower that time, and asked her in a sugar-sweet voice that would have made Grandpa Gus cackle at how fake it was. "How many do you think I have?"

"Okay," Jonah interjected in that too-calm voice. "Mum, that wasn't nice. Lenny…." He just turned his head to me and blinked.

I smiled at him.

His dimple popped out at me.

Fine. I guessed. God knows Grandpa had muttered worse in front of him before. "Yes, she's my one and only," I answered his mom grudgingly. I flicked my eyes back toward my little monster and did smile then. "She was my seven-pound, eight-ounce surprise."

She was too busy slobbering on her food to know I was talking about her.

Good lord this lunch was going to be something, and the only person I felt bad for was Jonah. And his sister. God knew I wasn't going to lose any sleep over it.

"So it wasn't intentional?" Sarah asked before clearing her throat. "Jonah, don't make that face at me. It's a simple question."

Natia, who had been busy making faces while still taking pictures of Mo from where she was sitting, coughed. "I can't believe you even talked to a girl long enough to get her to spend time with you, Hema. Much less have s-e-x with you."

I stopped breathing and had to fight for every second I didn't laugh. And that fight lasted two seconds—two seconds in which Jonah choked and his mom gasped—and then I asked, "*What?*"

"Yeh, you didn't know he's shy?" Natia asked, grinning wide.

"Natia," Jonah groaned, his face already turning pink.

Wait a second, wait a second... I looked at the man sitting across from me and tried to process what the hell his sister had just said and scoffed, "You're shy? Since when?"

"Always," his sister responded with a cackle. "You haven't noticed? If it's footy he's talking about, he's fine. Any other topic with a stranger?" She pinched her index and thumb finger together and drew a line across her mouth, then cackled again. "Really? You didn't notice?"

Shit.

Now that she mentioned it, I had noticed how he started talking with his Stuart Little voice every time he talked to women, and I know I'd wondered why the hell he was always whispering, but now...

Now it made sense.

And I couldn't help but grin at him. "I wondered why you were being weird—"

He huffed for the first time I had ever seen. "I was not being *weird*."

Oh my gosh. This sweet, little innocent soul. "No, you were not. I'm sorry. You have never been weird around strangers in front of me. You were being shy. Why didn't you tell me?" I straight-up asked him.

Natia started cackling a little more. "Did he do his small voice? The one that you can barely hear?"

Tearing my eyes away from his blushing face, I nodded at her, trying my hardest not to smile because I was trying to be understanding and supportive over the idea of this beast of a man being *shy*. Heh. Wow. I seriously couldn't believe I hadn't put it together before. "Not with me, but with other people, he has. I never realized that's what you were doing, Jonah. You talk to my grandpa and Peter just fine."

"Well, that explains it then," his sister said. "Wow. We've been making bets—"

Jonah groaned. "Nati, no—"

She ignored him. "Lenny, he's been shy for ages. I mean, *forever*. His entire life. Even with teachers he would get like that. Did you talk to him first?"

I nodded, switching back and forth between looking at him and then at her.

"I knew it," she bobbed her head triumphantly. "I knew it."

A thought entered my head that killed just a slice of the pleasure in my heart. "Wait, but you've had girlfriends before. So you're just shy around certain people?"

His sister didn't give him a chance to answer. "You mean Hanna and that annoying girl? They were our neighbors. We grew up together. They weren't strangers. I always thought they were more like your sisters." She snorted with a shake of her head. "Settled for them, he did."

Fuck me.

I raised my eyebrows and smiled at her, and she did the same right back.

And poor Jonah just sat there, still pink and at a loss for words.

I liked his sister even more now.

Jonah being shy. Who the fuck would have known? Jesus Christ. And his ex-girlfriends had been people he'd grown up around.

That shouldn't make me feel nice, but it really, really did.

He let out a deep grumble as he sat back in his chair. I'd cut him a break.

Turning to Mrs. Collins and going back to the question she had asked, I told her, "To answer your question, no, Mo wasn't intentional. I had never planned on having kids, if you really want to know." I smiled at how uncomfortable she looked... at me or at the conversation we'd just had about Jonah having girlfriends and having sex? I had no idea, and I didn't care. "But I wouldn't change anything. I'm just glad that Jonah's happy and wants to be part of her life. That's the most a mom can ask for, isn't it?" I was sure there was more I could ask for, but that was beside the point.

The other woman took a deep inhale, set her shoulders, and I got ready.

Natia must have sensed something too because she suddenly shot up in her chair and said, "Oh, I have a phone call. I'll be back."

And that was when Mrs. Collins spoke. "Jonah is a wonderful man, of course he would want to be part of his daughter's life." That was what she decided to pick up on of all things.

Did she want me to argue that? I wouldn't. So I kept my mouth shut to keep the temptation of saying something unnecessary down. Grandpa Gus had always said that if I didn't have anything nice to say, to just say it in my head. And most of the time I couldn't uphold that, but in this case, I could. Because she was right. He was a good man.

"But," she kept going, and something in me told me I wasn't going to like whatever was about to come out of her mouth next either. "I can't help but feel it's a bit convenient that you say that you didn't want to have kids, but you happened to have one with my son, a successful rugby player in every sense, who happens to do very well for himself. A former All Black—"

"Mum," Jonah said in a voice that was pretty damn close to a growl.

But I didn't look at him. I just looked at the woman who was staring right back at me without the smallest sense of shame or submission.

"That's no secret," she went on, apparently ignoring him too. "Jonah, I'm only speaking the truth. Aren't I? Your deal in France was well publicized. It was in the papers. On the internet. Seems a bit convenient to me, is all, that you just found out now that it's time for you to sign a new contract when you're still playing so well after your injuries."

Out of the corner of my eye, I could see him lean forward. Using that same tone as before, the one that was almost a low spit, he said very quietly, "That was completely uncalled for and unnecessary. You promised me you would listen."

Oh shit.

He kept going. "You said you would listen to the entire story later, but you've broken your promise and insulted Lenny. She's the mother of my daughter, Mum. She's my... mate. My partner."

I was his mate? His friend? Was that what he meant? And his partner? Like his partner in crime? I guess I had said he could be in the Mo League.

I sat there and let that soak in. I liked it. You know, if I ignored the fact that I liked him and that was all he saw in our… friendship. But what could I do? It was good enough. I should have been overjoyed we got along so well.

But I couldn't think about that for too long because he kept going in that voice that honestly sounded almost as deadly as the one he'd used the other day to defend me.

"I appreciate you worrying, but I'm not a child, and I haven't been in quite some time. I know whom I surround myself with; that's never been an issue," he argued. "I love you, Mum, you know that, but you can't talk about Lenny in that way or make those assumptions. Not if you want to be part of this, and I want you to be, but my daughter won't be surrounded by these kinds of dynamics. She won't be hearing anyone disparaging her mum. Not today, not tomorrow. Not ever."

I didn't move as I sucked up every single word he spoke.

And…. I thought my nipples might have gotten hard at his voice. At all those big words and the strength behind them. This kind, nice man wasn't always all that kind or nice, but he picked and chose his moments so well….

Goddamn, I was easy.

Or pathetic, which wasn't that true because I'd never thought I was pathetic. But here I was getting a little uneasy because someone—*Jonah*—was defending me. Who the fuck was I? Was this why women liked strong men? Because I'd known a lot of physically strong men, and I'd known a lot of bossy men, and I knew most of them would kick someone's ass for me, but talk to their moms in that way? Not so much.

And I must have been lingering over that for too long because the next thing I knew, Sarah was leaning back against the bench seat, looking a little pale, and I kind of felt bad.

Because really… *really*… if Mo were a boy and he came to me in thirty years and said he got some bitch pregnant that he wasn't dating, I would honestly probably do the same exact thing she had just done. I would think she was a gold digger, for sure, even if she wasn't. And I would more than likely hate her on principle for working magical vagina powers on my sweet, innocent child.

That's exactly what would happen.

But at the same time, I didn't give enough of a shit about what this lady could possibly think of me. Because I knew the truth. And Jonah knew the truth.

But...

She was going to be in my life for a long time. And she was just worried about him even though he was a grown man. Would I ever stop worrying or caring about Mo even when she was old enough?

Probably not.

"I'd like for you to apologize to her," Jonah said, still using that hard-ass voice that got me going. Then he added "Please," and I swear my ovaries just about exploded.

Well, it wasn't like I didn't know I had issues.

No one said anything for about three seconds too long, and I could feel the tension coming off him, until finally, his mom sniffed, sat up even straighter, and said very carefully, "My apologies for what I said, Elena."

We were going with Elena then. How the hell had she even found out my real name?

The man beside me groaned, more than likely, for the same reason.

I decided to be nice because that would be more annoying. "Apology accepted," I told her, keeping myself from smiling because that was a little much. "I know you're just watching out for him to make sure I'm not taking advantage of him."

That was definitely a groan from the man beside me, and if Sarah's eyes went a little wide... too bad.

"But I'm not," I told her, giving her a smile then and making sure not to break eye contact. "I had no idea who he was when we met. He made it seem like he was on vacation for the first few days after we met, but even if I had known who he was, it wouldn't have mattered because I don't know anything about rugby. And I don't need his money. Kids really had never been in my life plan, even with this much of a stud muffin."

Jonah choked right then, but I was on a roll and didn't want this awkward shit hanging over us, so I needed his mom to understand me. I just wanted her to suffer a little when I called her baby boy a stud muffin.

"I know I'm not that pretty, and I'm not fancy or that well-educated, but"—I looked right at her; I wanted her to know I meant the words coming out of my mouth—"I'm a decent person, and Jonah could have had a baby with someone a lot worse than me."

The other woman stared, and beside me, Jonah was still trying to stop choking.

I smiled at her even more sweetly. "Some people might even say I'm a catch. My grandfather won four world championships in boxing. My dad won a gold medal and a silver medal in boxing in the Olympics. I don't really know about my mom or her family because I never met her and my grandpa barely knew her, but I am…." I swallowed that word and blinked. "I was… a world champion judoka. I was undefeated for years in this country, and when I did lose, it was because I was injured. I've won multiple national championships in the junior and senior levels. I've won more Pan-American games than any other woman. The only reason I didn't compete in the Olympics was because I was injured each time, but I've beat the players who did win. And, most importantly, because none of that really matters anymore, I will work my ass off to be a good mom to your granddaughter. I don't know how to not try my best at anything, Sarah, so…."

I raised my eyebrows at her as I folded my hands on top of the table and gave her a long look.

And she…

She didn't say anything.

My job was done.

I peeked to my right and found that Sarah wasn't the only

one watching me silently. The difference was, I winked at the one to my right, all exaggerated and everything. Goddamn, Grandpa Gus would be proud. I was going to have to tell him everything later. Maybe.

That was my cue to pee. I stood up and patted Jonah on the shoulder. "I'll be right back."

That definitely could have gone better, but it definitely could have gone worse.

I made it to the bathroom and back out in no time. I spotted an elderly man approaching the table where Jonah, his mom, and Mo were at on the way. It wasn't until I was only a few feet away that I finally heard what the older man was saying and how Jonah was responding.

"You aren't?" the older man asked, frowning and wringing his hands.

Jonah shook his head solemnly. "No, sir. I'm a rugby player. Never played a day of American football in my life."

Holy shit. Was this really happening?

The older man looked pretty damn dubious as he squinted from beneath his glasses. "*Rugby?*"

My daughter's father nodded. "Yeh."

His squint got a little more intense, and even I could see the way his shoulders dropped. The man muttered his apologies before backing away, muttering under his breath, "Rugby?"

And the second he was a few feet away, Jonah turned to look at me with the fucking funniest face I'd ever seen.

But I beat him to it.

I was already grinning. "Who did he think you were?"

The funny face didn't go anywhere, but one of his hands went for his back pocket.

I opened my mouth just as he opened his wallet and thrust a five-dollar bill at me.

"A football player," he mumbled as he shoved his wallet back into his shorts just as I started fucking laughing.

CHAPTER 16

5:51 p.m
Please call me back.

"YOU INVITED HER?" GRANDPA GUS DIDN'T LOOK UP FROM shaking out the bag of baked chips into the one and only bowl he would be putting out that night. *"Why?"*

Holding Mo as she tried to stand on my thighs with her hands clutching my cheeks, I rolled my eyes at the man across the island from me. "Because she's Mo's grandma."

Those gray eyes flicked up to me as he started rolling up the bag, lips flat.

I made my lips go flat too as I took a quick sniff of the baby on top of me. Jonah had helped me give her a bath last night, and she still smelled good. *"And* it's more fun to be nice when you know someone doesn't like you since it'll just make them feel like they're the bad person, okay? Mind Games 101. You taught that class."

Grandpa Gus smirked, and I could see him trying to fight back a smile.

"She's your co-grandparent. You're gonna need to suck it up too."

That had him sneering, but before he could argue something about him and Peter being the only grandparents that mattered, I beat him to it.

"I think I impressed her by telling her about your world championships and Marcus's medals. Don't be surprised if she asks you to see them."

His back was to me as he hid the remaining chips in the cupboard. It wasn't until he moved toward the sink, back still to me, that he said, "I cleaned them a few days ago."

He cleaned them every other week like clockwork. He'd told me before that Marcus, my dad, had been meticulous about it. He'd been so proud of them.

"Jasper is coming tonight too, I'm guessing? I have to spend another night watching him ooh and aah over Mo?"

Speaking of, Mo decided to fart right then, and we laughed. The doorbell rang but neither one of us made a move to go answer it.

"You know... I think it's about time you started being nicer to *Jonah*, and I think you know that."

"You do!" a voice piped up out of the blue from the other side of the kitchen door, and I laughed thinking of Peter walking by right on time to overhear that.

Grandpa Gus groaned as he opened the refrigerator door and pulled out the tray of carrots, broccoli, and oranges he had prepped hours ago, and the hummus dip he'd made then too. "I am being nice," he tried to argue as he set the tray in the center of the island as Mo reached up blindly and snagged a handful of my hair, making me whine. "Yesterday, I taught him how to puree Mo's food, and I only criticized him once."

My mouth dropped open in pain *and* surprise as I started trying to pluck her little fingers off again. "Only *once*?"

"Your sarcasm isn't appreciated."

"But yours is?"

He made a face, but I knew he was just trying to keep from cracking up.

"He's all right, but don't hold your breath. I'll *think* about it. I'm still not crazy about the idea of him only coming and going a few months every year."

Which reminded me that I really needed to ask him what the hell his plan was—where he was going to go play, where he would live during his off-season, and maybe ten other questions too.

I told myself I wasn't ready for that conversation.

"It's a long time, Lenny," Grandpa Gus went on. "A real dad wouldn't leave his daughter for half the year."

I sighed, knowing he had a point, knowing how I felt about that point, but... "It's his job, and it's what he's worked for his entire life. You think I'm going to tell him to give up on it? How would you feel if someone told me that I shouldn't practice judo anymore all because I was a mom? If I still could compete on that level, I mean."

The face he made said he knew the answer to that question.

But the truth was, I didn't know how we were going to make it work either. A rugby season was long and brutal. We lived on different continents. Seeing each other only twice a year for a couple months wasn't enough, but what the hell could you do? We were going to have to figure it out someday, but that day wasn't going to be this one.

I'd looked at the calendar, and according to what I remembered about rugby season dates, we had a little over a month before he had to fly back to France or New Zealand or wherever the hell he was going to go for his next season.

"We'll figure it out," I said, only hearing the lump in my throat when it was too late.

Grandpa narrowed his eyes, and I was pretty damn sure he had heard the ping-pong ball that had taken up shop in my vocal cords. "What was that?"

"Nothing."

"I heard it. What was it?" he asked again, squinting just a little more, like that was going to help him sniff out my bullshit better.

I lifted Mo into the air and said, "Nothing."

"I swear on my mother's life—"

That had me breaking into a laugh.

"Don't laugh! She was a wonderful woman."

I laughed even more.

"Okay, she was mean and beat me every chance she had, but she was still my mother… and what were we talking about?"

I blew a raspberry against Mo's belly, earning me a squeal and a short stream of babble, before lowering her down to settle on her feet. "Do I need to start looking up homes for people with memory impairments?"

Grandpa Gus stood there and shook his head slowly, even reaching for his heart. "After everything I've done for you…."

"Just kidding. With your vampire DNA, you're probably done aging for the next ten years."

"I'm thinking fifteen."

I rolled my eyes with a groan and bounced my girl on her feet. "Did you close your bedroom already?"

My vampire grandpa sighed. "No, buy the pay-per-view while I do that."

I followed after him through the door, hitching Mo to my hip as she babbled from my shoulder. "I know kiddo, Grandpa is crazy. Can you say that? Cra-zy."

I glanced at the clock, knowing she was going to start winding down pretty soon. She hadn't napped long enough earlier, and I knew it was going to hit her hard and fast. Everyone said I was so lucky that she slept so much, but it still didn't feel like enough when I didn't go to bed at the same time she did.

By the time I had dropped Mo off on the floor in the living room and gone back and forth twice to grab the tray of veggies and the bowl of chips, the doorbell had rang twice. The first time, Vince and another guy from the gym had come in, heading back out toward the back deck after a moment to get the burgers that Peter was grilling, calling out a hi. But the second time, Peter, who had wandered back inside the house, had answered it, coming back with a tall figure.

"Hello," Jonah's voice greeted Mo and me from where we were in the living room. She was sitting beside me with three of her big blocks while I tried to buy the pay-per-view via text message.

"Hey," I replied just as Peter walked off holding a plastic bag. "Where are your mom and sister?"

"Long day. They decided to stay at the hotel, but Natia sends her love. Mum had me bring a plate over. I gave it to Peter," he explained. "Only me tonight, if that's all right."

I made a farting sound that had him smiling as he approached and dropped to his knees, Mo's face lighting up as two big—and now familiar hands—reached for her middle, the fingers doing something that made me think he was trying to tickle her, but wasn't too sure about it. I told my heart to close its eyes even as she laughed.

"Does she hate me and decided to stay?" I asked him as I leaned back on my free hand.

A hint of a smile crossed the side of the face closest to me. "Yeah, nah. I think you may have frightened her a bit."

"Me?"

The side of his mouth hitched up high. "My mum can't be the first person who doesn't know what to do with you. I still don't know what to do with you half the time. But she was falling asleep on the drive to the hotel after lunch. She is tired. They both are."

I was going to take that as a compliment.

Those trying-to-tickle fingers paused as Mo raised a hand to her face and made an agitated sound. "What's wrong, sweetheart? I'm sorry I'm late." He peeked at his watch. "Oh, no. You're tired. It's almost bedtime, isn't it?"

"She didn't sleep much when I took her back to the office with me."

"She stayed with you the entire afternoon?"

"Yeah. I left an hour early, but it's one of the benefits of being the underboss."

He looked up at me from under those thick, dark eyelashes. "I wouldn't use the word 'under.' Seems to me everyone listens to you just fine."

Mo decided right then she'd had enough and made another fussy, cranky sound. "Okay, I hear you, kiddo. It's okay," I told her, scooping her up. "I'm going to put her to bed. There are veggie and turkey burgers outside, and Peter is manning the grill, so you don't have to worry that Grandpa Gus will spit on your food or anything."

He got up right along with me, a lot more nimbly than I did and faster, and I wasn't going to admire it. "I'd rather come along with you."

I had a feeling that's what he would say. Every night, he stayed late enough to put Mo to bed. I lightly patted Mo's bottom and then ran my hand up her spine as she made a little whimpering sound against my chest, since she'd leaned totally against me, needing me to hold her up. My poor baby. "Come on then, you."

The three of us headed up the stairs, the sound of voices and laughter from the deck making their way up the stairs as well, the same sound I had heard so many times growing up when people would come over. There were always so many voices at the house it never felt empty. It reminded me of who I was and what I had.

I started humming to Mo, then turned into her doorway— the fourth one on the floor—the one in the middle of all the bedrooms, feeling the heat of Jonah's body directly behind me when I stopped briefly. Flicking the lamp switch on with my foot, I carried our girl in.

I glanced at him as I moved to lower Mo into her crib. "Can

you turn on the sound machine? Just press the button in the center," I asked him as I started to massage the bottom of her foot the way she liked; that usually helped put her to bed. Every other time he'd been upstairs with us, he'd been the one carrying her. For "practice."

He did it. And I took the time to move my eyes around the pretty neat room we had all pitched in to set up for her before she'd come along. It was the most well decorated room in the entire house. With light gray walls, a crib that one of Grandpa's friends had handed down to us for a deal of one hundred bucks, and with a white dresser she would grow into, an enormous stuffed giraffe that had also been a hand-me-down gift, and a rocking chair in the corner… I liked it. I liked it a lot more than my plain-ass room.

Jonah came to stand beside me as I kept on rubbing the tiny foot that had slowly stretched to get closer to me as she relaxed.

"Look how tired she is," I whispered, trying to stifle a laugh. "Her mouth is already falling open."

Jonah covered his mouth and nose to muffle his chuckle as he gazed down at Mo lying in her crib, trying her hardest to keep her eyes open even as her little mouth gaped wide enough for a fly to go into it.

It was so fucking adorable.

I wished I hadn't left my phone downstairs so I could take a picture.

"She's so cute. I can't even be mad or annoyed with her for keeping me up last night," I whispered to him.

"Did she keep you up a lot before?"

Before. Right. "I barely slept the first… four months. She was waking me up every other hour to feed her or change her diaper, and I'd still constantly wake up to come check on her even if she didn't make a peep. I worried that she'd stop breathing or someone would climb in the window while I was sleeping to steal her or something. It was kind of bad, but right after that, she started sleeping almost through the night." I had done some difficult things in my life, but none of them were anywhere near as hard as this parenthood thing. I didn't know the meaning of pressure until I had the responsibility of keeping a mini life alive.

But hey, she was still here, so I couldn't be fucking up the job too badly.

At least not yet.

"I had an air mattress in here at first so that I wouldn't have to walk all the way back to my room." AKA all the fifteen feet down the hall, which had been more like a mile and half when I could barely keep my eyes open and my body hated me for the trauma I'd put it through after so long of taking care of it.

Jonah didn't say a word, but I could hear his steady breathing beside me as I kept rubbing Mo's sole, her little eyes fluttering closed and then reopening with a jolt, over and over again. I'd read her book too early, I guessed.

The sigh that came out of his mouth had me glancing over at him.

"What's wrong?" I asked.

Those two hands went to the top rail of the crib, fingers curling over the edge, his attention totally focused on the squirming body inside of it. "I can't help but wonder... if I hadn't gotten hurt, if I hadn't gone off to my granddad's farm to sulk about for so long... if I would've hardened up and come before or answered the damn phone or messaged you back or checked my fucking email... if I wouldn't have felt sorry for myself like a selfish fucking arsehole...."

Oh.

That's what he meant.

"I don't know how you can forgive me for leaving you. For leaving you both," he whispered in a voice rougher than I'd ever heard him capable of before.

He sounded so damn upset, it made my heart hurt, and I wasn't expecting that.

His right hand reached inside the crib, and his thumb and

index finger took hold of the other tiny heel just as he sighed. "I should've been here."

Should've, would've, could've. One of my coaches had told me once that those were the most pointless set of words in the world. But you learn to live with them, you learn *from* them, or you let them weigh you down for life.

And maybe I had been pissed off at him for so long for not being around. But he was here now, and, mostly, I understood why he'd done what he did. Not totally, but mostly. He was sensitive and apparently shy.

I knew all about what I expected of myself. So I could understand the expectations someone else would put on themselves too. I wasn't that much of a hypocrite.

Those shoulders of his were enormous, but there are certain weights that no one could bear.

Especially alone.

And really, seeing his profile, hearing his words, I couldn't help but forgive him for what he'd done. He was going to beat himself up over it more than I ever would. He'd suffered enough maybe, I thought with surprise. I hadn't even made a shitty comment to him in a while because there hadn't been anything to complain about.

He should've been here, yeah. But he hadn't. But he was now.

I didn't hesitate to lean my shoulder against him, just a little, that ache in my heart still faintly there. "It would've been nice to have you around so I could blame you for all those months of morning sickness," I told him quietly, sucking up the heat of his clothing against my bare arm. "Or to bitch when I was sleepy all the time, didn't want to eat anything but fruit, and on the nights I couldn't sleep or be comfortable or hold in my pee. It was rough. I was mad. Then I went through a period of feeling sorry for myself and confused and scared. I was worried the baby and I wouldn't bond or that I would resent her because I thought my life was over.

"Those months were rough, and I wasn't the same person. To a certain extent, I'm not the same person I was then or even before then." That was the understatement of a lifetime. I hadn't just been mad; I'd been hurt too. "I thought you didn't want to have anything to do with us, and that pissed me off. But she's here, and I'm here, and you're here, and I love her so much I can never explain it, even to you. We can't turn back time, but I thought we were trying to move forward. I haven't thought about pushing you down the stairs in at least two weeks," I tried to joke.

But he didn't take it. Instead, Jonah murmured, "I'm so damn sorry."

"I know you are." Because I did.

"I wish I could go back in time and change it all."

Was my heart supposed to hurt like this? "Not everything, I hope."

Jonah turned to me, one cheek hitching up in a grave half-smile. "No, not everything." His nostrils flared at the same time his other cheek started to go up too.

"Had you even thought about having kids?" I asked him, realizing I had no idea how he'd felt about it.

His features got thoughtful for a moment. "I never thought about it much. I have a big family… but I think I would have been happy."

I gave him a flat look that had him giving me a slightly amused but pained one.

"All right, I would have been worried too, maybe even a bit scared, but I liked you so much…."

I barely managed to keep the snort to myself. Sure, he'd like me so much. He had liked me so much he hadn't reached out to me, regardless of how often he'd thought about me and how crazy he claimed he had been over me. But I was going to ignore that slight pain. I wasn't going to think about it. His career had been the most important part of his life. There was no competition there, and I understood it.

You couldn't change a person's priorities. I couldn't make myself more important. I was lucky enough to have been so high up on at least two other people's lists.

"I like you so much," he amended while I kicked my thoughts aside. "It would have been fine. I would have been there, here, wherever you were."

Should've, would've, could've.

And then there was that present tense.

"I'm sorry again for the things my mum said today. She thinks she means well, even when she meddles and says things—"

"She's just watching out for you," I told him. "She doesn't know me, and I'm sure you've had more than enough girls throwing themselves at you before because they know who you are." And because of that ass. And that face. And all those muscles. But he didn't need an ego boost right then, or ever, so I didn't mention any of that. Much less all the good parts that weren't visible to the naked eye, like his personality.

He had made a face when I said the last sentence, and I couldn't help but snicker at it.

"I've grown up around men in the spotlight, jackass. I'm not stupid."

Jonah let out a suffering sigh that made me snort, and I could tell he was fighting back a small grin that he wasn't totally feeling. "Did you not hear what my sister said?"

"What? About you being shy? I was going to ask you about that. You talked to me like nothing from the moment we met." I'd thought about that period again in the afternoon while I'd been with just Mo. Jonah had instantly started talking to me, smiling, being playful and teasing….

And just… maybe a little bashful, a little more easygoing by not being aggressive or cocky.

But we'd never struggled to talk or get along. He had been the one who invited me to go to dinner after our tour. The one who had asked me for my number so we could go to the Louvre together. He was the one who'd posted a picture of us together hours after we'd met.

The point was, he had never been shy around me. He had never used that ultra-quiet voice in my presence. But I'd witnessed it around others. I really hadn't thought much of it when we would go out to eat and he'd lower his voice or just tell me what it was he wanted.

And based on the face that he was making, he was struggling with explaining it, which was actually just more proof that he might be. "I've always struggled with strangers," he admitted with a half-smile. "I didn't start speaking until I was three. Mum had to take me to therapy for it. Then, when I did start talking, it was only around my family. In school, some of the boys, and the girls, teased me over it, and that made me want to say things less, I reckon."

The urge to go back in time and kick a bunch of little kids in the ass was really strong then.

Jonah gave me a twisted smile in the darkness of Mo's bedroom. "I told you I was this skinny wee thing. No girls liked me back then, and I'll tell you that messes with a mate's head. It changes the way you see things and people when you get teased for being yourself, like you've got some other choice in the matter. Once I grew, everything changed. The only thing that made me special to other people was my size and being good at footy. So, yeh. I had a hard time with people I didn't know then, and now it's worse, you know. Not just with talking, but with trusting another person to do... things like that with."

That? Sex?

And seriously, what asshole had been teasing him back in the day for being skinny and little?

He couldn't read my mind, so he didn't answer or explain, but he did keep moving right along. "Everyone is out for fame or for more than that. If I told you the stories I've heard about the things some women have done... asking for money, tampering with protection, phone footage..."

Unfortunately, I knew all about that.

"Women don't want me because they know me, Lenny," he explained softly. "They only see the jersey. Not *me*." He paused. "I'm sure you know that with all your manly knowledge."

"My manly knowledge?" was what my mouth repeated.

And it made Jonah smile like he hadn't just told me about being teased for the things he couldn't change as a kid and how it had affected him then and even now as an adult. He could go out there and play in front of thousands and thousands of people, but talking to strangers was what made his balls sweat. Because somewhere deep down inside, he expected them to make fun of him too, I guessed.

And I couldn't remember the last time something had touched me so deeply.

Or made me want to protect him that much more.

How hard must it be for him to play this sport he loved, be so good at it and popular, and get so much negative shit for it at the same time? It made sense now more than ever why he had fallen into such a black hole after his injury. Because of how other people had made him feel. Because they had made him think the only special thing about him was rugby. Hadn't his own mom brought that up during lunch multiple times? His career and success?

This fucking man.

I didn't know how someone I still wanted to hate could slip so deeply under my ribs. I really didn't.

"You said it," Jonah quietly teased back after a moment. "You grew up around professional athletes. You know what it's like for us."

I scowled at him.

He smiled. "But I don't want to talk about that anymore, eh. My mum was awful to you, and that's what's important. It's my fault, Len. All I told her was that I was off to holiday once the season ended. All I was expecting was to come and talk to you and see if you could forgive me."

I swallowed his words and tried to process what they meant.

"Then you told me about Mo and...." His plans had changed. His life had. I got it. "She was upset when I mentioned I was spending the rest of my time here instead of going back to En Zed. I was going to explain, but... I just wanted to enjoy this as much as I could. She must have known something was going on because she called every day. Most I've talked to her since I was a boy." The hand he had on the crib slid a few inches to the side. Closer to my own hand. "She came without warning me. I finally posted on Picturegram while working out and didn't realize the location had been tagged. That's how she found out where I was. She had no idea about Mo. No idea about you. Until now."

About me?

I rocked on my feet. "So she's usually really nice when she hasn't just found out randomly that she's a grandma?"

His laugh was awkward and said everything. "Eh... I don't know if I'd say that. She's always wanted the best for us. Always pushed us and supported us in her way. But only my second oldest brother has lived up to her hopes. The rest of us... not so much all the time. It's all good. It's easier to let her say what she wants and do what we want." He laughed again, still rusty and tense, his fingers moving even closer to the ones I had almost beside his. "But she'll be better with you. She promised. I told her everything. About the phone calls and the emails and the messages.... About why I came." He gave me a pointed look that I wasn't totally sure what to make of. Did he want her to know that he'd come... to see me?

"I reckon she understands now, and I'm sorry for that," he said. "You shouldn't have had to defend yourself or think you aren't good enough."

"I know I'm good enough," I said, earning a quick glance

and a quicker, slighter smile. "But I get it. I'm not winning any beauty competitions or charm awards."

Those big brown eyes widened. "What's a charm award?"

"The same thing you aren't winning either, stupid," I muttered, getting a big grin and laugh that he tried his best to muffle when Mo's eyes instantly opened in response. "Look, I get it. I'm not what any mom would want for her precious baby."

His laugh cut off immediately and so did the smile on his face. "Yeah, nah, Len. Why do you say things like that?"

I felt my lips drop out of the smile they'd been in.

"You're smart, and you're so damn funny." I'd swear his eyes twinkled. "I could look at you all day, if it was possible."

I shut the hell up.

"And I'd tell you what I think about all the rest of you if I didn't think you'd knock me to the ground again," Jonah admitted quietly, the smile he gave me afterward, small.

This big, massive man was smiling shyly.

God help me.

Even the hand I had on Mo's foot stopped moving at what he'd just said.

I'd had more than a handful of—mostly drunk—guys tell me that they thought I was hot or *goddamn, that fucking body*, but I took it with a grain of salt. Beer goggles were real. I'd seen them in action. And I didn't give a fuck what those guys thought. Or what most people thought. I saw myself in the mirror clearly.

But this man saying those words…? About me? To me?

Jonah kept on smiling—and fucking stealing my heart straight out of my chest even though I was trying to cling onto it for dear life—and then he did it some more with the "Heh" that came out of his throat.

All I could do was look at him, so that's what I did even as I swallowed again and said the words I should probably regret in the future but probably wouldn't. "If you're trying to get me to want to sleep with you again, it's working."

He blinked. "I...." He closed his mouth. Opened it again, said, "Sometimes I can't tell if you're joking with me or not."

I wasn't.

But I also wasn't sure I wanted to repeat that sentence either.

Instead, I smiled at him and looked back down at Mo like that would win me a break to get my own thoughts together.

Well, it wasn't news to me that I didn't look like Freddy Krueger.

And even though I knew it wasn't cool or mysterious or flirty or smooth, I found the words, and even though they made me uncomfortable, I still threw them back out into the world. Into Jonah's direction. "I had started to think that I'd forced you to talk to me." My lips moved to the side, and I had to fight the urge to grimace-smile at him. "I know I'm not soft or even that nice or sweet or girly. Not that there's anything wrong with being that way or not being that way, but I know not everybody is into... that." Me. And my sometimes bad attitude. And my bluntness. And a bunch of other aspects of my personality that I wasn't going to apologize for.

The lines across his forehead and at the corners of his eyes grew deeper as those eyes moved across my face, and it was right then that big, warm fingers covered in calluses covered mine. And Jonah's voice was a low, husky thing I didn't know what to do with. "You didn't force me to do anything, love." His Adam's apple bobbed as he shook his head. "And you are all those things, they're just mixed in with all those other traits I like even more."

His fingertips slid from my knuckles to my fingertips and back, and his smile grew a little wider, a little more brilliant, as he said, "You've got the sweetest face, even when you're throwing out every insult in the English language." Jonah's eyes bounced from one of mine to the other, and he asked quietly, "Do you know why I could talk to you when we met?"

I didn't.

"You were sitting on a bench at the architectural museum while we waited for the tour organizer to come around to sign everyone in."

I faintly remembered waiting around and sitting on a bench next to these two teenage boys who were trying to stay as far away from their parents as possible.

"An elderly couple arrived—do you remember them? The Canadians celebrating their sixtieth wedding anniversary?" he asked but didn't wait for me to answer. "You got up the moment you saw them, said a thing or two to those boys sitting with you, and they got up as well. You invited them to sit down. You went and sat on the ground right next to them and talked to them the whole time. Well, until the sammies."

I remembered all that. Or, at least, I remember talking to the older couple on and off all day. Frederick and Basil had been their names, from Toronto. But a question lingered in my head over what Jonah said. "I got under your shy shield because I talked to them?"

"No." If anyone else had given me the smile he did, I would have thought they were mocking me, but his was too sweet. "Because you were nice to them and the way you smiled at them made you look so much more beautiful. It made me forget all about how good you looked in those shorts. You know Akira gave me such a hard time afterward for talking to you. He was so disappointed it wasn't him you helped. He talked about you in those shorts all the way back to the flat until I told him to stop."

Why did I feel embarrassed? "I just like older people," I explained, knowing that probably lost me points. "They're honest and easy to talk to. It's why I liked working at the retirement home."

Those long fingers curled over mine, covering my entire hand, his thumb sweeping up the side of my hand directly below my pinky finger. "Lucky for me my French is awful, eh?"

My whole heart soared a little bit.

Okay, alotta bit.

And I'd be embarrassed to think that my fingers almost twitched under his, because I had touched hands with a lot of people before. Men and women. His. But never... never like... this. With someone looking at me the way he was, so openly.

Jonah held my hand. With his rough thumb sweeping up and down the bones under my pinky finger, being all honest and Jonah and heartfelt.

And fuck me.

At some point, Jonah looked over so sharply, I almost lost my train of thought. "How could you think I didn't care about you enough? I wrote you... so many times. I couldn't bear to look at my own face in the mirror, but I wrote you because I wanted you to know I didn't forget about you."

My stomach soured a little bit as I frowned. "You mean four times?"

He frowned. "I sent you thirty-two postcards, Len," he claimed. "One every other week just about. I missed a few right after... and before I came, but I sent them. My nan bought them and put them in the mail for me while I was with her. I bought the rest. I sent half to the box on your website." His gaze was bright. "I didn't know what to say in them at first, but I meant what I wrote about missing you."

Missing me? Something thick and sneaky went down the center of my chest and into my stomach. "I only got two to my address in France, and my friend who was staying with me forwarded another two. There wasn't anything on those." I squeezed my hand into a fist, thinking about what he'd said. "And the... the PO Box? On my website? I let it close a long time ago. More than a year. Maybe even closer to two years ago."

Jonah's face went soft, his forehead scrunching.

He'd kept sending me postcards? I did the math in my head even as my heart pumped and pumped like I was doing something strenuous. Thirty-two, one every two weeks, would be… the whole time we'd been apart. He'd kept on sending them to me?

And he'd still come?

If he would have just tried a little harder to give me a smoke signal or something….

Thirty-two?

"Jonah…."

His hand gave mine another squeeze.

"What are you doing?" Grandpa Gus whisper-hissed out of fucking nowhere, honestly scaring the living shit out of me so bad that I jumped.

The hand on mine didn't go anywhere—mine didn't either —but I felt Jonah's fingers tighten in surprise for a second just as we both looked over our shoulders to find the man I had seen a million times in my life standing at the doorway with his hands on his hips.

"What are you doing?" I fought the urge to take my hand from under Jonah's.

I wasn't doing anything wrong. I had been the first one to slip my hand into his about two weeks after we'd met. After that he'd been the one to initiate it. He'd been the first man to ever hold my hand like that. In public. Other than my gramps and Peter. But I'd think about all that later.

Even with only the side lamp on, I could see Grandpa Gus frowning from where he stood, his beady little eyes narrowing as he glanced from Jonah to me and back again, like he'd caught us having sex right on the floor.

"I came to check on my pal," Grandpa whispered, still looking like he was trying to figure out what the hell was happening, not knowing and still disapproving.

"We were putting her to sleep," I replied, glancing back inside the crib to see that the little body under my hand had stopped squirming. Maybe as soon as she'd felt the evil presence coming up the stairs.

Grandpa's mouth went flat as he hummed under his breath.

"I'm not giving him a hand job or anything," I whispered, feeling Jonah's fingers jerk on top of mine at the same time he hissed out, "Len!"

But what did the man at the doorway do?

He snorted. "If you get pregnant one more time—"

That had Jonah choking.

"—I get to name the baby," Grandpa Gus finished. "And the fight is starting if you're still planning on watching it and not standing there making kissy faces at each other."

All I managed to do was shake my head as he turned around and disappeared down the hall, having fired his shots and done his damage, aka ruining one of the most intimate moments of my entire life.

God.

Was I that easy? I'd never been deprived of attention or affection. I didn't regret for a second not having a steady romantic relationship at any point. I wasn't used to relying on people who weren't Grandpa Gus or Peter or even Luna.

But now all of a sudden, I wondered...

I wondered what it would be like to have someone hold my hand and smile at me and for me to be there to do the same for them in return. To have an... extra special friend that was only mine. To have a... partner.

Not just anybody, but this one right here, with his biceps touching mine. His bare skin over my own. A person who claimed he'd sent me thirty-two postcards over the last seventeen months.

This one whose smiles made me feel better, whose playfulness seemed so attuned to me, who I could look at all day every day.

"I wonder how long it will take me to get used to the way you two are with each other," the softly voiced man noted a few seconds after my grandpa disappeared down the hall.

"A few years at least, I bet," I told him, still holding on a little to that piece of me that was suddenly way too curious.

I didn't move my hand and neither did he.

"Lenny," he said quietly.

I looked away as I pulled a blanket over Mo with my free hand and swallowed up every inch of that sweet, sweet face. "What?"

"I meant to tell you before my mum arrived...."

My stomach churned. Why did I always have to expect the worst?

"I want to start sharing Mo's existence."

Oh. I had a feeling I knew what he meant, but.... "What does that mean?"

"I know my mum. She would have already called my dad and told him. Word will get out sooner than later. There will be questions, there's no stopping that, but I don't want to make it seem like I'm hiding her. She's no secret, and I'm thinking we should front foot, that way we can control it so the journos don't."

I wanted to wonder why the hell people would care if he had a child or not, but I knew better than that. I had been on his social media accounts. His Picturegram account alone had four hundred thousand followers. I'd read some of the comments, his followers even got into arguments over his hair when he got it cut.

Of course some people would care about him having a daughter. He still sold papers. Magazines. Ads on websites.

"I'd like to keep the details as vague as possible, and I'm sure there will be criticism—on me—but this is between us. The whole story, at least. People will ask questions and look you up. I've got nothing to hide, but I don't want to put you into a situation you wouldn't want to be in either. I'll try to protect you from the media as much as I can."

Drawing my hands back toward me, I turned to Jonah and took in his face, tossing and turning his words over in my head.

He didn't want to hide Mo's existence, and that made me happy. I understood why he hadn't told anyone else about her until now. But how did we handle the rest of it?

I hadn't taken into consideration what it would be like for him to suddenly show the world this adorable baby and say, "She is mine," out of the blue and there not be any questions. Of course there were going to be questions. He was one of the most high-profile and highest paid players in a sport that was played in dozens of countries. He couldn't just say "Surprise!" and have people roll with it.

And he couldn't have a child without a mom. Well, he could, but I wasn't about to hide that Mo was mine. Especially not because I was afraid of people talking shit. Ooh. Let me shake in my flip-flops. What were they going to do? Look me up? What would people say about me? He could have done better? That I could be prettier?

Fuck 'em.

And, when I really thought about it, I wasn't about to let people drag Jonah through the mud because of whatever they might think.

Fuck that.

But…

There was the part that had nothing to do with me and what I wanted. This was his career. His lifetime of hard work.

And even though my chest suddenly ached at the idea that he would prefer to keep me hidden…. "I'm fine with you letting people know you're a dad and that you have Mo, but I don't know what you want to do about me in the equation. I know you keep a lot private"—I knew this from my brief period as a hormonal stalker, whatever—"and I get it, you know I do. So, I guess it's up to you what you want to do about me."

He blinked.

"If you don't want people to know I'm in the picture. For the future." I swallowed and then added hastily, "But I'm not going to lie if somebody asks. I'd just tell them it's none of their business with maybe a cuss word or two thrown in there. Just warning you."

He blinked again, and a tiny part of me wanted to squirm for the first time in my life.

"You know, that you had her with me," I threw in before making myself shut the hell up.

Those long lashes dipped down over his cheeks, and Jonah pinned me with a gaze that felt heavier than any body I'd ever tried throwing in my life. His words held the same weight. "I only said that because I thought maybe you wouldn't want anyone to tie you to me. I'm the one who lives with the criticism. It's always going to be there, at least while I play.

"It's you who will be tied together to me forever, Lenny," he went on. "You will always be in my life. It's my responsibility to worry about you, even though I know you have experience with criticism and opinions. I know you can handle yourself, and more than likely anything, but I want you to know you have a choice. It's up to you how much that is. If you want others to know that we... made Mo together. If you want your name connected to mine. But I know what I want."

It was his responsibility to worry about me.

I could handle anything.

I had him.

Was he trying to tell me all the things my subconscious wanted to hear? It fucking seemed like it. And that made me itchy.

This was my decision.

In it or not in it.

There was no middle ground.

I was scared of being a bad mom. I was scared of spiders crawling into my ears while I was sleeping. I was scared of fucking birds. But I wasn't scared of screwing up. I'd fallen a lot of times in my life. You might get bruised and it might hurt for a while, but you didn't die.

And what? He was worried I would get turned off by people talking shit about him? Ha.

So I told him what he hadn't yet figured out about me. "You're stupid handsome and you're a good person too. You can tell whoever you want. I'm not ashamed of you." I went up to my tippy toes and gave him the most direct look I could muster. "I could've had Mo with worse. Actually, I can't think of anyone else I would rather have had her with, and I will never repeat that out loud again. If anyone wants to talk shit to you with me around, they're going to regret it, and that's what they'll deserve. The only person who gets to call you a dumbass is me... and your siblings... and maybe Grandpa Gus."

The silence between us, ignoring the sounds in the background, was deafening.

And that was why I wasn't expecting Jonah to throw a hand up and cover his mouth with it before he turned around and walked out of the room as he started fucking chuckling.

All right.

That went well.

No one in this country would ever care about who Mo's dad was, but in other places, they would. And none of those people mattered. The only thing that mattered was what *we* knew.

Why the fuck would Jonah think I'd be turned off by people criticizing him? I wasn't joking when I told him that anyone who talked shit to him would end up regretting it, if they got me involved. They could all shut the hell up.

Too afraid to wake up Mo, I turned her baby monitor on even though I wouldn't need it, turned down the white noise machine just a little, and headed downstairs.

On the way, I stopped in the kitchen and filled up a glass of water while I talked to a couple of the guys from the gym who had showed up while I'd been upstairs, and then eventually made my way toward the living room, which was packed with at least twenty male and female bodies wedged on the couch, on the floor, and on chairs that had been dragged from the dining room we only used on Thanksgiving and Christmas.

"Len!" and "Lenny!" all came out from half the people in the room.

"Where's Madeline?" one of the guy's girlfriends asked. I couldn't remember her name.

I pointed upstairs as I looked around the room to find somewhere to sit. "Sleeping."

"Aww," one of the other girls groaned. Amanda? Mandy? She was a new-ish girlfriend I had met twice, and I liked her. "That's why I came. I wanted to see her."

Her boyfriend made a comment about how he thought she'd tagged along to spend time with him, while I went back to looking around the room for a spot.

Grandpa Gus and Peter were both hogging the love seat that everyone knew was theirs, but it was when I glanced toward the couch that I found one big body taking up a whole lot of it, a beer wedged in between two enormous thighs.

Jonah smiled at me, one of the only people in the room who wasn't totally focused on the television, and I smiled back at him, just as one of the guys who had been training with Peter on and off for years called out, "Len, you can come sit with me if you want."

Jonah's smile fell off.

What he didn't see was one of the other guys from the gym hitting the guy who'd piped up in the thigh and whispering something in his ear that had him leaning forward and looking across the room at the man sitting on the couch.

"I'm good," I replied, still watching the biggest man in the room.

Clutching the baby monitor under one arm and my water in my other hand, I waited until the end of a round to hop across the floor, stepping on someone's toes before I made it to the far end of the room.

"Lenny," Jonah called out, sitting up straight on the couch, scooting forward enough so that he was perched on the end of it, one hand on the armrest. "Sit here."

I shook my head as I took another step closer, so close I was directly beside him and the couch. "If you pass me that pillow, I'll be fine on the floor," I said just as the commentators on the television started talking about what needed to happen in the final round of the fight that was on.

The father of my child shot me a look.

I shot him one back, already slowly lowering myself to the floor to his right. "I'm serious," I promised him. "If I wanted to sit on the couch, I would. Cushion, please."

That serious-ass expression didn't go anywhere as he pulled out the toss pillow that was wedged in between his side and the couch before handing it to me. I set it on the floor, and then parked my ass on top of it, my back against the front of the armrest part of the couch. I scooted over an inch to the left to bring the long length of Jonah's lower leg closer to me, so I could lean against it slightly.

He didn't move away as I scooted in, setting the baby monitor down on my other side along with my glass of water.

The last thing I remembered was yawning as I focused in on the television and tried to recall any information I could about the two men fighting in the cage.

I passed out.

At least, I didn't realize I had passed out until sometime later when I woke up because something was hurting from the general vicinity of my neck.

I opened both eyes slowly, not surprised at all I'd fallen asleep and licked my lips as I focused in on a few things.

One: apparently I'd started hugging and leaning against Jonah's leg because I had an arm around it, and there was a wet spot over his jeans right by his knee that had to belong to me.

Two: The main fight was over because what was playing on the television wasn't anything that involved two highly trained fighters trying to win a lot of money. Instead, on our eighty-inch TV, there were a lot of sweaty men running fast across a field, passing a ball from one person to another. Some of them were wearing red jerseys, others were wearing blue jerseys. But it was the short shorts on the screen that confirmed they were watching rugby.

Three: At least half the room had emptied, but Grandpa Gus was still there, so was Peter, and I didn't know who else to my left.

But most importantly, Jonah was talking quietly. Not in his Mighty Mouse voice, but in a very, very soft one.

And it had to be Jonah who had his fingers loose and heavy over my head as he murmured to someone, "The scrum only happens when there's been a minor infringement and play has to be restarted."

"But how do you know when play has to be restarted?" a voice I faintly recognized asked.

"You're a dumbass. How do you know when any play in any game has to be restarted? When somebody fucks up. Like a foul. What do you think an infringement is?" another voice I also recognized answered.

I yawned as Grandpa Gus's voice piped in with, "The big one right there is bleeding, and he's getting into that… what'd you call it? Scum?"

"Scrum," Jonah corrected.

That word reminded me of how he'd told me so long ago that he had started wearing a scrum cap to protect his ears at his grandmother's insistence.

"But they aren't taking him out of the game?" Grandpa asked.

The fingers on the top of my head stirred over my hair. "Yeh. Rugby isn't… like that. Unless there's a head injury and an HIA is needed—"

"What's an HIA?" that was Peter who asked.

"Head injury assessment. Concussion protocol, you'd call

it," the man whose lower leg was giving me all the warmth in the world answered.

"That guy's nose is still bleeding though."

Jonah's laugh was soft. "Yeah, he doesn't need staples. He'll play the rest of the match, you'll see."

"What the fuck?" another voice echoed. "I still can't get over that none of y'all wear pads or helmets, and you still tackle the shit out of each other."

"Yeh," Jonah said, and those fingers on my head sifted over my hair some more, moving so that the pads grazed my temple. "It's like what you do with the MMA. They don't take you out if you bleed a bit, do they?"

I could see Grandpa Gus stirring on the couch, his eyes glued to the game on the screen. "Yeah, but fights happen two, maybe three times a year. You play, what? Once a week for four months?"

"Eh… once a week for eight months sometimes, depending on the schedule and the league. Depending, too, on if you play on the national team or not, then you're in it for most the year."

"*Eight months?*" Grandpa Gus spit out.

Did he sound… impressed? Was that the sound of my grandfather being *impressed*?

I might have *almost* felt jealous. Almost.

Jonah's soft puff of laugh had me lifting my chin so I could peek at him. His eyes were down on me like he'd felt me moving around, and the next thing I knew, a finger was grazing my temple, and that was nice… but confusing. And he looked right at me as he answered back, "Eight months with a two-week break in there."

"How old are you?" Grandpa asked.

His gaze went nowhere, his thumb still on me, brushing up and down a half inch or so as he said, "Thirty-one in June."

A little younger than me.

"It's a young man's sport," he went on, still doing that thing with his thumb that was pretty much the equivalent of a snake charmer to me because I wasn't moving away and had no freaking plans to. "If I'm very lucky, I've got another four, five years at best. Maybe less, maybe more. Depends what my body decides."

Four years left playing?

But what I really heard was… four years left of him living wherever the hell else his career might take him?

And, realistically, wasn't it a reminder that he had the rest of his life to live somewhere else? I wasn't expecting him to move here, to Houston, just because of Mo. A person couldn't just pick up their entire lives and move to another country where they had no one. Especially not someone like Jonah who, as I'd just learned, was close to his family.

What were we going to do?

I turned my head, taking my cheek out of the reach of his thumb and facing forward again, forcing a yawn out of my body to play off the fact that the idea of him being gone for four years, five years, the rest of his life… sucked.

Of course I wouldn't have a baby… maybe be even a *little* in love… with a man who was simple. Of course it wouldn't have been with someone who trained at the gym. Someone who did MMA. Someone who lived in the same city, much less the same fucking country. Someone who didn't love what he did as much as I had probably loved judo when that had been all my life revolved around.

But I had barely thought that when something that felt an awful lot like a finger grazed the top of my ear.

"And you play where?" a familiar voice asked.

"I finished my season in Paris not long ago," he answered, without really answering, which made me wonder.

The same voice huffed. "Wasn't that where Lenny was last year when she—*hold up*. That's where y'all met, huh?"

"Yeh. On a tour together. She translated for me while we were waiting on the bus," he said to them for no reason at all.

"Best decision I've ever made was buying that sammy that day."

I held back my sigh because I knew Grandpa Gus could hear me do that in a crowded room with the television blaring and sagged against the leg at my side, my arm still wrapped around it.

I stayed right there, listening to the voice of the man on the couch go on for the next forty minutes of the remainder of the rugby game, and tried my best not to think about how I felt about him or about the time we had left or about how buying my own sandwich that day might be the best decision I'd ever made too.

CHAPTER 17

11:11 p.m

> I can't believe you're this much
> of an asshole.
> All I need is to talk to you for
> two minutes.
> That's it.
> It's important.

11:13 p.m.

> It's really fucking important

I WAS SO TIRED THE NEXT MORNING THAT I COULD BARELY KEEP MY eyes open as I headed down the stairs holding a wide-awake Mo in one arm. I'd jinxed her the night before and ended up waking up twice to her little kitten cries, once because she'd pooped—super soft poop that reminded me of what she'd done to Jonah, which had made me laugh despite being exhausted—and the other because she'd been hungry after crapping out everything she'd eaten and wanted more calories right the fuck then. I had ended up telling myself I'd nap after the second time she'd woken me up, and that "nap" had ended up being a three-hour mini coma, and my back, shoulders, and hips were hating me for putting them through that.

At least the little booger had let me sleep in until nine, but even then, it wasn't the same.

"You're lucky you're a cute little monster," I told her with a side-eye.

Mo rattled off some animated babble that had me raising my eyebrows at her.

"I didn't give you a sloppy butt; don't blame me," I replied to her, giving her a smile.

"What do you think about going to the park later and giving the swing a try? Maybe we can ask Grandpa to go with us and talk him into getting on one, and we can push him so hard he falls off," I told her, taking another two steps down the staircase.

Mo just kept on grinning, pulling my hair hard enough to make me wince.

I snuck a quick kiss to her neck that had her squealing and pulling on my roots some more. "You're right, that's probably not the best idea. Then we'd have to listen to him whine, and nobody likes that, huh?"

I swore she lifted her chin so I could give her another kiss to the neck, so I did it again, getting another squeal and hair tug, as my feet took another two steps down, finally hitting the bottom of the landing just as I heard a female voice coming from inside the door that led into the kitchen. And that was a split second before a voice said, "Aren't you two a sight?"

I stopped, instantly looking up to find Jonah standing there in the hallway in black sweatpants that shouldn't have been fitted but were because he was just that muscular, a clean and crisp long-sleeved white T-shirt with a logo over the chest, and white quarter-length socks, looking totally and completely awake and with a smile on his face, like he didn't know what being tired was like.

God, I missed those days when I had no problem sleeping nine to ten hours a night because I *had to*. Because of judo and because sleep was so important for your body to reenergize and heal, and I had needed every advantage I could take because the sport was so hard on everything. I could remember the times I'd groaned at Grandpa Gus when he'd ordered me to head upstairs even though it had felt too early.

It's the little things you take for granted. Like sleep. And bladder control.

I gave him a sleepy smile. "Beauty and the Beast," I yawned. "Mo's the beauty in case you're wondering. She woke me up twice in the middle of the night."

The pleased expression on that handsome face fell away, replaced with a concerned one. "Is she all good?"

"Yeah. Her poop was pretty loose, and she took her time going back to sleep. Then she woke up hangry and took her sweet-ass time going back to sleep that time too. Look, she wants you." Because she did. Mo had already started leaning forward, even her little arms going up in a reaching gesture for him. "What a bandwagoner."

His worried face didn't go anywhere, but his hands did, coming up and toward the daughter who was straining even more to get out of my hold and into his. Little traitor. Once he had her and had placed a kiss on each of her cheeks, he glanced back at me and asked, "Are you all right?"

I blinked, eyeing his clothes—and him—again. "Yeah. Just tired and my back and hips hurt from sleeping on the floor in her room. It'll pass." I scratched my throat and eyed my girl who stared dreamily up at the man holding her like *wow, who is this?* She was such a double-crosser, but her little face made me so happy. "Why are you here so early?"

He smiled at my blunt-ass question, hiking Mo up a little higher on his chest as her hand smacked at the corner of his lips, even as his attention remained on me. "Peter invited me for breakfast."

He had?

"I like your pajamas."

I didn't have time to think about the tiny shorts and loose shirt hanging off my shoulder, because I was too busy trying to think about what had happened the night before. The last thing I remembered after basically crawling up the stairs from how sleepy I was was waving at the remaining five people who were still there after another forty minutes of Jonah trying to explain rugby to people who knew absolutely nothing about it and kept comparing it to football and soccer, when it wasn't either. Those five people had included Grandpa, Peter, Jonah, and two other guys. It had been midnight, which was hours after my bedtime when I could help it.

And now… it was nine. And he was here.

"Did you get any sleep?" I found myself asking him with another yawn, taking in again how bright and alert he was. Lucky bitch.

"Some," he answered, finally focusing down at the baby in his arm who had grabbed his T-shirt with two bossy hands to more than likely get his attention.

I didn't need to do the math in my head. "Shouldn't you be getting more?"

Jonah did that small, shy smile, but leaned his forehead toward Mo's as he said, "Yeh… but this is more important." He tickled her belly with an index finger.

I let that answer hang in the air. And in my heart.

Those honey-colored eyes moved toward me, and the little smile he gave me was deceptive. "My mum is here."

I glanced down at my clothes. Or lack of clothes.

Then I decided, it was Sunday, it was nine in the morning, and he was at my house. If she wasn't going to like me because I walked around in my pajamas, then she wasn't going to like me for the hundred other real reasons I could give her.

"Cute socks."

It was my turn to probably turn a little pink as I ignored the fact they were flamingo socks that Luna had given me. They clashed perfectly with my red T-shirt from the last time I'd donated blood. "I've seen your Spiderman underwear, champ, you don't have room to talk."

His laugh made me smile, but I wasn't the only one; Mo grinned up at the man too as she said a string of consonants and vowels that didn't totally work together.

But I knew right then that she knew. She had to know somehow who he was. She was already trying to crawl out of my arms to go into his every chance she had, and that said something major.

"Is your sister here?"

"No, she went shopping."

"Lenny! Stop running your mouth and come eat!" Grandpa Gus hollered from the kitchen, making me roll my eyes.

"Want me to take her?"

He shook his head.

We headed into the kitchen a second later, and I instantly spotted Sarah, his mom, sitting at the island with a cup of tea in her hand. It was a good thing I'd ordered some for Mr. Innocent, I guess. Grandpa was at the stove, dealing with his whole-grain pancakes, and Peter was at the island, cutting up berries because apparently we were spoiling our guests instead of eating thawed frozen berries.

"Morning," I said, holding the door open for the two and then letting it swing closed as I headed straight for my grandfather, giving him a kiss on the cheek first—we both made eye contact with each other because he could've done me a solid and texted me a warning but intentionally hadn't—and then did the same to Peter, who I wasn't going to blame because we both knew who the mastermind behind all rude things was: the ancient evil in the house.

And it was that awkward moment as I was pulling away from Peter that I made eye contact with Sarah and had no idea what the fuck to do. Wave? Handshake?

Fuck it.

I went around the island and gave her a kiss too, ignoring the surprise on her face as I did it, but not being able to ignore the man smiling from where he was standing at the other side of the island holding *our* girl.

"Good morning, Elena," the woman said, surprise all over her voice too.

Heh.

I shot Jonah a sneaky look as I stretched my arms over my head—my shoulder shooting me a slight *fuck you* in the process —and asked, "Need help with anything?"

From the looks of it, we *were* being fancy and shit. We usually fended for ourselves after Grandpa made pancakes or waffles or whatever he was gracing us with, but from the platters I suddenly spotted on the counter, he was done. There was fruit salad, tofu scramble with potatoes, onions, tomatoes, and bell peppers, a bottle of maple syrup and another bottle of honey, and as soon as Peter got done, there were going to be berries too for topping, along with the pancakes.

Whether he was trying to fuck with Sarah or with Jonah, I had no idea. We hadn't done anything special any other time Jonah had eaten with us but knowing Grandpa, maybe both, because except for the holidays, we didn't do buffet-style meals. So I knew he was up to something. Showing off? Killing them with fake kindness? I should've been surprised he hadn't run out to the store and bought placemats at the rate he was going.

But as I looked at my grandfather's profile, he didn't look like he was up to no good, and I didn't know what the hell to do with that.

He was purposely not looking at me either, so….

"No, everything is done," Peter answered as he pushed the bowl of berries toward the middle of the island, catching my eye as he stood straight and then winked at me.

What's going on? I mouthed, not able to keep from frowning because I could expect some devious shit from Grandpa—of course I could—but Peter being in on it?

The grin he flashed me didn't make me feel better, but it did at the same time.

"Jonah, coffee or tea?" Peter asked.

"Tea, please. Herbal if you have it," he replied, standing there while the baby in his arms slapped his cheeks and made his eyes go wide. He whispered something back that had her talking back to him.

Peter's head swiveled toward me, and I nodded.

"I'll drink whatever you have," Jonah amended, I guess noticing our back and forth.

"We have herbal," I told him as Peter went back to the container where he had grabbed Sarah's. I'd told both him and Grandpa about it a few days ago when the box had arrived with my regular shipment of matcha tea I took to Maio House.

"Lenny ordered you some," Grandpa mentioned under his breath, peeking at me as he turned the knob on the range to turn it off.

I felt my nostrils flare.

"You got what? Four different kinds, Len?" the other man I was planning on disowning as soon as we were in private said as he turned toward the island holding a plate with what looked like twenty pancakes stacked on top of each other.

"Yes." I glanced at Jonah before moving around the island to grab forks from a drawer while everyone else sat wherever they wanted. In my head, I could sit by myself on one end, he could sit with his mom, and The Traitor and Up to No Good could be beside each other.

No one said anything, and when I turned back around with silverware in my hand, my hopes for the seating arrangement had disappeared.

Fortunately—or unfortunately—Mo's high chair was beside Sarah, who had already angled her stool toward her. There was an expression that I wouldn't have believed she was capable of yesterday on her face as she watched Mo, like she was a fucking unicorn or something. Which she was.

Jonah, though, was on the side I'd planned to sit on next to Peter, with a free stool beside him. I slipped into it and looked around expectantly.

What the hell was everyone waiting for? Did they… did the Collins family pray before eating? Because it was a Sunday? Was that why Peter and Grandpa weren't moving? Jonah had never prayed before a meal.

Uh….

"Baby Jesus, thank you for our food. Amen," Grandpa Gus rushed out all of a sudden out of fucking nowhere, startling the fuck out of Peter and me, who both stared at him like we didn't know who the hell he was anymore.

And….

Did he say baby Jesus?

The cough beside me had me glancing at Jonah, who had his lips pressed together and his gaze straight ahead at the wall behind his mom and Mo.

Glancing back at Grandpa, his cheeks were pink like he didn't know why the hell he'd said that and was debating whether or not he regretted it.

"Ah, amen," Sarah managed to get out, sounding pretty damn graceful and not like my gramps had just thanked *baby Jesus* of all people.

"That's the last time I let you watch *Talladega Nights*," I muttered under my breath just loud enough for my grandpa to hear.

And apparently Jonah too because he coughed, a lot.

"I don't know what you're talking about," Grandpa replied before nudging the plate of pancakes closer to the middle of the island, avoiding eye contact. "Okay, let's eat unless someone else wants to… pray or make another useless comment that I have no reference for."

I laughed.

But it was Jonah beside me who cleared his throat, reached for the spatula, slid two pancakes onto it before transferring them over to my plate first, as he said, very quietly, very calmly, "I do have a question, were you praying to eight-pound, five-ounce baby Jesus or...."

I threw my head back and laughed a second before I slid off the stool and onto the floor.

It was a long, long time before I managed to start eating.

"So...," I said a while later as I swallowed the last piece of tofu scramble. Beside me, Jonah mopped up the maple syrup he had left over with his final triangle of pancake. I hadn't kept count, but I was pretty positive he'd eaten at least six of them. Grandpa Gus had mastered the whole grain pancake game a while ago. They were the shit—nutritious, with very little sugar and even a little banana and flaxseed thrown in. "I was going to take Mo to the park and sneak her onto a swing if I can pay some little kid to hop off for a few minutes. Do any of you want to come?"

Please God, please God, don't let Sarah come....

"I'm meeting Allen for a matinee at noon," Grandpa was the first one to answer as he wiped his mouth with a napkin.

"I promised Frank and Carl I'd watch the last day of a jiu-jitsu tournament," Peter added after taking another sip of his coffee.

Please. Please. Please, please, please....

"My only plan was seeing the two of you. It's my day off from conditioning," Jonah replied, shooting me a much gentler smile than the rest he'd been shooting me after the baby Jesus incident had landed me on the floor and had Grandpa Gus scowling for an hour. "Mum? You can take the ute if you would rather do something else."

Sarah, who had been pretty silent the entire breakfast,

picking and choosing very specific questions and conversations —but maybe that was because she'd been too busy looking at Mo, handing her pieces of pancake and basically touching her every chance she got—chose that moment to look away from the messy baby who had eaten a record amount of soggy pancake. She blinked. And what I was pretty sure was dread poked at my chest as she said, "I could go for a walk."

Shit.

I forced a smile onto my face that my grandfather and Peter could recognize from across the fucking galaxy, and I hoped that Jonah couldn't but wasn't totally convinced. It was one thing for his mom to be the one who was snappy at me, but it was another for me to be bitchy toward her.

Plus, she'd come today. So that had to be something, I guess.

"Okay," I said, trying to keep my inner whine out of my tone. "Let me take my little monster upstairs and get her dressed, put some clothes on so I don't moon anyone, and we can get going."

"I can get her dressed," the man at my side claimed.

I lifted a shoulder and nodded before shifting around in my seat and getting up. I grabbed my plate, Jonah's, Grandpa's, and Peter's—Sarah had already rinsed hers and left it in the sink—stealing a smooch against the small head as I passed by, and rinsed those off too.

"Leave them in there, Len. I'll set the dishwasher later. I found a couple recipes for Mo I wanted to try before I leave," Grandpa said, still sounding annoyed his baby Jesus thing hadn't gone unnoticed.

"What kind of recipes?" Sarah asked in a polite voice.

"Apples and chicken."

That had me making a face. "In the same mush?"

Grandpa Gus shot me a look that said he hadn't forgiven me yet and wasn't going to. "Yes. Apples and chicken. I don't remember what else goes in there, carrots and cinnamon too, I think, and don't make that face at me. You ate everything I put in front of you when you were a baby and everything I didn't put in front of you." He snorted. "You still do."

I frowned. "These muscles don't feed themselves."

"I thought I was the only one who noticed how much Lenny ate. It's impressive." This fucker Jonah was nodding at Peter, who was telling him with his own dip of a chin that *yeah*, he wasn't imagining how much food I put away every meal. "I've wondered a time or two where it all goes."

That was a nice compliment, at least.

"You should have seen her when she was competing in a higher weight class. She was packing in around five thousand calories a day," Grandpa Gus said, sounding pretty damn cheerful all of a sudden.

"How many kilojoules is that?"

How the hell he knew the conversion was beyond me, but it only took Peter a second to reply. "About twenty thousand kilojoules."

"I was doing physical activity for several hours every day," I tried to explain drily, not enjoying the stunned face Jonah was making.

"I eat around twenty-thousand now to maintain my weight," he said, his expression turning into an amused grin that still didn't amuse me at all.

"I have a high metabolism. It's a gift," I threw out again to the haters. "And I needed to gain weight. Thank you. It was your idea, Grandpa, for me to go up a weight class."

No one was listening to me.

"We used to joke that one of us was going to need to get a job at the grocery store to get an employee discount," Peter chuckled.

"Darling, you have no reason to tease," Sarah commented out of nowhere with a properly contained smile.

I turned my head to cheerfully gaze at the man who was still looking extremely pleased by the conversation.

"You would eat your meal, then eat whatever your brothers

left. Did you forget about hiding cans of Watties when you were in primary school?"

Color rose up on his face instantly, and I couldn't fucking help it. I couldn't. "What kind of food did he hide?"

That got the first laugh out of Sarah I'd heard. "Canned spaghetti. Baked beans. Loved them. He would try taking them in his school bag so he would have a snack to eat on the walk home from school."

I opened my mouth and turned to look at Jonah with it still open. "Did you have to carry around a can opener to eat cold spaghetti and beans?"

His face just got even pinker. "I was growing."

He *had*. I was going to die from cuteness overload. My body didn't know what to do with that.

"Darling, you didn't grow hardly any until you were sixteen, or did you forget that as well?" Sarah egged on with another light laugh that seemed totally opposite of the distance she'd been showing.

"I was saving up the calories and the energy for the future," he replied under his breath.

I snickered.

"It's hard to see it now, but he was a skinny thing for so long. We thought he was going to take after me instead of his dad. Do you remember all those talks we had with you when you were younger?"

"Yeah," he responded with a normal smile. "Used to tell me how it wasn't important that I was smaller than the other boys. That all that mattered was that I use my ticker and that I try my best and work harder than the rest of them. Dad would have a list of all the shorter players who made careers of it, so I'd know it was possible. If I remember correctly, you fed me all that food to get me to bulk up so at least I wasn't all skin and bones."

Then he sniffed and blinked, and I had to swallow because was he getting fucking emotional thinking about his parents trying to make him feel better about being short and scrawny?

To tell him that he could still pursue this dream of his even though biology worked against him? Damn it. Goddamn it.

I pressed my lips together and forced myself to keep my eyes open for a few seconds.

The heavy chuckle that came out of Sarah told me I wasn't the only one thinking this over a lot. "Then you grew and kept on growing. If I thought you ate so much before, it was nowhere near as much as you did after that."

For some reason, I glanced at my grandpa to find him side-eyeing Jonah with a heavy-lidded expression on his face like he was contemplating something. Whether it was a good something or a bad something, I had no idea. I wasn't sure I wanted to ask.

"Bigger than your father now. Bigger than all your brothers and grandfathers too," Sarah finished with a smile.

That reminded me he still hadn't shown me a picture of his siblings, other than the ones I'd come across when I'd been looking for him.

"Do you have any siblings, Lenny?" the woman asked all of a sudden.

But it was Grandpa Gus who answered with, "No. She would have tried to drown any other brothers or sisters if she'd had them."

I blinked.

And the silence was fuel for the man who had even less shame than I did. "I hope Mo takes more after her dad than her mom because Lenny took things to school, but it wasn't anything food related."

I knew where this was going, and there was no stopping this train of memories I had never been allowed to forget.

Grandpa reacted the same way he had every time he brought up this story for the last... twenty-five years. He fucking closed his eyes because he instantly started laughing so hard it was difficult to understand him.

A glance at Jonah showed him looking really expectantly.

Grandpa Gus had his hand over his face as he kept on losing his shit, recounting this story. Probably one of his most favorite stories of my childhood. It was one of mine too, not that I'd admit it to him.

"What did she take?" my girl's dad asked.

It was hard to understand him but not impossible as he answered, "She took... she took nunchucks to school and got suspended for two days when she was in kindergarten. The principal said it was a school record."

I groaned again. "All right. I'll be upstairs now."

He ignored me. "Remember? You told Noah the night before you were going to beat him up if he pulled your hair again and he did, so you took them to school to do the job so you wouldn't get in trouble with your coach?" Grandpa Gus cackled, grabbing at his middle like it was seriously the first time he'd recounted the story when it was probably the millionth, and he still thought it was as hilarious as it had been the first.

I glanced at Jonah as I undid the tray of Mo's high chair and lifted her out of it. The dark-haired man was smiling, but it was... it was a weird smile. Like he was thinking about something a little too hard.

"Nunchucks?" Sarah was too busy gasping. "Where did those come from?"

Only Grandpa Gus would laugh his fucking ass off at a six-year-old having nunchucks. "Her godfather. She asked Pierre for them for Christmas."

Even Peter chuckled. "He was never able to tell her no. All she had to do was ask, and he would do whatever she wanted. She'd ask if he was coming to one of her competitions even though he was in the middle of filming a movie, and he would come every time."

"Like a sucker." Grandpa Gus chuckled. He put his hand on his chest and smiled almost dreamily over at Sarah. "I really hope Mo ends up taking more after Jonah than Lenny. I really do. My heart can't handle another Lenny in the world."

Liar.

But maybe not.

I edged my way closer to the door with my girl, shooting a glance toward Jonah again who still had the same thoughtful expression on his face that was almost a confused one. "I was a precious angel, and you know it." I flicked Grandpa Gus behind the ear as I walked behind him. "Jonah, you coming?" I asked as I shouldered the door open, and he got up.

I had barely made it about three steps into the hallway toward the stairs when he came up behind me. "Lenny?"

"Hmm?"

"Peter said something about your godfather, Pierre...."

Oh. That. "Yeah?" I started up the stairs.

"Making movies...," he kept going, following me up. "Is he referring to Pierre St. Cloud? The actor?"

"Yeah," I told him, stopping to shoot him a glance over my shoulder. "He filmed a couple movies here in the 80s. Grandpa trained him during them."

His face was blank with surprise. "*Blood Games* Pierre?"

I nodded.

"Karate master Pierre?"

I lifted a shoulder. "A second dan black belt. I wouldn't call him a *master*...."

Jonah blinked.

"I used to call him Pew-Pew because I couldn't say Pierre," I told him. "You'll probably meet him one day. I still see him a couple times a year." You know... if Jonah was around in the four months he had off from work.

Fuck.

I turned forward again and kept heading up the stairs, listening in to the fact that I was almost all the way to the top before I heard his footsteps again.

"Why didn't you say anything about it?" he called out after me.

"Because it's not a big deal." I paused. "And because sometimes people make fun of him when they know. People say he's cheesy and stuff, but he's always been great to me. I don't like him being made fun of. If it hadn't been for *Blood Games*, I don't think MMA would have ever blown up the way it has because he inspired so many kids who are now adults, you know."

His footsteps stopped again as I made my way down the hall, passing the master bedroom, the spare, and finally getting to Mo's room, separated from mine by the bathroom in between. Jonah stopped just to my side and, without prompting, took the baby out of my arms and into his, his biceps bunching and showing off the fact that one was just about as big as Mo's entire body.

The boy was ripped.

And that wasn't saliva pooling in my mouth at the memory of running my hands up and down those arms while he'd—

Nope.

I forced a smile onto my face. "I'm gonna brush my teeth and change. Just holler if you need anything."

I ducked into the bathroom. Brushing my teeth, washing my face, and rubbing some moisturizer into my skin didn't take long and neither did applying deodorant. On the walk from the bathroom to my room, I heard Jonah talking quietly, but I had no idea what was being said or done. He'd been around long enough. He knew what he was doing.

I stripped down to my underwear and sports bra, deciding to leave that sucker on because the last thing I needed was a boob to pop out in mid-swing push, and had just put on my high-waisted black leggings when I heard a cough from the doorway.

"The door was open," Jonah murmured as I turned, one hand in my drawer as I pulled out a sweater.

Mo was holding a toy in one hand, gnawing and drooling on it at the same time.

I had never been too-too ashamed of my body even after having her. I wasn't back down to pre-baby weight yet—and I sure as hell wasn't at my competing weight or body composition—but I was getting to what was becoming my new normal. And, well, a lot of things had changed and moved around a bit, but I had expected that to happen from the books and blogs I'd read while I was pregnant.

But now, all of a sudden, standing there in my high-waisted pants, I got self-conscious for what might have been the first time in my fucking life.

"I'm almost ready," I told him, tugging the sweater out, suddenly aware of how much of a mess my room was. There was a pile of laundry on the floor in one corner, another rocking chair I'd used pretty often with Mo over the last few months that was covered in clothes that I'd worn but could wear again. Then there were the handful of toys all over the floor that I hadn't put back up after bringing them over for my booger to play with while we hung out in my room.

The bras hanging off the doorknobs of my closet were a nice touch too, I thought, knowing there was no way to miss the giant bra cups.

And that was where his gaze went straight for.

I'd swear on my life that his eyes moved down to my boobs for a second. And I'd swear on my life too that his Adam's apple bobbed as he looked at them. They'd always been big, and had only gotten bigger with Mo, even if she'd decided a couple months ago that she was too good for breast milk.

Was this kinky bastard....

"Are you staring at my boobs?"

His gaze flicked back up, eyes wide. "No," he spat out before pausing, shaking his head and giving me the start of a bashful smile. "All right, yes."

Well, well, well.

I pulled the sweatshirt over my head and only let myself smile when it was covering my face, wiping it back off once my head popped through the top.

In the three seconds it took me to do that, he'd maneuvered

further into my room and deposited Mo on the floor, sitting, by some of her toys.

"Only one trophy?" he asked in that beautiful accent, lingering by the drawer chest closest to him. Over the last few weeks, he had been in Mo's room plenty of times but never in mine.

I tugged my sweater down as far as it would go over my hips. "Just my last national title. The ones from Worlds are downstairs, and the rest are in the shed out back."

One single finger touched the plaque at the bottom of the trophy, swiping across the gold-plated face. "You aren't fond of looking at them?"

"Not really," I told him. "Peter always said it was good to not get hung up on the things you've done but on the things you will do. And no one ever comes up here anyway." Which reminded me of the fact that *he* was up here, and for about the twentieth time, I wondered if I should worry over the idea of him noticing that things were... off or not. "There's a lot of them."

"That many?" he teased.

I shrugged my good shoulder with a smile.

"You'll give me a complex. I have one."

I raised an eyebrow as he bent over to inspect my trophy closer. "Is it a participation trophy?"

Jonah's grin spread when he glanced at me. "Close."

"What's it for?"

"World Rugby Player of the Year."

I'd forgotten that lovely fact that I'd learned when I'd looked him up online. I also forgot that it had annoyed me that he hadn't *told* me about it either. I'd only learned about it from his public page.

World Rugby Player of the Year. Fancy, humble fucker.

I knew for a fact he'd been on the last national team that had won a World Rugby Cup title, but he kept that to himself.

"Excuse me," I joked.

He shook his head, and I didn't imagine the quick glance he shot down to my chest one more time, before coming back up again like it hadn't happened in the first place.

I could see his feet out of the corner of my eye move around my room. It wasn't anything flash, like he would say. Light gray. The furniture was from the last six years, all black and low, covered by a teal comforter to add some color. Really the only personality in it was the knickknacks all over the place, things I'd been given or collected when I went on trips—shells, rocks, random figurines or souvenirs from different countries, picture frames of periods throughout my life. There was nothing on the walls.

Jonah continued moving, stopping at my bed and setting a hand on the mattress. "Big bed."

I raised my eyebrows at him as I hopscotched a block across the floor in front of Mo. "For me and all my boy toys."

His eyebrows slammed down into a straight line.

"I'm kidding," I told him, not able to keep from smiling because *seriously?* Like, for real? How did he not know I was fucking with him?

Mo threw a block at my face that I didn't have enough time to block or dodge out of the way of. It hit me right in the center of my forehead, and I couldn't help but laugh as I said, "No, Mo. No."

Jonah had a tight little smile on his face as he watched us, but his throat bobbed and something funny came over his face as he asked in that still, still voice, palm lingering over the mattress, "Your granddad brought up a Noah earlier. Is he an old friend?"

I should have known this was coming. "Yeah. I've known him since I was three."

His fingers brushed over my comforter some more, and I was pretty sure I wasn't imagining that his voice got deeper. "Where does he live?"

This was the conversation he wanted to have? I would have

rather told him about the hemorrhoid I'd gotten while I'd been baking Mo. Or tell him about how I had gone three days without pooping during that time too and thought I was dying.

But I guess Jonah had told me about some of his darkest moments, so there was that.

Glancing back up at his face, I lost my train of thought because... well, because of the fucking face he was making.

"What?"

I was so used to seeing him smirking or smiling or just looking like the world was an okay place that *this* was something else I didn't know he was capable of.

But I think I kind of liked a scowl-y, serious Jonah.

At least in tiny doses.

"I think I'm beginning to regret asking," was his low answer.

"Why?"

"You're thinking about it a bit much. Seems to me that's a sign the answer is complicated, and I don't know how I feel about you feeling conflicted over someone."

I dropped from my crouching position to flat on my ass as I stared up at him standing beside my bed, looking down at me with a seriously aggravated fucking face. And I took my sweet-ass time asking yet again, "Why?"

If I had ever doubted the fact that this guy clicked with some part of me that I wasn't sure I would ever understand, his fucking answer, without hesitation, without any sort of shit I would have faced from any other man in the world, came at me. "I'm jealous, and I'm not much of a fan of that, but I want to know what happened even if I regret it more than I do already."

My hand reached out toward him on its own, without a single thought, until I had my fingers wrapped around his calf —because it was the closest body part to me—and, chances were, I probably had a dreamy look on my face as I did it.

Was this why some women played games? Because it made

them feel like a champ? Because I liked it. I liked it a lot more than I had any business liking it, because Jonah was jealous.

Because of me.

And as his eyes slid down to look at the hand I was touching him with, a tiny part of his expression faltered, and the next thing I knew, he was dropping onto the edge of the bed and saying more quietly than a moment before, with a little less of an edge, "Tell me, would you?"

The words just about got caught in my throat, but I grabbed them and flung them out at him. Humbled. Honestly. Feeling way too good for something so dumb. Because he really didn't have a single thing to be jealous over.

"Noah and I grew up together, like I said."

Even the way he nodded was grave.

"We met in tae kwon do when we were three. It turned out his family lived down the street from us, and his parents were nice. Do you remember that first day we went on a walk? When the woman honked at us? That was his mom," I explained. "He was an only child too back then, and I guess it made sense for us to be friends. When I got old enough to start judo classes, Grandpa moved me over to that, and his parents did too because he wanted to do the same thing I did, I guess," I started to explain, noticing the way one of his eyes started to narrow a little.

This story wasn't exactly going to go the way he expected.

This wasn't one of those kinds of stories.

"We were in all the same classes in elementary school; I don't know what you call it in New Zealand, but I'm sure you get the picture. He was my best friend, my brother kind of, I guess. His mom picked me up from school twice a week and kept me at her house until I got picked up. Grandpa Gus dropped us both off every morning. We went to the same middle school too, and everything was the same.

"When high school started—that was grade nine—he followed me to the same school then. I remember he got mad that I was going to go to a school further away instead of the one we were zoned to, but…." Mo slapped a hand on my thigh, forcing me to glance down and smile at my little turkey. I grabbed one of her toys and started walking it up one of her legs as I kept on talking to him.

I squeezed Jonah's leg a little more, still looking down at Mo who was watching me trot her toy down her opposite leg. "Anyway, one day, I was seventeen, I woke up, looked at Noah and thought I was in love with him. He was still my best friend, but it was like this switch flipped, and I found myself getting jealous—literally all of a sudden—over him dating other girls and fooling around with them."

If only I could go back and kick myself in the vag.

"I never planned on saying anything because he was closer to me than a brother would be, and I was too scared to ruin our friendship. I knew he didn't like me the same way. I knew how he thought of me, and it wasn't romantically. And then one day, he had sex with my friend and I got so mad, it killed what I thought I felt. Literally, the next morning, I woke up and was just over it. I know now it wasn't his fault. He hadn't known how I felt, but anyway."

Jonah was full-on frowning at that point, eyes totally thoughtful and narrowed. His whole body was tense.

And I started to regret being this honest. Maybe I should have just… skewed the truth a little. Oh well now.

"I graduated a year early because the Olympics were coming up and I wanted to try my best to be able to compete in them. I went straight on ahead with training; he stayed in school to finish like normal. That summer I came home for a weekend because I'd been at the big training facility they have in Colorado, and out of the blue, he told me he was leaving for Oregon. I talked to him on the phone every two or three days for months before that, and he never hinted that he was thinking about leaving. He never said a word. I felt so betrayed. I trusted him, and he kept that from me, you know? I didn't keep anything from him. I wouldn't have cared if he'd just said something, fucking anything, but it was like he kept it a secret on purpose to hurt me. Then a few weeks later, I slipped and broke my wrist the day of the opening ceremony."

I had to roll my eyes as I thought about how much I had cried, thinking I was getting away with hiding my heartbreak even though apparently Peter and Grandpa Gus had known from the fucking beginning. I'd been so stupid. Of course they had known.

"He left, and he never reached out to me once he was gone. Not even a fucking picture message after he'd spent every other weekend at my house for just about fifteen years. He came back for Christmas break, and I made it a point not to see him even though he went by Maio House almost daily. Grandpa Gus and Peter were both on my team, I realize that now, and lied for me every time. And when that following summer rolled around, I saw him, but by then, I was going full steam ahead with competing, and I was taking a couple classes at the university, and he'd quit judo, and that felt like another kick to my fucking balls. And that next year, he called me twice in twelve months, can you believe that? Twice.

"And, I guess to wrap the next ten years up, I think he grew up a tiny bit and realized what he'd done and tried his best to be my friend again, but I was over it. It was the beginning of the end. Four years after telling me he was going to leave, he broke my fucking rib when I came home *again* from Colorado, like a dumbass, and even though I know it was my fault for putting myself in that position, I was still mad at him. I know I'm a hypocrite. Our friendship was never the same again. I tried to be there for him when I could, but it was totally different.

"And you know the rest. I went to France and came back pregnant. Grandpa, Peter, and I decided to keep it a secret for the first few months, and then one day, when I realized I wasn't going to be able to hide it anymore, and I was scared as hell and sad and pretty fucking pissed off at you for ghosting me, I finally put on a tight shirt that showed off the whole grain loaf I was baking in the oven and everyone saw.

"An hour later, he showed up while I was in the office doing some accounting work, and just… tried to rip me a new one. *How the hell could I be pregnant? How could I do something so stupid? Why wouldn't I tell him who the dad was? Where the hell was the dad? Why would I do this to him?* Blah, blah, blah, like he had any say in my life. I almost went to jail that day, Jonah. I was going to rip his nipples off and stuff them down his throat. He made me feel like a slut. This asshole who went through girls like they were toilet paper after he took a shit made me feel like I had done something unforgivable. This prick who hadn't been a real friend to me in a decade made me feel like trash."

Mo decided to put her hand on my thigh, like she could sense my frustrations from before she'd even been born, and I couldn't help but drop a kiss on the back of her head, seeing the fucking finish line of this shitshow of a story and sprinting toward the end. "I didn't say anything to him, for the record. My hormones were crazy then, and I guess I was in shock, but it made me cry, and I don't ever cry. And the next day, Grandpa Gus called and told me that Noah had cleaned out his locker at Maio House. Two days later, he posted a picture on his Picturegram that he'd joined a new *family* at a gym in New Mexico."

Jonah, who had been sitting on the edge of the bed, slowly melted off the edge, sliding down and down and down until he sat directly in front of me, his long legs crossed, his knees bracketing my own. But it was his facial expression that made me swallow and blink. Noah hadn't hurt my feelings in a long time, but the look on Jonah's face had something churning inside of me.

It was a scowl for sure, and it was sad for sure, but it was mad and something else I couldn't completely understand, and those honey-colored eyes were totally and completely focused on me.

Then, *then*, it was then that those big, rough, tan hands came to my face, cupping one cheek in each, and he leaned forward, and I leaned forward too for some reason, until our foreheads touched, and I could smell Mo from how close she was. And Jonah kept us like that. Foreheads touching. His breath and mine mixing together. His hands on my face, gentle and comforting and sweet. And his voice was a low wave as he asked, "And what happened after that?"

I stared at the freckles on his cheeks as I answered. "He called me a few days later and tried to apologize. I answered because I told myself that I wasn't him. That I hadn't done anything wrong and I wasn't going to hide from his hypocritical ass. He said that he loved me, that he had always supposedly loved me, but he was full of shit—you don't have to squeeze my cheeks so tight, hey—and he tried to claim that he thought he would be the one who would give me kids one day and that he was hurt and confused and a bunch of other bullshit.

"Stop holding your breath, Dimples. I'm telling you the truth. He was jealous, and for some reason, he had the impression that my dumb ass was sitting around and waiting for him to decide he wanted to settle down. But now he couldn't, and it was my fault because I hadn't *loved* him enough in return. For the record, I'd never given him a single impression that I cared about him like that. He didn't know about what I'd felt in high school, so that even more so didn't make sense.

"Anyway, he got mad when I called him out on why that was stupid. You know, like there hadn't been a thousand girls over the years and like our friendship hadn't devolved to the point we only spoke to each other if he wanted or needed my help once he'd started doing MMA at Maio House. Then he hung up, and I didn't hear from him again until you showed up.

"Grandpa Gus refuses to speak to him, and after knowing and training with Peter for most of his life, all he gets out of him is distant politeness. And I know that chafes his ass big-time. I know it. It's easy for people to love you when you're doing things for them, when they get something out of it. But it isn't so easy to find people who will still love you when you're down and need help getting up. That's when you really find out who's with you for the right reasons.

"My best friend, Luna, told me once that everyone has a threshold for what they're willing to forgive. That you can forgive someone but never forget what they said, and you shouldn't. A real friend wouldn't have said and done the things he did. So if you are getting jealous"—I looked right into those bright eyes and smiled at him because he was still looking sick and pissed and jealous, and I was eating that shit up—"there's no reason for you to do that."

All I could manage to do was feel the soft puff of his breaths on my lips as he breathed long and deep, and I couldn't begin to imagine what was going on in his head. So when he spoke next, the last thing I expected was to hear strain in his tone. "I left you too, Lenny. I never said those ugly words, but I wasn't there when you needed me either. I reckon that might be worse."

Honesty is a funny thing. It's brutal and wonderful at the same time, somehow. And it was the best response he could have ever given me, and that was how I knew how totally and completely different Jonah was from Noah. They weren't even in the same country together.

"Yeah, you did, and you're a dipshit for that, but you didn't know I needed you," I replied carefully. "That's the difference. He knew and he didn't give a shit. You were an idiot, but you left because you were worried that your own life was basically over. Yet, you came back, even if it took you almost two years, you asshole."

He made a noise in his nose that might have been in amusement or pain. Both, knowing him. Definitely both.

"I thought my life was over when I found out I was pregnant, and if I could have run away, I would have. So I get it. But you wouldn't have disappeared if you'd known, right?" I made myself ask, and I got my answer by him shaking his forehead against mine.

"Not for anything." One of the hands on my cheeks moved to rest on the nape of my neck, cupping it, his breathing getting even deeper. "I'd like to have a word or two with this arsehole, if it's possible."

Fourteen words were all it took to change my fucking life.

To tip my face up. To say *fuck it* and press my lips against his for the first time in so long. It was just a second, then two, of my mouth pressed against his like it was my first kiss before I pulled back.

But he followed my retreat. Jonah's mouth dipped back to mine, his warm lips against my own, so soft, so lingering. I'd look back on that moment and think that it was the most intimate kiss of my entire fucking life. No tongue. No sexual shit at all. Just long, endless touches of our lips meeting in lingering pecks. Kisses on the corners of my mouth, over the bow of it, just below my bottom lip, and more and more and more and more across them.

Jonah Hema Collins was kissing me like he handled most things in his life, I was coming to see: seriously and deeply and carefully.

But it was the touch of what I knew was a hand on my ankle that had me pulling back and glancing down at the body trying to scoot over onto my lap that broke our mouths apart.

It was then as I looked down at my chunky monkey that I felt the tear slide down my cheek and off my chin.

I watched with my own two eyes as a big hand, that was becoming more and more memorable to me by the day, reached up and wiped the trail off. It was after that that his other hand came up and cupped my other cheek, and Jonah said in that voice that I had tried to exorcise from my life, in that voice that felt like a warm, heavy blanket, "I missed you."

Oh hell.

Oh, fucking, fucking hell.

He had no idea that someone could come and scrub my memories clean, and I doubted I could ever forget that moment, even if they tried to do the same a hundred times. I really did.

I pulled back at his comment, wanting to stay where I was but not wanting to stay there either because… I liked it too much. And no fucking sooner had that thought entered my head than I asked myself what the hell I was doing. Running away? Ending this sweet-ass moment because I was scared of what it might mean? *Really?* Me?

God, I couldn't remember the last time I'd been so disappointed in myself.

I didn't do shit like that. That wasn't *me.*

Then again, it was one thing to do something risky that only caused physical pain. Physical pain you could manage with ice, rest, and anti-inflammatories. It was the other kind of pain, the one that snuck under your skin and settled up in quiet places you didn't go visit that often, that wasn't so easy to get over. That was the difference, wasn't it?

"What are you thinking?"

I glanced up at the intent face focusing on me, and just went for it because why not? Because I was scared of what he'd say? That should make me want to do it more often.

Life was short. You either took what you wanted or you didn't. You either regretted not doing something or you regretted failing. Not doing something would keep me up at night. But it was failing that I could laugh at eventually and get over.

So I told him, because that was who I was. Who I had always wanted to be. "That I had wished you had liked me more before—"

He groaned. "I did, Lenny. I liked you heaps. I never forgot about you."

"You didn't let me finish," I said. "And that I also really like you, and I was thinking that maybe I shouldn't, but maybe I should because you might end up breaking my heart, but you might not. What do you think?"

His slow blink had me smiling at him.

"Too blunt, huh?"

His own small smile crept across that handsome, happy face. "Nah, just perfect." He shook his head, that smile growing. "I won't be breaking any hearts. You can take my word for it." He held his hand out toward me. "You ready to go?"

I took it, but I didn't stop looking at him.

Jonah's big grin didn't go anywhere as he picked his daughter up, dodging out of the way of a stray hand aiming straight at his beard to grab it and pull. "Let's go, yeh? Before my mum comes up?"

I nodded. "Yeah."

He kept me company as I grabbed a pair of ankle socks and put them on, getting a pair of tennis shoes from the rack in my closet before all three of us headed downstairs. Sarah was still in the kitchen with only Peter that time, and it didn't take me too long to pack Mo's backpack with formula, fresh diapers, wipes, and a premade snack because I wasn't about to lug Grandpa's homemade food around with me since they were in glass containers.

If Sarah watched me the entire time I got Mo's stuff together, I ignored her. The person who watched me the closest was Jonah, who looked into the bag, took out his phone, and I bet wrote notes about what was already inside, adding in what else I put in there afterward.

And if my little heart fawned all over him being so... aware... I wasn't going to fault that bitch either. Meticulousness, giving a shit, that was attractive. Paired up with that body....

I'd swear he had been made to ring every single one of my bells.

This guy who had to fucking leave.

∽

AN HOUR LATER, AFTER SPENDING ALL OF FIVE MINUTES PUSHING Mo on the toddler swing before she started hanging over the edge like she was measuring the distance to the ground for a dive, we loaded her up into her stroller and decided to make a walk out of it.

I'd spotted Jonah and Sarah both taking pictures of Mo on the swing, happy and excited, talking nonstop, and acting like she didn't have a care in the world.

Because she didn't.

Because she had people who loved her and would shoulder every burden so she didn't have to until it was necessary.

I couldn't help but glance at the person walking right beside me, a big man whose size alone caught the attention of most people we passed by.

That was when he decided to glance down at me, as his mom pushed Mo in the stroller a few feet ahead of us. "What's that look for?"

"Just admiring the weather," I lied.

He knew because he made a face.

"You haven't been here long enough, but this is pretty nice." Mid-sixties and blue skies? It was.

His hand went to his head, but he didn't exactly look like he believed me. "What's it like during the summer?"

Shit. "Hot and a little humid."

He didn't even try to keep himself from wrinkling his nose.

"What? New Zealand doesn't give out pleasant doses of humid air and heat so bad that you can burn bare thighs on leather seats?"

He was still wrinkling his nose, still being just fucking adorable, when he replied, "Ah, no. It's not too hot or too humid compared to here, sounds like."

"And the winter?"

I didn't miss the pause he took, but I didn't think much of it either because he hadn't lived there in years, maybe he'd forgotten. "It's pretty great in the winter too."

All I could do was "huh" him. "Better than France in the winter?"

He flashed me a funky smile as he nodded. Then he kept going, not letting me linger. "It's summer back home now."

Home. That was a fucking word. I fisted my hand at my side and asked, "Do you miss it?"

He didn't instantly nod, but when he did, it was heavy. Direct. "Yeah, I do. When I think of *home* that's where it is. I've moved quite a bit, but that's where my family is. Mum, Dad. Natia. Two of my brothers; the oldest lives in Aussie. My sister's in Melbourne too. My nan, granddad, aunties, and uncles… they're all home. I was planning on seeing them, but…." He trailed off.

He wasn't sure what his plan was now.

Because of Mo. Me too technically.

And I couldn't help but feel a little guilty. Just a little when I thought about how long his season was. How short his time to relax and refresh himself was. And he was staying with us now.

If it was me who didn't get to see Grandpa Gus and Peter on the regular and only had three months to spend with them when I loved them so much, and then I didn't *get* to see them when I more than likely had looked forward to doing so all year….

Family was responsibility. Family was family. At least when you had a good one. And mine might be small, but it was the best. His might be a lot bigger than mine, and I might be on the fence with how I felt about his mom, but it was clear he loved them.

And he was sacrificing his only time with them to be here.

Fuck.

But most importantly, I knew we had to have this conversation, finally. We had put it off long enough. *I* had put it off long enough.

But I had to go one topic at a time first.

"Jonah…." I forced a smile onto my face as I nudged his hand with the back of mine. "You should probably go see them before your vacation is over."

The lids on his light brown eyes slowly lowered. "You want me to go?"

"I don't *want* you to go, but I'd understand if you did. You said it yourself that you had plans to see them, didn't you?"

He didn't respond, which confirmed that *yeah, he'd had plans.*

Of course he would. More guilt stirred up my chest.

"They're your family. My soul would probably die if I didn't get to see Grandpa or Peter every once in a while. And you've been in France, what? At least since you were cleared to play again? So what's that been? At least five months?" I forced another smile onto my face. "You should go. I get it. Mo will understand."

Jonah gave me a long look over his shoulder before nudging my hand back with his. "I was planning on going home to help at my granddad's farm," he finally said. "It's what I do for a few weeks every holiday, Lenny. And you're right, family is important. Family is the most important." He glanced at me again, the edge of his mouth tilting up as he made a noise that sounded a hell of a lot like a sigh. "But you and Mo are my family too."

Should the f-word out of his mouth have felt the way it did? Like a sharp, thin knife sliding straight into my gut in a good way? Was that normal?

"I've told you. I've missed too much time." His hand nudged mine again a moment before his fingers wrapped around mine loosely. "Too much, love. I'll make it up to them for missing out on this holiday, but they would want me here. They would understand why this is where I need to be."

This is where he needed to be.

Here.

I hated him as much as I didn't hate him. That was the truth. The annoying truth.

All right, I didn't hate him at all.

And because I would never admit that, I reached forward, trying my best to ignore the ache in my chest, and tapped the knuckle of my index finger against his forehead.

One corner of his mouth went up. "What was that?"

I dropped my hand. "I'm making sure it sounds like you have a human skull in there and you aren't some kind of perfect fucking cyborg that killed off the original Jonah and now you're here to take his place and planning to kill me in my sleep in twenty years."

Those long lashes fell again, and he asked very slowly, "What are you talking about?"

I didn't even bother not groaning. I groaned. "You're too perfect, numbnuts. You're too good of a person, and you're too good with your words, and it annoys me."

That earned me another blink and the slowest, creeping smile I'd ever seen in my life. So slow that I was mostly prepared for the huge, blinding one he aimed right at me. His eyebrows had crept up too, lighting up his face that much more. "Is that what you think? That I would wait twenty years to kill you if that was my plan?"

I couldn't help but laugh. "Yeah, probably. But I know there has to be something wrong with you. I bet you're totally tone deaf and can't sing to save your life."

This asshole cocked his head to the side, dimple popping, and said, "Nah. I've been told I have a lovely voice."

"If your mom said it, it doesn't count."

He laughed. "More than just my mum, love."

It was my turn to blink before I nodded slowly. "Yeah? That's where you want to go with that?" I socked him in the stomach with the back of my hand.

But in true fucking Jonah style, all he did was laugh as he

caught my hand in both of his, holding it lightly. "Oi! I was talking about the other members of my family!"

"Sure you were."

"I was!" He laughed some more, still blasting that full-watt smile. "I don't have much experience with these types of things, but even I know not to bring up past girlfriends with your partner."

I was his partner. In crime. I liked it.

Jonah brought my hand up in his, tucking it against his wide chest as we kept on following his mom up ahead of us. "I wanted to tell you, since we're on the topic of families...."

Where the hell was this going?

"I called my brothers yesterday before I came over."

I left my hand where it was. "That's... nice."

"They both remember you messaging them on Picturegram. I spoke to one, and the other left me a voice mail. Would you like to hear it?"

I nodded, and he pulled his phone out of his pocket and started tapping at the screen.

"He's the one in Melbourne. I left him a voice mail telling him about you and Mo, but he didn't answer. Here. Listen," he said before holding the cell in between us and pressing Play on the screen.

"Aw, maaaaaate. Your girl messaged me ages ago. I'm sorry, bro. Thought she was after a root..." There was a sigh. *"Call me back, yeah? I want to hear about this niece of mine."*

Well, well, well.

He did remember reading my message.

Jonah gave me a sad smile that I immediately wanted to smack off.

"Told you," I said, but without anger in my voice. "And what's a root?"

That sad smile turned into a funny one as he reached up to scratch at his temple. "Ah, sex."

Huh. "Which brother was this again?"

He didn't wait long to start going through his phone again. Up ahead, I saw Jonah's mom turn around to look at us, so I waved.

She didn't wave back.

Fuck her too then.

Oblivious, Jonah held his screen to my face. "This is my brother, Arthur. The one in Melbourne."

Not as broad at the shoulders and his eyes were lighter, but the family resemblance was still there.

Two steps later, he shoved his phone into my face again. "My younger brother, William. We call him Bill."

With the same colored eyes as Mo and Jonah, he was slightly slimmer, which wasn't saying much considering that Jonah was basically Hercules.

"This is Garrett. He's the one who still won't speak to me," he explained before showing me yet another photo.

This one was a professional picture off the internet. The guy looked a hell of a lot like Jonah too, except his brow bones were more defined and he looked thicker. And I remembered why he looked familiar. He was the one even more famous than Jonah. The one who was the captain of the national rugby team.

And I suddenly didn't like him so much for ignoring his brother.

But setting that notion aside, all four of the Collins men were handsome as fuck. Big surprise.

Yet I still couldn't get away from the Garrett dude. "Why isn't he speaking to you?"

"A few different reasons," he hedged, almost thoughtfully. "He was mad when I left Auckland."

"Why?"

"We played on the same team together there," he said, like that explanation as enough. "We played on the All Blacks together too."

It wasn't. "So is he mad at your other brother for playing in Australia?"

"No...." He trailed off, considering that with a tiny frown. "We were close when we were young, but since I left home...."

"What else is he mad at other than you making a decision that made you more money?"

"He said it shouldn't be about the money."

I rolled my eyes. I was sure his brother, who I figured wasn't hurting for endorsements, didn't make any decisions based on financial matters. Yeah, right.

"But he hasn't spoken to me since I was injured. I told you I didn't speak to anyone other than my nan and granddad for months." I knew he grimaced because I peeked at him right when he did it. "Including him. When I finally did call him back, he told me to fuck off. Called me a tall poppy, an embarrassment... heaps of other things I don't want to repeat. So, yeah, we haven't spoken in ages."

The urge to kick his brother in the backs of his legs was strong.

So was the urge to look up what a tall poppy was, but that was for later. Because right then, all I wanted to do was wipe off the sad look on Jonah's face. So I went with the first thing I thought of.

"Want me to sweep him if I ever meet him?"

His laugh went straight to my heart.

The arm he threw over my shoulders before tugging me into that enormous side was the topping on the damn cake.

"I don't think I've ever wanted to give you a cuddle more." He chuckled, dipping his head down to look at my face as he said that.

I smiled, relieved that had done the job. "I like hugs," I told him honestly.

He grinned at me as he planted his mouth on my forehead and gave me a kiss there like it was the most natural thing in the damn world.

And I wanted it to be.

But I took the happy silence between us as we walked along

the path with his mom and Mo up ahead. Moments later, with his arm still over me, our thighs brushing together as we walked, he broke the silence between us.

"Would you like to look at some of the pictures of my nan's farm? Of home?" he asked, sounding almost... hopeful? "You loved that time we went out of the city and into the country-side, and I like to think that home is even more stunning. Most beautiful place I've ever seen."

Home.

Damn it, hadn't I just thought we needed to talk about that? How the hell had he sidetracked me so easily?

I nodded anyway. We could discuss it later. Tonight, I figured when he handed me his phone. I looked through at least one hundred pictures, maybe even two hundred. Beautiful green landscapes that looked straight out of a movie. Of sheep. Of a countryside, and if I was to use the word charming correctly, a really fucking charming little house tucked into a spread of grass and fence line.

One picture after another was filled on his phone of random things. Of an older woman who had to be his grandma, a man who looked like an older replica of Jonah who definitely quali-fied as GILF material with equally massive shoulders, dark hair, and rich skin. There were more pictures of people around his age with about the same skin color as his—the nicest blend of olive—a testament to their heritage of Samoan, Māori, Scottish, and who knew what else grandparents. There was this family mixed up of so many shades between cream and brown, it was unique and beautiful.

When I got to the last picture in his gallery, my finger hesi-tated over the options button.

And like a sneaky fuck, I hit the info button. The first picture had been taken months ago. Right around the same time he'd said he'd come back into the world, when he'd been sure he would be able to play again.

Something that was so much more than just relief filled up

every cavity in my body, and I had to steel myself against it, just so I could handle it.

"So you left New Zealand just to make more money?" I blurted out, trying to sound casual but not feeling anything close to it.

That might have been the only time I would ever witness Jonah stumble as he looked at me over his shoulder and seemed to hesitate for a second before scratching at the back of his head. "Ah...."

"I'm not judging. I'm just asking." Because it was the truth. "They pay you more overseas?"

He flashed me an uncertain smile. "A bit more, yeah."

"Why do you sound embarrassed about that?"

He went back to scratching at his head. "I'm not, but not everyone is supportive of it." He grimaced. "My mum wasn't. My brother wasn't. Most of Auckland wasn't either."

Ohhhhh. God, I was dense. "They're mad at you for leaving?"

The sigh that came out of him said everything. "I can't play for the New Zealand national team if I don't play there. They take it like I've been unfaithful to them by going, but...." He sighed again, and I watched his eyes drift forward in the direction of his mom and Mo. "If I could still play for the All Blacks and play in France or Japan, I would, but it's a sacrifice. I'm not getting any younger." He glanced at me again before adding, "You understand."

I did understand. "It's the same thing with professional fighters," I told him. "Or I guess most professional athletes in general. You don't have to be ashamed of that. Anybody would have done the same thing. You work your ass off for yourself. You have to do what's best for you." Something he had told me in the past clicked in my head. "Wait. So if everyone is mad at you, and I'm sure you can't exactly go walk around without anyone recognizing you, where the hell did you go for those months while you were recovering? I thought you said you were at your grandma's farm."

"I was." He nudged me with the back of his hand. "I, ah, didn't leave the house much in those days. If I did leave, I stayed out of the way. By the time I did head into town with my granddad or nan, they had warned everyone off. That or risk facing the wrath of my nan. She even went to the physio with me every week."

That had me perking up. "She's scary?"

"Firm. Everyone knows better than to go up against her. She's something, even now."

"Your dad's mom?"

He nodded. "Small town. No one said a word to me, and I wasn't in the mood for it."

I grabbed his arm. "Your mood was that bad? *You*?"

He laughed and shook my hand off, his palm sliding against my lower back. "I have bad moods from time to time, Lenny. You've seen it."

If bad moods consisted of him being silent and broody for a little while… well… "I can deal with you being pouty."

"*Pouty?*"

"Whiny?"

The hand on the small of my back slid up along my spine until his palm cupped the shoulder furthest away from him and he tugged me toward him a couple of inches, his laugh the soundtrack to the movement. "I don't whine," he hissed but chuckled at the same time.

I snickered and soaked up the wall of muscle alongside me.

And it was in the middle of me coming down from that, that I glanced toward my car and spotted the figure standing right by the hood.

The figure that even at this distance looked a whole hell of a lot like a woman. A woman who looked a lot like Grandpa Gus's ex-wife. What the hell?

I must have made a noise that had Jonah looking in the same direction as me because he asked, "Is that…?"

"I think so." Fuck. Digging into my back pocket, I pulled out my phone and dialed Grandpa's number. "I don't know what she's doing here, but I'm about to find out."

"Are you calling your granddad?"

I nodded as the ringtone came on.

"Why would he tell her where you are?"

I slid him a look as the phone kept on ringing. "I don't know. He hadn't wanted me to meet her in the first place. Goddamn it, he's not answering." He wasn't going to answer. Ending the call, I dialed Peter's number next. "Let me go talk to her and see what she wants—hold on."

The "Lenny" came at me really quickly. Then, "I told him not to tell her where you were, but she insisted she wanted to talk to you." He paused. "I'm sorry. You know we would never have wanted to put you into the middle of this."

Fuck.

"Sorry, Len," he said gently. "Good luck."

"Love you. Bye," I muttered into the receiver. *What the fuck?*

I got a "Love you" back a second before I hung up.

Jonah raised those thick eyebrows at me. "Bad news?"

I just shook my head.

That big hand went back to the base of my spine, and it stayed there. "I'll come with you, make sure to pull you back before you say something you'll regret."

I made a face. "Good luck with that." What the hell did this lady *want*? Why was she here? "Are your grandparents nice?"

"The best."

The best. He was going to make me vomit.

"Do you think they'll want to meet Mo?" I asked, more to kill the time while we got closer and closer to the woman who had spotted us and stood up straight.

"More than anything," he responded. The hand on my lower back moved slowly over to my hip, and I let it, eating it up. "I was planning on giving her a call today to tell her the news now that I've talked to my brothers. She'll have me promising to bring her over as soon as we can."

"We? You want me to go too?"

Jonah leaned in. "There's no place I wouldn't want you to go with me."

This fucking asshole had magic in him. That had to be it. Sorcery. Witchcraft.

Because this wasn't right. My heart shouldn't be doing this. My whole body shouldn't be reacting like he was fucking crack.

Why? Why did I have to like him out of millions so much?

"Good morning," the woman said before I could formulate a response to what the hell he'd just dropped on me.

"Morning," I told her distractedly with all of the five manners that Grandpa had instilled in me,.

"Good morning," Jonah threw in, with his immaculate manners.

Grandpa's ex flashed him a hesitant smile a second before her eyes flicked in the direction of where I knew Mo and Sarah were. They moved back to me in the blink of an eye, and I could see her straighten, see her grasp for maybe strength, and then say, "Gus said I could find you here."

"I know," I replied. "Something I can help you with?"

She glanced back to the spot behind me, and I ate up the fact that I didn't feel even a tiny bit guilty for not rushing Sarah over. "I didn't know you were with your family," she said, still looking away. "I wanted to see if you were interested in having lunch with me."

Of course he'd left that part out.

I swear I didn't mean to ask it the way I did, but the word just came right on out of my mouth like I was pouring syrup out of a bottle. "Why?"

She tried her hardest to mask it, but I could see her flinch. "Because—" She cleared her throat. "—I'd like to speak to you."

Her gaze moved to Jonah and back to me. "I'd like you to know my half of the story too."

The words seemed so shallow, all I could do was look at her and feel the weight of Jonah's hand settle even heavier on my lower back.

Her half of the story? That's what this was about?

"You are my granddaughter," the woman said when I just stood there and looked at her.

Okay, I could say this a little nicer. Just a little. "Well, yeah, technically. Biologically." I squinted my eyes because I couldn't keep that much of the smart-ass out of me. It was in me like I knew I had A positive blood. "I'm not trying to hurt your feelings or anything, but I don't really care to hear *your half of the story*, as you put it."

She didn't wince or flinch or anything, this woman who looked more and more like me with every second I looked at her. Instead, she lifted her chin up higher. Her fucking nose too. "Well, I think it would be fair if you gave me the opportunity to explain what happened."

I understood suddenly why my grandpa hadn't told her to fuck off when she'd shown up to ask him for advice, or whatever bullshit had led to her showing up to Maio House. I really did. But the thing was, I didn't give a shit. I didn't give a shit about this woman who had never given a shit about me.

But for them, for them I would try and do this as politely as possible. Because I would never want to do anything to hurt them.

And this woman had the opportunity to do that if she wanted.

"Look, you haven't been in my life in thirty years. You've had zero interest in it. I don't know you. You don't know me. You haven't wanted to know me, and I'm fine with that. You don't have to explain anything to me," I said, wishing that I had my stress ball with me.

I couldn't believe this bitch.

"It isn't that I haven't wanted to know you," she tried to argue.

"How many times have you come to Houston over the last thirty years?"

That had her face going slack, her eyes brightening, her nostrils flaring. To give her credit, she answered. "Every few months."

Every few months.

Wow.

I couldn't help the smile that came over my mouth as I made sure to keep my gaze on her instead of looking at Jonah. I had to straddle this line as cleanly as possible. For Grandpa. For Peter. For Maio House. "I know why you got divorced. I understand, and I don't blame you. Neither does Grandpa Gus. But I just don't care to hear whatever it is you want to tell me. Not when you've come to Houston who knows how many times over the course of my life and not cared to contact me. Not when you went to Maio House and didn't make an effort then either, and the only reason I saw you was because I got curious and showed up. I know I'm not important to you, and I'm fine with it. You just don't want me to think of you as the bad guy. I get it."

My grandmother, because that's what she was, blushed. I could see the hesitation—the *anger*—in her eyes. Yet somehow she managed to lower her voice as she said, "Your grandfather *lied* to me."

"But I didn't."

"You don't understand," she tried to argue.

"No, I do. I'm a mom now too, and I understand better than you will ever imagine, Rafaela. You didn't want anything to do with me or my dad, and you never will. How much more do you want to rub that in?"

CHAPTER 18

Subject: IMPORTANT

Lenny DeMaio:
    Wed 3/22/2019 1:29 p.m.
    to Jonah Collins

Jonah, please. For real. Call me back.

Email me back. I don't care, but I really, really need to talk to you.

I don't want or need anything: I just have to tell you something important, and I don't want to do it over email.

"BUT I DID PAY."

I stared at the phone sitting on my desk and pictured the face of the man on the other end of the line. A man I couldn't stand half the time I had to deal with him. Then again, anyone who continuously lied to me annoyed the fuck out of me. He did this shit every other month. I took a deep breath in through my nose and let it back out again, feeling all my facial muscles get tight. "Damon." I sighed. "Do you know how many times you've said those words to me?"

What that question got me was silence on the other end.

"I just checked Pablo's bank account"—that was one of my rare lies—"and nothing has been deposited. It isn't some magical glitch in the computer system that the payment didn't go through. You haven't transferred the money. Why do you put me through this every single time Pablo fights?" I asked him, leaning back against my chair and staring blankly at the wall in front of me in exasperation.

"Look, Lenny, I sent my assistant over, and she said she made the deposit."

What was this? 1990? We both knew he was full of shit. She could have mailed a check if he was being cheap, wired the money if he wanted to spend the fee, or used one of those apps to transfer money across banks. I used that shit all the time.

"Let me ask her to check the deposit receipt, and I'll call you back. You know I'm good for it, and tell fucking Pablo to call me if he's got a problem," the man tried to throw.

I gripped the cord of my work phone in my free hand and shook my leg under my desk. "He did call you. I saw it. He called you five times last week." Silence. "And I know that you're good, but you're good at paying two months late instead of two weeks later like you're supposed to. If your assistant deposited money into wrong bank accounts, you would have fired her the day after you hired her. Don't play the dumb game with me. Come on, I know I don't look that stupid."

There was another beat of silence before a rough, short bark of laughter filled the line. "Jesus Christ, Lenny. If you ever want to come work for me, I'll have a position open for you."

That got a snicker out of me.

The promoter laughed some more. "Listen, the money will be in there by five, all right?"

"Uh-huh. I hope so."

"It will," he tried to assure me like I hadn't known him for the last ten years. "Tell Gus to give me a call, would you?"

That had me smiling at least. "Ooh, now I know you're for sure going to make the deposit if you want me to bring you up in front of Grandpa."

He laughed again.

"I hope I don't talk to you later, Damon. Bye."

"Bye, Lenny," the promoter on the other end muttered before hanging up.

I dropped the phone into the cradle with a snicker.

"I didn't know you managed athletes."

Damn it!

The back of the chair I was leaning in went back even further when my whole body jerked at the sound of the voice that had come *out of fucking nowhere*. I threw my arms out at my sides to grab onto the desk, or something, anything so that I wouldn't tip the seat back and fall out of it.

Out of the corner of my eye, while I flailed around since I'd basically just scared the shit out of myself, or *Jonah* had, I saw the dark-haired man start to sprint forward like he was going to catch me. Before he could get to me though, the second that my instincts realized that I wasn't about to go feet-over-ass and break my chair in half, I sat up straight, slapped my hand over my chest because my heart hadn't beat so hard in forever, and slid him the nastiest look I could conjure up.

Stopping right in front of me, stopping *right on the other side of the desk*, Jonah looked at me and grinned.

That smile grew with every second that passed. One after another and then another until he was basically beaming at me. All handsome, straight, white teeth, and looking like a million-dollar asshole.

"I wish I could have filmed that," he said way too brightly.

I didn't even think about it.

I grabbed my stress ball and threw it at him, seeing his

hands cover his balls like I would really try and hit him there, as he laughed. *Laughed*.

"I can't stand you," I hissed, rubbing a circle over my heart because it hadn't gotten the memo that we weren't about to die from an intruder alert. "How do you move so quietly when you're so damn big?"

He was still laughing, but his hands were falling away from his crotch area when he replied, starting to bend over, "Practice. I move fast too."

"If I had another stress ball, I'd throw that one at you too," I told him as he tossed the ball back at me.

I caught it and dropped it on top of my desk.

"You all right?" he asked, smiling wide and slowly dropping into the seat that still looked too small for him.

"Besides that minor heart attack I just had, and the fact I probably pissed myself a little too, yeah, I'm fine," I told him drily, earning me an even bigger smile that made it totally worth the fact that I wasn't lying. I probably had peed a couple drops out. Mo's fault.

"As long as it was just a bit of urine, eh?" the cheeky bastard asked.

"You know, I don't remember you being this sarcastic two years ago."

He didn't break eye contact with me for a second. "You're a bad influence, love."

I smiled.

"As I was asking before I caused your palpitations," he started. "I didn't know you managed anyone."

Oh. That. "Not officially or anything, and not really, but I'm a good third party. Especially when they want to get paid more for fights, the amateurs I mean, I have the connections. And I don't mind haggling for them."

"They pay you?"

"A little bit. I don't know how much you heard, but this last time, one of the guys hadn't gotten paid, and he asked me if I could call the promoter because he wasn't getting through. So I did. I've known him for a long time, and he knows better than to screw around with us."

"You mean you and your granddad?"

"Exactly, but I've been told I'm worse than Grandpa Gus." I smiled. "Deep down, I probably enjoy it too much. It's my high now." I thought about that for a second. "You okay? Need anything?"

"Everything is good as gold," he replied, leaning back into the too-small chair, his upper arms crowding over the armrests. "Just came to check on you."

"Me?"

"Yes." But that was all he said.

"Why?"

"Yesterday. We didn't get a chance to talk about it."

I played dumb. "What happened yesterday? Your mom asking me all those questions?" Because she had asked me a lot of questions on the ride back from the park. She went right in and laid them out one right after the other.

"ELENA," THE OLDER WOMAN SAID MAYBE TWO SECONDS AFTER we'd gotten inside the car after I finished speaking to Grandpa Gus's ex-wife. "Did I hear that correctly or did you refer to the woman at the park as your grandmother?"

She'd heard that. I was still feeling pretty riled up after our conversation, but it wasn't the time to think about it, so I'd do it later, in private. When I could really let it set in.

Or maybe I would never think about it. Who knew? I still, and more than likely forever would, want nothing to do with her.

"She is biologically my grandmother. She was my dad's mom," I replied, flexing my fingers around the steering wheel.

Out of the corner of my eye, I could see Jonah fidgeting in

the seat beside me and knew without looking that he was watching me.

"Your father, where is he?" Sarah went on to ask.

I heard Jonah grunt, but I answered her. She wasn't the first person to ever ask, and she wouldn't be the last. "He died before I was born."

The silence in the car for a few moments after that honestly made me feel just a little bad. I bet she hadn't been expecting that. And she wouldn't be the first person either to feel bad for asking that specific question.

So I decided to be the better person and not let her feel so shitty. Mostly because making someone feel guilty was kind of a cheap shot. Like *Rafaela* showing up out of the fucking blue just to make herself feel better.

"He was in a drunk driving accident. He wasn't the one drinking or driving. The woman who gave birth to me hadn't even known she was pregnant when he died, so he didn't know I was on the way either," I explained, and for once, I realized just how similar in a way my story with Jonah and Mo was to this.

I didn't like it.

And I was glad, obviously, that it wasn't tragic too.

Because maybe I hadn't known Marcus, but Grandpa had always talked about how awesome he'd been. And if he was Grandpa Gus's son, of course he had been that way. "I know he was my biological dad, but I've always thought of him as being like a brother-figure I never got to meet."

"I'm so sorry to hear that," Sarah said in a surprisingly gentle and honest voice that I was only partially expecting. "And your mum?"

I had glanced in the rearview mirror to take in the back of Mo's car seat. Poor little monster. We'd be at the house in five minutes, so I hoped she stayed awake so we wouldn't have to wake her up all over again. "My biological mom gave her rights up and let my grandpa take me. Supposedly she was only twenty years old and wasn't ready to have a baby, so she did the right thing. My grandpa and Peter raised me, and I couldn't have had better parents. It's always been the three of us. Grandpa Gus didn't have brothers or sisters, and Peter's only sister died a while back."

Memories of the thousands of times they had been there for me had made my heart clench up. The countless hours spent at judo, with one or both of them always there. The family vacations, the weekend trips they had snuck in as much as possible to give me a normal childhood. The infinite amount of unconditional love they had given me, even if sometimes it was tough love. I really couldn't have had better parents. "They loved me enough for five whole families though, so I was the lucky one."

There was more silence, and I'd bet my ovary she regretted asking that question too.

Awkward.

And because I had still been feeling pretty gracious and could only imagine what was going through her head as she tried to piece things together, I decided to just wrap up the whole story so she would know.

We were family, after all. Maybe I didn't like her yet and maybe she didn't like me yet, and maybe we would never really and truly like each other, but that didn't change shit. She was here, and she seemed to truly love Jonah in her own way I wasn't totally feeling, and she was being all about Mo, so....

"My grandpa divorced that lady when Marcus, my dad, was five, and she wasn't really in their lives after that. She moved somewhere else, and after he turned eighteen, they never saw her again until she showed up at my family's gym a few weeks ago."

Jonah was for sure watching me as I drove, but I didn't dare glance at him.

But in the back seat Sarah made a noise that sounded somewhere in between shock and outrage, and that surprised the fucking shit out of me. "I don't mean to be intrusive—"

Sure she didn't.

"—or be rude and make assumptions, but you're at least in your late twenties, and you have never met your own grandmother until recently?"

"Correct," I confirmed, trying to figure out where she was going with this. "Today is the second time I've ever seen her."

"I'm sorry for asking about such an upstanding family member. I don't see how any person could leave their child, *or grandchild,* their own flesh and blood, like that. I would never be able to do that."

"Me neither," I agreed with her, glancing in the rearview mirror again and catching her eyes.

Luckily I hadn't expected that little moment to change anything, because it hadn't. Thirty minutes later, Sarah had criticized the bottles we were giving Mo and then tried to grill me on what we were feeding her. I started zoning her out ten seconds in.

But I wasn't bothering with that. I knew we were doing our best and had done a lot of research on everything we used on her and for her. Sarah meant well, and I wasn't going to get pissed off for her giving a shit about my daughter.

Apparently Jonah was well aware of that because he gave me a playfully exasperated face at me playing dumb by answering my previous question. "The conversation with your granddad's ex-wife, Len. I want to know you're okay with it."

I eyed my stress ball but kept my hand on my lap.

"Not that all right then, I'll take it," the man who probably saw and understood too much—obviously since he was bringing it up—claimed easily and carefully.

Opening up my mouth to say that I was all right, I shut it right back. Because I'd be lying if I said I was. He didn't need to know that I hadn't even been able to tell Peter or Grandpa about that conversation because I didn't trust myself to explain it in a reasonable voice. I could tell them anything and everything. Every cell in my body knew that.

But, *that*... that I hadn't been able to share. *That* I had let settle in my chest to pick up and look at while I had stood under the shower that night once everyone had left. Jonah and his mom had bounced after spending all day with me and Mo at the house. Natia had showed up in the afternoon, and I found that I really fucking liked Jonah's sister. She was cool as shit. Even Luna had showed up with Ava and her husband, and we'd all had dinner together.

It had been the first time that my best friend met Jonah, and the second she'd gotten a chance, she'd elbowed me in the ribs and given me an enormous grin. She'd texted me from home that night and said he was great and even Rip had mentioned liking Jonah. But my favorite message had been:

Luna: And he's better looking in person, Lenny. WOO.

It had been a nice day that had made me forget all about Rafaela and her bullshit. So it wasn't until the shower that I'd let myself think about her. Then I'd thrown that moment in the park with my grandmother into the imaginary trash after thinking it over while I'd washed and conditioned my hair.

Until now.

"I just...." My voice came out a little high. "I'm fine."

The look he gave me was enough for him to not have to verbally call me out on my bullshit. He wanted me to tell him the truth on my own. Fine.

"I am," I insisted, trying to think about it. "Realistically, I am. If I don't see her again, I don't think I would regret it. I don't think I would even think about it much. Really."

His face was so patient. "But?"

Was this my second Peter? Another person about to see a loose end sticking up and decide to pull at it gently to see how much came free? "But," I continued on, not totally wanting to, "I am a little mad about it." I thought about it. "Maybe more than a little."

Jonah didn't make any kind of physical gesture to get me to keep talking, but the way he just looked, straight, his facial expression totally blank, made me keep going.

"It's been thirty-one years. Longer than that if you want to be technical. The last time she saw my dad was when he was eighteen, seven whole years before I was born. So that's a whole lot of time."

He still didn't say a word, and I could *feel* my eyelid get twitchy.

But I didn't touch it. What I did do instead was keep talking. "She didn't *miss* out on anything. She gave it up. She didn't *want* it, and that's the difference." Fuck it, I reached up and gave my neck a scratch with my index finger, just one quick scratch, and I dropped my hand again. "Who the hell cuts their kid off because of something someone else did? How do you just... leave them behind? I've been mad over things. I've been hurt. But I would never do some shit like that. She didn't come talk to me because she wanted to. She only did it to make herself feel better for getting caught."

Jonah still didn't say a word, but it made me think about what had just come out of my own mouth.

I scratched at my neck again. "It bothers me more than it should, and I know that. I didn't even tell Grandpa or Peter what she said. I just said I'd tell them later, but it's not that easy to talk about someone not wanting you." I swallowed. "I should be used to it by now though, you'd figure. I shouldn't let this— her—piss me off. She doesn't even deserve that."

Then, then, he decided to finally open his mouth, and when he did, it wasn't to say the words I might have expected. "There's nothing wrong with being mad, love. And you shouldn't be used to... that. None of it is your fault."

I tried to swallow, I really did, but there was a rock in my throat. Suddenly, a rock the size of a fucking Rhode Island-sized meteor sitting in my throat, blocking anything from going in and everything from leaving.

"She has no idea what she missed out on," he said in that quiet voice. "Leaves more for us who do know what we have, eh?" Those eyes sparkled. "A good friend. An incredible family member. A loyal, practical, brave woman. One of the most amazing women I've ever met."

My entire life, I had never known how to be anything other than how I was. Even if it made other people uncomfortable or mad. That I was too mouthy, too bossy, too determined, too blunt, too *much*.

Despite all of that, I was and had been loved by a lot of people. People who knew the best and the worst parts of me. Some knew more, some knew less.

Yet, no one had ever said something like what had just come out of Jonah's mouth. Not a single one of those people who loved me, and who I loved right back.

And wasn't that fucking something?

But my big fucking mouth went crazy on me as my brain struggled and I found myself asking, "One of?"

Jonah's smile was tender. "Yeah. My nan is pretty amazing too."

It made my chest go tight, it made my nose sting, and it forced me up to my feet and around my desk, ignoring the curious expression on his face. It made me bend over in front of this man who I'd had a child with and hug him. My forehead went into the warm side of his neck, slightly damp with the sweat of the workout he had probably just finished, my arms loose around his neck and shoulders.

And I responded the only way I could manage. "Thanks, Jonah."

Words weren't what replied to me. It was a forearm around the middle of my back. It was a hand cradling the back of my head, holding it gently like it was precious or something instead of hard as hell. It was the great big breath that made his chest puff closer to my own.

A big hand palmed my head. "Come here," he said to me.

Most special of all was the way he turned me—or I guess, I let him turn me—to the side and then inward, my arms not going anywhere. They stayed exactly where they were around his neck, my forehead staying in the same exact place because it liked it there and didn't want to go someplace else. And before I really thought about anything other than how warm he was, how much I liked the scent of a man who was a mix of salty, clean sweat and a deep-scented deodorant, I was on his lap.

I was sitting on his thigh. Again.

My butt was high on his lap, one of his arms loose around my back and the other on my hip. And I didn't make a joke about being too heavy for him. I didn't make a joke about how we weren't in high school anymore and people didn't sit like this. I just sat there, on this man who I knew could handle my weight and, apparently, maybe even all the other little sharp pieces too.

I had sat on my friends' thighs before but not like this. Not even close. Not by a mile.

So when the office phone rang, I didn't answer it. I was too busy listening to the measured breaths that came out of him. And when my office phone stopped ringing and started up again, I still didn't pry myself away.

I soaked in that nice smell of him deep into my senses… the steadiness and sturdiness of his body…

And that was when my cell phone rang.

Five years ago… three years ago… I would have let it keep ringing. But I had Mo now and that changed everything.

The thing was, Jonah must have thought the same thing, because he leaned forward, the heavy arm around my back keeping me in place, and grabbed it off the counter, handing it over.

"MAIO HOUSE" was across the screen.

I answered, my voice more hoarse than normal, at least to my own ears, "Hello?"

"Lenny," Bianca's whisper came over the line. "I tried calling you on your office line."

I sat up straight, leaving the warmth of Jonah's wide chest. "Everything okay?"

"Um, this guy just walked in without scanning his pass. I've never seen him before, but one of the girls just said he used to train at the old Maio House."

I groaned. I hated it when old members just randomly showed up. Well, it depended on the person and why. Most of the time they were just around to come and kill time and distract people even though they didn't train here anymore.

"What do you want me to do?"

Bianca was five foot two and had the kind of petite body most women would never cry over. She was literally one of the least intimidating people I knew. She was friendly, I had never seen her in a bad mood, and worked hard. And she seemed to me to be all marshmallow fluff on the inside. Basically: Bianca was the last person I would ever expect to tell someone to get the fuck out, and she wasn't paid enough to do that either. I would never ask it of her, period.

"Give me a second, and I'll go over there and deal with it. Just keep an eye on him," I told her. "Thanks for telling me."

She hung up after thanking me, and with a sigh, I slid off the thigh under me, stood up, and turned to smile down at Jonah.

But he was already beating me to it.

Lord, I loved this man.

My insides froze as I processed that thought.

I flipped it one way and the other and let it settle right under my throat.

I did love this dumbass, didn't I?

The surprising part was, it wasn't a horrifying thought or even close to it. I looked at this grinning idiot and… it felt good. *Right.*

My blood pressure didn't go up. My eye didn't start twitching. I didn't feel itchy or uncomfortable or anything like that. It was like… putting on my favorite pair of sweatpants.

How about that? I was going to have to process this some more later.

"Thank you for that," I told him, unable to keep from smiling as I held the l-word real close to me. I was going to have to think on it some more.

"I'm always here when you need a cuddle," he said, totally serious, watching me as his right hand went to wrap around the back of my thigh. "Or more."

I flashed him a small smile. "I need to go deal with someone walking around here that shouldn't be. Are you done for the day or—"

The knock at my door came a second before a voice I hadn't heard in person in months came from the direction. "Lenny, you in there?"

Before I could get another word out, the figure appeared, hands already on his hips, eyes aimed in the direction of the chair I had just gotten off of.

His blond hair was cut shorter than in the past. Those blue eyes were still the color of the navy shirt I'd worn yesterday, and he still had the same body I had seen expand and grow throughout my life: trim and muscular.

The hand on the back of my thigh slid an inch higher, the fingers curling around it even more than they had before, and it was that, that snapped me out of it. Not the numbness that came over my spine, replacing the joy and happiness that had been there moments ago. Or at least in the context of the man standing there, *years* ago. The vision of him had once brought me comfort. Trust. I had hugged this person more times than I could ever count.

I had loved Noah. As a friend. Like a brother. For a tiny amount of time I had thought as more than that.

But it was Jonah's hand on my leg that grounded me then.

And the fact that it didn't go anywhere.

The only part of my body that moved as those navy-colored eyes flicked to the man touching me was my mouth. "Hi, Noah," I said pretty fucking calmly.

That had his gaze moving up to my face. I watched his nostrils flare and his hands—hands that had touched me ten thousand times—form fists.

I stayed right where I was. Like I always would. And if a small amount of grief slid along my back, it shouldn't have been surprising.

"Hey," the man who had once been my best friend said, his gaze moving back toward Jonah for a moment and lingering there in a way I didn't like.

I didn't touch Jonah's shoulder to be an asshole, but I did because he was special to me. Because I would never pretend not to feel something for him just to make someone else feel better. Especially not when that someone else didn't deserve anything from me anymore. "Jonah, this is Noah. I told you about him, remember?" I moved my gaze back toward the blond, sliding my hand to Jonah's upper arm, his biceps bunching under me. Then I said the words that I hoped would mold the direction of whatever was going to happen. "We grew up together."

That was the sum of us now, and *that* made my chest hurt, just for a second; the tinge of pain flaring with intensity. He looked exactly the same. Handsome. Buff. So sure of himself.

"Noah, this is Jonah," I kept going, the muscles under my fingers flexing some more.

I put the pieces together that made up Bianca's call about a former Maio House member coming in like he owned the place. Of course Noah would do that. If anyone had a right to feel like they would always belong here, it would be him.

Even if that wasn't the case anymore and never would be again for the shit he'd said and done.

"Her partner," Jonah threw out suddenly, so quickly I didn't get a chance to step back before he was up on his big feet, towering over me with all of an inch of a space between us as he thrust a hand toward Noah.

There he went calling me his partner again. How was a man this big so adorable?

Noah took in the hand being held out in his direction, and I watched him look up at the face that stood a couple inches taller, then back at the hand… and not do anything. Really? *Really?*

I went to fucking seven, or maybe eight, instantly.

"You're not going to shake his hand?" I asked, anger settling right at the base of my fucking neck, making the skin on my arms prickle as this fucker still didn't shake Jonah's hand. He wasn't my grandpa. He didn't have a right to be this way, or any way, really.

"Why should I?" the man I hadn't seen in almost a year asked, that face that was so handsome it had gotten one endorsement deal after another screwed up into an expression that was pretty much outraged. Outraged at what, I had no idea. What the hell did *he* have to be mad about? "This is him?"

Jonah's hand, still in the air, curled into a fist and dropped.

And that only made my anger spike up even more.

"Is this who?"

"You know who."

I stared into the face I had thought of as my friend for half my life. More than half my life. Into the face of the person I had been teenage-in-crush with, who hadn't cared about me the same way.

I tried my best to grip onto that memory, onto that rope of love and vines and lifetime, and not lose my shit at the completely uncalled for aggravation on Noah's face and in his voice. I only partially succeeded, not able to keep my tone civil. "You mean Mo's dad?" I asked him, taking the words and owning them officially.

Noah's cheeks puffed. They always did that when he was upset or angry. Or both.

"Then yeah, Jonah is Mo's dad," I confirmed, hanging onto those memories of this being someone I had loved, someone I still loved in a way, at least enough to try to do that. I didn't want to go apeshit. I didn't want to make this ugly. There was no reason for it. "You should have told someone you were coming to visit."

He knew that wasn't what I was implying and didn't try to hide it as he tipped his chin up in Jonah's direction. "They told me he was here."

"He's been here."

"*Now*," he tried to throw out like that would mean something.

I nodded because yeah. *Now* he was.

That was when Noah's eyes flicked to Jonah once more, and his face went ruddy as he said, "Two years later. Or did you forget that?" He gestured with his chin toward me that time.

"I haven't forgotten anything," I said, losing hold of my temper just a little, just enough for the sharpness to come out. "None of this is any of your business anyway."

I was going to kill someone, and that someone was either going to be Noah or it was going to be another member of the gym for having a big-ass mouth.

"Why are you playing stupid, Len? Since when do you forgive someone who let you have a baby by your fucking self?" He shook his head, his face getting redder and redder. "The girl I knew would've had his ass ten feet in the ground, not—"

Before I could ask if that was the same girl he'd been friends with ten years ago, another voice in the room spoke up.

"You and I have enough issues to talk about, mate," Jonah said in a voice even more rough than I'd heard before. It was cold. Hard. And I liked it even more. "But you imply she's stupid again, or you raise your voice that way one more time, and we're going to have bigger issues to deal with. Understand?"

Noah said something, but I was too busy taking in the man standing beside me, firing off a glare that gave every other glare I had ever seen in my life a run for its money, and trying to comprehend that my sweet, sweet Jonah technically laid people out for a living too. I remembered reading once that he usually led his team in tackles, or something like that. Back in my brief stalker days.

"I don't care who you are," Jonah with a capital J said, responding to whatever it was that Noah had just spilled out. "That means nothing to me."

"Who the fuck are you anyway?" Noah demanded.

I was over this.

"Stop."

He glanced at me for a second, the words out of his mouth and into the air before maybe he even realized it. "I'm not talking to you right now."

Was this fucker *for real?*

My shoulders went back, and if I'd had earrings on, I would have taken them off because I was about to beat the shit out of Noah. No one knew his weaknesses better than I did.

I'm not talking to you right now.

Mother. Fucker.

"Who the fuck do you think you're talking to?" I snapped, as beside me, Jonah said in that deadly, crazy voice, "Meet me outside, bro."

That snapped me out of it.

Shock could do that to a person, I guess. How the hell had we gotten to the point where one of the two calmest males I'd ever met was telling people to meet them outside? *Jonah?* My shy Jonah who could barely speak to strangers? *Whaaaaa?*

I didn't know what the fuck was wrong with me that I all of a sudden wanted to laugh. That comment alone had put this whole shit into perspective. What the hell was going on? What were we *doing?*

"You want to meet up outside? Let's go," Noah responded like the hotheaded dumbass he was.

I rolled my eyes that time because *get the fuck out*. I wanted to laugh. Noah would go straight to jail if he got into an unsanctioned fight. He would be suspended. Was he that dumb?

And Jonah had to be fifty pounds heavier than him right then, and maybe he had no official training, but he had amazing reflexes and he was strong in a way that wasn't just for glamour muscles. His whole body was a machine. An expensive, well-maintained machine.

And I wanted to kiss the shit out of him for being one of the best things ever.

After I dealt with this dipshit.

"Stop being stupid, Noah," I said, taking him in with what I was sure was disgust. "I don't know what you're doing. I don't know why you're doing it." He choked like he knew the answer to those questions and didn't like it. "But you need to stop. Don't talk to him like that. Don't even look at him either. And don't you dare use that tone of voice on me. You have zero right to be over here being a fucking jackass, and I will call your mom and tell her what the hell you're doing if you don't quit making that face right now."

His eyelid twitched as the words penetrated his brain.

Noah's mom was no one's quiet, tender mom. She'd still beat his ass if it came down to it. I'd watched it happen more than a few times myself. Plus, Grandpa Gus had gotten the scoop on how his mom had reacted after she'd found out how Noah had treated me that one day before he'd left. I wished I could have seen it.

I loved that woman. Admired the hell out of her. But that was beside the point.

"You need to go," I finished, staring straight at him.

It was that sentence that dug in the deepest. I'd shocked him. "You're telling me to leave?"

"He's a member. You aren't anymore."

Those dark blue eyes focused in, surprise still all over his eyes and features. "I need to talk to you."

"No, I don't think you do," I replied at the same time Jonah said, "Too late for that."

I glanced over at him and had to fight the urge to smile again.

"*I need to talk to you*," Noah repeated himself, frowning, finally ignoring the other man. "It's important."

"About what?"

His shoulders rolled backward, and his chin went up in defiance. "It's private."

He was full of shit.

If I could go back in time and slap the shit out of myself for all those times I'd clung onto our friendship for the sake of being loyal to someone who had once meant a lot to me, I would. How many times had he been a stubborn dumbass and I'd been left to help him or deal with his shit once Peter and Grandpa were fed up with him and his bullshit? How many times had I been the person who tried to talk some sense into him when he'd forced everyone else to exhaustion?

A hand that wasn't so familiar anymore reached out and wrapped around my forearm, distracting me so much, I didn't process quickly enough. "Let's talk over dinner."

Was this happening to me? All I could do was stare at him like he'd lost his fucking shit. Because he had. The last time we had been in the same room together he'd called me a slut.

He was lucky he was still alive.

So it wasn't hard to look at him like he was fucking nuts and give him the only answer possible. "No."

Noah swallowed as his eyes moved toward Jonah and back, shoulders bunched tightly. "I really need to talk to you."

I repeated myself, genuinely asking myself how the hell my life had gotten to this point.

"For old time's sake. You owe me that much," he tried to insist.

The *'I don't owe you shit'* was right on my tongue.

"Please."

Jonah tensed up beside me, and I couldn't help but think about how he felt.

But... this was Noah. He'd put Band-Aids on me. He'd gotten a unicorn painted on his face by my side on my fifth birthday. He had carried me on his shoulder when we had been fifteen and I'd won my first Pan-American game. Before he'd turned into such a dipshit, he had been my closest friend.

But....

Then again, he'd also pushed me down a few times and caused me to need the damn Band-Aids in the first place.

Unfortunately, I knew him. At least I had known the person he'd been before becoming this. And if he was feeling entitled and genuinely thought he felt a certain way about me, there was only going to be one way that he'd stop all this shit and just let me move on.

"I'm not going to dinner with you. But if you want to talk, we can do it at the juice bar later. I have to work, and I've got Mo at home, and I want to spend time with her."

His nostrils flared at the mention of her.

And it made me sad.

It made me real sad.

Friends were supposed to support each other. They were supposed to be there for one another even if you thought they were being dumbasses. Even when things weren't perfect and easy.

I realized then better than I ever had before, that things between Noah and I would never be the same. Not even close. Not when he flinched when I brought up the joy waiting for me at home. The kid that was as much a part of me as my own hand was. Even more important than my stupid-ass hand.

And he was never going to be okay with where I was in my life now. Jonah or no Jonah. It didn't take a genius to see that either.

It made me really sad, and I'd have to save that up for later.

The arm right next to my own went hard again, but I wasn't going to think twice about it. Not right then.

"You don't have time for me?" Noah asked, going there like I owed him something.

He should have known better. "No, I don't. I barely have time to take a poop in peace. Are you good with five thirty or not?"

He could see it. I saw that. He could see that I wasn't going to budge. Not anymore. Not when spending time with him had once been second nature. But that had been a long, long time ago.

The way he said "fine" almost got to me.

Almost.

But I had an imaginary Kevlar vest on, so it bounced right off.

And when Noah sneered at Jonah before basically stomping his way out of my office, all I could do was regret not giving him the official kick out of my life when he had ruined one of my dreams by being a careless prick.

"That went well."

Jonah turned toward me. "You're going to talk to him?"

I blinked. "I'm going to listen to him. At the juice bar. In the gym. I thought I said that out loud?"

That wasn't the answer he'd been expecting based on the scowl on his face.

The scowl that honestly pleased me a hell of a lot more than I would ever admit.

I'd had friends before who got all pissed off when their boyfriends and husbands got jealous, but I couldn't find even the tiniest bit of anger inside of me. Annoyance, yeah. But just a little.

Because *hadn't he fucking listened?* Did he not understand that I'd downgraded our conversation from *dinner*—when we hadn't had dinner together by ourselves in… never—to being here at Maio House in front of people? Hello?

I had to keep my face neutral. I wasn't about to ruin this shit. I was going to soak it up, eat it up, and gorge on it. Then do it all over again.

"You know what he's planning on saying," he accused in a voice that was almost that deadly one but not.

He was *mad*.

Hehe.

"I don't understand why you need to listen to that fucking arsehole."

Seriously, my heart *soared*, just flew right out of my chest and straight into the sky, and I had to keep my face straight so I wouldn't give myself away, and it was a lot harder than I ever would have imagined.

This beautiful, handsome, amazing man was jealous.

Was that what joy felt like? It had to be. It fucking had to be.

It was because of that joy, and the borderline anger on his face and the fact that he had no idea that he was making my whole year by being mad, that I put a hand on that beefy-ass upper arm and told him calmly, "I'm only going because if I don't, he'll never drop it. Whatever it is he's thinking isn't going to go away with time. He needs to totally understand what the situation is, and he won't listen if I do that in front of you, Jonah."

He opened his mouth, but I kept going.

"I'm not going to dinner with him. I don't even want to meet with him period, and I'm only doing this because he was my friend for a long time."

"He hasn't been your friend for a long time either."

That was a good point. "But he was my friend for a long

time first. I know what I'm doing. I know who I'm dealing with. I'm talking to him for thirty minutes at the juice bar. I was trying to be considerate of your feelings, if you don't see that."

This man I had so rarely seen lose his shit, huffed, shook his head, and then nodded all in less than a minute. "Bloody considerate." He took a step back and swallowed hard. "I need to finish my workout. Good luck over *juice.*"

I didn't say shit as he walked out, and I waited to smile until he was way out of the office.

That little jealous asshole.

I loved it.

~

HOURS LATER, AFTER I'D SPENT TWO OF THEM ON THE PHONE arguing with the cleaning company about how they had double-charged me—Maio House—I was still feeling a little on edge as I headed toward the juice bar.

It wasn't that I was dreading my conversation with Noah, because I wasn't.

I already knew what the outcome would be, and it was going to suck, and it was probably going to be uncomfortable, but… it had to be done. That chapter of my life, the one that had him in it was over. He'd made his choice, and even if he changed his mind now, it was too late.

The thing was, he wasn't going to change his mind.

I could see that by the way he had reacted when I had just *brought* Mo up.

The other thing was, I didn't regret shit.

The training facility part of the building was starting to fill up with guys filtering in slowly, taking their time talking outside of the locker rooms and making loud noises inside them. Peter was already leading his group of ten men through warm-ups that consisted of jogging the perimeters of the mats with their full gear on: head protection, shin, chest, and gloves.

I had spilled the details about Noah showing up an hour ago when he'd first arrived, and it hadn't been hard at all to notice the way Peter's normally easygoing eyes had narrowed and the way his head had lulled to the side more than normal while I'd recounted most of the incident.

Minus Jonah getting all butthurt and jealous over it. That was my own personal little treat I got to indulge in.

The other thing I got to enjoy was the long, warm hug that Peter had given me before we'd noticed the time; he had to get back out on the floor. His arms had still been around me while he'd said in that calm way he had about him constantly, "We outgrow clothes the same way we outgrow people, Len. We change inside the same way we do outside."

It was that thought that I had in my heart and my head as I pushed open the door that led to the walkway and then a few moments later as I opened the connecting door to the main part of the gym. It was in its early stages of getting packed. In fifteen minutes, the cardio machines would be filled and three-fourths of the dumbbells would be missing from their racks. I waved at a few people I recognized but kept on walking, not wanting to get distracted. I had thirty minutes for this; then I was going to tell the assistant manager on duty that I was going home.

Turning toward the juice bar, I smiled at Bianca when she caught my eyes, and she smiled back at me a second before I noticed that Noah wasn't there. The employee behind the counter was moving quickly through whatever the customer in front of him had ordered, with a line of two more people. I fought off the irritation that Noah wasn't around and took the last stool along the counter, hooking my knee over the top of the stool right next to me to save it.

Under normal circumstances, I would have helped make the juices, but I really did need to get this conversation over with.

But as one minute went by and then another, and those two turned into five and Noah still wasn't there, this feeling of just… being resigned… of being *over* this shit fully hit me.

I glanced down at my watch to see that it was five forty-four.

"I'm sorry I'm late," the voice that belonged to Noah said over my shoulder a second before the stool I'd been saving for him got pulled out from under my thigh.

Five forty-six.

Some form of disappointment made my chest tighten. Pasting a blank look on my face, I waited until he'd taken the stool, watching his movements. The expectant look on his face was almost enough to get me to want to be nice to him while we did this.

But... nah.

Grandpa Gus said that when you made your bed, you had to sleep in it. So don't shit or piss in it.

And like with a lot of things, he was fucking right. You made your choices in life, and you had to deal with them. There weren't take backs. You could never and should never expect a second chance.

"Don't be pissed. I forgot how much traffic there was," he said in a huff that pierced my chest a little tighter. He was apologizing because he knew being late drove me nuts. Because he'd known me so well for a while there.

"I'm not," I told him honestly, because I wasn't. "I've got... thirteen minutes before I have something else I need to do, so I hope you can summarize whatever it is that you need to say in that amount of time."

"Thirteen?"

I'd told him I was busy, hadn't I?

"Jesus, Lenny, you can't reschedule to hang out with me?"

Did he not know me at all? He remembered enough to know that being late drove me fucking batshit. The fact that he didn't care enough about me and my time to leave early enough and spend the time he wanted to spend with me didn't bother me.

This was what I expected.

Sometimes you really did outgrow people, no matter how much they meant to you at some point.

"No, I can't," I told him calmly. "Twelve minutes now, Noah. What's up?"

His face went red, and he said, "Are you—" He cut himself off. Of course I was serious. He knew it. His hand went up to his face and brushed the short blond hair to the side, the back of his hand going up to draw a line across his forehead. "Len, I'm sorry. Jesus. I thought you were bull-shitting."

No, he hadn't.

I slid my gaze to the right so that I wouldn't roll my eyes.

And when I did that, I immediately spotted the three people sitting at one of the tables across the walkway from the juice bar. There was one green and one beet red drink in between them. And a bottle there too.

A baby bottle.

The two biggest—the two *adults*—were both staring over at where I was sitting. And if my eyes weren't deceiving me, Grandpa Gus and Jonah were sitting there muttering to each other, with Mo standing on top of Jonah's thighs; she was the only innocent party in this entire thing.

I wanted to be surprised. I wanted to ask myself if they were fucking for real. These two people who barely spoke to each other—mostly because Grandpa Gus still hadn't allowed himself to join the Jonah bandwagon—apparently deciding that they were each the lesser evil, and they were now banding together to spy on me.

Goddamn it.

Goddamn it.

I couldn't fucking laugh.

I could not fucking laugh even if it fucking killed me.

These *idiots*....

Out of the corner of my eye, I saw Noah move his body so that he faced the stool I was on, reminding me of why I was there and why I had to ignore the wannabe retired CIA agent and whatever secret service New Zealand had. *Those two....*

Peter was going to die with me when I told him about their little meetup.

One of Noah's hands went to rest at the top of the bar counter, those navy eyes focused directly on me, searching and searching... like he hadn't seen me before. He looked sad and a little tired and stressed. I'd forgotten he'd lost his last fight, and there was no way that hadn't stung his ego.

But I didn't feel pity. I didn't feel bad. I just wanted to get this over with. To be done.

The hand he had on the counter inched closer to where mine was, and I wasn't sure whether to look at it or at him as he said, in a voice too soft, "Look, I... I miss you, Len."

I faced him again, expecting some level of tenderness to flood me, but getting nothing.

"I miss talking to you about shit."

A hundred different examples of proof of how that couldn't exactly be true and hadn't been in a decade went right through my head, but I was proud of myself for keeping my mouth shut.

"I know that I've fucked up a lot. I know that I've said a lot of stuff to hurt you, but I love you." His fingertips grazed mine, and I had to make sure not to look in the direction of Inspector Gadget or Pink Panther again as much as I wanted to.

"We've been through everything together," he kept right on going, and I knew I was going to have to stop him because this little declaration was pointless. "No one knows me better than you, or ever will. I'm sorry, Lenny. For everything. I just... I don't know. I got so mad at you for getting fucking pregnant. It felt like you cheated on me."

Cheated on him? *Okay.*

My eyes strayed toward the table beyond, where I could see Grandpa Gus's lips moving, probably talking shit—all right, not *probably*, for sure talking shit, this was Grandpa Gus after all—and Jonah nodding in response.

I had wanted these two to bond, and what the hell did they have to bond over?

Hating Noah.

I swear I didn't understand my life sometimes.

"Lenny?"

He'd caught me. I glanced back at him and raised my eyebrows. "Yeah?"

"Are you listening?"

"Yeah. Mostly," I told him the truth because, well... it was the truth. And if he looked butthurt about it, I didn't know what to say.

He did look butthurt on second glance. His forehead was wrinkling, and he was frowning, insulted. "You don't give a fuck about what I'm telling you?"

I couldn't help but give him a long look as I thought about the two goobers sitting together. "It isn't that I don't care, Noah. I do. I care about you. I wouldn't want anything to happen to you. But you telling me that you love me and that you're sorry for the things that you've said...." I drew my hands up at my sides as I shrugged at him. "I will always love and care about you, frankly, and maybe I missed something, but we haven't been in each other's lives in forever."

The fingertips on mine jerked away, and I couldn't say I wasn't glad.

"Noah, come on. You were here a year ago, but the only time you ever talked to me was when you wanted me to help you train."

He opened his mouth like he was going to argue but shut it right back.

"But you don't love me."

"Yeah, I do," he insisted, leaning forward, expression intense. "I always have."

It was way too hard to keep a straight face. "No, you haven't. Maybe you've convinced yourself that you do, but it isn't real. If you're going to feel that way about someone, it should be honest. It shouldn't be because my daughter's dad is here and you decided to get all possessive for no reason. You care about me, in your own way, but you don't love me, Noah."

My words weren't sinking in. I could tell. "I've loved you my whole fucking life, Len!" he claimed, eyes moving around to see if anyone had heard him. I didn't give a fuck if someone did, so I didn't bother caring. "*Always.* There's never been a fucking day when I didn't."

"You should've thought about that at some point before I was pregnant, and I wanted my friend around. When I needed some support and you made it out to seem like I was walking around with radiation poisoning. You called me a slut." I gave him a smile that wasn't a happy one by any means. "I needed you, and you left me. Not just now but years ago. I used to fucking take you to the hospital, Noah. I stayed with you the whole time, and that was when you needed *stitches.*"

He tipped his head back. "You're going to bring that shit up? I was eighteen. I wanted to go away to school, and you're still pissed off about that? I didn't give you shit for graduating early."

Oh hell. Yeah, none of this was doing anything. I couldn't help but snort and look up at the ceiling as I shook my head.

He wasn't the boy who had been my brother and best friend. He wasn't anyone I knew anymore. And that really did suck.

"You know what, Noah? Yeah, I'm going to bring the past up. Because all of this goes back to you not being a real friend to me since then. I never would have just been a chickenshit and gone away to school without giving you a fucking warning. Without telling you I was thinking about it. You never even apologized to me over fucking up my ribs back then either; you know how fucking shitty that is?"

Noah opened his mouth, but I wasn't letting him get another chance. I'd given his ass enough chances, and I was done. I had been done years ago.

But fuck it.

I didn't give a shit anymore.

"But none of that matters anymore, Noah, because you don't really love me. You don't even really care about me. Because now I know what that's supposed to be like, and it isn't supposed to be like this. You don't get to be territorial and ugly to anyone in my life. Sorry you realized too late that I'm pretty fucking awesome and that I have no gag reflex. But I love Mo and wouldn't trade her for fucking anything, and I love her dad too, and they're what I want. And I don't say that to hurt you, but so that you know that even if Jonah wasn't around, Mo always will, and if I could go back in time, I would still have her. And I can see that you could never look at her and see a child you could love. You don't love me enough to love something I do, and that right there is the biggest neon sign in this shit."

I pinned him with a glare and shrugged. "I get it, I really do, and I don't blame you. It's fine, but you don't have a single right to say anything to me about anything."

I saw his face change. Saw the anger take over his features. But he let me finish talking. He listened, at least to part of it.

Not enough based on the comment he went with next.

"You think you love that asshole?" was what he asked. "I've known you our entire lives. We used to be able to look at each other and know exactly what we were thinking."

When we had been teenagers.

"And you're going to choose some dipshit you've only known for a couple months *over me?*"

Oh fucking hell.

I just sat there and watched his features twist and turn as I leaned back into my stool. I was done with this conversation. I wasn't about to waste my time going over this shit in circles, and unfortunately, words had never been my strong suit, but they were going to have to be enough. "Noah," I told him as calmly as possible, digging in real deep for all that "mom patience" I'd developed... not that there was much of it, "he's not an asshole. He's not even close to being an asshole, and I could give you all the reasons why he isn't, but I'm not. But, yeah, I do love him, and it isn't choosing one person over the other. That's not at all what it's like, and the fact that you think that says everything."

"What the fuck is that supposed to mean?"

I shook my head and couldn't help but smile. I had known exactly what I was walking into. Hadn't I? Yeah, and that only made the next words out of my mouth a little easier. But they came out after I slid off my stool and paused before pecking Noah on the temple. Standing up beside where he sat, I told him as seriously as I could, "It means that it isn't that I love him because I don't want to love you. It's that I know him, and I can't help it."

I made sure to look him right in the eyes. "If you ever want to try and be my friend again, you know my number, and if you don't, I don't know what to tell you. But I hope you'll be happy and quit doing dumb shit like not doing enough cardio before a fight and then you end up running out of steam too fast."

Taking a step away, I thought of something else and added, "You probably shouldn't try talking to my grandpa anytime soon. Just saying."

I wished I could have said that his face wasn't bitter and angry as I gave him one last look, but it was. And as I weaved my way through the tables by the juice bar, going forward some more and alternating eye contact between my gramps and Jonah—who both had no shame because they didn't even try to pretend like they were around for any other reason other than to snoop—I thought about life and how it worked out.

When I got to the table that held three of the five most important people in my life, I was already shaking my head at the two older ones even as I drew an arm over Grandpa Gus's shoulders. "You two are the worst," I said to both of them as I leaned down and started kissing the old man's cheeks over and over again, hugging him tight in basically a chokehold.

"What are you doing?" He tried to squirm away.

I started kissing his other cheek repeatedly. "I love you so much, Grandpa. I love you, I love you, I love you."

He made a choking sound and attempted to lean away from me. "Why are you doing this to me?" he tried to ask but started laughing almost instantly.

"Because you're the best grandpa in the entire world, Count Chocula." I pecked him on his forehead, one kiss after another after another as he pretended to try and get out of the hold I had him in.

But I knew he was just faking it. He was eating this shit up. He used to do this to me all the time.

"I just love you so, so much," I told him, giving him two more kisses as he whispered, "Mo, help me."

I laughed as I pulled away, seriously flying inside by the fact these two stalkers cared about me enough to be so meddlesome.

Grandpa moaned as he sat there, eyeing me like he was expecting me to give him another kiss attack as he said, without any remorse or embarrassment, "That's my payment for making sure you didn't do anything dumb?"

I kept my arm around the top of his shoulder and looked down at his old Dracula face before glancing over at Jonah, who was still sitting there with that weird look on his features. "What would I do that's dumb?"

"You decide you *loveee* him or something," Grandpa answered with a sly, knowing look in his eyes, and I witnessed a nerve under Jonah's eye start to jump.

Did he... know? How I felt? I wondered, eyeing my grandpa suspiciously.

I wasn't even sure why I was wondering it. Of course he knew. He had more than likely known before I did.

"Sure, because that's me, falling in love left and right," I said, glancing over at Jonah right as that nerve popped once more, and being pretty damn gleeful over it.

Grandpa tilted his head to the side and looked up at me in this way that warned me that he knew.

Hm.

I was going to give him shit over his temporary truce or new bromance later in private. And tell him what Noah had said too. He'd ask.

I pecked him on the cheek once more, set a hand on Jonah's shoulder, hesitated for point five seconds, and then pecked him right beside his mouth as he eyeballed me quietly. Finally, I picked Mo up out of her dad's arms, gave her a snuggle as I told her how amazing she was and then landed a couple kisses on her neck, forehead, and both hands.

With my mouth to her cheek, I glanced at both of them. "I'm going to leave in a minute. I'll see you at home?"

I didn't miss that Jonah didn't say anything as my grandfather smirked, looking pretty pleased with himself, and said, "Yeah, yeah, see you at home."

Noah was nowhere to be seen as I headed to the manager's office after leaving Mo with her two protectors, and I couldn't say I wasn't glad that he didn't witness me smiling on the walk there.

CHAPTER 19

Subject: I'll pay you

Lenny DeMaio:
> **Wed 3/22/2019 1:29 p.m.**
> **to Jonah Collins**

I will literally pay you if you could just respond back to me. You don't even need to say anything. I can do all the talking: $100 for 15 seconds of your life, Jonah. It's the least you could fucking do.

ABOUT AN HOUR LATER, AFTER GETTING A CALL FROM LUNA WHO wanted to do something on Saturday, grabbing my things from the office, and making a quick stop at the store, I was finally pulling up at home to find that there wasn't a rental car parked anywhere on the street.

Grandpa Gus's Camry was in the driveway. Peter was still at Maio House like usual. He didn't get back home until nine on Thursdays.

I got out of my car, fighting back the flare of disappointment that Jonah wasn't around, grabbed my backpack on the way out, and opened the door in the kitchen, straining my freaking ears to listen to what could be going on. The second I had it open, I found Jonah and Grandpa both standing at the stove, with Jonah stirring something, my grandpa watching him. Mo was sitting on the floor, a toy in each hand, apparently the only one who heard me open it because her gaze was instantly on me, shouting out with glee, "Ma!"

"Hey, booger," I called out, swinging the door fully open and heading straight for that little body.

She babbled, really excited and animated, as I picked her up, going straight for that baby neck as she pulled at my hair like it wasn't tied up in a ponytail.

"Your day was that good? What else happened?" I asked her, eating up the baby sounds coming out of her and how good she smelled and putting one baby fat wrist in my mouth and pretending to munch on it. "Oh my God, I can't believe your poopy-face Grandpa did all that with you. Wow."

"Are you going to give poopy-face Grandpa a hug or am I going to die before I get one?"

I groaned as I turned with Mo toward the stove where the two men were, but instead of looking at whatever was being cooked in the pot, they were watching us.

"Yeah, poopy face," I said before going toward them, shifting her to one hip and giving Grandpa Gus, who was the closest, a one-armed hug and a kiss on the cheek, getting one back in return.

There was no hesitation in me before I let go of him and went for Jonah, wrapping an arm around his waist, surprising him if the way he tensed at the contact meant anything.

But just as quickly as he tensed up, he relaxed and put one arm around the middle of my back, his mouth being the one that dropped to my cheek—the corner of my mouth, really—before mine did that to his.

When he moved his face to Mo's and kissed her too, I tried not to let my heart do anything.

I failed.

That pink mouth touching that soft face....

Yup. I was gone. This was over.

I had thought about it the entire drive home. I loved him, there was no arguing it. It worried me, sure. I wished that I didn't, of course.

But I did.

And I was 90 percent sure he liked me a lot. Enough to get jealous over Noah. Enough for him to come spy on me.

To come here.

I didn't need much more than that. It was something to work with. Not that I knew what the fuck I was doing or what the fuck we could do or even what the fuck was going to happen sooner than later when he had to get back to work.

But I wasn't scared, and I sure wasn't about to give up on something good because it wasn't going to be easy, especially not when he didn't seem to want to give up on me—us—either.

Fucking *please*.

I had this. I'd been *made* for this. It was all good.

So when Jonah's eyes drifted over to me as he pulled away from our girl, I couldn't help but not make total and complete eye contact with him.

And this fucker, who hadn't even told me bye because he'd been so aggravated earlier, gave me a tiny and possibly apologetic smile.

I wanted to punch him in the stomach and kiss him at the same time. That sounded about right. Sounded great, actually.

"Hi," he said in that soft voice that I was a total sucker for, even now, when I should probably be mad but wasn't. Not even a little bit.

"Hey," I told him, keeping my face straight. "Is Grandpa teaching you to make poison?"

Gramps snorted from behind.

"I'm showing Jonah"—the fact he even called him that surprised me, but I kept that to myself—"how to make Mo's food."

Jonah sucked in a breath. His eyes widening, and he temporarily forgot he was annoyed because he mouthed, *Did he call me Jonah?*

I nodded.

The adorable little jealous shit grinned.

I grinned too as I peeked into the pot to find there was beans and quinoa inside, just on the verge of becoming mush. Then I glanced at my grandpa with a face that said *oh, he's Jonah now?* And the face he made back at me said *yeah, so?* I felt the smirk on my face and saw his own.

Honestly, right in that moment, I couldn't remember ever being happier.

"I got you something," I told Jonah.

His eyes lit up. "Yeah?"

I nodded. "It's in the front pocket of my backpack. Get it."

Giving me a suspicious look, he went behind me since I still had it on, and I heard the zipper open. There was a pause and a slight jerk as he stuck his hand inside and then... "Len!" He burst out laughing.

"You like it?"

Jonah groaned as he stepped around to the side and held up the can opener I'd bought him. "Thanks, love," he chuckled before bringing it up against his chest with a grin. "I'll never go hungry again."

I grinned at him just as the old vampire let out his own groan.

"Your turn to make dinner tonight, Len. What are you making us?" Grandpa asked.

"Depends." I glanced at my girl's dad. "Where's your mom and Natia?"

Those honey-colored eyes were bright and moving back and forth between the little monster in my arms and my own face.

"On their way. They should be here soon, but you don't need to worry about them. If you show me how, I can order a pizza."

I slid him a look. "There's enough. I'm just going to prep to have bowls for dinner. If they don't want it, then order the pizza, but your sister didn't cry about our veggie cheese-less pizza last night, and I saw your mom eat vegetables. They'll probably like it."

"You don't—"

The doorbell rang, cutting him off.

"I'll let them in," Jonah said before giving me another tight, small smile and heading out the kitchen door after setting his can opener down on the island.

The door had barely begun to swing shut when I glanced at Grandpa and asked, "Are you doing anything Saturday night?"

"Allen is coming over with Lydia. We're going to play cards. Why?"

Play cards. It was easy to forget this man who still played fucking basketball once or twice a week did something like play cards with his longtime friends. "Luna asked if I wanted to go to that bar by her job for her coworker's birthday," I explained. I didn't insult him by immediately suggesting I'd contact a sitter. I knew better.

Grandpa didn't let me down either with his words or his eye roll. "We can keep her." He even shrugged. "You can never be too young to learn how to play poker."

I snorted. "That sounds like the beginning of a gambling problem."

He was still rolling his eyes when the sound of voices coming warned us that the door was about to be opened. Jonah came through first, holding it wide as his sister followed right after, with his mom trailing behind, saying "Why would you do that, Jonah?"

His gaze was on the floor as he replied with, "Can we talk about this later, please?"

"No," Sarah answered immediately as she headed straight

toward the three of us. She gave Mo a kiss on the cheek that my kid only slightly tried to dodge, shook my grandfather's hand, and then gave me a nod before going straight back into it with her son like she didn't give a single fuck that whatever they were talking about he was trying to keep private. "Why would he need to go through Garrett to speak to you? You have to harden up. You can't ignore his calls anymore. Do you have any idea how upset he was with you after your injury? We had to plead with him to take you back."

Had to plead with who? And what the hell were they talking about?

Jonah let the door close, and he finally looked up, making eye contact with me first before switching it over to his mom. "Mum, he makes more than enough money off me. Your pleading wasn't necessary. And I will speak to him when I'm ready."

His agent? Who else would make money off him?

Natia flashed her teeth at me as she came over and gave me a hug, gesturing with her hands for Mo. Someone had experience with them discussing shit. I nodded and handed her over, still listening.

Sarah was fully facing Jonah again; she even had her hands on her hips. "When you're ready? Jonah, the season starts in two months. You have to make a decision now. If you wait too long, the rosters will be filled and then what?" Her back straightened, but somehow her head went forward and her voice got creepy quiet—I noticed Natia stopped walking and just stood where she was, looking too—and asked, "You are planning on playing this season?"

Jonah's face got pink at the same time it all clicked.

They were talking about his plans for the future with rugby and how he really hadn't made a decision yet on what he was going to do.

Because really, what were his plans? He hadn't said a word

to me. Then again, I hadn't asked either because I didn't want to know yet. Even though I should.

Jonah's hand went to the back of his head, and he said quietly, "Can we discuss this later? I should get the bags you left in the boot. I'm sure Mo would love to see what you bought her."

Being raised around someone who didn't give a fuck had prepared me for her answer. "No. Her gifts can wait. We need to talk about this now. You need to make a decision *now*. Garrett said that there's a team in Japan interested in you, another club in France has reached out. I reckon that, if you can get past this issue you and your brother are having, he would be more than willing to talk to the selectors in Auckland about you coming back."

Goose bumps broke out across my arms, and I found myself holding my breath. France, Japan, or New Zealand? That shouldn't be such a surprise. It wasn't like there were any teams any closer, unless he went to the UK. Even then, that was still an eight-hour flight.

Why was my heart beating so fast?

I looked up at the ceiling. Well, none of those places were fucking Mars. There were planes, and I didn't have that many expenses other than Mo, insurance, my car note, cell phone, and the electricity and gas bill. I swallowed and lowered my gaze, but as I did it, I caught a pair of honey-brown eyes across the room.

I smiled at Jonah. A real one. One that I hoped said he shouldn't worry about us.

I was too busy looking right into my favorite eye color in the world that I didn't notice his mouth start to move until he said my name. Then, "What do you think I should do?"

Who? Me?

"Yes, you," he said in that quiet, strong voice. "What do you think I should do?"

His mom turned to look at me, so did Natia, and I was positive Grandpa Gus was mentally doing binocular hands.

"Whatever you want to do?" I offered, not knowing what to say.

One of those dimples popped, and he was partially smiling as he asked, "But what do you think I should do?"

I didn't mind being put on the spot, but in this case, I didn't want to. So I shrugged at him. "Whatever makes you happy, Jonah with a little j."

His other dimple came out to party, and he wasn't even trying to hide his big-ass grin.

"Seriously, go wherever you want," I said. "Go to the team that offers you the most money and has the most potential for winning. Or go where they offer you less money if it'll make you happy. Do whatever you want. We'll support you anywhere you are."

"And what if I decide to retire?"

I'd swear the neighbors were able to hear the gasp that Sarah let out. Hell, the neighbors down the street might have been able to as well.

But Jonah put a hand in between him and her and said, "Mum, wait." He speared me with a look. "What would you say if I told you I wanted to retire?"

Now I could see why he wanted to have this conversation in private. I didn't even want to be a part of it. But… he was asking me to be involved, and I wouldn't tell him no. So what I did was tell him the truth.

"If you want to do that and it'll make you happy and you won't regret it, then do it," I said. "But, if I were you, I wouldn't be a little bitch and quit. I'd play as long as I could if I still enjoyed it and it didn't screw my back or my knees up too bad. You don't give up on shit you love, Jonah. Not until you don't have a choice. But that's just what I think, and I told you, we'll support you with whatever you decide to do or wherever you decide to go." I looked at my girl sitting in her aunt's arms and said, "Right, Mo?"

And Mo agreed with a very loud, "Da!"

∽

HOURS LATER, AFTER GIVING MO A BATH THAT ENDED UP WITH Jonah and me both nearly soaked, putting her to bed, and walking Jonah out to the porch so he could leave with his mom and sister, I went and found Grandpa. My lips were still tingling from the kiss Jonah had given me before taking off. He was sitting in front of the television with a basketball game on the screen, one of his romance novels spread open facedown on his lap. He didn't even look up as I sat on the couch next to the love seat he was on.

What he did do was jump right into it. "That was an awkward dinner."

I couldn't help but laugh. It had been awkward as fuck after Jonah had asked me what he thought he should do. His mom had kept trying to bring it up, but my girl's dad hadn't let her, changing the subject and telling her that he would make a decision when he was ready.

Basically, she'd been shooting him annoyed looks all night, even after dinner, and Natia had sat there with a shit-eating grin on her face that she kept aiming at me so I could join in too.

And I had. Because what was their mom going to do? Get mad at me?

"Peter's going to be disappointed he missed out."

Grandpa snickered, and it was because of that snicker that I wasn't expecting him to say, "He's a good kid, Len."

My mouth gaped, and I raised my eyebrows at him. "Now you think Jonah's a good kid?" I asked, finally realizing just how much of a drama-filled day it had been. It had to set a new record for us.

"Yes."

"When did you decide that?"

"Earlier."

The only person in this world who could out stubborn me was my grandfather, but I'd still give him a run for his money. "Earlier when?"

"Earlier."

"An hour before you went to Maio House or while you were dropping bombs after dinner?"

A smile crossed his features, and he made a little puff of a muffled laugh. "Earlier, nosey." He couldn't help but laugh out of fucking nowhere. "He came to the house to ask if he could have Mo for a couple hours."

"And then?"

It was his turn to sigh. "*And then*," the smart-ass went on, "I asked him why."

Obviously.

"He told me that Noah showed up at Maio House. He said he was pretty positive there was no way you were going to forgive him, but that he wasn't going to take the chance, so could he have Mo so they could go together, and he could remind you of what you had together. *To be sure*."

Grandpa Gus raised his own eyebrows back at me. "He said he'd understand if I didn't want to use Mo because it was a dirty move or something like that, but that he didn't want to take any chances because he was running out of time.

"He also said that he knew I didn't like him, but that he loved you both." He blinked, pressing his lips together. "Then he said that even if I hated him for the rest of my immortal life and kept calling him names from that vampire book, it wasn't going to change anything. So could I please help him?"

Fuck me.

I sniffed, trying to pick up the barest hint of onions somewhere in the house, but there wasn't any.

Not a single hint.

Maybe because I hadn't used a single onion in the bowls I'd made for dinner.

But still, I fucking tried to find the scent because there was no way my eyes would tear up like this for no reason all of a sudden.

And when my grandpa looked at me and kept his expression nice and even, pretending like he didn't see me struggling to keep my shit together, he made an expression that said he was going to tell me something and he wasn't sure if he wanted to or not.

"You know how I feel about Noah."

I didn't say anything because, yeah, I did have more than an idea. He'd referred to him as *that no-loyalty weak little bastard* months ago.

"I thought of that boy as family for thirty years, Len. I thought of him as my… nephew." Grandpa shot me a long look before he kept going. "Even after he left for school like a spoiled, selfish kid without warning you, I was still fond of him. I thought, *he's just a kid; it's just a phase*. You've been so mature over most things; I knew you were an exception. Your dad had been a shithead at that age. I was a shithead at that age. It pissed me off that he did that to you, yeah, but I figured I could forgive him, and you bounced right back. You didn't let him get you down for long.

"But I've seen him since then. I've seen him grow up. At least I've watched him physically grow, and I've got to tell you, I told Peter at least once a week for years, that I hoped the rest of him never grew up. That he didn't get his life together and get his head on straight, and finally *see you*. I prayed, Len. I prayed that you wouldn't end up with him, even if I was confident that after what he'd done by leaving, that you wouldn't forgive him for it."

I had to hold my breath his words felt so raw. He wasn't done either.

"And the more time went on, the more I knew that he was

going to be too stupid to see what he had in you. That boy's loved you his whole life, but he doesn't have, and never will have, the focus you do. You're better than him at everything, and you always have been. He doesn't have half your heart or your brain. I'm grateful for that, because he wasn't what me, or Peter, would have dreamed of for you. So I'm glad. I'm real glad he's too late. You did the right thing, Lenny. I'm glad you're smart like I am," he decided to end with.

I just sat there, almost holding my breath, but mostly just staring at him and taking in every word he said. I picked one at a time and went with the last thing he probably expected. "So... you've decided Jonah is a better option?"

He made a face. "I think you're going to be too good for anybody." Then he took his face to a whole new level. "But that Jonah kid—"

"He's almost thirty-one."

It didn't matter apparently. "If he cares enough about you to come over here and use Mo to gain an advantage...." He tipped his head to the side. "That boy does not give a *fuck*. He's not afraid to do what he has to do to get what he wants, and he told me. He was pissed off, but he was ready to fight. He didn't run away.

"I'm impressed," he kept going. "If somebody cares that much about what you're doing, how can I hate him? Especially when it's Noah, the little shithead. If I had to choose between the kid who used to stick beans up his nose—the same one who won't even come around anymore because he knows I think he doesn't have any balls—or the kid who still comes by even though I'm not nice to him. You *know* who's gonna win that. I'm going to want the one who stuck around even when he wasn't welcome. I want my girl to be with the kind of person who fucked up but learned from it. I want someone for you who knows your worth and wants you to be a part of his life. There's not much more I can ask for."

Something twisted and turned inside of me.

"You might as well ask the kid to come stay with us the rest of the time he's here. He's already over here all the time anyway," Grandpa threw out.

I blinked. I wasn't dumb enough to ask him if he was sure. Of course he was. Grandpa never said shit unless he meant it.

Yet it still surprised the hell out of me so much all I could do was stand there as he kept talking, cementing my opinion that whatever had happened today sealed the deal on how my gramps felt.

Because if Jonah were to spend the night, there was only one thing that would mean. The biggest secret of all. The one thing in this world we kept under wraps as much as possible. Only a select handful of people knew, and they were the closest and most trusted people in our lives.

And now... now Grandpa Gus was inviting Jonah into the circle. The second, and final, circle of trust. It was pretty much shocking.

My grandpa didn't give me a chance to soak it in because he kept on talking.

"Did you know he's the third highest paid rugby player in the world? His brother is the first? I looked him up while you two were upstairs giving Mo a bath while I eavesdropped on his mom on the phone complaining to his dad. Did you know he had sixty-three caps on the New Zealand national team? Except for some people who were pissed off that he left the country, and the bad coverage he got two years ago when everyone thought he was done—and all the criticism he got this past season with people saying he wasn't playing like he used to—I couldn't find anything bad about him. A couple of pictures of him with two different girls a long time ago, but that was it. I'm going to offer to train him before he leaves, but I don't want to tell him too soon. I'm going to wait maybe three days before I do."

~

Was I doing this?

Yes, I was, I told myself for about the fifth time over the last fifteen minutes. I'd been going back and forth since I was in the shower. Was I doing it or not?

Fuck it.

I was doing it.

I grabbed my phone and found Jonah's contact info and sent him a message.

Me: Want to go out with my friends this weekend?
Me: And how do you know the character names to that vampire book?

If that wasn't the invitation of a lifetime, Jonah wasn't who I thought he was.

My phone started vibrating fifteen seconds later.

"JONAH" flashed across the screen as an incoming call.

I was already smiling when I answered. "Hey, Dimples."

His laugh made me smile even more into the receiver. "Hello, love," the calm, controlled voice came over the line.

I lay back against the pile of pillows behind my back. "Can I help you with something?"

"Can't I call to see how you're doing?"

"Considering I saw you an hour ago, just sent you a text, and this is the first time you've called me at night… no."

"First time I'm calling this late because I don't want you fed up with me," he replied. "I can call you every night if you'd like."

I grinned like an idiot at the white ceiling. I could get fed up with him, but I figured it wouldn't be that easy.

Then his words settled in, and my inner jealous bitch reared up.

But just as quickly as she did, she disappeared.

But I still asked anyway, "Do you talk on the phone a lot once you get back to your hotel room?"

His chuckle filled the line, making me smile again. "I talk to my grandmother every other night. I take turns calling my father and sisters. I was thinking about calling one of my brothers when your message came through."

The message.

He could tackle starting that conversation, while I thought about how cute it was he called his grandmother so often.

"I would like to accept your offer before you change your mind," he said.

"You're sure you're up for it?" I asked. "You can come by and hang out with my grandpa and his friends instead. Or take Mo with you if you want to do something."

He hummed. "I feel like I'm obligated to go to fill your requirements."

"Requirements?"

"Your best friend. No asking questions. You said."

My cheeks hurt from my smile. "You're right," I said right before a yawn tore its way up my throat from out of nowhere. "Speaking of questions, did you read those books?"

His laugh warmed my heart. "I watched them on marathon with my sister once on holiday."

"Ah."

He chuckled again.

So I went for it. "How would you feel about saving hotel money and coming to stay with us the rest of the time you're here?"

Honestly, it sounded like he dropped the phone, or himself, but he was back on the line so fast, I wasn't sure. "Stay? At your house? With you?"

"There are three more people here than just me...." I trailed off, still stunned by my grandfather's offer.

"Are you sure?" he asked with so much hope it hurt. "Your granddad—"

"Is the one who brought it up," I cut him off.

It sounded like he dropped his phone again, and that time I couldn't help but laugh.

"Granddad Gus told you to invite me?"

"Yeah." But he still had no idea just how much trust and respect went into the invitation.

But he would know soon enough. Because he needed to know so that it wasn't a shock.

"You don't have to say yes if you'd rather stay at a hotel."

Jonah laughed. "Give me a chance to answer, Lenny. Yes. *Yes.* I would love to. Wow."

I smiled and decided to fuck with him. "But you'd have to stay in my room with me."

There was a pause and then, "I will?"

"If you want to."

He let out another cute little laugh. "Sweet as. Was that your granddad's idea as well?"

"No. Mine." I pulled in a breath through my nose and knew I needed to go ahead and initiate him. "Jonah, I want you to know that you're being invited into the final circle of trust in the DeMaio family."

"Awesome… but did I imagine you saying there were three?"

"I lied." All right, I could do this. "If you're planning on staying with us—"

"I am."

I smiled. "There's something I need to tell you so that you aren't surprised."

"All right." He made a noise. "I know you snore sometimes. We did spend several nights together, Lenny. That isn't a surprise, and I think it's adorable when you do. You don't need to warn me."

I smirked. "You snore too, and that's not what I'm talking about." There was no doubt in my mind that this was going to go well. I knew Jonah, and apparently so did my grandfather, otherwise he never would have approved of him coming over.

"There are only very few people who know this, and it has to stay that way, okay? It's... a secret, and it wasn't mine to share, that's why I never said anything. They have good reasons for keeping it in the family and the circle of trust, and I trust that you'll never say anything to anyone. Okay?"

"Okay."

Part of me braced for his surprise and all the questions that might come. When I'd finally gotten the clearance to tell Luna, *nine years* into our friendship, she'd had at least... thirty. So it was totally saying something that we were months into this and it was happening.

I went right into it. "My grandpa and Peter have been in a relationship for the last twenty-eight years."

My body prepared....

And all Jonah said was, "Yeh, I know."

What?

"What do you mean you know?"

"I know. I assumed," he said easily, not sounding even the slightest bit surprised. "They live in the same house together, share a room, always sit next to one another. I've seen how they look at each other. Those comments your granddad's ex was hinting at helped too. I hoped you would tell me when you were ready. I couldn't imagine how hard it must be for them to keep it a secret, but I understand why they've had to. It made me a bit sad the first time I thought about it, Lenny."

How observant was this son of a bitch?

It really didn't throw him off at all, because the next thing I knew, he said, "I'm excited to be part of this circle finally."

I was too stunned to reply. But okay. If he wanted to brush this off and go with it... great. Perfect. All right.

It was amazing he'd figured it out, but okay. I wasn't going to make a big deal about it if he wasn't. Their relationship was the single most guarded secret I had ever known, and Jonah had taken it like nothing.

I wasn't imagining the love that pulsed through my chest as

I thought that over. I wasn't imagining it at all. I really did love this wonderful, intuitive, easygoing man who took things and rolled with them.

He kept on going like we were talking about the weather, forcing me to do the same. "Can I make a booking to stay with you starting two days from now when my mum and sister leave?"

I pumped my fist, but managed to keep my voice casual as I asked, "So soon?"

Jonah chuckled. "I can hear your heartbreak, and, yeah, Dad asked her to come back."

"Why? Is everything okay?"

"Good as gold, but I may have asked him to make the request."

Not that I wasn't grateful, but… "Why?"

"To get to spend more time with you and Mo," he answered easily.

And my brilliant-ass answer? "Oh."

"Did you mean what you said, Len?"

"About what?"

"About supporting me with whatever decision I make?"

Did he have to sound so hopeful? I rolled my eyes. "Yes. Duh." And just as quickly, my heart started beating fast, and if it was mostly just over the idea that he was going to have to leave eventually—sooner than later according to what his mom had said—well, it wasn't like I hadn't known. "Do you know what you want to do?"

"I thought I did," he answered, voice softening again. "But you gave me something to think about today."

Yeah, that was my heart beating fast. "And what was that?"

"That most blokes would kill to have the opportunities I do, and mostly… if you and Mo will be supportive of wherever I go, then…."

I was happy for him. I really was. I wouldn't want him to do anything else. Give up his dream. Or at least cut it off so early. But…

He'd still leave.

But that's how shit worked sometimes. Some people had loved ones in the military who got deployed. Some people had loved ones who worked in transportation and were gone all the time. You had to do what you had to fucking do, and I wasn't about to make him feel guilty.

"I'm calling my agent tomorrow, finally, and having a chat with him. See what can be done," he let me know. "Makes me feel heaps better now than I did earlier."

I squashed my dread down and got myself to ask, "What was wrong earlier?" Wait. "Noah? Or your mom?"

"Both I suppose, but that arsehole more," Jonah replied. "Most difficult thing I've ever done, sitting there, watching you talk to him," he admitted, sounding genuinely pretty put out about it.

Heh. It made me smile despite the hint of dread I felt at him leaving sooner than later. "I just gave him shit. Don't get all butthurt."

"What did he say?"

I crossed one leg over the other and grinned at the ceiling like I had probably never grinned before. "Well, it was more of what I told him. He showed up almost fifteen minutes late, if you didn't see that. And I don't know if you know, but I hate tardiness. I hate being late and having my time wasted." Especially when we were supposed to be having a serious conversation, but I didn't need to bring that up. "And after that…."

Was I going to tell him that I said I loved him? When he hadn't said those words to me? When I didn't even know what we were going to do in the near future with him leaving?

But those words clung onto my tongue, staked through my heart.

He cared about me. He got jealous. He was *trying*.

And according to Grandpa, he loved me.

So I had to try too if this—he—was what I wanted. And it was. There was no question there.

"He tried to bring up a bunch of old shit, and I had to remind him that he hadn't been my friend in a long time." I paused, knowing this was a leap and taking it. "I told him that I didn't feel the same way about him."

Jonah literally fucking grunted, and I could hear him breathing loudly over the line. It must have been at least a minute before he spoke up again. "What else did you tell him?"

You snooze you lose, right? And I hated losing.

So I went for it. Fuck it. "Well, I told him I was in love with your dumb ass."

I heard him exhale.

And I definitely heard him when he said in a clear, clear voice, "Did you tell him that I love you back?" There was a pause. "Or that his time had passed, and that I wasn't going to make the same mistake again?"

I pressed my lips together as my eyes started to sting out of nowhere. "No. I didn't tell him that."

His voice was a husky grumble. "You should have. Because it's the truth. Because I love you and Mo so much, I'm going to make up the last seventeen months to you both, Len." He paused. "If you'll let me."

CHAPTER 20

Subject: COME ON

Lenny DeMaio:
    Wed 3/22/2019 1:29 p.m.
    to Jonah Collins

Can you please fucking call me back?

Text me back?

Send me a fucking letter if you're too much of a chicken to communicate with me: one on one?

You need to know something.

I'm not trying to get you to like me again, but I have to tell you something important

---

IF I WOULD HAVE BEEN THE KIND OF GIRL TO KEEP A DIARY, I WAS sure every entry for the next three weeks of my life would have been something along the lines of TODAY IS THE BEST DAY OF MY LIFE.

And it wouldn't have been an exaggeration.

I couldn't remember ever being so… happy. Not in a way that I was smiling or laughing all the time, that wasn't me, but happy in the way that it was on the inside. Almost like wearing a life jacket even though I knew how to swim. I felt just… better than usual, and I had always been pretty good.

I was still tired and didn't want to kill people at the gym any less, but it was different.

Jonah's mom and sister had flown back to New Zealand right on the date that he'd told me, leaving me with a big hug from Natia and a pat on the back from his mom. She, of course, didn't leave without a long, long look that might have made me uncomfortable if I wasn't used to getting ugly looks from people and a question of, "You'll bring Mo to visit?" that didn't really feel like she was asking me but telling me.

I promised that I would.

Then I'd surprised the shit out of myself by inviting her to come visit whenever she wanted.

Every ten years or so.

I was just kidding.

Kind of.

No sooner had Jonah dropped them off at the airport, then he came knocking on the back door with his luggage duffel and a new rolling suitcase. Peter had let him in while I was busy flying Mo around the house. When I heard his voice in the kitchen, I kicked the door open and carried her in, belly down, her head up, fingers and toes wiggling in the diaper and shirt she was in.

"Don't be afraid; it's just the flying incredible Mo," I told them as I zoomed her around the island and flew her straight toward them.

Peter laughed as I stopped her in midflight and asked her to give him a kiss—she did, and he gave her one back—and then said "Pssshew" and fake threw her at Jonah, who had his hands open and wide at chest level, taking her with an ease that made me smile. He grinned at me before brushing his lips across my own briefly. He lifted her up over his head, elbows nearly locking, her body inches from the ceiling as she shrieked, "Da!" with absolute fucking joy.

"She loves me," the big man gasped, grinning as he lowered her back down to earth and planted a kiss on each cheek.

Ugh. They were too cute. It was sickening.

And amazing.

I couldn't stop smiling as Jonah lifted her back up high toward the ceiling, lowered her back down to his chest level, and then asked me, "May I continue the tour of the house?"

"Yup."

Off they went, with Jonah using his butt to push the door open and them disappearing through the house, with Mo laughing and giggling, back in airplane mode.

An arm came over my shoulder, and I felt Peter's kiss on the side of my head. I leaned against him before turning to him and raising my eyebrows, a smile stretching across my mouth.

He wasn't smiling, but I could tell he was happy. "Did you tell him?"

I knew what he was asking. "Yes."

He nodded, and I felt the deep, deep breath he took.

So I dug my knuckle into his rib and said, "Speaking of, when are you going to make an honest man out of my grandpa?"

Peter laughed like he always did when I asked him that every six months.

But we both knew the truth. If it ever happened, it wouldn't be until they both retired and had nothing to do with MMA anymore. But despite keeping it a secret for so long, I understood the reason behind the sacrifices that they'd made to make what they had work. Especially for so long.

And I guess, if they could make it work for so many years....

Well, if you tried hard enough, you could make anything work for that long.

You just had to have some heart. And patience. And a whole lot of will.

Luckily, I had all three.

~

LATER THAT SAME NIGHT, ON THE NIGHT THAT STARTED THE BEST three weeks of my life, we were all hanging around the living room. Grandpa Gus and Peter were sitting on their love seat, Grandpa half reading a novel and Peter with his eyes glued to a television program about police officers in the Pacific Northwest. I was sitting on the couch with Mo tucked into my arm, over my chest since she'd just finished her bottle. I had *Where the Wild Things Are* opened on my lap as I read to her while she tried fighting falling asleep. Jonah was in the middle of the couch, his thigh pressed against mine, with one hand resting on my thigh, holding her foot in his palm.

We'd had a nice, normal dinner like usual… except this time, Jonah wasn't leaving.

And I was feeling a little excited over it.

Nervous too, but mostly excited.

I had just finished flipping to the last page when Grandpa Gus let out an enormous yawn a second before he climbed up to his feet, palm going to his back with a groan, and said, "Well, I'm beat." Grandpa made a face as he raised his arms overhead and gave them a stretch with another yawn. Something told me to expect whatever was about to come out of his mouth, so I wasn't totally caught off-guard when he dropped his arms, focused in on Jonah, and asked, "Jonah, I'm gay. Is that going to be a problem?"

Peter's head immediately swiveled in my direction, and we made eye contact.

Yeah, he'd gone there.

And it was while I was processing that, that the man sitting beside me said, "You're a bit older than what I'm usually interested in, but...."

I was already snorting by the time Grandpa Gus shook his head and started walking out of the living room, calling out behind him, "You two deserve each other. Goodnight."

Even Peter had a grin on his face as he got up too, came over, gave Mo a kiss on the forehead, me one on the forehead too, hesitated for maybe a second, then planted one on Jonah's forehead too before disappearing out of the room. "Love you guys."

"Love you too," I called out after him.

Jonah and I both looked at each other the second we were alone. I smiled at him, and he smiled right back at me. "Are you tired?" I asked, leaning over to give Mo a kiss on her forehead too as I closed her book at the same time with my other hand. It was nine.

"A bit," he answered. "What's your usual routine?"

"I put Mo to bed, shower, watch some TV until I get sleepy... you?"

"Call my nan or sister for a bit, then go to bed." His gaze drifted down to the little girl resting against my boob. "Would you like me to put her in her crib?"

I shook my head. "I'll do it. Then I'll go shower afterward. Make your call and go upstairs whenever you want."

"Are you sure?"

I made a face at him as I started to get up as quietly and less bouncy as possible so that I wouldn't wake up Mo. "I got it, Dimples. Tell your grandma I said hi. I've got some pictures on my phone of Little Mo Peep she might like, if you want to steal them."

Jonah's hand reached for the back of my thigh and gave it a light squeeze. "I know you don't need me, but call down if you do. I won't be long."

His comment rode with me all the way up the stairs and

while I put Mo down and got her all set up for the night with her sound machine and baby monitor. And I kept on thinking about it while I showered and then hung under the spray a minute longer than I needed to. *I know you don't need me....*

It wasn't exactly a lie, but it still didn't sit right with me. Actually, it bothered me a little. He hadn't sounded mad or even a tiny upset or anything, but....

In my room, I eyed the two new bags that had been moved in there at some point during the day. I hadn't moved them in, and I couldn't remember Jonah doing it either. I wondered if it had been Peter, and the idea made me smile as I went about moisturizing my face and legs.

I took my time stretching; touching my toes, taking some deep breaths in and out, doing a few neck and shoulder exercises to loosen up. By the time I was done and Jonah still hadn't come up, I climbed under the covers as I yawned and grabbed the novel about the firefighters that grandpa had been reading weeks ago. He had checked it back out for me. About three pages later, I heard creaking down the hallway that stopped for a couple of minutes and then got louder before a big body stopped in the doorway.

Jonah was already smiling when his hands went to the doorframe, the sigh that came out of him so deep I raised my eyebrows at him.

"What?"

His dimples popped, and his voice was quiet as he said, "I wasn't sure I'd ever get to see you in bed like this again."

"I didn't think you would either," I told him honestly, then patted the half of the bed beside me. "Only if you want though. There's the guest bedroom too, if you would rather—"

He groaned. "The day I would rather sleep alone than with you...." His arms dropped from the doorway as he took a couple steps inside then paused. "Do you close your door?"

I smiled. "Not unless I have a reason to."

Those honey-colored eyes settled on me, and I could see his

cheeks puff in and out with the breaths he took. "Would you like me to close it?"

Under the blankets, I scrunched my toes. "The day I tell you not to close it…."

Jonah smiled shyly as he took two steps back and quietly closed the door, flipping the lock.

"My nan says hello," he said as he turned back, those big hands going to the bottom of his long-sleeved T-shirt.

I was watching those hands as I said, "How are your grandparents?"

The shirt was being tugged up, exposing an inch of tanned olive skin, and then another inch, and another…. "They're well. She was telling me that Granddad hasn't been feeling well, but he refuses to see his doctor."

The damn shirt went over his head, revealing that wide, naturally smooth chest that tapered to solid, flat abs. I'd asked him once if he shaved, and he'd laughed and shaken his head, claiming the only hair he could get to grow out was on his face. *It's a family curse,* he'd claimed; apparently neither of his grandparents or his dad were hairy. And there was that narrow, trim waist….

"Does anyone live close enough to go check on them?"

His thumbs were flicking at the button and zipper of his jeans as he replied, "No. Not often enough. They live in Hawke's Bay, it's a bit south of Auckland."

I tore my eyes up to his face to find him still watching me, his smile somewhere between shy and smug. I groaned and earned a big smile with a hint of pink blossoming on his cheeks. "Hopefully you can go visit them sooner than later."

I meant it.

The smile that had been on Jonah's face mostly melted away as he stood there, fingers tucked over the loops of his jeans. "My agent has started talks with a couple of different teams to see if they even want me."

I couldn't see anyone ever not wanting him.

"Talks should go by fairly quickly. I should know in a matter of weeks where I'll be playing… if I'll be playing."

My heart ached, but I still offered him a smile. "You will. I don't know how you played this last season after your injury, but you'll go somewhere. I know it."

Jonah didn't say anything for so long I almost thought that he changed his mind about bringing this up, but he moved toward me after a moment, half the skin of his beautiful body exposed as he settled in beside me, his butt against the side of my thigh, angled to face me. One of those hands came up to my face, and his thumb stroked across my chin. "Lenny, I—"

We weren't doing this. He wasn't doing this.

I turned my head and brushed my nose against the finger closest to my mouth. "Don't say it, Dimples."

Those lips pursed, and his index finger moved across the eyebrow closest to him. "I don't want to…."

Yeah, the idea of him leaving hurt me too.

But…

He had to go. I would never ask him to stay. I reached up for his hand and dragged it over so I could press my lips against his palm.

His hand went to my cheek, and those eyes met mine for a moment, unblinking and so serious, and then he was leaning over and that mouth was on mine. Jonah pulled my top lip into his mouth before releasing it and then sucking the other one. Then it was my turn; his lips parting under mine, and I didn't hesitate to slip my tongue against his.

His mouth was warm, and his lips were smooth as we brushed tongues. His hand slipped to the back of my loose, wet hair and held my head in place as he deepened the kiss, slanting his mouth even more. I moaned into him as he turned his head and kissed me the other way.

When he pulled back a moment later, the tip of his nose brushing against mine, he asked, "Okay?" all I could do was nod.

Then he kissed me some more, soft and slow and deep, brushing tongue and lips against my own. The hand on the back of my head moved to cup my nape, his other hand sliding over my lap to grip my hip over the covers that had fallen to my waist. Both of my hands were on his shoulders before sliding them over the soft skin of his upper arms, then back up and over the warm flesh spread tight over his shoulder blades.

"I love your mouth," Jonah whispered as he pulled back slightly, I could still feel his lips move. He kissed each of my cheeks, taking his time, moving down to do the same along my jaw. "Love kissing you. Looking at you. Touching you. Holding you," he let me know between kisses.

Something hard formed in my throat at his words, at his affection. When I had the chance, I caught his mouth again in another deep, deep kiss that made my skin tingle. It was while we were kissing that I let my hands drift down his pectorals, dragging my fingertips over the lean skin covering his abs, one hand brushing over his belly button, which had the faintest little trail of hair beneath it, leading down until I touched the band of what I knew was tiny boxer briefs.

Jonah pulled his mouth away, sucking in a breath as I dipped my fingers under that elastic band, the backs of them brushing even more warm, smooth skin.

"Oh," he gasped in a hoarse whisper a second before I felt the short, curly hair hidden in there.

I snuck my hand in a little farther until I touched the base of his cock... and Jonah jumped. I met his eyes and smiled, stroking what I could reach of the thick root there. His big, thick cock twitched in his underwear at the same time a shudder worked its way through Jonah's spine, earning me a hiss and a "Len!"

I was grinning when his mouth covered mine again, and every other part of me was smiling as his body turned and moved toward me, over me as I scooted down in the bed to lay flat on my back. I felt the comforter over me get tossed to the side, the cool air hitting my bare legs for a moment before Jonah slipped a hand under my knee and moved it aside as he kneeled there, jeans open into a V, his boxer briefs lower than before, giving me a good view of the trail of hair leading from his belly button down to the treasure he had hidden.

Jonah braced himself on his elbows as his lower body curled against mine… reminding me that I only had a big T-shirt and panties on. I hadn't been able to find a clean sports bra and had been too lazy to go downstairs to look through the laundry room.

A palm stroked the outside of my thigh over and over again, sliding up and up until he was cupping my ass cheek, kneading the muscle and skin there as his mouth opened over my neck and gave the skin there a soft suck.

"Jonah." I arched my back under him, my nipples brushing against his chest through my shirt, and Jonah moved to lick and then suck at the other side of my neck.

His lips trailed further down as I wrapped my legs around his hips, loving the feel of his worn jeans on my bare inner thighs. A hand covered my breast, cupping it, as his mouth descended as well. Jonah sucked through the shirt, his tongue flicking over the hard nub.

I wiggled under him, arching my back again as my hands went to his hips, sneaking under that waistband again until I had a hand full of his perfect ass cheeks, tugging him in toward me. Wanting him in.

When Jonah's mouth switched over to my other breast, sucking that one too into his warm, warm mouth, I wiggled and arched my back more. His hands tugged my shirt up to my waist, and Jonah scooted down the bed. When his finger hooked into the stretchy material of my underwear and tugged it aside, I only had a second to hold my breath before his tongue was there. Down there. Dipping in before those lips pursed over my clit and sucked that too.

My hands clutched the pillow under my head as he tucked

his tongue inside of me again, replaced by one slow-sliding finger and then another. They scissored as I held my breath and my thighs jumped around his ears. Jonah moaned low and hoarse as he pushed in and out, flexing and moving his big fingers inside of me over and over again until I could hear how wet I was, his mouth opening and closing, nibbling and sucking. He licked one lip and then the other before tracing his tongue over the sensitive skin of my inner thighs before going back... until he stopped. The flat of his tongue gave me another swipe down my lips before he dipped both fingers into his mouth. His smile was huge.

I sat up enough to grab at the band of his underwear and tug the material down so that his long, thick mass bounced out, tipping up to slap at his lower stomach. I settled my eyes on the tip weeping clear, nearly white tears. Wrapping my hand halfway down the length of it, I gave his dick a soft squeeze, his precum warm and sticky under my palm. "I forgot how pretty this big thing is," I told him a second before I leaned forward and gave the head a lick that had Jonah jerking his hips back with a smile and a shake of his head.

"One more of that and it'll be over in no time," he whispered before ducking down and giving me another kiss that distracted me enough so that I didn't know where he was until his hips were between my legs again and the head of him was nudging against my clit. "I don't have a condom."

I raised my hips, letting his head slide over my clit and back down while I said, "I'm on birth control, and I'm not ovulating." I dragged my tongue over the column of his neck, giving the tendon there its own suck.

Jonah didn't wait. His hand went in between us, and the next thing I knew, that big plum of his head was pushing through, in and in and in, and....

I groaned at the sting of his size in me after so fucking long and the pure fucking pleasure of having him in me, his upper body over mine... his mouth taking my own as he pushed slowly to the hilt with a grunt.

You could say the last thing I was expecting was the husky, gravelly laugh that bubbled out of Jonah's mouth when he was seated deeply in me, filling me up like nobody and nothing else ever could or would.

I sucked in a breath as the movement of his laugh made him twitch inside of me, and even then, I started laughing too. "What the hell are you laughing over?"

Jonah looked down at me, pain in his eyes, and groaned before saying, taking his time with each word, "I'm sorry, love." His throat bobbed, and he took my mouth again, pulling out about halfway before thrusting back inside just as slow. "This isn't going to last long, and I think it's funny how short this is going to be. I'm sorry."

I smiled just as he pulled a few inches out before shoving back, hard, forcing me to suck in a breath as the base of his dick hit my clit. "It doesn't matter," I whispered into his ear before taking the lobe between my lips for a second. "I'm real good at making myself come."

He groaned as I slipped my hand between us, fingers brushing the wet root of his cock before I set the flats of my fingers right above where they were most needed and started a slow circle.

I watched as he pulled half of his dick out and then pounded it back in like it had never retreated in the first place. The sound wet and so fucking hot as he pulled a quarter out and then pushed it back. Jonah was slow and intense as he took my mouth, filling me up with that thick, thick length that was already throbbing. With my free hand, I grabbed his ass again, holding one cheek as his hips rolled and pushed and pulled, taking their time, making it intense as I rubbed at my clit slowly.

"You feel amazing. I missed you so much," he whispered before taking my mouth for another deep kiss. "I love you."

I wrapped my legs around his hips and moved my hand faster and faster. I had to tear my lips away from his when I came, burying my mouth against his neck as I pulsed around him, inner thighs shaking, wrapping my arms around his shoulders to hold him against me while I caught my breath. It was while I did that, that his forearms slipped under my shoulders and he did the same, holding me so close, his mouth against the column of my throat, dick throbbing and twitching as he impaled me with every inch, hugging me to him like he feared there was really somewhere else I would rather be while he shuddered through his orgasm.

He lay over me panting, my legs still around his waist but loose, my arms still over his shoulders. I swept my hand up and down the column of his damp spine. Jonah kissed my jaw and neck as his palm stroked my thigh from hip to knee and back up.

After a long time of him softening in me, kissing as much of my chest as he could as he tugged at the collar of my shirt, I couldn't help but smile at him after he brushed his nose against mine some more.

"We don't have to do this every night," I told him, kissing his chin. "But we can if you want to."

His white teeth flashed. "If you're going to insist...."

I laughed, and he kissed me, his mouth hovering over my ear.

"Lenny?"

"Hmm?" I pecked his neck.

His breathing turned heavy. "I wasn't going to ask you to come with me."

That had me dropping my head against the pillow and blinking up at him.

His thumb moved over my eyebrow before his mouth descended and his lips brushed my temple, and he whispered, "Because of your life here. Because I don't want to take you away from here. But…." Those lips trailed over my forehead, pausing right there in the middle. "But I want you to come with me. You and Mo. I want us to be together. I want my family with me."

He… he wanted me to go with him? *Us* go with him?

"I don't want to be without you."

I lost every single one of my words.

"I don't need an answer now, or any time soon. I don't deserve an answer to begin with… but I'm leaving soon. And I have you to thank for it. You were right. If I can keep playing, I should. *I want to*. I missed it so much while I was out, but now… I'll have to miss you and Mo if I do. But I've been think-ing… even if you don't come… I'll come back as soon as I can. My contract could be for a year, after that, I could… I could retire. Come here, possibly. Or you could go with me to see home. You and Grandpa Gus and Peter. I've saved most of my income. I could build us a house big enough for all of us. I just want you with me, Len. And if I have to wait a year or two or three, I'll do it, but I would always rather have you now than not."

I hadn't even….

Go with him? Mo and me?

I wanted to ask him if he was serious, but this was Jonah. Of course he was serious.

Go with him?

Go with him?

His mouth trailed over my forehead, dry and warm, until his nose was there too, and he was nuzzling me. Then both of his hands were there, under my shoulders, holding them tight. "I don't make up for everything you would leave behind, but I would try my best, Lenny. I would try my best every day if you'd consider it."

~

AND THAT WAS WHAT I DID. EVERY CHANCE I HAD. EVEN IF IT FELT like a lead weight that had been dropped on top of my soul.

We did other things too.

I loved brushing my teeth with him beside me in the mornings. I loved seeing him greet Mo first thing, with cuddles and kisses and his lovely voice singing Māori lullabies into her ear. I loved his sleepy face and the way he smelled and how unafraid and open he was to touching me all the damn time. A hand on my hip. An arm over my shoulders. A chin against my head. Fingers threading through my own every chance they had.

If I hadn't already been in love with him, it would have been over for me in those following weeks.

Regardless of what he was training, he would come and get on a bike with me any time I got on and we'd race.

If I was weight training, he'd come and spot me.

If I was working in the MMA building, he would sit and watch me like he had nothing better to do. When I'd do something he thought was impressive, he would clap, and later on tell me how amazing he thought it was. Then he'd ask me to do it to him *to know.*

My heart grew and grew with every day with him. And grew even more every night that we were together with Mo. Like a big family.

At night when it was just the two of us holed up in my room like horny teenagers… baby Jesus would have been traumatized. We might have even had an addiction problem. I sucked him off when my period hit, and he'd shoved my shirt up high to suck on my nipples and rub at my clit over my underwear at the end of my period. But mostly, it was the way I woke up with his arm thrown around my waist most mornings that was the best. Or waking up with my face in between his shoulder blades, my toes touching his calves.

And then when the day came that his agent called with news that he'd been signed and would have to leave….

That was the worst day I'd had in a long time.

CHAPTER 21

Subject: Email me back

Lenny DeMaio:
    Wed 4/8/2019 1:29 p.m.
    to Jonah Collins

I hate you. I really do.

MY HEART WAS HEAVY AS FUCK, AND THERE WAS NO USE DENYING IT or trying to hide it.

I was moping. Big fucking time. Massive fucking time.

So far, I'd been fortunate enough to never lose anyone really close to me, but I had a feeling that my body was going through the closest thing to grief it had ever known.

And Jonah hadn't even left yet.

It had been three days since the call had come through confirming that he had been picked up by a team. That he'd signed another massive deal with more than a handful of zeroes behind it. That he had to leave.

Two years. That's how long his deal was for. Two years with the Kobe Chargers.

The bittersweet smile on his face while he'd held the phone to his ear as he'd laid in bed beside me, bare-chested with Mo sprawled over him with her bottle, had been awesome and painful.

Awesome because he was going to keep doing something that he loved doing. Something that he was meant to do. But... painful because of what it meant.

I'd still slapped a smile on my face and kept it there. I'd hugged the shit out of him and kept on hugging the shit out of him since. I'd booked his plane ticket for him. I had even downloaded the app that may or may not work once he got to Japan so that he could see Mo at daycare through the cameras.

One week was all the team had been willing to give Jonah to arrive since they had already started practicing for the upcoming season.

One week didn't give me enough time to leave with him. If I was going to.

The fact was: we could go visit him no problem. I knew that. He had already eyed his game calendar and circled off clots of days, times that he could squeeze a quick trip to visit, days when he'd be home for longer than three or four days so we could fly over for a visit. Bye weeks when we could meet up somewhere.

I'll take any time I can see you both, Jonah had told me when we'd sat beside each other in the kitchen with his calendar. *An hour. Three. A day. Whatever you can do, I'll take.*

Whatever I could do he would take.

Two days later, that comment still pounded away at my head. And my heart.

My entire fucking body.

I hadn't said a word to Jonah about how much my chest hurt every time I looked at him—which was half the day because he'd been picking up Mo from Grandpa and bringing her to Maio House in the afternoons, where they would hang out with me in my office. Half of my family. Half of my heart.

And a fourth of it was leaving me in four days.

This man I fucking loved the shit out of.

He was going.

And he'd asked me to go with him. To fly halfway across the world, away from half of the people I loved with all of my heart, away from my job, my life. And be with him there. In Kobe.

I had no idea what the hell I should do. Leave everything behind or… not. It wasn't just me I was deciding for. I had a ten-month-old life relying on me to do what was best for her.

I was in the middle of trying not to think about what was going to happen—and how I was being a selfish asshole and didn't want it to happen—when the knock on my office door came. I called out "Come in" to whoever was on the other side as I minimized the screen I'd been reading, a thousand and a half thoughts going through my head that had nothing to do with Maio House or any of the guys and women in it.

The size of the shadow warned me it was Jonah, and my stupid-ass heart squeezed itself tight at his big smiling head as he came in holding Mo, his fucking mini-me from the color of her hair to her skin and eyes, in one brawny-ass arm. "Busy?" he asked, circling around and coming to stand beside my chair before he dipped his head and brushed that mouth over mine before giving me a peck on each cheek that had me smiling.

I grabbed Mo's foot and pretended I was about to eat it, my other hand wrapping around the back of Jonah's knee, giving it squeeze. "Nah," I answered him once Mo had squealed and told me all about her day. I met my favorite eye color in the world and smiled up at him, even though I was pretty sure he could see right through me and what I'd just been in the middle of doing.

He didn't disappoint me.

His index finger grazed my eyebrow as he stood right there, towering over me with our girl cradled in the crook of his arm, and asked, "What's that sweet face for?"

How the hell was I supposed to go so long without seeing him? Could I do it? Yeah. But I didn't want to.

I really didn't want to. That was a fact, and it was always going to be, my gut said. *What the hell was I supposed to do? How was I supposed to choose between the loves of my life?*

"Honestly, I was thinking about how much I'm going to miss you, and how I don't want to only see you..." I had to think about it for a second. "Eight times over the next eight months." I'd already memorized the dates he'd circled.

That smile of his didn't go anywhere, and his fingertip brushed over my cheekbone again as he hoisted Mo up a little higher. "We'll make it work. It won't be forever," he told me with that sweet-ass expression on his face that said he totally believed every word coming out of his mouth.

"I know." I blinked, soaking in what he *wasn't* saying. What he wasn't asking. And I hated feeling so vulnerable, hated not just being straight-up happy he was leaving, but... at least there was something for me to be sad over. I didn't want him to be sad. I didn't want him to lose something that meant so much to him again. Of course, I would rather him have this dream of his for a few years longer, even if it came at a cost to me. Of course, I would. After what had happened with his Achilles, I knew it was wishful thinking that he would get to choose when his career ended, but any more time he could get would and could be all I wished for him.

But...

I still couldn't help but ask the one question that had been bouncing around in my head since that call about the Kobe Chargers had come in. "Do you not want us to go with you anymore?"

That handsome face fell so instantly, I felt bad, but before I could say anything, Jonah dropped to his knees after moving Mo to his other arm so that they were both looking at me. "*Yeh,*" he answered immediately, his gaze bouncing from one of my eyes to the other. "You thought I changed my mind?"

"You haven't brought it up since you got the call," I explained, lifting a hand to tap at a freckle right over the bridge of his nose as something uncomfortable slid into my chest. He'd mentioned us tagging along with him almost daily in the weeks before his offer.

But not since.

Mo slapped a little hand over her dad's cheek then, and he smiled at her before dipping his head to give her a kiss that ended up on her mouth. When he turned his attention back to me, his eyes were brighter than I had ever seen, but his lips were flat, not in a mad or sad expression but more... resigned, I guessed. "I will always want you to be with me, do you understand? I know this isn't a decision you can make in a day or a week or a month, Lenny. I know what you have here, but that doesn't mean I've lost hope that one day you'll make that decision," he said, gazing right into my fucking eyes. That same index finger as before made a loop around the shell of my ear, his gaze bright.

"Time and distance... that's nothing for us, is it? Whatever time we have together, I will cherish every minute of." That finger dragged over my cheekbone, and his expression went to the next level with the understanding and patience reflected in it. "My body is leaving, but the rest of me will be wherever you and Mo are, Lenny. I'd hoped I'd made that clear."

Oh, this son of a bitch and his fucking words.

I pressed my lips together, soaking up every single one of his sentences and saving them for later. Later when I would need them. Later when he wasn't around to say them in person and remind me that he felt the same way I did.

Later when I was going to miss the fucking shit out of him.

I loved him, and I wasn't going to make him feel bad about this. I wasn't. Not ever.

Sometimes you had to do the right thing for the right person, even if it hurt.

"I can't leave just like that, Jonah," I told him, not meaning to whisper the words out, but that's how they arrived into the world. Weak. Sad. "I want to be with you. I'm going to miss you, but you're leaving in four fucking days, and—"

He placed a hand on my thigh and squeezed it. "I know."

"I'd have to find someone else to manage this place. Train them. And there's Grandpa Gus and Peter too. I love them too, and I can't just leave them like that either. Mo and I are all they have, and they were all I've ever had for most of my life," I whispered to him, my eyes burning just a little but more than enough because they weren't used to it. "But I'm going to miss you so fucking much, and I don't know what to do."

It wasn't my imagination that his eyes were getting glassy, and it definitely wasn't in my head that I heard his voice get just a little hoarser as he said, "You didn't ask me to stay."

"No, and I wouldn't," I told him. "I love you, and I'm not going to make you pick. You don't do that to someone who means the entire universe to you. Grandpa Gus told me once that when you love someone, you threw them up into the sky to fly, Dimples. You don't just open your hand to let them go. Because you know who they are, and they know who you are, and that's all that matters. You don't hold back someone you love. Even if I don't want to go so long without seeing you, you have to go." It was my turn to reach over and cup his lean cheek. He'd shaved, and I could just barely feel the prickles of his beard growing back in. "And I was just looking into it. Literally, right before you walked in, I was reading up. I can stay in the country for ninety days at a time on a tourist visa, and I don't know if you knew this or not, but I'm the boss of this place, and I bet they could survive without me for a while once I train the assistant manager to do more of the things that I do."

"Yeah?" he replied, those golden-brown eyes sparkling, or at least to me, it seemed like they were. He slowly eased forward until his forehead was against mine, and Mo was there, digging a hand into my hair until we were both giving her kisses on each cheek. After a few moments, it was his turn to whisper. "I've looked it up too, and there's a better option as well."

I moved the pad of my thumb right under his fat bottom lip. "What is it?"

"I reckon it's our best option," he replied, easing away just a little, the corners of his mouth edging upward. "At least the only one that makes the most sense. Our only option, really. If you're ever ready. If you ever can, but you have to know that I'm fine with whatever you decide, love. But it would be better all around."

"I know I could get a work visa." I kissed one corner of that mouth. "Grandpa Gus has got friends in Tokyo that—"

Jonah touched his lips to mine. I sensed him fumbling for a second before his mouth brushed a light kiss across the bow of mine and then one more on the other corner. Only then did his big, free hand take mine in the same way it had so many times lately. "Lenny," he murmured. Those fingers stroked over my own. I could feel his breath on my lips, and it made me want to kiss him again.

So I did.

And it was then that I felt it.

Something cold and hard, followed by the heat of fingertips right after.

In the wake of his fingers as they moved across my skin, I glanced down and sucked in my breath.

Those hands, so big and rough and careful and gentle at the same time, threaded themselves through mine, squeezing.

"I'm coming back," that soft voice stated with so much conviction I felt it. "And you're coming to see me. This is just the beginning, Lenny. It's nowhere near the end. I love you. I love you both, and we'll be together again." His voice dropped even lower as his fingers rubbed over my ring finger. "Marry me. Before I go. If you change your mind, I can get you a visa, easy. If you don't change your mind, you know I'll always come back to you, yeh?"

I was too busy looking at the ring sitting on my finger to manage to find a word to say.

Marry him? Marry Jonah?

Holy fucking *shit*.

Here I'd been just thinking and stressing about being apart from each other.

Here I'd been, never even thinking about the "m" word in the first place.

And here Jonah was telling me to marry him.

To be with him, even if I couldn't be with him.

Marriage. *Marriage*.

Forever. For some people. Not forever for other people.

And he wanted *this?* From me? With me?

My heart started pounding away at my fucking chest, and I could barely say, "Jonah, we don't—"

"Shh."

I blinked up at him, laughter erasing the fucking panic instantly, just wiping it right off. "Did you just shush me?"

He was already grinning when he nodded.

I laughed again. "You *shh*."

That smile grew even wider before he proceeded to ignore me. "It's a gray rose cut diamond," Jonah explained, like I knew what the hell that was.

My fucking eyes strayed to the delicate yellow gold band and the two white, almost triangle-shaped diamonds tapered on each side of the center rock sitting on my finger.

He was serious.

There was a ring on my finger. And not just any ring, but a real one. One he'd bought for *me*.

Because he was telling me to marry him.

"It made me think of you," he went on, his fingers taking each one of mine and massaging one at a time lightly as Mo slapped at his cheek. "But if you don't like it..." He lifted my hand to his face and gave two of my fingertips a kiss. "Too bad, eh."

What the fuck?

Something that was either a snort or a fucking crying choke snapped out of my throat. And then I couldn't fucking help it. I couldn't help but grin even as a thrill shot through me like a damn lightning bolt, straight down the middle, heady and brutal and beautiful and terrifying, but not really.

Not at all, actually.

I laughed again, right from my gut, from my soul, from the place inside of me that housed all of my joy. *"Too bad?"*

He nodded and settled my hand on his cheek, letting the tiny bristles tickle my palm. "We don't have time to change it if we have to wait three days after getting the license to marry." He smiled. "The office closes at five today."

That beautiful, amazing fucking feeling filled my chest, but it still made me gulp, still stole my words and my thoughts and everything. "Why do I feel like you aren't asking me?"

"Because I'm not." He leaned forward again and brushed his lips across mine so softly it almost seemed like I could have imagined it. That mouth went to one cheek and then the other before he drew back and beamed me with an enormous smile I'd remember for the rest of my life. Jonah Hema Collins wrapped an arm around the back of my neck and drew me into that wide chest, and I let him. His voice soft in my ear as he informed me, "If I don't ask you, you can't tell me no, love."

Three days later, when we got married in front of a justice of the peace, with Jonah holding my hands tight, with Grandpa Gus holding Mo on his shoulders beside Peter, with Luna, her husband, her sister, daughter, and my grandpa's friend and his wife, I smiled so much my cheeks hurt.

The very next day, when Mo and I dropped him off at the airport, and he gave us a hug that lifted us into the air as he told us how much we were loved, and how there was nothing we couldn't handle together, I made sure I was smiling then too...

Even though it broke my heart.

CHAPTER 22

Subject: Please

Lenny DeMaio:
    Wed 4/29/2019 1:29 p.m.
    to Jonah Collins

I'm about to give up on you.

Please. Just call me back.

"SOMEBODY'S DISTRACTED."

I blinked up from the salad I'd been poking at for the last few minutes. "Yeah. I've got my mind on some things," I told her, stabbing at a falafel before shoving the whole thing into my mouth.

I *was* distracted. Mainly by a six-foot-five man who weighed two hundred and fifty pounds year-round, was too handsome for words, and had a heart of fucking gold. A person I enjoyed being around. A person that I loved.

The guy who'd put a ring on it before leaving.

The guy who'd video messaged me every day over the last two weeks since he'd left. Who had sent me multiple texts every day with pictures of what he was doing, what he was eating, of his teammates, the hotel room he was living out of. The man I missed the shit out of, mostly because I knew how far away he was.

I'd bet anyone would be distracted with that over their head.

And heart.

And fucking soul.

Luna frowned over at me as she slowly chewed part of the huge grilled chicken salad she had put together not even fifteen minutes ago when we'd met up at our favorite salad buffet place for lunch. She was still frowning a moment later when she swallowed what she'd been eating and asked in a way that was way too careful for how long we'd known each other, "Want to talk about it?"

There was my Luna. Always there and never too into prying.

That thought felt like a tiny little sliver off my heart as I thought—again—about me leaving everything and everyone behind. Including her. The best best friend with boobs I'd ever had.

"I can keep a secret," she kept going. "I'll only tell Rip. Promise."

That almost made me snicker. But not even her being herself was enough to ease my heartache... and confusion... and how torn I was about going with him to Japan.

Leave my job.

Leave Grandpa Gus.

Leave Peter.

Leave Luna.

Leave Luna's family.

Leave Maio House.

Leave our house in the Heights.

Leave… everything behind except for Mo and Jonah with a little j.

Was I *really* considering it?

And did I have to feel like such a fucking traitor for thinking about it as much as I had?

The thing that got under my skin the most though was that the more I thought about it, the more I realized I didn't exactly feel scared when I contemplated leaving.

The biggest problem was that I couldn't imagine my fucking life without Grandpa Gus and Peter.

And how could I just leave Maio House months after I'd taken it over?

How the hell was I supposed to choose between the loves of my life?

Something soft landed on my shoulder, giving it a squeeze. "You look so sad, Lenny. What is it?"

I glanced up at Luna and raised my eyebrows as I gave her a brittle smile, dropping my fork into the huge metal bowl. I wasn't that hungry. I couldn't remember there ever being a time, other than when I was getting over being sick, where I wasn't hungry. If that wasn't a huge fucking sign that there was something wrong with me, I didn't know what else would be.

"I'm not sad," I told her. "Just… conflicted."

She fucking took it. "Because of Jonah?"

I nodded.

"Because you miss him a lot?"

She'd known all about him leaving; we had seen each other the day after he'd flown to Japan. Plus, we'd kept up our lunches even while he'd still been in Houston. She knew everything. Except for his invitation. I hadn't told anyone about that.

I rubbed a hand over my chest as I glanced down at my salad.

I had known my entire life that Maio House was going to be my place.

How was I supposed to leave it? Leave everything? I had a place here. Responsibilities. *My fucking loved ones.*

But there was Jonah. And Mo. Mo who lit up every time she was around her dad. She'd cried the whole way home after we'd left him at the airport. I doubted it had been my imagination that she'd been fussier than normal, especially at night, since he'd left. And I had liked Japan. I had lived there for three months years ago; I'd been back twice since then.

What the hell was I supposed to do?

Not be a whiny little bitch, that was what.

I looked up, grabbed my fork again and stabbed at a cherry tomato before popping it back into my mouth. When I was done, I focused on my friend who looked so worried it made me feel bad. We barely got to see each other in the first place, and here I was being a vibe kill.

Luna scooted forward on the bench she was sitting in, a frown over that face that hadn't gotten any less pretty over the last decade. "You look so sad, Len. I can tell by your eyes."

If I couldn't talk about this with Luna, who could I talk with? This was what friends were for anyway, wasn't it? She would be the last person to ever give me a hard time for loving someone and wanting to be with them. Fuck it. "I'm not sad," I answered. "But yeah, I do miss him a lot more than I thought I would." I thought about it. "A lot more."

She sat up and aimed bright green eyes at me, thinking. "So then go be with him," she said, like she was giving me an address to meet her at.

I opened my mouth to tell her something but realized I didn't know what to say.

"Or not. But if he's going to be gone for, what did you say? Two years? And you're going to miss him, go too. I'm sure he'd love it if you went. I've seen the way he looks at you. He looked so happy at the courthouse, Len, like you made his whole freaking life. And I've seen the way you look at him. I've never seen you smile so much. Not even close." Her smile was tighter than normal but just barely, just noticeable only because I knew her so well. "Do it, Len. Go."

Do it, Len?

"He did ask me to go. A few weeks ago," I admitted, feeling just a little bad that I hadn't told her that from the beginning.

She lifted her hands palm up. "See?"

This wasn't exactly what I'd been expecting, and I couldn't keep the surprise out of my voice. "Go with him? That's your advice?"

She nodded. "Yeah."

I blinked. "But it's not that simple." Was it?

Luna smiled and it wasn't tight at all anymore. It reminded me of that eighteen-year-old version of herself who had beamed at me from across the mats at the original Maio House, like she'd known exactly how much I was going to need her in my life. "What's so hard about it? You quit your job. You go."

"Quit my job? It's Maio House. It isn't like I'm quitting the retirement home again. My last name is outside. Grandpa Gus—"

"It is just a job," she told me seriously, her smile gone. "And if you say something dumb like *but I don't want to leave you either*, you're going to hurt my feelings. Because you're always going to be my best friend, even if we see each other a little less and have to talk on the phone more to make up for it."

That was a low blow. She knew damn well she was one of the last people in the world I would ever want to hurt. And then dropping that *you're always going to be my best friend?*

Fucking hell.

"So then what's the problem? Because you're not getting rid of me even if you move to Japan and end up with a bunch of new friends. I'll fight 'em."

"I've got friends here."

"I thought I was the only real one left now that you still talked to."

Fine. She had a point there. "Family—"

That had Luna rolling her eyes with a scoff. "You think Grandpa Gus would let you leave without him? Or Peter? I'd give them a month before they followed you out there."

I—

Huh. *Huh.* She did have a point. Kind of.

"Maio House," I found myself bringing up too.

Luna reached over and placed her hand over mine. She rarely did that, and it made me freeze up and really look at her. Really, really listen. "Give me a break. I didn't think you were scared of anything, Len, except maybe your grandpa. I never thought it would be a little ocean that would freak you out."

A little ocean.

I flipped my hand over and held hers back, something weird and tight and freeing and terrifying at the same time making me hold my breath. "Maio House is my family business though, Lu."

She set her other hand on top of our pile, her expression full of love and understanding and that thing that was all Luna and her endless compassion. "And this is your life. This place isn't going anywhere. Grandpa, Peter, and I aren't letting you never see us or talk to us again. There are phones, video calling, emails, *planes*, credit card miles... the only things you lose are the things you give up on."

CHAPTER 23

Subject: Done

Lenny DeMaio:
   Wed 5/5/2019 1:29 p.m.
   to Jonah Collins

I had your daughter yesterday, asshole. She's beautiful and she's perfect. I'm done trying to reach out to you. I'm done bothering you and: begging you to contact me. She's here and she's not going anywhere. If you ever want to see her, we'll be here. But I'm done trying.

Bye

"Lenny, sit with me."

I didn't even bother looking at my grandfather as I undid Mo's bib, wiping her cheeks off with it afterward. "Why the hell do you sound so serious?" I asked him with a smirk as I brushed off the crumbs of her lunch of beans and mushy rice into my palm a couple days later.

"Because we need to have a serious talk, Len."

I froze as Peter came to my shoulder, setting a hand on it as he said, in a voice that was too quiet, "I'll take her. You talk to him."

Okay.

This was weird. I tried to think back on whether Grandpa Gus and I had ever actually had a "serious" conversation, and nothing came to mind. What the hell was going on?

I swiveled my head to look at the man who was gazing down at my baby with so much love, I had to suck in a breath. He flicked his gaze to me and smiled, a big, real, tender smile. Then he leaned over and kissed me on the cheek, his hand covering mine for a moment as he said, "Stay and talk to him."

I eyed him, alarm filling up my belly even more. "Uh, why are you two being so serious?" Oh God. "Are one of you sick? Because I swear to—"

"*No.* Talk to your grandpa, Len," Peter insisted, turning his attention back to Mo before dislodging the tray of her high chair and pulling her up and out of it.

I watched as he brought her close, kissed her cheek, and headed out of the room, whispering something to her I couldn't totally understand. I almost dreaded turning around and finding Grandpa Gus sitting at the island, hands linked together on top of it, a cup of decaf sitting to the side of him. But he was smiling at me, so maybe this conversation wasn't going to be totally serious despite what he'd said.

As long as they weren't sick, that was all that mattered.

I made a suspicious face as I headed over to him, snagging my glass of water and refilling it from the filter on the counter. After pulling out the stool with my foot on the bottom rung, I dropped into it, crossed my legs, told myself it couldn't be so bad as long as they were both healthy, and asked, "What's wrong?"

"Nothing." He reached up and tugged on my earlobe. "Other than you being a sad little shit."

I laughed, a tiny bit of relief sliding over my shoulders. "I'm not sad."

"But you are a little shit?" Grandpa smiled.

"It runs in the family."

"Yeah, on your mom's side," he replied. "But you are sad, and we both know it, so quit trying to lie to me."

"I'm not sad, Grandpa. I'm fine," I insisted, even as everything in me called me a damn liar.

The look on his face definitely said he thought I was full of shit.

Which I was. Just a little. When I thought about it, it was like back when I'd first decided I was having Mo and knew I'd have to give up judo if I didn't want to risk hurting myself so badly that I might not be able to do fun shit with her. It hurt. It sucked. But I knew I'd survive.

That didn't mean that I didn't miss Jonah down to my fucking bones.

But I'd hoped I wasn't that fucking obvious about it either.

"I'm not," I repeated, not appreciating the *bullshit* face he was making.

He blinked. "Now you're going to choose to lie to me? *Now?* After all the things you've done? All the things you've said? You're going to lie to me about *this?*"

I shut my mouth and pressed the tip of my tongue against the inside of my cheek. "Fair enough," I agreed, earning me a knowing smirk. "I do miss him, okay? But I'll be all right." Mostly.

Grandpa Gus was smirking by then, and he didn't bother curbing his sigh as he reached over, took my hand, and said, "Lenny, you're full of shit and we both know it."

I blinked. "You're... full of it."

He squeezed my hand. "Yeah, but not right now, am I?"

"You always are."

Grandpa grinned. "We're not talking about me. We're

talking about you being a sad little panda because your boy is gone."

I opened my mouth to tell him that he wasn't a boy, but he held up a finger that told me to stop talking.

Grandpa didn't say anything for so long as he watched me with those thoughtful eyes and smirking mouth that I wasn't sure what to expect. And that put me on edge because there were very few times I could ever remember where he didn't know what to say. Grandpa always knew.

"Tell me something."

"Okay."

He squeezed my hand. "What is it about Jonah that made you pick him out of all the other men you've met?"

"Why?"

"Just answer the question, Len."

All right. "He's the nicest person I've ever met. The kindest. He's so calm, it soothes me, and when he isn't calm and he's pissed off and grumpy, I still want to be around him." I had to think about that. "He just makes me happy, Grandpa. More than anyone else I've ever met, not counting you guys."

He still didn't say anything. All he did was just keep on staring at me as he contemplated whatever it was that was going through his head. And it made me want to squirm.

He stared at me, and I stared at him.

For a minute.

For two.

Finally, out of fucking nowhere, he beamed at me.

And that scared the fuck out of me.

As I sat there, worried and alarmed by the fact him smiling made him look like Jack Nicholson in *The Shining*, he reached forward—scaring the shit out of me again—and cupped my cheeks in his hands.

Yeah, that kicked it up to me being basically terrified.

Grandpa Gus squeezed my cheeks together, kissed me on

the forehead as I stiffened because *what the fuck was happening*, and then said it.

He said it.

He said, "Lenny, you're fired."

His hands were still on my cheeks and his lips were still on my forehead as I fucking froze again.

"What?"

He pulled back and smiled at me. "You're fired."

I blinked. "What?"

He squeezed my cheeks together with every word. "You. Are. Fired."

I blinked again and then squinted. "From?"

My cheeks were squeezed together, definitely making me look like a million bucks as he answered almost cheerfully, "From Maio House, genius. What else?"

He... he... was firing me?

"Why?" I murmured, looking at him like I didn't know what the hell he was talking about. Because I heard his words. I understood what each one meant separately, but together....

What?

"You're fired," he repeated himself. "Either effective immediately, or I'm giving you a two weeks notice. It's up to you."

I leaned back, out of his reach, and kept on squinting at him. "Grandpa, what are you talking about? I'm fired? Why?"

He grinned. "Yeah."

He... was firing me? From Maio House? I looked up at the ceiling, then back down at him and felt tears well up in my eyes, telling myself not to feel betrayed. This was Grandpa Gus, the last person in the world to ever not treat me right. "But why?"

His throat bobbed, and my cheeks were squeezed together again. "Because I love you." This savage literally pinched my cheek. "And because I don't want you to work there anymore."

He was really trying to fire me. My own fucking grandfather

was trying to fire me. From his business. From the business that was supposed to be mine. And I didn't understand.

"You can't... you can't fire me, Grandpa," I stuttered.

He ticked his head to the side. "Pretty sure I just did, Len."

"You're joking, right?"

"Nope."

Panic, it was panic that swelled up inside of me as I sputtered, "But... but... why? Because of Jonah? I thought you liked him. Why are you—"

"I do like him," he confirmed, still smiling that creepy smile. "But I'm firing you because... you stole pens from the gym. I saw them in your purse."

I drew back and stared at him. This wasn't about fucking pens. Of course it wasn't about pens. Grandpa had bought all of my school supplies as business expenses my entire life.

Why the hell was he doing this to me? "But why? I thought"—I had to reach up to wipe at my eye as more panic spilled into my chest at the idea that he was doing this to me for no fucking reason—"Maio House was going to be mine one day. You told me. You told me that when you died it was going to be mine, and that's why I've been working there since for fucking ever. And I've been managing it because it's ours. Because it's our family's, and I'm your family. I'm your... I'm your...."

I was panting.

I was fucking crying. Holy shit. I reached up to touch my face, and there were real tears there.

"Why are you taking this away from me?" I croaked, feeling... feeling so fucking confused. "I've been doing a good job. Most of the time. Half the time."

My grandpa just blinked at me. Then he used his reasonable voice on me. "I'm not taking anything away from you."

"Yeah, you are." I wiped at my face with the back of my hand, feeling... feeling... holy shit. This had been the plan. My entire life, this had been the plan. "You said... you said it was going to be mine."

"Is that what I said?" he asked.

I wiped again, trying my hardest not to get upset but failing miserably. "Yeah."

"When, Len?"

What? "I… I don't know. A bunch of times. You know you did."

He crossed his arms over his chest. "Yeah, I did. When you were ten. When you were three, four, five, six, seven, eight, nine, and ten."

What the hell was he talking about?

He aimed those gray eyes at me steadily. "I haven't told you that this was going to be yours since you were ten years old."

He hadn't?

"It's been twenty years since I did that, Len, and part of me regrets so much that I put that responsibility on you when you were a kid. Do you know why I stopped?"

I didn't even answer him. I couldn't.

Luckily he wasn't really waiting for a response. "Do you remember that was the year I made you enroll in gymnastics?" I didn't nod. Of course I remembered. I had really liked it, and I'd been pretty good at it. "Your coach told me how good you were. How much talent and athleticism you had, and he said he regretted that you were going to be so tall because you would never make it to the elite level."

I jumped in. "What does that have to do with you firing me?"

"Give me a second," he requested. "I came home and told Peter how much of a badass you were, and he agreed. He said *she's good at everything. Lenny's going to be able to do anything she wants when she grows up.* And that was when I realized what I'd been doing."

I blinked.

"Before you were born, Len… I had been a wreck because of losing your dad. My heart was broken. It was… dust. I had thought… I had thought for a while there that I didn't want to live in a world that would take my son away from me," Grandpa said quietly, more quietly than I'd ever heard, I knew for a fact. "I missed him so much, and I was so angry. And then your mom came to me. I told you this story a long time ago."

He had. But he retold it.

"She told me she was pregnant with my grandchild. She said she was five months along, and that it was too late to have an abortion." I knew all of this. "And she wanted to tell me that she was going to put the baby up for adoption because she wasn't in a place to raise her, but she wanted me to know.

"And I knew without a doubt, in that instant, that there was no way I would ever let her put my boy's child up for someone else to raise. Not when this, you, were the last piece of him I had left. I didn't know how I was supposed to live without him in this world, and then you were born, and it took one look at you being all ugly and wrinkly—"

I laughed and wiped at my face, not realizing until then that I was full-on crying.

"—and I knew that I was going to have to break the world record for being the oldest man alive because there was no way I would ever let anything happen to you. You gave me life back. You gave me a damn purpose, Lenny. You have been the greatest gift I have ever been given. The greatest joy I will ever have. You were my best friend from the moment those cloudy demon eyes looked at me, like you needed me more than anything or anyone.

"I would fight to the death for you, Len. You were—" He smiled at me before correcting himself. "You *are* my everything. My soul mate. My best friend. My enemy."

I laughed again and watched as he blinked at me, eyes glittering even more.

"And with that comment, Peter reminded me of everything I had seen in your face when you'd been born. That I would do anything for you. That you were a supernova. And look at what I'd been doing to you. How could I bottle you up and decide your future for you? How could I tell you what to be? I wanted the world for you. I *want* the world for you. And that's why I stopped telling you that this place was yours since then. That's why I made you get jobs outside of here. That's why I made you get a degree and I didn't let you work full-time here until Mo came along.

"Because I wanted to give you a chance to be whoever you wanted to be. Do whatever you wanted to do. All I want, Lenny, is for you to be happy, because that's what matters to me at the end of the day. That's what I lose sleep over; that's what I will always lose sleep over. I want you to be happy in whatever way that is, being yourself the whole time. Do you understand me?"

At some point, the need to gulp in breath was making it hard to breathe. My cheeks were *wet.* But somehow, someway, I managed to ask him in a voice that was barely intelligible, "But Maio House is our family legacy."

The old fart rolled his eyes even as he smiled. "Maio House is our family *business*, Len. You, *Mo*, you two are our family legacy."

Oh hell.

Oh bloody hell.

I was so grateful right then that this wasn't the man who had raised me. That this sweet, nice grandpa wasn't the one I had grown up knowing.

Because he would have killed me with his sweetness, with his kindness, and I never would have grown up to be the person I was if this was what I'd grown up with.

More fucking tears came out of my eyes as I slowly started to realize what he was trying to tell me. What he was doing. For me. For Mo.

A million times in my life, I had thought that I couldn't love my grandfather more than I did right then, and every single time that was proved to be a lie. Just like it was in this case. Right then.

And he kept on going.

"I love the gym, loved running it, loved having you there with me all the time. I love Peter being there. But it's just a business, Len. It's four walls and some concrete that could disappear in a day, in a flood, in a hurricane or a tornado. It's a part of me, you, and Peter, but it's not everything." He reached up to wipe under his eye with the side of his index finger. "Some people are lucky to find one person in the world to love. Some people are even luckier to find more than one person to love and be loved back. Some don't find anyone. If you find someone, you don't let them run away. We love them the way we need to love them. The way they need to be loved. And we don't give up on that. We don't throw that kind of thing away or push it to a better time, because there is no better time. If you love that kid the way you say you do, you don't give that up. You fight for it, you stick with it, and you go for it. You keep it."

I felt like a zombie as I pulled myself into a standing position and then draped myself around my grandpa, giving him the tightest fucking hug and feeling him give me the tightest fucking hug right back.

I could barely understand what the hell I was saying as I muttered, "Are you telling me to go? To go be with him across the fucking world and leave you?" I hiccupped. "How the hell could you tell me that? How could you tell me to not be with you and see you and…"

Those strong, safe arms—the strongest, safest arms I had ever known for the majority of my life—didn't let me down. They cradled me. They loved me. They adored me right then, as my grandpa said, "I'm telling you to go live your life, Len. I'm telling you to go be happy. That's what I'm telling you to do." Those hands of his palmed my face and pulled me back just far enough away so he could look right into my eyes. "And who the hell says you're leaving us behind? Jonah invited us to come along too. My bag has been packed for weeks."

CHAPTER 24

9:30 p.m.
>**Me:** Are my messages
>coming through?

9:31 p.m.
>**Me:** Our flight just landed.

9:32 p.m.
>**Jonah:** Yes :)

9:33 p.m:
>**Jonah:** Awesome. Take your time.
>**Jonah:** Can't wait to see you.

TWENTY-FIVE HOURS AFTER LEAVING HOUSTON, WITH SIX SUITCASES between the three of us and a promise from Peter that he would be flying out right after his next big fight, Grandpa Gus, Mo and myself went through immigration, baggage claim, and customs, half-delusional but happy.

With our brand-new, very special visas courtesy of Jonah's rugby club's connections.

The fear and the worry hadn't left me totally in the three weeks leading up to our trip. Three weeks that had been a mad rush to expedite a passport for Mo, get our most important shit together, and train the assistant manager as best as we could. I was leaving almost everything behind, and I'd almost cried once on the flight right after we'd boarded. Almost.

But as I pushed the trolley with our luggage through those glass doors that led to Arrivals, with Grandpa trailing behind me with a Mo who was so over all of this travel bullshit, all it took was one look at the head towering over everyone else's in the crowd of people waiting around for that fear and worry to ease away.

Because Jonah was there, surrounded by a large group, signing an autograph while also trying to duck into a selfie with another person, but the *second* he spotted us, the small, polite smile on his face exploded. The man I loved lit up. His mouth moved with what I could only imagine was an apology, and then he was coming for us with that bright, beaming face full of love and excitement and relief.

Jonah Collins was there for us, like he always would be.

EPILOGUE

I wasn't going to cry.

I wasn't going to cry.

The hand holding my right one gave it a squeeze a second before Jonah, knowing exactly what was going through my head like he always did, whispered, "You're not going to cry."

Damn it.

I pressed my lips together and stared out at the endless turquoise water in front of us, making my eyes go wide so that they wouldn't backstab me and do something I had promised myself—and Grandpa Gus—I wouldn't do.

I wasn't going to cry, damn it. *I wasn't.*

Curling my toes into the soft sand beneath my feet, I took a deep breath in and let it back out as I gave Jonah's hand its own squeeze. In return, his thumb swept over the back of my hand, his fingertips even more callused now than they had been back when we'd first met. When he'd first started to hold my hand… twenty-two years ago.

Twenty-two years ago.

Goddamn time had flown by.

That's what happens when you're having fun, Grandpa Gus would have said.

And just thinking that made my throat close up, made a

choke catch right at the base of my throat, and it made my eyes want to water again. My heart started beating faster, my fingertips tingled, and it took every single ounce of discipline in my body not to bring my hands up to my face and lose my shit. *I had fucking promised, and I wasn't going to go back on my word.* Instead, I made myself keep my eyes forward on that blue water that hadn't changed in the least bit since the last time we'd been to this beach so long ago.

I clung to that memory like it was a lifeline sent to save me. A lifeline to one of the best days in my life—and a reminder that I'd had so many best days over the course of it. A reminder of just how fucking lucky I was that maybe life hadn't always been easy, but it had been—it *was* — amazing.

And *that* was what my grandpa had always wanted for me. For all of his loved ones.

Which was why I tied that memory to my wrist and let it lift me up like an oversized balloon.

This was the beach where Grandpa Gus and Peter had gotten married after nearly thirty-one years together. Right here. Well, close by. Under the Hawaiian sun, with enormous smiles over both of their faces, while my gramps cracked jokes at his groom and at the not-so-small party they'd invited to watch them each put a ring on it. A marriage thirty years and a lot of sacrifices and a lot of love in the making, that had only happened once Peter had retired and Grandpa Gus had decided to sell Maio House.

"You and Peter are Maio House to me, Len. And I'm tired of keeping it a secret. You have a life here, a career. You're not giving that up for the gym," he had reasoned with me a month after Jonah's contract with the Kobe Chargers had ended, days after he had signed a new three-year contract with his old team in Auckland.

And sure enough, six months later, Maio House had been sold to a group of three former fighters who had pooled their money together. It had been a little bittersweet, but just a little. Because how the hell could I have been upset when the moment after we'd talked about his decision, he'd asked, *"What do you think about a wedding on a beach in Kauai?"*

I'd swear I could still hear the way the ordained minister had asked my creature of ancient evil if he took Peter as his lawfully wedded husband, and how he'd answered, *"I guess so"* with his trademark little smirk before his face had sobered and he'd added, *"Yes. For the rest of my life."*

Another fucking choke appeared in my throat, and I decided maybe I shouldn't have delved into that memory so deeply because that time, I couldn't keep my shit totally under wraps. The choke sprang up and out of my throat, and one single tear escaped my eye at the same time Jonah's hand slipped out from under mine, and he threw a heavy, still-muscular arm over the tops of my shoulders. He sidestepped into me, his cheek slotting over the top of my head, and he snuggled me even as his own throat bubbled with deep chokes he was trying to hold back and mostly failing at. My sweet, wonderful man. The same man who had never given me a single reason to doubt or regret any of the decisions I'd made for him—for us.

"Are you remembering the wedding?" Jonah asked in a voice just barely an inch tall, weary and about as soft as he was capable of as that still big body shook against mine with so much emotion it triggered another tear out of me.

"Yeah," I answered him, taking a sniff and wrapping my free arm around his waist to hold him right back. My other hand gave the one I was holding a squeeze.

I wasn't the only one mourning and trying hard not to, I remembered.

We had all lost Grandpa Gus two months ago.

My fucking watery nose betrayed me and made something wet that I wasn't going to bother wiping off drip over the top of my lip and down the side of my mouth as I thought about the day that Peter had come into the kitchen, face pale and eyes stunned at first. How he had stood there for a moment while the rest of us looked at him expectantly. Not knowing what he was about to drop on us. Not knowing what had happened.

And then he'd smiled gently, his throat had bobbed, and he'd said the last words I would have ever imagined, "Gus is gone."

He had left us at ninety-five years old, in what was probably the quietest moment of his life. In his sleep. Not fighting or arguing or being sarcastic or loving or anything like he was normally.

I had lost my grandfather.

Peter had lost his *partner* of half his life.

Jonah had lost the man who had helped him with conditioning during each of the four off-seasons he'd had left in his career. A man who had become not just his children's nanny or his wife's best friend/grandpa/business partner in sports management, but his friend. His confidant. His own Granddad Gus.

And Mo and Marcus had lost their Grandpa Gus. Their nanny/playmate/number one cheerleader. The best great-grandfather in the history of great-grandfathers.

The greatest man to ever own the title of grandfather.

A man I had missed every second of every day for the last two months. That we all had. Not just me.

A man buried in a natural cemetery in his adopted country of New Zealand per his wishes. *Why would I want to be all the way in Houston when you're all here?* he'd asked when he'd given us his instructions after becoming a permanent resident.

The hand fitted against mine squeezed it for a moment before a lanky body turned into mine, threw his arms around my waist, tucked his head under my chin, and muttered in a choppy voice, "I miss him heaps, Mum. He made me promise him I wouldn't cry, and it's so… hard."

"Me too, buddy," I agreed, wrapping one arm around him and keeping my other around Jonah. "We all do. It's okay if you cry. He'd know it was just because we love him so much."

"He can be mad at both of us," Jonah piped up as he turned his body toward his son too.

Marcus, our fifteen-year-old who was a perfect physical mix of both of us, nodded against me even as he sniffed again. He was loud, opinionated, energetic, and fiercely loyal. Not as olive-skinned as Mo, his eyes grayer than brown, and hair lighter and straighter like mine, he was lanky and growing. I had a feeling that one day, when I wasn't fighting back the black hole in my chest that had only shrunk a fraction in size over the last few weeks, I'd look at him and see that he was a replica of Grandpa Gus.

One day.

But for that day, he was still our baby.

"Mum, Dad," a familiar voice said from behind us. "Everyone is here. I think we can get started."

"All right, darling," Jonah replied from over my head a moment before giving the top of it a kiss. "Ready, love?"

I could do this. I could do it.

I turned my head and gave the hand he had resting on my shoulder a kiss before nodding up at his so-loved face that had stayed just as handsome as ever over the years. "Yeah, let's do it."

The three of us turned around to face away from the water then. There were easily thirty people scattered closely around the beach, but it was Peter I focused on. He was sitting in a chair with his cane leaning against his knees, with Mo kneeling on one side of him and Luna, my forever best friend even after being separated by an ocean nearly constantly for the last two decades, standing on his other side. Her husband and their three kids were right behind her. Their presence was just another reminder of how lucky I was. We had vacationed together just about every year, and I saw her when we'd traveled to Houston once a year to check on Grandpa's house.

My house now, actually. A house that had only been lived in

for a month or two a year for a while. A house we could vacation in, but that would never be lived in full-time again.

Oh, Grandpa. I miss you so much.

The rest of the people on the beach were a mix of Jonah's family members and people I reached out to who had kept in touch with my gramps over the years. People who had supported him after coming out. People who had called and emailed and visited while he had been with us.

Jonah gave my shoulder a squeeze before letting his hand drop away for a moment before he rifled through his pocket and pulled out a folded piece of paper that he'd been entrusted with. *"He's the only one I trust not to read it before it's time,"* Grandpa had claimed, sliding me a look that said *yeah, you know you'd read it if I left it with you.*

And he would have been right, because I had tried to convince Jonah to let me read it at least twice.

And it was that thought that brought the first smile onto my face that day.

He'd always known me better than anyone.

Well, maybe he was tied with Jonah. And he would have been totally fine with that.

Holding the paper with two shaky hands, one of the six loves of my life sidestepped into me until his biceps touched me, the side of his bare foot touching mine. I was his reassurance then, I knew. And this enormous man who had fought for every year of his career, who had put his family first every single time he was needed, who was the best friend, best father, best person I knew—tied with Peter—cleared his throat as he unfolded the piece of paper as he said, "I have a letter Granddad Gus wanted me to read to everyone."

He cleared his throat just as Marcus took my hand again and Jonah's little toe touched mine. Peter smiled from where he was sitting, glasses shoved up onto the bridge of his beloved nose, and let out a deep, deep breath. It was then that I saw that Mo, twenty-one years old and as beautiful as her dad, had her hand through his, and Luna had his other one. Her left hand was linked through her oldest daughter's. Her husband's hands were on her shoulders.

Her shiny eyes met mine, and we smiled at each other just as Jonah started again.

"*Dear everyone,*" Jonah read. "*Fuck you*—wait."

Beside me, Marcus snorted this watery noise, but I looked up at Jonah to figure out what the hell he was reading. Sure enough, the lines across his forehead were wrinkled in confusion as those beautiful eyes moved across the sheet of paper… but it was the slow smile that crept across his face that surprised me. And the tear that bubbled up in the corner of my husband's eye that he wiped off with a big index finger before saying, with laughter and pain in his voice, "He wrote in parentheses to point randomly around and say *fuck you*, point at someone else and say *fuck you*, and do that at least eight times."

I wasn't expecting the laugh that burst out of my throat, much less Peter's or Mo's, but it happened. Even Marcus fully laughed. Jonah smiled over at me, lips pressing tight together before he read on with a shake of his head like he should have expected that.

We all should have.

That was Grandpa Gus. Even in death, he would want to fuck with us. I had loved that man with my entire heart for the entirety of the fifty-one years of my life, and somehow I loved him even more then than ever, and I hadn't thought that was humanly possible.

Jonah's hand snuck over to squeeze my wrist for a moment before lifting the paper back up to his face and continuing on, but this time with laughter on his face and in his voice. "*If you're reading this, none of y'all better be crying. I'm not kidding. Not a single tear. But if you really need to, it's okay. I would miss me too.*"

I laughed again as tears streamed out of my eyes and down my face, and I had to stoop to use Marcus's shoulder to wipe them off as he dragged a skinny fist across his face to do the same. I glanced at Peter to find him smiling huge, not a single tear in his gaze as it focused on Jonah. But everyone else… we weren't that strong.

And my husband, my love, kept going. "*I didn't want a funeral because there's nothing to be sad about, and I hate the color black. I hope at least one of you is wearing a Hawaiian shirt. I wanted you all to come and be together, to be happy, in one of the most beautiful places in the world. To remember the most important part of life is living it with people that you love and people that love you right back. It's the greatest gift we can have.*

"*Where you're standing right now is where the best man I've ever known finally married me. He gave up his family, his career, and our home, for me. For our family. We had to keep what we had a secret for over thirty years so that our business would prosper, because we were scared of being judged and losing everything.*

"*He gave me the best years of his life, and I tried to do the same, but as I look back on it now, I wish we wouldn't have had to hide it for so long. I wished I had told every person in my life to fuck off, as my Lenny would say, and have had more years of our rings on each other's fingers. But I think I would have felt that way even if we'd had a thousand of them. But it's what we had to do, and it all worked out. What I'm trying to tell you all from the grave—*"

There were a few watery snorts, because he'd gone there.

"*Is this: I love you all, and I want you to remember now that I'm not around, to never forget what's important. You're each important. You're each loved. And if you love something or someone, you don't ever give up on it. Life's not easy but hold on to the things that matter, even if you have to use some fingernails. I told one of you once that you don't throw away the things that matter. Hold on for me. Fight for me, or like I'm behind you telling you that you better not quit,*" Jonah read.

He had told me that. I remembered. When he'd fired me so Mo and I could go to Japan to be with Jonah, that had been the sentence he'd said when he'd hugged me tight and set me free.

Kind of. Because he'd followed me there and stayed with me for ten months out of the year.

Jonah read a little more of the paper that was directly meant for his friends and the members of Jonah's family that had come, and then this wonderful amazing man I had been lucky enough to spend the last two decades of my life with said, *"Mo and Marcus, I love you two so much, and I'm so proud of you. I'm always here. I'll always be listening for you. Jasper—"* Jonah's voice broke off with a laugh at the nickname the old vampire had never managed to totally drop even after so long. *"—you are the second best man I know. It was a privilege knowing you—"* He swallowed and glanced at me to whisper, "He called me son."

I couldn't help but smile at him as I wrapped my fingers around his forearm and said, "He's been calling you that behind your back for years, Dimples. He loved you."

He knew that. I knew he knew that. Jonah smiled before ducking down to give me a kiss on the nose. He straightened, swallowed hard, and nodded to himself. "Okay. There's just a little more. *To the two loves of my life—"*

Peter and I made eye contact then. My second dad. His smile hadn't gone anywhere, and I'd swear his eyes sparkled from behind his glasses. I smiled at him too then, knowing he was fine between Mo and Luna, while I gave my own strength to these two guys of mine who needed me.

"—you gave me a reason to live. And I'm going to haunt you both for the rest of your lives. That creaking noise you hear in the attic? It's me. The shadow you see out of the corner of your eye? That's me too. I love you both. You know that. You know what you mean to me. I love you all. I'm never far away. Do what you have to do to be happy, okay? No one else is going to do it for you."

Do what you have to do to be happy.

Goddammit, Grandpa.

I was not going to cry. I was not going to cry. I was not going to cry.

Slipping my hand through Jonah's arm, clutching Marcus's hand close, I led them all toward Peter, and the next thing I knew, I had my cheek against his. Marcus was on one side of me, arm over his Grandpa Peter's shoulder, and I had Jonah on my other side again, holding me close to his body with one arm, and the other around his mini-me, Mo. And Mo had her arm around Grandpa Peter too. From the weight on my back and on my arms, I knew we had been surrounded as well by another layer of love.

Grandpa Gus was there too.

I could feel him in my heart, and I knew he was in everyone's then like he always would be. Where he belonged. Exactly where I knew he'd want to be.

With his family. With the people who loved him the most. The group of us who loved each other the most. My past, my present, and my future. The best things to ever happen to me.

And there was only one person in the world I could thank for it all.

For the life I had that even on the worst, most frustrating day, I could smile.

I love you so much, old man. Every good thing in my life has been because of you.

Thank you for being the best grandpa/grandma/uncle/brother/best friend/soul mate/enemy I could ever ask for, I threw out to him, knowing he was always listening, because some things never changed.

No vampire has ever been loved as much as you, Grandpa Gus. Tell my dad I said hi.

ACKNOWLEDGMENTS

Thank you so much for reading THE BEST THING! I constantly sound like a broken record saying it, but I really do have the best readers in the world. Thank you so much for all of your support and love. You guys believe in me more than I believe in myself some days, and that's something I can never repay.

Eva, I don't know what I would do without your eagle eye, honesty, friendship and your ability to do math, haha. And especially for knowing when I can do better. I can't thank you properly with words, but I know you know how much I appreciate everything you do for me (and my books).

Sita, I can't thank you enough for your kindness, assistance with my kiwi slang, and awesome suggestions with Jonah's character. Thank you so, so much for your help. Ryn, my blurbs would be pathetic without you. Thank you for always being willing to help. Letitia at RBA Designs, I've told you before and I'll tell you again: please don't ever leave me. Thank you to Virginia and Kim at Hot Tree Editing, and Ellie with My Brother's Editor for making my book less of a hot mess. Jeff, thank you for always squeezing me in for a formatting even when I have to change my dates at the last minute. Kilian, I'm so grateful for all your help.

Thanks also to Jane Dystel, Kemi Faderin and Lauren Abramo of Dystel, Goderich & Bourret for all of their work with getting my books into different markets.

To my friends who I know I'm forgetting: thank you for everything.

To my Zapata, Navarro, and Letchford family, thank you all for always being so supportive and bragging to all your friends about my writing, haha. You're the greatest families a girl could ever ask for. A very special thank you to my mom for being a great travel partner, always agreeing to be my assistant even before I tell you where we're going, and for being more organized than I am.

To my love, Chris, I don't know what I would do without you.

Last but not least, to my two best friends on the planet, Dorian and Kaiser. No character will ever love another character half as much as I love you guys.

ABOUT THE AUTHOR

Mariana Zapata lives in a small town in Colorado with her husband and two oversized children—her beloved Great Danes, Dorian and Kaiser. When she's not writing, she's reading, spending time outside, forcing kisses on her boys, harassing her family, or pretending to write.

www.marianazapata.com
Mailing List (New Release Information Only)

Facebook: www.facebook.com/marianazapatawrites
Instagram: www.instagram.com/marianazapata
Twitter: www.twitter.com/marianazapata_

ALSO BY MARIANA ZAPATA

Under Locke

Lingus

Kulti

Rhythm, Chord & Malykhin

The Wall of Winnipeg and Me

Wait for It

Dear Aaron

From Lukov with Love

Luna and the Lie

Made in the USA
Coppell, TX
10 November 2019

11064606R00277